THE VAULT BOX SET

EDEN SUMMERS

Copyright © 2017 by Eden Summers

This book is a work of fiction. The names, characters, places, and incidents are products of the writer's imagination or have been used fictitiously and are not to be construed as real. Any resemblance to persons, living or dead, actual events, locales or organizations is entirely coincidental.

All rights reserved. With the exception of quotes used in reviews, this book may not be reproduced or used in whole or in part by any means existing without written permission from the author.

The author acknowledges the trademarked status and trademark owners of various products referenced in this work of fiction, which have been used without permission. The publication/use of these trademarks is not authorized, associated with, or sponsored by the trademark owners.

A SHOT OF SIN

To passion and love.
To naughtiness and risk.

CHAPTER ONE

"*R*aspberry and vodka, thanks. And in a tall glass this time."

Shay Porter acknowledged the order with a nod and prepared the guy's drink with the last shot of vodka in the bottle. The man was a loner. Three nights a week, every week, he came to Shot of Sin. He ordered the same girlie beverage, chatted up the same high-class women and then went home sulking, as if he was the only one here who hadn't anticipated the rejection.

Dumb fucker.

"Do you want a straw with that?" she called over the heavy club music, her smile insincere.

His hazel eyes narrowed. "The drink is for me," he snarled and handed her the correct change.

She turned her back with a shrug and placed the money in the register. "Still a legitimate question, asshole," she muttered, retrieving the empty liquor bottle from the overhead dispenser.

"Taunting the customers again, Shay?"

Her spine tingled at the gravel-rich tone. Leo Petrova, aka Mr. Boss Man, was one sexy hunk of masculinity. Skin tanned from an unending kiss of the Beaumont, Texas sun, hair long enough to be pulled into a short ponytail with wisps falling around his face to highlight intense blue-green eyes.

Change of panties needed at the main bar, please.

"He can't expect to score when he orders girlie drinks like that." She dumped the empty bottle in the bin beside his sexy muscled legs covered in coal Chino's. When she lifted her gaze over his white buttoned shirt and met his focus, she subtly licked her lips, inwardly rejoicing at his narrowed gaze. She had to do these little things—smile seductively, plump her breasts, accidentally trip over invisible objects and find herself plastered against his body. How else could she weaken his defenses? "The single women think he's gay. I can't stand to watch the carnage anymore."

She turned on her heel and headed for the storeroom, hoping Leo would follow. As she flicked on the light in the darkened room behind the bar, she smiled, sensing his dominant presence at her back.

"Then quit." He slid the door closed behind them, lessening the harsh thrum of music.

Quit? No.

Under the thick layers of his hard-ass bravado, he was joking. She knew that. And he knew she would never leave. She loved working at Shot of Sin and the adjoining restaurant, Taste of Sin. This place was her second home. The bar staff she managed might not always appreciate her temperamental attitude, but her three bosses valued her contributions... Well, most of the time.

More importantly, they listened to her suggestions on improving the business. After five years of hopping from one employer to the next, she'd finally found a place worth sticking to. The eye candy her boss provided was an added bonus.

She glanced over her shoulder with a raised brow. Her body hummed with his proximity. What she wouldn't give for him to push her against the side of the shelves and make her whimper in pleasure.

He leaned against the wall, arms crossed over his chest. "We've spoken about your sassy mouth before. Either stop it, or take a walk."

She cleared her throat to cover a chuckle. "Is that how you plan to work around the no-sleeping-with-staff policy?" She turned to the shelves in search of another vodka bottle. "Fire me so you can have your way with me? 'Cause I'm okay with that, as long as I'm a kept woman."

His growl reverberated off the walls, making her nipples burn.

"Don't push me tonight, Shayna."

No nickname? Two points for getting under his skin.

"Or what?" She retrieved a bottle from the high shelf and faced him.

"You know you won't fire me. I'm the hardest worker you've got." And hopefully the only one he was attracted to.

She stepped forward, bringing them toe-to-toe. His gaze held her captive, staring her down. She knew he wouldn't break the connection. One, because Mr. Dominant would never heel to a woman. And two, because she had the impression his aversion to kissing her weakened if he glanced lower to her lips. Or better still, to the cleavage he liked to eye-fuck whenever he thought she wasn't watching. "I'm sure you could shut this sassy mouth without the threat of sacking me."

His nostrils flared. There was attraction in those ocean eyes, no doubt about it. Only she knew he wouldn't act upon it. Not yet, anyway. He'd made it clear their first heated interlude had been a mistake. It wouldn't stop her from taunting him with something she was more than willing to give, though. One day she'd break through his no-relationships barrier, she just had to be patient.

He leaned in, positioning his mouth deliciously close to her ear, making her skin prickle with awareness. "I could shut you up, little girl, but I'd be scared of choking you with this big dick of mine."

Shay pressed her lips together, fighting the burst of laughter threatening to break free. "I've got an exceptional gag reflex." She let the vodka bottle fall between them, the heavy weight brushing his crotch.

Voices echoed from the bar and Leo stiffened, moving out of reach moments before the second boss in the trio of broodish men slid the door open. T.J. frowned as he cautiously entered the room. His brown-eyed gaze narrowed on Leo before turning Shay's way.

"This doesn't look inappropriate at all," he drawled. "What are you two doing back here?"

Shay held up the liquor bottle in her hand. "I came to get a refill. I'm not entirely sure why he followed."

Leo rolled his eyes. "What do you want?"

T.J. shook his head with a knowing grin and turned his attention to Leo. "Tracy broke her arm. She's going to be out of action for a while."

"Tracy?" Shay frowned.

"She works downstairs."

Ahh. The illusive VIP lounge she'd never been allowed to step foot in. Apparently, being the most valued employee upstairs didn't hold enough merit to see where all the beautiful people went each Saturday night.

"We don't have anyone to replace her shift next week when Travis is away," T.J. continued. "Bryan and I thought Shay could take her place."

Shay's eyes widened, not only at the new opportunity, but more shockingly that Bryan, aka Brute, would suggest she was capable of such a highly-coveted role. He'd earned his nickname because of the harsh way he dealt with life. He was merciless, clinical, and rarely showed emotion. Most of the time, he was an accomplished grump who liked to hide any enthusiasm under snarky insults. This suggestion proved her theory that underneath all the angst, he truly was a soft, cuddly bear.

Like hell she was going to point out the uncharacteristic comment though. Downstairs intrigued her. She'd already spent months in the adjoining Taste of Sin restaurant earning their respect before they'd let her work in the dance club part of the business. Now she wanted to hit the big time. The door leading to the private part of the club was always protected each Saturday by a security guard. Not even long-term Shot of Sin staff could enter, and she'd never met anyone who worked behind the sacred walls.

"No." Leo's tone brooked no argument.

"Excuse me?" She straightened her shoulders and raised a brow. She wasn't a daddy's girl or a wealthy socialite who expected her every whim to be adhered to, but when it came to devaluing her, in any way, her hackles immediately rose.

"I said no." He turned his focus to T.J. "I don't want her down there."

"What's your problem?" she snapped. Yes, he was her stubborn, slightly nauseatingly gorgeous boss, but they were meant to be friends. Even more if he'd finally lower his guard and allow it. And now he was treating her as if she couldn't handle a simple night's work at a different bar.

"She isn't trained to work in that environment." He no longer acknowledging her presence. "We'll find someone else."

T.J.'s brow furrowed. "Shay, can you give us a sec?"

She held tight to the liquor bottle in her fist. "Fine." Clenching her teeth together, she fixed her arrogant fantasy with a glare and then pushed past him to the open doorway. "Convince him, T.J. Otherwise, you might find yourself looking to replace more than one staff member."

*L*eo watched Shay's ass storm from the storeroom and then winced when she slammed the sliding door. The woman drove him crazy. She was wild and sassy with a delectable body capable of making his cock twitch on a hair-trigger. She was also predictable. Now that she was sporting a mammoth case of fury, he knew she'd go back to work and bat her lashes at every pretentious asshole in the building just to piss him off.

In other words, she was trouble. And as drawn to her as he was, he didn't need another complication in his life. The restaurant and bar kept him, T.J. and Brute busy, and with the private club downstairs increasing its clientele, none of them needed a distraction. Especially one with pretty light-brown eyes and dark wavy hair.

"Give me one good reason why she can't work down there," T.J. muttered, the shadowed smudges under his eyes more prominent than earlier in the evening.

"Like I said, she hasn't been trained."

"And like I said, give me one good reason."

Fuck. Leo let out a heavy breath and wiped a hand down his face. "I just don't want her down there, okay?"

T.J. and Brute weren't aware he'd once succumbed to her sassy charm. He'd practically dry-humped her in this very room—his tongue down her throat, his fingers in her panties, sliding through her slick juices. He'd strode away soon after she'd climaxed around his digits, his jaw tight with regret. Unbeknown to Shay, she'd proven she wasn't what he needed, no matter how much she thought she was. His sexual appetite was raw, demanding, and not suitable for someone with a narrow scope on pleasure.

In the few moments they'd shared, he'd seen her innocence. She wasn't a virgin by any means, but neither was she a female equipped to handle his desires. She'd gasped at his ferocity, stared at him like he was an entirely different man, and he'd learned long ago to back away when his needs didn't match those of the woman he was interested in. Things would only become complicated later. Been there, done that.

He had the emotional scars to prove it.

So, he'd run, and hoped T.J. and Brute didn't hear about his fuck up. For weeks, he'd distanced himself from the hope of commitment in her eyes. He'd hated fracturing the defenses of such a strong-willed woman, only he hadn't had a choice. With her penchant for tantrums, he'd had to snap out of the attraction in an instant. Or at least pretend to.

"Unfortunately, with the limited staff employed downstairs, we don't have any other options. Travis has already scheduled annual leave and I'm not going back on my word when it's the anniversary of his dad's death." T.J. huffed in frustration. "Look, I know you have a thing for her, but you've gotta decide—are you her manager or the guy who wants to get in her pants?"

Leo scowled. "I don't want to get in her pants." Been there, done that, too.

"Then why is it a hard decision?"

Sadly, when it came to the sassy wench, things were always hard. For Leo, anyway. Problem was he didn't have a legitimate excuse to stop her from getting them out of the staffing issue.

"Fine." He stabbed his fingers through his hair, loosening his ponytail. "But I'll be the one to show her around. Brute can take my shift up here next Saturday and I'll take his downstairs."

T.J. shrugged. "I'm cool with that. You could take her down tonight if you wanted. We aren't likely to get overrun up here."

Leo's palms began to sweat. "Yeah, okay."

He closed his eyes and rubbed the back of his lids. Shay didn't have a good track record of reacting with professional calm when surprised. And the contrasting environment downstairs would definitely be a bombshell.

One of his pet peeves was judgement from others, especially friends and family. Yes, it was human nature for every fucker to have an opinion, even when the situations they were criticizing were none of their goddamn business. He was just sick to death of narrow-minded people opening their mouths and spewing hatred about shit they didn't understand. He didn't know how he'd handle that type of commentary from Shay. And she'd definitely have an opinion about the activities in the downstairs area.

"You sure this doesn't have anything to do with you wanting to slam your cock down her throat?"

"Christ, T.J." Leo scowled. "Don't you think downstairs would be the first place I'd take her if I did?"

"Just askin'." He held up his hands in surrender and backtracked to the door.

"Well, don't." Leo jerked his head toward the hall and hoped T.J. would leave him the hell alone so he could think shit through. "Look after the main floor tonight. Leave Shay to me."

CHAPTER TWO

Shay raised a questioning brow at T.J. as he strode behind the bar toward her. He waited until she finished serving one of the bleach-blonde regulars before sidling up beside her.

"You okay?" he asked, always the gentleman.

She liked T.J. He was sweet, caring and always had her back, even when she didn't deserve it. His dark features and drool-worthy appearance didn't hinder her fondness for him, either. She doubted there was a woman who entered Shot of Sin who hadn't fantasized about him, or the other two owners. And if the women were anything like Shay, they'd fantasized about all three of the men at the same time, because she was creative like that. Only now, she was too pissed off to appreciate the gorgeousness of T.J.'s dark-brown eyes.

"I suppose that depends." She wiped her hands on her jean-covered hips and eyed the bar staff to make sure they didn't become overrun with drink orders. "Is Leo committed to being a jerk?"

"He's only looking out for you."

"Bullshit." She met his gaze with a glare. She'd been through this before, having worked with more than one manager who didn't believe she was as capable as her male counterparts. There was no way she would allow her time here to go down the same path. "I've never disappointed you. Not once. Yet, Leo's initial instinct is to claim I'm incapable of handling new duties. Christ, T.J., how hard could it be? I rarely see anyone go down there."

T.J. winced while his focus strayed over her shoulder. Moments later, Brute strolled up beside them and leaned against the back counter as staff members buzzed around them.

"What's going on?" His blue eyes were devoid of expression. As always. The dark-blond, clean-cut beard also helped to hide any emotions he had going on in that stubborn face of his. "Did you ask Shay about working downstairs?"

"We were just discussing it," T.J. muttered over the music. "Leo was a little apprehensive about the suggestion, but I think I won him over."

"Won him over?" Shay bit out. "He shouldn't need to be won over. I'm the most capable bartender you have."

T.J. and Brute exchanged a glance she suspected held hidden meaning.

"What?" she asked. "Aren't you happy with the way I've been running things?"

"No. It's not that." T.J.'s response was immediate. "Leo's being protective. Downstairs isn't as..."

"Straight," Brute added. "It'll definitely keep you on your toes."

Shay focused on them both in turn. T.J. no longer made eye contact. His attention hovered anywhere but her face, as if he were apprehensive, or maybe nervous. Brute met her gaze head on, but his vacant expression gave nothing away.

"I can handle it." At the very least, she deserved the opportunity to prove herself. She only wished Leo had as much faith in her as T.J. and Brute.

"I know you can." T.J squeezed her shoulder. "Leo does too. He's just a little touchy when it comes to downstairs."

Touchy she could handle. What she couldn't stand was the hit to her pride from a guy she had a female boner for.

"I better go check that Taste of Sin closed properly. I'll catch you both later." T.J. gave her shoulder another gentle squeeze and then made his way around the bar.

Shay watched him disappear into the crowd of dancing bodies and cursed herself for crushing on the wrong bar owner. Leo was too stubborn. The only problem was that he was exactly what she wanted in a guy. Apart from having the ability to melt her panties with a single glance, he was confident, capable and too deliciously sexy when he growled at her.

Their one scorching play session in the bar storeroom had been enough to cement her attraction to him. Confident and capable, Leo always exuded dominance and possession. Shay was certain he'd be the same in the sack. A wicked combination to tempt a woman who had never truly been satisfied by the opposite sex...or the same sex for that matter.

"So what's the real problem here? Are you annoyed at Leo for not giving you the job opportunity, or are you pissed because he won't sleep with you?"

Shay turned her gaze back to Brute with a gaping mouth. "You really need to research social filters."

"Why? We're close enough to cut the crap and I'm not going to waste my time dancing around the topic."

Of course he wouldn't. Brute was the type to take pleasure in asking the questions nobody wanted to voice. "His aversion to sleeping with me has nothing to do with my annoyance." She used the term loosely. They all knew she tended to bypass the annoyance stage and head straight to fury. "I can work any bar. Leo's just being an ass."

"Fair enough." Brute shrugged, seeming unconvinced. "I'll leave you to it. So don't sweat the simple stuff, sweetheart. If he hasn't changed his mind by closing time, me and Mr. Attitude will have a chat."

Even though he wasn't the guy her libido craved, the term of endearment made her heart flutter. He may have been nicknamed for his brutality, but it didn't stop her from searching for the soft and gooey center he pretended not to have. The guy had a heart. Somewhere. He just didn't like to show it.

Brute strode away at the same time she noticed Leo standing in the doorway leading to the storeroom. His gaze was fixed on her, his jaw tight, chin raised. In an instant, the heart fluttering began to pound, from fury or attraction, she wasn't sure.

She turned her back, unable to look at him without losing the last of her withering professionalism. Fucking asshole. His appeal defied logic. Not only was he worthy of naming rights to her vibrator, she was pretty sure toy manufacturers would kill to mold the package outlined in the crotch of his butt-hugging Chino's. The annoying part was that he wasn't just a panty-wetting machine due to his looks. He actually had a surprisingly enjoyable personality—for a male. Well, he used to. He used to be playful and flirty and charming…until the night he slid his hand into her pants and then backed away like he'd armed a bomb.

"Now I'm just another easy bar wench."

"Excuse me?" He came up behind her, his shadow falling over her shoulder.

She turned and pinned him with a death stare. "I said, get out of my face."

He raised a brow, the side of his heart-stopping lips tilting. "You're quick to bite my head off tonight."

She scoffed and nudged passed him. "Yeah, and funnily enough, you're the one acting like you've got PMS." She strode around the bar and into the dancing crowd illuminated in purple light. This time, she hoped he didn't follow. She needed space from all his self-assured gorgeousness, and she was owed a twenty-minute break.

Palming the phone in her pocket to make sure it didn't fall out, she bumped through the mass of gyrating bodies and headed toward the opposite side of the building. As she approached the guarded entrance to the fancy-schmancy private club, she scowled at the guard manning the door. It wasn't his fault she was crabby, but the fucks she gave about who took the brunt of her anger were nowhere to be found.

"*Shay*," Leo yelled over the heavy pulse of music. "Hold up."

She paused, crossing her arms over her chest like a petulant child.

"You really want to go down there?" he asked over her shoulder.

She turned on him. "It's not about wanting to go down there." She raised her voice, hoping it didn't waiver. "It's about you not giving a shit about how hard I work. I'm the one who stays late to help clean up." She tapped her chest with a pointed finger. "I'm the one who works overtime in the restaurant if someone calls in sick." *Tap*. "I'm the one all the regulars come to because they know I remember their drink order." She poked him in the sternum. "Your attitude is a kick in the face to all the effort I put in."

Leo glanced around with disinterest. "You finished?"

"Do I look like I'm finished?" she grated and then thought better of continuing the hissy fit when clearly he didn't care. "Forget it."

Turning, she pushed passed a couple making out and stormed for the nearest exit. As she strode by the guard at the private entrance, a hand grabbed her upper arm, pulling her back.

"Hey, Jeff, you mind letting us in?" Leo asked.

The colossal guard's brows knitted as his gaze lowered to the grip tightening on her arm. "Sure thing, boss."

He pushed open the bulky door and stepped to the side, eyeing them with concern as Leo hauled her into the darkness. When the door closed, Shay's heart rocketed into her throat.

In here, it was quieter, almost deafeningly so, and the faint thump, thump, thump of bass barely breached the walls. The light from the club had been extinguished too, making her eyes work to adjust to an even darker environment.

A quick glimpse to her left showed a narrow staircase with crimson wallpaper lining the walls and plush carpet under her feet. The area was more compact than she imagined, more intimate, especially when she stood toe-to-toe with a man who stole her breath.

"You know your grip is bordering on harassment."

His hand fell away as she gazed up into his shadowed features.

"Sorry," he murmured. "I didn't expect you to throw a tantrum."

Tantrum? "If I wasn't furious right now, I'd be belting you with a plethora of insults."

She shouldered him out of the way, no longer giving a shit about what treasures lurked below. He could take his private club and shove it where rich people didn't shine. She was a fucking brilliant bartender, and if Leo didn't appreciate her skills, she might have to leave and find a bar owner who did.

Stupid lust-filled crush be damned.

She gripped the door handle and plunged the leaver, but as soon as she pulled, Leo wrapped a strong arm around her waist. Time stopped, along with her breathing, while the heat of his chest invaded her lungs. She could smell his sweet, exotic aftershave. Could feel his warm exhalations tickling her neck as she fought to keep her posture straight and defiant.

"Being a great employee has nothing to do with my reasons for not wanting you in here," he hissed under his breath.

She raised her chin, hating the way her core contracted and her nipples beaded beneath her bra. "Then why?"

He dropped his arm from her waist and the heat from his body disappeared. She turned in the silence, wishing she could make out his face clearly as he stepped back.

"Why, Leo?"

The sparing dim lights stretching along the ceiling didn't reach the far corner where he stood. She couldn't see his eyes, only the faint jut of his chin and his straightened shoulders. She could sense a bravado settling over him, yet she had no clue why.

"This game we play..." he started, leaning back to rest against the wall. "I enjoy it. The banter, the tension. Even the way your flirting grabs hold of my dick and won't let go." He paused, as if sensing she needed a moment to let his words sink in. "I don't want to ruin that."

Her heart lurched. "Okay..."

She'd never played games. Every time she'd flirted, she'd done it with intent, with the sole focus of not only getting in his bed, but in his heart. She sure as shit wasn't going to correct him though. Not when he was being such an ass. "Where is this speech going? You've already made it crystal you don't want to be with me, so why all the dramatics?"

Silence. Then there was a long, drawn-out sigh that dried her throat.

"Follow me."

He started down the stairs, and she cursed herself for following behind so quickly. No matter how willing she'd been to walk out the door, curiosity still won. She needed to know what was at the end of the staircase.

As they descended, crisp, cool air danced around her heels, filtered in through air vents near the floor. The atmosphere was different to the bubbly purple and silver of the main area of Shot of Sin. In here, she struggled to fight unease. She could see picture frames lining the walls, and when they reached the first, she stopped and did a double-take. She expected a landscape, or maybe autographed images from people who'd made their way into this exclusive part of the club. But it was neither.

The first frame held a black and white photograph of a naked couple, intimately entwined. It was erotic, graphic, and when Leo glanced over his shoulder, she felt like she'd been caught with a hand in her own private cookie jar.

The beauty of the image made her feel inadequate. Here she was in a tight black Shot-of-Sin tank and jeans, while they bared their bodies and souls for art. It was spectacular and oddly confounding. Why would Leo, T.J., or even Brute for that matter, pick out something so graphic to decorate their private club?

She shook away the confusion and followed after the sculpted shoulders continuing down the stairs. More images passed by, all with couples in erotic poses—men with women, women with women, and more delicious than she would've imagined, muscled men with sexy muscled men. Each shot was beautiful in its own striking way, but now Shay was beyond bewildered and heading for freak-out central.

The darkness, the silence, the sex lining the walls, it set her fertile mind to work on some pretty heavy ideas. By the time she reached the last step, she was staring at Leo's back in contemplation, her palms sweating and not from exertion. Finally, his warnings had sunk in, and she thought better of pushing him to the point of dragging her down here. For the first time since becoming an independent adult, she felt anxious.

"That's the locker room."

Leo's voice startled her, and she glanced from his back to see him pointing to a closed door highlighted with one small light above the frame.

"Patrons are encouraged to leave valuables at home, but everything else gets locked up in there."

"Everything else?" She tagged along behind him.

He ignored her, not faltering in his dominant stride as he pointed to another closed door. "And that is the change room."

"Change room?" she asked louder. "What is all this for?"

He continued to the end of the hall, to a padded door bathed in glowing light. A keypad was positioned on the wall at chest height, the numbers aglow in bright blue. She glanced from the keypad to the back of Leo's head with growing apprehension. What required all this secrecy and security?

"Are you going to answer me?" Her voice waivered.

He always had a quick word to say. In fact, he usually had the final word in every conversation, yet now he was silent. *Toot toot.* All aboard the freak-out train.

"Leo?"

He turned to her and waved a lazy arm toward the door. "This is what you wanted."

She couldn't tear her gaze from him. She was looking for a clue, a tiny hint to make her laugh off the impending heart attack. Only, in the brighter light, she could see the worry around his eyes, the troubling furrow to his brow.

"Ladies first."

He indicated for her to step in front and she reluctantly complied. Once she was a foot away from the door, he moved behind her, leaned close, and hovered his fingers over the keypad.

"On the other side of the door isn't just a VIP lounge. It's an exclusive club, something someone like you wouldn't be familiar with."

Someone like me?

Now he was trying to make her feel inferior for not being wealthy or famous? She turned her head, glaring at the side of his face. "Insult me one more time..."

"And what?" His mouth quirked and he met her stare with a raised brow.

She got in his face, close enough she was caught between wanting to slam her fist into his perfect nose or smash her mouth against his. "And I'll..." She bit back her anxiety-riddled reply. "Don't worry, Leo," she snarled his name. "I won't embarrass you in front of whatever pretentious, high-powered people you have in there."

He chuckled, soft and low. "It's not them I'm worried about."

Before she could question his comment, his fingers were on the keypad, entering a four-digit number. The door buzzed, and he flung it wide. A fresh burst of cool air filtered forward, and her eyes widened, not only at the porn playing on the huge television in front of her, but at the unmistakable sounds of sex that weren't coming through in Dolby digital quality. Oh no, the noises she heard were real-life, unscripted feminine moans and brutal grunts coming from another room.

Holy shit.

"Welcome to Vault of Sin, Shay," he drawled.

Her mouth worked, unable to form words as her gaze went in search of where the lust-filled sounds were coming from. "Is this a brothel?" she blurted, her focus now glued to the woman being hammered on screen by two men.

"No."

"A sex club?" Her voice was suddenly high-pitched.

"Surprise." He nudged her into the room and closed the door behind them.

Holy adolescent hormones.

Her mouth gaped. How had she not known this was going on right underneath her feet? And for how long? Shay glanced around in a daze, scoping out the small room with an archway at the far wall. Apart from the screen full of orgasmic undulation, there was a leather sofa, a dimly lit lamp, and a basket in the corner with items she wasn't sure she wanted to know about.

"This is the chill-out room." Leo strode forward, heading for the archway. "A place for newbies to settle in before joining the fun."

Fun?

She released an awkward chuckle.

Leo's relaxed stride added to her horror. She tried not to contemplate how many hours it would take to become nonchalant about this type of setting. How many women he'd seen. How many orgasms he'd heard. She shook her head, ignoring the bite of jealousy nipping at her ribs, the cloying adrenaline rushing through her veins, and the slight buzz of arousal.

"You coming?" He stood at the archway with a raised brow.

"Obviously not right at this very moment." She straightened her shoulders and took pleasure in the way Leo's gaze lowered to her breasts. He was smart enough to figure out she was fighting her discomfort through sarcasm, and she didn't have the sense to care. It was the only reliable strategy she had to calm down and stop her from rushing back up those stairs. "It takes more than porn to get this motor running."

"If memory serves, it can take a lot less."

Argh.

How did he do that? Take all the rushing emotions flowing through her body and replace them instantly with the need to choke him.

Ignoring his deep chuckle, she ground her teeth and strengthened her resolve as she came up behind him. Together, they stepped into a larger room and her knees threatened to give out. She'd tried to prepare herself, yet her imagination hadn't been equipped to create the cavern of carnality before her.

There were beds. A hammock. Leather sofas. A sex swing. And half were occupied with writhing naked bodies. Numerous television screens played different porn scenes while the bar stood alone in the back corner, the only surface in the room currently safe from copulation.

The whimpers, groans, grunts and screams hit her like physical blows, making her step back, dizzy with adrenaline. She didn't know where to look—at the huge cock plowing into the woman to her right, the spread thighs of the female giving head to a muscle-ripped black guy, or the safe and easy bartender who polished a glass, unfazed by the room filled with the smell of sex and sweat.

"Ready to put your tail between your legs and run back upstairs?" Leo taunted.

She raised her chin. "Bite me."

Asshole.

He gave a predatory chuckle and leaned into her, his lips brushing her ear. "You're in my territory now, Shay. Don't tempt me with dares I'd be more than willing to fulfill."

Her knees weakened, her breathing became labored as he turned and strutted like a fucking peacock toward the bar. She didn't like this. Not one little bit. Upstairs, she held the upper hand. The bars were her domain. She was king of that freaking castle.

Down here was the opposite. This was Leo's territory. The way he baited her only proved how comfortable he felt in this environment. And unfortunately for her, she was entirely out of her depth.

"Leo," she scolded, trying not to distract the patrons from their...patronage.

He ignored her, giving her no choice but to follow in his footsteps like a lost puppy. She came up beside him at the bar, still shaking and skittish when he placed his hand at the low of her back and indicated to the bartender unpacking the dishwasher under the counter.

"Travis, this is Shay."

The mocha-skinned man threw his dishcloth on the counter and hit her with a seductive grin. "Hey, Shay." He held out a hand. "Welcome to the fun house."

She shook his hand, letting the warmth of his palm soothe her, holding on longer than necessary for the support.

"Don't look so petrified." His smile warmed. "You'll be okay."

She wanted to clarify, to tell him whatever horrified expression crossed her features was from shock, not cowardice, but her addled brain had packed up and left the building.

"Shay's the bar manager from upstairs," Leo interrupted, his tone gruff. "She won't be here permanently, only the remainder of tonight and next Saturday to cover Tracy's shift." He pressed his hand harder at the low of her back. "There's no hanging around after closing tonight, Travis. You feel me?"

The bartender stiffened and released Shay's hand. "No problem." Then he turned and moved back to the middle of the bar to continue his job at the dishwasher.

It wasn't until she glanced at Leo that she realized why Travis had fled. Her boss was glaring, still focused on the guy with an unwavering feral stare. "No playing between the staff." He tilted his head, turning those hard ocean eyes on her. "Understood?"

"You're worried about me sleeping with him?" she grated. "Christ, Leo, back off." She was trying her best to remain level-headed about the switch from dance-club bartender to beverage dispenser on a porn set. But there was only so much she could take. And apparently, it wasn't as much as the woman moaning around a mouthful in the corner. She had a guy down her throat, one doing her doggie, and another caressing her breasts, trying to get in on the action.

"I'm not joking, Shay." He turned into her, gripping her chin to hold her attention captive. "No one touches you."

Why don't the rules apply to you? She wanted to ask but bit her tongue instead.

"I'm going to do a scan of the rooms and make sure everything's in order. I'll give you a full tour later, once you've digested the basics. I don't want to scar you for life."

"I've had sex before, Leo. None of this is new to me."

He smirked. "I know from experience, remember? But have you had sex like this?" He quirked a brow, waiting for her response even though the arrogant bastard already knew the answer. "Yeah, I didn't think so."

She leaned toward him, lowering her voice and adding menace to her tone. "Well, maybe I'll convince T.J. to let me down here as a guest. That way I can gain the experience you seem to think is so important." The lie flew from her mouth without pause. He kept baiting her. Her only defense was to retaliate, especially when her own body betrayed her with lust.

His eyes flashed. "You will never come down here without me. You understand? Never."

Her nipples tingled with his command. Traitorous fucking nipples. "You can walk me down those stairs as often as you like, but you've made it clear you won't be making me come again. This is the perfect place for me to find someone who will." Again, the untruths rushed forward, and this time she couldn't help the accompanying smirk.

He released his grip and the anger in his eyes increased. "Never, Shay." And then he was gone, striding away with his head held high and his shoulders straight with arrogance.

CHAPTER THREE

*L*eo continued walking through the main area and into one of the private rooms where Shay's gaze couldn't tickle the back of his neck.

Motherfucker.

This wasn't what he'd expected. She was meant to run, to glare at him in disgust, call him a perverted asshole and vow to never come down here again. Instead, she was still a sassy-mouthed viper and the lust in her eyes hadn't dulled. She was shocked as hell, that much was clear, but she hadn't fled. And now he didn't know what to do.

This was a first for him. Every woman he'd introduced to this part of himself had done a runner. Whether he brought it up in conversation to prepare them, or they made the entire journey to the club door, they all ended up fleeing from his life. Yet, Shay had stuck around, remaining true to her typical reaction to shock—hitting him with a healthy barrage of sarcasm.

Maybe he'd misjudged her. Or maybe she was too proud to admit defeat after stamping her foot and demanding to work down here. Either way, he'd come further than he had with any other woman he'd cared about. He should be relieved, shouldn't he?

"Leo?"

He blinked the half-empty room into focus and smiled at the leggy blonde sauntering toward him. Curvy, with deep-brown eyes and flawless skin, Pamela was a sight to behold. Yet, she was the anomaly in their environment. For an attractive woman, she was shy, apprehensive and didn't like showing off the assets hidden under her shiny red corset and panties. In fact, he'd never seen her participate at all. Like T.J., she only ever watched.

"Are you playing tonight?" She came up beside him, her eyes weary.

"No, sweetheart." He couldn't play. Not with the image of Shay still firmly plastered in the forefront of his mind. "But have fun without me."

She lowered her gaze, nodded and began to slink away.

"Pamela? You okay?"

She paused, glancing over her shoulder with watery eyes.

"Pamela?"

"I'm just frustrated," she murmured. "I want to join in."

He bridged the distance between them in two steps and cupped her upper arms with an encouraging smile. "Then go for it."

"It's not that easy. I haven't been with a man since my husband died."

Husband? Leo jerked back. The beauty couldn't be older than twenty-eight. How the hell was she a widow?

"Don't look at me like that." She gave a half-hearted chuckle. "It happened almost two years ago, but I haven't been able to convince myself to…" she shrugged, "…get back on the horse." Her eyes twinkled and a soft grin tilted her lips. "Could you help me?"

Shit. Talk about insensitive. He had no idea what to say. Shay had rattled him. "What do you need?"

"Guidance." She looked at him with hope. "I know you don't want to play, but could you get me started with someone? Maybe stand beside me and give directions. My husband was very…" she paused, biting her lip, "…instructive. I loved how he took control."

Leo scrubbed a hand over his jaw, trying to wipe Shay from his mind. Tonight was getting more complicated by the minute. "Of course." He scoped the small room, looking for an unoccupied guy. Two hetro couples were in the darkened far corner, the male positioned over his partner, giving her a massage. His hands were on her back while he ground his pelvis against her naked ass. The other couple sat on a leather sofa, murmuring words between slow kisses.

"Give me a sec." He strode from the room, unable to stop his focus from wandering to Shay. She was talking to Travis, a grin plastered across her beautiful face. When her gaze found his, he glanced away, finding what he needed on the chaise to the left of the doorway.

"Jack," he barked.

The guy continued to stroke his cock as he dragged his attention from the two men pleasuring a chesty blonde in the sex swing. "Yeah?"

"I need a little help in here."

"Sure thing." Jack stood, unabashed by his nudity or the stiff dick in his hand.

Leo jerked a thumb in Pamela's direction and waited for the man to pass before he chanced another glance at Shay. Shit. Their gazes collided and her brow furrowed in a silent question. Great. Exactly what he needed—an inquisitive, sassy wench. He ignored her and turned on his heel, making sure the frustration was hidden from his expression when he reached Pamela's side.

"What's up?" Jack asked.

Leo cleared his throat to stop a smart retort and gestured to Pamela. "I want you to help me with this beautiful lady."

Pamela's cheeks turned a darker shade of pink.

"It'd be my pleasure. What do you need me to do?"

Leo waved a lazy hand at the bed to their right. "Kneel on the mattress and go with the flow."

Jack did as instructed, surveying his upcoming conquest with hungry eyes.

"Do you have any rules?" Leo swung to Pamela.

Although members did have paddles, nipple clamps, restraints and floggers at their disposal, this wasn't a BDSM club. Safe words weren't a necessity. However, Leo respected everyone's limits and wanted Pamela's first step back into the world of pleasure to be enjoyable.

She tore her focus from the bed and met Leo's gaze. "No kissing on the mouth. I'm not ready for that."

"No problem," Jack replied. "We'll do whatever you're comfortable with, and don't be scared to stop at any time."

Leo eyed the man, giving him a subtle nod in thanks. Jack had no way of knowing Pamela's history. Yet, his response was exactly what the club was all about. It wasn't all hard fucking and fulfillment. It was about growth through experience, finding likeminded people and learning about yourself as well as others. More importantly, it was about respect.

Most people were quick to judge the less-inhibited lifestyle, not taking the time to understand the safety that accompanied a controlled environment. Women didn't need to be vulnerable and bring a stranger home to experience a one-night stand. Men didn't have to offend their hook ups when they left in the morning without leaving their number. It was also a place where people like Pamela could feel comfortable taking the first step.

"Lay on the bed, sweetheart," Leo murmured.

She complied, climbing onto the mattress to rest her head on the pillows.

"I know you asked for direction, but first I want Jack to make you feel good." Leo focused on the other man. "Go down on her. Use your hands and your mouth to bring her to the brink. Just don't let her come."

Pamela whimpered, biting her beautifully straight teeth into her lower lip as she clenched her thighs together.

Jack grinned and shuffled to her side, gently spreading her legs with his large hands. He hooked his fingers under the waistband of her red satin underwear and slowly pulled them down, exposing the clean-shaven pussy beneath. "You're gorgeous." His gaze was riveted as he placed the material beside him on the mattress.

She was. Blushing with a lustful glow, her breasts heaving against the tightly strung corset, Pamela was a sight, one he hoped her deceased husband had savored.

Jack lay between her spread knees, his mouth hovering close to her core. "Relax," he purred, keeping his focus on Pamela as he swiped his tongue out to brush her clit.

She gasped at the first lick, arching her back off the bed.

Fuck.

Tonight was testing Leo on too many levels. He ached to be the one positioned between heavenly thighs, tasting the heady flavor of arousal. He closed his eyes, picturing the image on the bed with two different people. Shay would be against the pillows, her legs parted for his touch, her cream resting on the tip of his tongue. He'd lap at her, delving his fingers into her smooth heat until she started to whimper. Then he'd back off, kissing her thighs, nipping her skin until she begged him to continue, tangling her fingers in his hair, pulling at the strands.

His dick was hard as stone at the thought. Tap, tap, tapping against his zipper, pleading for release. He wanted her. Naked. Now. If he got through the night without a waver in his step from his growing case of blue balls, he'd be fucking surprised.

Pamela's moan had his eyes opening, and he grinned to find her writhing under Jack's touch. She clutched the bed sheets, her pelvis raised for more, her sounds increasing with every flick of her lover's tongue.

"Enough," Leo ordered, his tone harsher than anticipated.

Jack growled, Pamela whimpered, and they both looked at him with annoyance.

"On your hands and knees, sweetheart." Leo softened the command. "I want you to take his dick in your mouth."

Pamela swallowed as she pushed to a seated position and Jack moved to his knees. Her sights were set on the thick erection jutting toward her, a large fist slowly pumping the length.

"Can you..." she turned to Leo and grimaced, "...can you instruct me?"

He inclined his head, his throat too dry to speak. He could still feel the shiver of Shay's gaze on his skin, could sense her nearby, could almost smell her. His blood rushed with lust and adrenaline, his forehead beaded with sweat. Never had he fought so hard with his self-control. He wanted to stride to the bar, to kiss the sass right out of her and sink his cock into her heat until she screamed.

"T-take." Fuck. He cleared his throat. "Take the head of his shaft in your mouth."

His own dick threatened to explode. He could imagine Shay's lips around his length, her tongue brushing the underside, her delicate hands cupping his balls. Without thought, he stepped forward and palmed the back of Pamela's head, guiding her, testing her gag reflex as she took Jack to the back of her throat.

With his other hand, he adjusted his erection, trying to make the fucker comfortable when it was hard enough to drill through stone. His breathing grew heavy and his eyes rolled to the back of his head as he listened to the suction of her mouth.

Jack began to groan with each gently guided stroke, and the pressure increased to breaking point in Leo's sac. He released his grip, fumbling back as he opened his eyes.

"Are you all right if Jack takes it from here?" he asked. Guilt built in his chest, but unless he got out of this room, away from sex and the temptation of Shay, he was going to make a fool of himself.

Pamela released the cock in her mouth with a pop. "Yes." The word was breathy, her smile genuine.

Thank fuck. He stroked her loose hair behind her ear, letting the sense of achievement dilute some of his lust. "If you need anything, find me."

She nodded as Jack's hand raked through her hair, his palm guiding her mouth back to his cock.

Leo spun around, eager to flee from the potent scent of sex, and found Shay leaning against the doorframe. His cock jerked. His heart stopped. She stood with her chin raised, her jaw tense, her brows pulled together, with her arms crossed over her chest.

You are fucking kidding me.

She had pissed off written all over her face, and although he was thankful her blatant jealousy made his dick wilt, he didn't need her to cause a scene. Downstairs was low drama. Anyone who caused trouble was booted without a second thought and never allowed re-entry. He didn't want that to happen to Shay, because there was no way T.J. or Brute would allow him to make an exception for her behavior. No matter how much they all liked her. The trust of their patrons was paramount.

As he approached, she parted her lips and he shook his head in warning. "Think before you speak, Shay."

She narrowed her eyes and pushed from the doorframe, straightening. "I only wanted to ask a question," she cooed, her tone sweet yet full of menace. "Is that all right?"

"Sure," he muttered.

The need to slam her against the wall, cup her cheeks and kiss the look of defiance off her face was cloying. He wanted to fist her hair, to pull her head back and make sure she knew who was in control down here.

"I was just wondering what job description you file on your tax return," she spoke softly. "Before tonight, I would've considered you a businessman, but after watching your little show, you could also be defined as a pim—"

He grabbed her wrist and yanked her to his side, his eyes burning with anger. "Finish that sentence and we're done." His nostrils flared, his chest pounded, and through it all, he wished she would see past her misconceptions and understand him for who he was.

This was the reason why he hadn't wanted her down here. This was why he'd fought hard to have another staff member take over the vacant shift. He didn't care what any of the other upstairs bartenders thought of him. But with Shay, it was different.

"Don't you dare judge me," he ground out.

Her eyes glinted as he continued to hold her wrist. He could feel her pain, understand her sense of betrayal, yet there was no future for her at Shot of Sin if she didn't get over it.

"This is who I am," he grated. "I don't need your judgment. If you don't like it, you know where the fucking door is."

Her forehead creased into a mass of wrinkles and her bottom lip quavered. He lessened his grip as she fought for control, raised her chin and took a deep breath. She yanked her arm free, gave him one last tortured look and then stormed away, heading for the bar.

Goddamn it.

"And that's why I'm single," he muttered, shaking his head as he made his way to the next private room.

CHAPTER FOUR

An hour later, Shay was still sulking. She knew it. Travis knew it. And wherever Leo was, he knew it too. She wasn't to blame though. Drooling over a man for months and then finding him doing whatever the hell he was doing was reason for any heart-fractured woman to lose a little composure. Well...a lot of composure. She still winced every time she ran the conversation over in her mind. The look on Leo's face when she almost called him a pimp would haunt her for a damn long time.

She hadn't meant to be such a bitch. Her emotions were out of control. He'd walked into view, demanded a naked and fully aroused man follow him into one of the rooms, and her curiosity had been piqued. Along with her jealousy.

With growing dread and an unhealthy amount of unencouraged arousal, she'd watched him from the doorway. Her heart had pounded like unforgiving thunder as he'd focused on another woman's pussy. Her eyes had burned from the erection straining against his zipper. But it was the way he gently cradled the woman's head, guiding her with adoration as she deep throated another guy that made her throat painfully tight.

Shay's confidence had dwindled with every one of Leo's heavy inhalations until she'd been a mass of mental insults. Why was this woman able to gain his attention when Shay had only been able to keep it for mere moments? Maybe her breasts weren't big enough. Maybe she was too short or made herself appear too eager. Damn him. Whatever it was, she had to get over herself. No man had the right to make her feel worthless.

Fuck that.

After next weekend, she would gladly take her position behind the upstairs main bar, tail between her legs, and never shamelessly flirt with him again. Curiosity had not only killed the cat, it had slaughtered the optimistic anticipation in her pussy, too.

"How you doing?" Travis turned his back to the room and resting against the counter.

She shrugged. Anger had made it easier to get over the shock of what was happening in the room. The blood rushing through her ears dimmed the animalistic sounds of sex, and the constant slow stream of drink requests kept her busy. Still, all she could think about was Leo and what was going through his mind.

"I'm okay." She jerked her chin to the left. "The guy in the corner is freaking me out a little, though."

Travis peered over his shoulder to the man seated on a black chaise. The stranger had been staring at her on and off for the last hour. Every time she glanced up, his gaze was focused on her, his hand on his boxer-covered erection.

Travis turned back to her. "I can get Leo to make him stop."

"No." She shook her head. God, no.

All she wanted was to get through the remainder of her shift without seeing her boss at all. She owed him an apology, but she wasn't in the right mood to give it at the moment. "It's fine. I noticed another woman doing the exact same thing to you earlier. If it's normal, I can deal." At least for the next hour until her shift was over, then she'd go home, scrub her skin until she no longer felt dirty and drown her sorrows with chocolate.

The tops of Travis's cheeks darkened.

"Are you blushing?" She grinned.

"That was Melissa." He broke eye contact, busying himself with wiping down the already clean counter. "She gets off on people watching her get off."

And he loves it.

"But I'm used to it," he added. "If that guy makes you feel uncomfortable, just say so."

She shook her head dismissively and glanced past the man in the corner one more time. No matter how ripped the guy's abs were or how sexy his jaw line, he still made her skin crawl. Only dealing with Leo wasn't an option. She'd have to ignore the sleazy masturbation stare.

"So give me a rundown of the rules." She needed a distraction. "How does someone get access to this part of the club? And why do I rarely see people entering from upstairs?"

"There's a long list of rules." Travis threw his dishcloth into the sink and moved to lean against the counter beside her. "The club isn't advertised. It runs merely on word of mouth and is only open on Saturday nights. Anyone who wants to attend has to pass guidelines set by T.J., Leo, and Brute."

"Guidelines?"

"Haven't you noticed that most of the guys are ripped?"

Shay frowned and scanned the patrons. He was right. There wasn't an overweight man in sight. They were all reasonably athletic, some more so than others.

"Men have to be to a certain standard—physically fit, no love handles. I think there's even a rule on chest and back hair."

"And how is it policed? They walk through the club, bare their chest and can't get access if they're too hairy or overweight?"

Travis chuckled. "An application has to be submitted via email every time someone wants to join the fun. Men have to attach an image of themselves in nothing but their underwear. And women have to provide a headshot. If they don't fit the criteria, they don't gain entry, and if the photos they send are bogus, either the security guards will turn them away at the door, or whoever is on duty down here will have a quiet word with them."

"And what's with the different standards?" Shay was all for women's rights, but most of the females down here weren't held to the same standard as the men. There were a lot of curves and full breasts jiggling around. "How come women don't have to meet the same criteria?"

"Would you fuck a fat and hairy guy?"

Shay winced. "I guess I never really thought about it." She wasn't into hairy men, but if Wolverine found his way into her bed, she sure as shit wouldn't kick him out. Yet, she had to admit, she'd never been with a man with weight issues.

"See? Women are more selective than men. Everyone pays a hefty price to enter the doors. So, Brute vets applications and selects guests based on who is more likely to interact better with others. Guys tend to want to get naked with any woman with a good dose of confidence and sexuality, no matter what size, shape or color."

Travis grabbed a tall glass from the dishwasher rack, scooped in some ice and filled it with water from the soda dispenser. "We have couples' night, where most attendants are in a long-term relationship but want to play with other likeminded couples. Ladies' night has a ratio sixty-percent female, to forty-percent male, and vice-versa for people looking for more man action."

Shay's mind buzzed from the onslaught of debauchery. "Wow. I'm blown away, not only at being in a fully functioning sex club, but the amount of detail the guys have put into it."

Travis smirked. "*Blown* away?"

She rolled her eyes at the innuendo and nudged his shoulder. "I guess I had that one coming to me."

He snorted, showing a dazzling smile. He was an attractive guy, clean shaven, nice build, light-green eyes against his smooth, dark skin. No wonder women stared at him while they rowed the boat. He was capable of inspiring scream-worthy orgasms from his looks alone.

"Do you ever play?" She broke eye contact as the question fell like a stone between them. It wasn't a pickup line, yet it sounded like it once the words left her lips.

"The more you work down here, the more open-minded you become. I suppose it's only natural that staff are allowed to participate on their nights off, or after the last call for drinks."

"You didn't answer my question." She gave his shoulder another nudge.

"Oh, you noticed that, did you?" He placed the glass of water against his lips and slowly sipped.

Hint taken. "How about the owners? Do the same rules apply for T.J. and Brute?" And Leo, she added silently.

The jealousy from earlier hadn't faded. She still pictured the man of her dreams caressing another woman, staring at her longingly. Please tell me management have their own set of rules where they can't participate.

"Do you really want to hear the answer?" He placed his glass on the counter and looked her in the eye. "You've got a thing for Leo."

It wasn't a question, so she didn't bother answering.

"He's active, Shay." His eyes softened as he spoke. "They all spend a lot of time down here."

Damn.

That hurt more than she'd anticipated. She nodded, breaking eye contact. It was over then—her infatuation, the flirting, the heart-fluttering moments she always hoped would turn into something more.

As if called from her thoughts, Leo appeared at the doorway of one of the rooms. His gaze sought hers, and before she could look away, he broke the connection and moved into the next room.

Shit.

She didn't even have the upper hand with glance-aways. This sucked…harder than the woman in the corner making slurping sounds around a bodybuilder's cock.

She couldn't stop the throbbing ache in her chest from intensifying. It hurt to think of him with other women. Not only because she was jealous, but because she genuinely liked him. Leo was a great guy, sex-club tendencies or not. He held a certain charm she'd never seen before. She'd even go as far to say he was a true gentleman under the layers of arrogance, stubbornness and the inability to believe he was ever wrong.

Shay was thankful when a guy wearing silk boxers sidled up to the bar, dispersing her pity party. With a silent jut of his chin to Travis, he turned his back and concentrated on the threesome taking place in front of the mega porn screen.

"He's a regular," Travis murmured. "He'll probably be here next week. Always orders bourbon on the rocks."

She acknowledged the drink with a nod, but her gaze kept drifting back to the room Leo had entered. Her insides were being torn apart, one side of her wanting to know what he was doing, the other not willing to find out.

"Where's the bathroom," she spoke above a whisper. She needed a live-porn breather, to get the sounds, the scent and the images out of her mind. At least for a little while.

"First door to the left." He pointed a lazy hand to one of the open doorways. "At the end of the room, there are female and male amenities with showers and anything else you or any of the patrons should need."

Shay frowned. What the hell did that mean? "Okay. I'll be back in a minute."

"You should call it a night." Travis slid the drink along the bar to silk-boxers guy, and met her gaze. "You're starting to look pale, and your shift is almost over anyway. Go home and regroup before next weekend."

Shay let out a sigh. The guy she liked was a deviant, she didn't know how she could continue working at the job she loved, and now she apparently looked like shit. "Yeah. I might do that." She continued to the first room on the left, staring at her toes, concentrating on each footstep so she didn't falter and draw unwanted attention.

When she reached the doorway, a shiver of apprehension ran over her skin. This room was quiet, no orgasmic banshee calls or heated moans, just the faint sound of a female giggle and the deep murmurings of more than one male.

Curiosity grabbed hold of her ovaries and held tight until she raised her gaze to the three people on the lone bed in the room. Comfy-looking sofas and ottomans lined the walls, but the main focal point was the bed, illuminated by tiny lights in the ceiling. A curvy blonde reclined in the center, her face bright with a beautiful smile, her body entirely naked, her thighs slightly parted to expose her smooth sex.

A man lay on her right, propped on one elbow, his gaze focused on the woman with adoration while he idly drew trails around the smooth skin of her hip with his fingers. On her left lay another, his head bowed to her chest. It wasn't until Shay took another step that she could see him placing delicate kisses around the side of the woman's breast.

Shay held her breath, overcome with an emotion she couldn't pinpoint. Envy? Distaste? The scene before her was mesmerizing. The gentle way the men paid attention to the beaming woman. The way their cocks stood hard as stone, yet they weren't rutting on their prize like a dog in heat. It seemed almost romantic... In a sex club? Holy fuck, Shay was confused.

"Hey." The man facing her greeted with a genuine smile.

The connection was enough to make her footsteps falter. "Ah. Hi."

She wasn't familiar with the protocol of sex-club conversation. What was she supposed to say? How's it hanging...when clearly it wasn't hanging at all.

She lowered her gaze with a frown and increased her pace to the bathroom. Once inside, she pushed the door shut and leaned against the wall beside it, breathing deep to control her anxiety.

This was ridiculous. She was a strong, self-assured, grown woman.

Not a fumbling, blubbering mess. This shit had to stop. Only she didn't know how to curb the unfamiliar flutter of butterflies in her belly, or shake the sordid thoughts in her mind.

Going back to her main bar job and acting normal was going to require an Oscar-winning performance. She wouldn't be able to look T.J., Brute or Leo in the eye again. Not without picturing them entangled in a mass orgy of beautiful people. And it pissed her off even more when her pussy began to tingle at the image.

She usually owned her sexuality. Getting herself off wasn't something she was embarrassed about. She had toys, watched porn and had the occasional one-night stand. But this...a sex club, was way beyond her depths. Travis was right. Going home early was the best option.

And what the hell was on the vanity? She straightened and made her way to the basin, ignoring her reflection in the mirror. Along the ceramic counter stood a myriad of deodorant bottles, all different brands placed neatly in a line. Beside them were bath towels, plush and dark with some already discarded in the thick wicker basket beside the vanity. In front of the towels was a laminated list of rules taped to the counter. Her management trio really had thought of everything. The page listed privacy requirements, the need for regular STD checks, instructions on washing after every play session, right down to the necessity to place condoms on sex toys before use.

She groaned, reaffirmed in her decision to leave. Her brain was fried, and every compiling aspect made her overreact. She turned, about to flee, when the door swooshed open and the attractive blonde from the bed walked in.

"Are you all right?" The woman stood before Shay with a whole heap of exposed tits and pussy.

With no control to stop it, Shay's gaze raked the woman's body, over the hardened nipples, the glint of jewelry in her navel, the crevices of bare vagina, to the smooth thighs and finally her dark painted toe nails.

Awkward. Stare at those toes. Do not take your focus away from those fucking toes.

"Umm." Shay cleared her throat. "I'm fine."

"Do you mind handing me a towel?"

Shay was thankful for the excuse to turn her back, and gave the woman what she wanted.

"Is that better?"

Shay raised her gaze to the woman now covered in the large towel, feeling a slight reprieve to the massive case of holy-fuck-get-me-out-of-here. "Thanks," she murmured, ignoring the heat climbing up her neck.

"Now tell me what's really wrong."

Shay frowned.

"Come on." The woman strolled past her and jumped to sit on the vanity counter. "Spill. You look like you're caught between disgust and shock."

Ouch. "Is it that obvious?"

The woman nodded. "Kinda. I've been around the club for a while. I've seen a lot of virgins walk through the doors."

"Oh, I'm no virgin." Shay shook her head. The situation continued to worsen. Not only was her distaste evident, but she was acting so childish people thought she was pure.

"Sex-club virgin, honey." She chuckled. "It's nothing to worry about. You just look out of place."

The clarification didn't help. "I don't think I'm cut out for this type of scene. Even as a working environment."

"Why are you apprehensive?"

Shay didn't know where to start. The list in her mind seemed a mile long and it was all exacerbated because the man she liked was a participant and the owner. "It's...so..." She shrugged. She didn't know this woman, and she certainly didn't want to offend her any more than she probably already had.

"Would it help if I told you why I come here?"

The woman focused on Shay with genuine concern, like they were best friends trying to get through a challenging situation. There was no reason for it, but Shay felt a slight connection to the woman's sincerity. Maybe it was because she wanted to cling to the only person who didn't currently have exposed assets.

"I guess."

"I'm single." The woman grinned, as if her status was a badge of honor. "I work. Hard. Every damn day, and at the end of the week, I want someone to snuggle up to. My job doesn't give me time to date, and I don't really want that drama in my life at the moment. But what I do want is a little attention every now and then."

The woman paused, waiting for a reaction. Shay could only nod in acknowledgement.

"I love sex." The woman's smile widened. "However, men can be selfish assholes."

Shay released a soft chuckle. "You're preaching to the choir."

"I guess it's hard to explain. And I suppose, even harder for an outsider to understand. But down here, it's like family." The woman cringed. "Wow. That came out wrong."

Shay snorted with delirium and came to rest against the vanity, listening intently.

"Everyone down here wants sex. And I guess, because we are all somewhat assured of getting what we crave, people are more giving. The guys..." her eyes glittered, "...they are ah-may-zing. If you say no they immediately back off. There are no questions, no recriminations, no judgments."

It sounded amazing, in theory. "But don't you feel weird having a crowd of people watch you?"

"Have you ever been watched?" The woman raised a brow. "Have you ever fantasized about someone watching you?"

"Maybe." Shay shrugged and felt the heat crawl back up her neck when the woman grinned.

"It's a rush. And most of all, for me, it's uplifting. Knowing another man, or woman, is aroused because of what you're doing." The woman crossed her legs, making the towel rise up her thighs. "Security is also a big bonus. I come here knowing I won't be assaulted or abused. I don't have to seduce men and risk my safety by leaving a public place with them or taking them back to my home, which is secluded and would make me vulnerable. For me, there's no other option, until I want to settle down and focus on finding a husband."

Shay broke eye contact and stared at the polished tiled floor. It made sense. Picking up men involved risk and wasn't usually worth the effort.

"I'm Zoe by the way."

"Shay."

"Well, Shay, I know you're down here as a staff member, not a participant, but try and look at the club without reservations. Imagine what it would be like if two guys were smothering you with affection, their sole focus on your pleasure."

The fantasy heated her nipples and she crossed her arms over her chest in frustration. "I'm not looking for more than one partner."

"That's understandable. And I bet you already have someone in mind." Zoe quirked her sultry lips. "Rumors are already spreading about Leo commanding you aren't to be touched. He's a great guy. You'd be a lucky woman if you gained his long-term interest."

No luck there. Shay was far from gaining his interest.

"He's a sexual man, though. You'd need to get over your inhibitions."

Shay released a heavy breath, unsure if getting over her inhibitions was an option. Or even worth it. From Leo, she wanted love. And it didn't seem possible to establish a relationship in this environment.

A loud bang sounded on the door and Shay startled. "Shit."

"Shay, are you in there?" Leo's voice boomed from outside the bathroom.

"Wow." Zoe pushed off the counter. "The boss sounds like he's going caveman on your ass. Do you really want to miss the opportunity to have all that raw masculinity to yourself?"

"But that's just it—" She wanted to discuss her issues concerning monogamy but another loud knock cut her off.

"*Shay.*"

"I'll leave you to it." Zoe unwrapped the towel from around her body and placed it in the wicker basket. "I have two very lovely men to get back to."

Shay straightened and had to stop herself from begging the woman not to leave. She didn't want to be left alone with Leo. So far tonight, all they'd done was argue. She wanted to go back to the flirting and fun, the innuendo and batting eyelashes, and forget this discovery had ever been made.

Instead, she swallowed the nausea creeping up her throat and rubbed at the rampant butterflies in her belly. "Thank you."

"No problem, honey. Come find me if you ever have any questions."

Shay gripped the counter behind her, oblivious to the naked curves strutting from the bathroom, and focused on the man who reached to hold open the door. She'd never seen Leo so furious. His eyes were narrowed slits, his jaw tight, his hands clenched in fists at his side while wild strands of hair shadowed his features.

"What's going on?" His harsh tone hit harder than the current glare he fixed her with.

She could understand his aggression. She'd insulted him earlier and it would take more than a few hours for him to get over it. An apology was necessary. She just couldn't find the strength to say it.

Not tonight. Not when her heart was bleeding and her temples throbbing.

"I'm going to the bathroom." She pulled a face. *Duh.*

"Cut the crap, Shay. You've been in here for fifteen minutes." He strode inside the women's bathroom like his shit was red hot and let the door fall closed behind him. "Are you capable of working the bar next weekend or not?"

She straightened, taking his question as a fresh insult to her capabilities. "Of course I am. You know that."

"Do I? You made it clear you don't approve of the scene. I don't want you spreading hate toward the patrons. They pay good money to be here."

Fuck you.

She returned his glare. "I'd never do that." And besides, she didn't have hate to spread. Every passing minute made her realize her aversion was from being clueless about the lifestyle. For singles, it seemed like the perfect way to have fun. She didn't know if she'd ever try it herself or understand the reasons why someone in a committed relationship would join, but her horizons were inching a tiny bit wider.

"Really?" He shrugged. "I guess I don't know what to expect from you anymore."

"From me? Are you kidding?" She raised her voice. "*You* blindsided *me*, remember? You knew I had feelings for you, and you strung me along like a lost puppy. And all this time I never had a chance."

"Because I knew you'd act like this," he snarled. "This is who I am, Shay, and I knew you'd never want a part of it." He stepped forward, closing in on her. "I didn't lead you on. I tried my fucking hardest to stay away. Do you think I haven't imagined spreading your thighs a thousand damn times since you started working here? Or wondered what it would be like if you enjoyed the club scene. I've been living in my own private hell, unable to stop you from dragging me round by the dick."

His angered breaths brushed her lips as her mouth dried.

"You never gave me a chance." She swallowed over the gravel in her throat. He didn't have the right to make assumptions about her sexuality, just like she hadn't had the right to insult him earlier.

"I did." His voice lowered to a whisper. "Months ago, when I touched you in the storeroom."

Shay narrowed her gaze on his ocean eyes. "I don't understand."

"I was testing you. Once and for all, I needed to know how you reacted to sex. If you'd be open-minded enough to try things out of your comfort zone. Yet, even in the privacy of a storeroom, you acted shocked and distraught at what we'd done."

No. Fucking. Way. She blinked at him, not sure whether to set him straight or claw his eyes out. "I wasn't distraught."

She'd been shocked, yes, because it was the first time a guy had unselfishly pleasured her. Usually, she was the one giving sexual favors without her own gratification. She'd been flustered, trying to hide her growing infatuation and adoration because he'd treated her the way she'd always wanted to be treated. In that moment, her feelings had passed the point of infatuation and she'd struggled to disguise it.

"You should've given me the opportunity to make my own decisions." She stepped to the side, needing space from his cloying dominance. "I might have tried."

He bridged the gap between them, hovering over her. "Prove it."

"Prove what?" She shuddered, trying to ignore the throb beginning to pulse in her pussy.

He took another step, backing her into the counter, bringing them thigh to thigh. "That you'd try." His gaze was bleak as he pressed the hardness of his erection against her abdomen. "Try for me. Now," he whispered.

She shook her head. Not tonight. Not when her heart was barely beating and her mind couldn't control her rampant thoughts. He didn't deserve it. Nor did she. No matter how much her pussy throbbed in encouragement. "No."

Slowly, he leaned forward, his light dusting of stubble brushing her cheek. She shivered, her thoughts and body swaying as he murmured in her ear.

"Your lips say no, but your body says otherwise. Which is it?"

She closed her eyes, unable to decide, unable to breathe. She ran her hand around his neck for grounding and prayed the right choice would hurry up and make itself known. All she'd ever wanted was his attention, his desire, but the timing and her insecurities were tainting the X-rated fairytale she'd imagined.

"Shay." Her name was a whisper against her neck as he brought one of his hands to rest on the counter, the other on her hip, and then slowly moved upward. "Please don't torture me."

Him?

He'd been endlessly tormenting her for longer than she could remember. "I don't know what to do."

Her body was on fire, her nipples hard, her sex fluttering. But people were on the other side of that door. Naked people. Anyone could walk in. Anyone could see them and think their intimacy was a show to be watched. Did that matter? Right now, she had no fucking clue. The heat of his body made it hard to rationalize.

He parted her legs with his knee and ground the hardness of his thigh against her mound. Her sex creamed in response, bursting to life in a mass of tingles. Damn her treacherous body.

A whimper escaped her throat and she clung tighter to his neck. She wanted him so much it hurt, but she didn't want to hate herself afterward. If she did this, it needed to be for the right reasons. And all of her had to be onboard—mind, body and soul. Not just her pussy.

"I can't." She released him and placed her hands against his chest. "I need more time."

He stiffened, killing her slowly in the following silent seconds. "Okay." He stepped back, keeping his focus lowered. The hard length of his erection strained against the crotch of his pants, and it suddenly hit her that he might go elsewhere for relief.

"It's almost time for you to knock off anyway. You may as well go home and get the extra sleep."

Alarm bells rang in her ears. His instant dismissal only exacerbated her theory of him taking another woman. Her stomach nose-dived, freefalling while she silently sucked in a deep breath. The distress must have been written on her face, because when he glanced up, his features softened.

"I don't want to hurt you."

"But you will, right?" she choked. "I'll drive away the same moment you drive your dick into someone else."

She instantly regretted the words, even before the look of loathing crossed his face. Calm under pressure, she was not.

"I'm not a fucking animal," he spoke through clenched teeth and spun away from her, heading for the door. "Go home, Shay."

CHAPTER FIVE

*L*eo slid onto one of the bar stools and kept his head lowered, his hands fisted into tight balls below the counter. He was on the cusp of losing his shit. He'd never been this angry in his life. His heart was pounding, his head throbbing, and if he clenched his teeth any tighter, he was sure he'd crack a tooth.

"Scotch," he barked at Travis.

Shay continued to come out swinging, and he only had himself to blame. He was the reason she was acting like a wounded animal backed into a corner. He should've waited until she came out of the bathroom, into the open, instead of storming in on her. Only he hadn't been able to curb his worry when he couldn't find her behind the bar. He let panic choose his actions instead of common sense, and yet again, he was nursing wounded pride.

"Here you go, boss."

Leo grasped the glass that slid in front of him and downed it in two burning gulps. Sweet Jesus, that stung. He wanted to order another, to get shit-faced and bury his troubles in the depths of another woman's body just to piss Shay off. It wouldn't take much for him to be the asshole she thought he was. But no matter how angry he became, he wouldn't stoop that low.

He had a heart. And although he wanted to, he couldn't blame Shay for her backhanded comments. She was in shock and always flew off the handle when she didn't have tight control of her emotions. He'd seen it happen too many times to count. It was one of her not-so-endearing charms—the way she showed she was hurting by shooting out a rapid, uncensored response.

"I'm going home." Her voice broke his thoughts.

He held tight to his glass, trying hard not to raise his gaze. She wasn't speaking to him anyway. From his periphery, he watched her grab her cell from the counter and shove it in her pocket. "I hope to see you again, Travis."

"You too, Sas-Shay."

Quit the endearments, Travis, or I'll break your face.

She strode back around the counter, not acknowledging Leo's existence, not bothering with a see you later, asshole, and stormed away. The need to chase after her clawed at his back. He even had to fight not to glance over his shoulder and watch her leave.

"Fuck that."

He'd walked down this shitty path before. He was stronger than this. She was only a woman, after all. Nobody should have a tight rein on his dick like she did. Then again, she'd always been more than a typical woman to him. He'd been attracted to her since the day she'd handed in her employment application.

Tempting looks aside, he was drawn to her for too many reasons. She worked hard, played even harder, and owned her independence. She didn't placate others and never hid behind a fake façade. He needed a strong-willed woman like that. He needed her, period.

"Want to talk about it?" Travis asked.

Leo raised his gaze and glared.

The bartender held up his hands in surrender. "I guess not." He began polishing the beer taps. "Let me know when you cool down. I need to speak to you about a minor issue with Shay earlier."

Issue? As if he wasn't going to bite at that statement. "What issue?"

"It isn't major, and she didn't want me to make a big deal about it." He shrugged. "Glenn kept staring at her from the corner while he jerked off. I don't think she was prepared for that sort of thing. It freaked her out."

Of course she wasn't fucking prepared. Leo hadn't given her the time to be. He'd crumpled under Brute and T.J.'s suggestion, not wanting to out his infatuation for her and completely cocked up the situation. He pushed from his stool, ready to...he didn't know what, and stepped back into a human wall.

"It's just me," T.J. spoke from behind him. "Where's Shay?"

"Shh," Leo snapped and raised his brows at Travis to continue.

"There was no issue," he reiterated. "She was cool about it and made it clear she didn't want anything said to you or Glenn. But I thought I'd let you know, I had a quiet word with him anyway. I told him tonight was her first night and she was a little skittish."

"Fuck." Leo huffed out a breath and rubbed his forehead. "We're going to lose our best bartender." He was going to lose her. "Shay's out of her fucking mind." He rounded on T.J. "And it's all your fault."

He ignored his friend's frown of annoyance and scoped the room. "Where is he? I want to speak to him."

"I dunno," Travis answered. "Maybe he left. Everything was fine, though. Glenn was apologetic. He didn't realize she was new."

"Well, he should've fucking realized." Leo hoped to hell Glenn had gone home, otherwise the target of his frustrations would wish he'd never showed up tonight.

"Calm down," T.J. muttered. "Travis took care of it."

But what about Shay? Who was taking care of her?

Leo slumped back onto the bar stool. "Tonight was a total fuck up."

"Why?" T.J. asked. "Couldn't she hack it?"

"I thought she did a great job," Travis added.

Leo glanced over his shoulder at T.J., not bothering to hide the vulnerability itching to break free. "No." He shook his head. "It didn't go well. I'm not sure if she'll come back." To the club, or back into his life. And after all the women who'd dismissed him due to his sexual proclivities, Shay's rejection was by far the worst to take.

~

Shay fled up the staircase and rushed through the Shot of Sin dance crowd. Without a word to her bar staff, she snatched her handbag from the main bar storeroom and headed for the entrance of the club. She needed to blow this pop stand. Fast. Her chest was throbbing with regret, a sensation she was too familiar with but unfortunately couldn't control because of her shitty temper.

It was her one downfall. She couldn't hide her emotions. It was either blow up or tear up, and she fucking hated crying. But she would apologize. She always did. All she needed was a little time to ditch the fuzzy, blindsided sensation, then she'd make amends.

Once she sucked in a few deep breaths of clean, night air, she would calm down. The hope of relaxation almost had her running through the crowded entry hall to the lights illuminating the street outside.

"Leaving so soon?" Brute stepped away from the small group of females and blocked her path. His gaze narrowed, the slightest hint of concern tightening his brows. "You look ticked."

"I am ticked." Deep breath. Deep breath. "You could've warned me."

He shrugged a shoulder. "I did. I told you to stay away from Leo months ago. You didn't listen."

What?

"Was tonight about proving a point?" Her eyes burned with humiliation. "Was Leo in on this?"

"No on both counts. Tonight was about filling in for Tracy. But I admit it was an added bonus that I didn't have to spell out why the two of you aren't compatible."

Shay let out an angry breath. "Nice, Brute. Real nice." She shook her head and stepped around him.

"I care about you. We all do."

His admission made her halt. She kept her gaze on the street light beckoning her to flee. Defeat had firmly set in. She'd been humiliated, devalued and heartbroken, all in one night. And the worst part was the waning hold she had on her confidence.

"Believe me, Shay, if you two had any chance of being together, I'd be the first in line to give my congratulations. But it's not going to happen. Leo doesn't do normal. None of us do."

She released a derisive laugh. "I never knew being normal was such a repulsive attribute. I suppose I should thank you for the reality check." She turned to him with a raise brow and a fake smile. There was still no emotion to his features, no comforting smile, no pleading eyes. "Good night, Brute."

She strode away, trying to rebuild her broken walls. This wasn't the end of the world. It was only the death of an infatuation. It didn't change the love she had for her job. It didn't make her less of a person because she hadn't experienced the joys of communal fucking. All she had to do was go home, pull on her big-girl panties and spend some time online looking at Gandy candy. Mr. David Gandy would fix everything. He always did.

The cool night air comforted her as she stepped outside, not bothering to acknowledge the bouncers standing at the door.

"You need an escort?" one of them called.

She shook her head, unable to speak. They usually made sure she reached her car safely, but she didn't want the company tonight. The two-minute walk to the staff parking lot at the back of the building wasn't going to kill her.

She needed to get home. And the sooner the better. The thin material of her figure-hugging top was making her skin crawl. Even the light breeze against her cheeks was beginning to make her whimper.

What a fucking disaster.

Turning the corner, she slowed her pace, needing to calm herself before sliding behind the wheel.

"Hey, miss."

Her gaze snapped around at the deep voice. Oh, shit. It was the guy from Vault of Sin, the one who'd thought she was God's gift to masturbation. She ignored him and increased her pace. Adrenaline spurred her faster, her legs almost breaking into a run.

"I just want to talk."

In a darkened parking lot? In the early hours of the morning? After jerking off in front of her?

No thanks.

"I'm not interested." She palmed her keys, ready for anything. Everything.

Turning the far corner of the building, she chanced another glance over her shoulder and stumbled across the loose asphalt. Her bag slid from her shoulder, falling to the ground, and the spike of fear almost had her doubling over.

With a squeal, she yanked the handbag strap from the ground and began to run to her car. She fumbled with the button in her hand, finally unlocking the doors as she reached for the handle. He was right behind her, she could feel it. Her senses were on red alert, waiting for a rough hand to grab her.

She yanked the door open, jumped inside and pressed the lock as fast as she could. Her hands shook trying to get the key in the ignition, and she almost sobbed in relief when they slid into place. Without pause, she gunned the engine, yanked her gearstick into reverse and floored it.

God help anyone behind me.

As she pulled out, she caught the shadow of the man standing at the corner of the building, one hand raised, asking her to stop. Okay, so maybe he wasn't right behind her, but he had more chance getting a blowjob from one of the alley cats than he did of her hitting the brakes.

Buh bye, asshole.

She watched him jog after her car from the rear-view mirror, following her to the front of the building. Pressing harder on the accelerator, she pulled onto the road, thankful for no oncoming traffic.

Two blocks down the road, she was still breathing heavy, her heart gradually descending from her throat. What a douche. Mr. Masturbator was the perfect ending to an equally perfect day. There wasn't a hope in hell she would sleep tonight, or the rest of the week for that matter. She would dread seeing Leo on Tuesday when she worked the lunch shift at the Taste of Sin restaurant. Even if she did regain her confidence, it would take a lot of effort to hide her wounded pride.

Flicking on her indicator, she pulled to a stop at the traffic lights and inwardly cursed her stupidity. If only she'd kept her mouth shut. Leo wasn't a jerk, he'd probably had no intention of sleeping with anyone tonight…until she'd overreacted and driven him to it. And who knew, in the light of day she might've been able to understand what the whole sex-club thing was about.

She wasn't a prude. Her mind was as open as a hooker's thighs. He'd shocked her, that's all. She'd never seen him with another woman, and having the mental image of him diddling the masses was heart shattering.

"Stupid. Stupid. Stupid."

She blinked back the sting in her eyes and winced when the lights from a car behind her entered her rear-vision mirror. They flashed their high beams and she glanced up to confirm the traffic lights hadn't changed.

"Nope," she muttered. "What's your problem?"

Focusing back on her mirror, her skin prickled as she zeroed in on the car behind her. No way. It was the guy from the parking lot. He'd followed her.

"Son of a bitch."

He opened his car door and her heart stopped in fear. She had no intention of sticking around. She checked for traffic and then turned through the red light, reaching for her bag as she pulled onto the main road.

He was going to follow her home and then rape and murder her. Holy shit, she was going to die. She riffled through her bag for her phone and unlocked the screen as she drove. Calling Leo wasn't an option. He already thought she was weak, and she wouldn't give him the satisfaction of rubbing it in. Instead, she clicked on T.J.'s contact and bit her lip as the phone rang.

"Hey, Shay, what's up?"

Flashing lights glared at her through the rear-view mirror, and she whimpered. "Please help me. A guy from the club came after me in the parking lot. He's following me home. I don't know what to do."

"Baby, calm down." Concern laced his words. "Where are you?"

"I'm on the main road, a few blocks from work, heading toward the city."

"Can you turn around and come back?"

She shook her head and puffed out an anxious breath. "I don't want to take a side street and risk him running me off the road. Please, T.J., I don't know what to do."

"Don't worry, I'm coming after you. Stay on the main road and slow down so I can catch up. But don't stop. I'll be there in a minute."

"Okay." Her voice waivered. She lifted her foot off the accelerator, slowing the car well below the speed limit. The guy behind her continued to flash his lights, his arm now waving out the window, his finger pointing to the side of the road.

This was karma. She'd been a raging bitch to Leo, and now she was paying the price. Either her stalker was going to ram into her car and drag her out the door, or she'd have a heart attack while she waited.

Chill.

She sucked in a shaky breath, let it out slowly and turned on the radio. The lethargic, early morning music did nothing to soothe her. All she could do was continue to hyperventilate and wait.

As she reached a yield sign, a horn blasted, startling her. A car sped up beside her on the wrong side of the road, and Leo's face stared at her from the passenger window. Shit. She didn't know if she should be relieved or more frightened from the heat in his eyes.

"Pull over," he mouthed, his lips set in a solemn line.

She did as instructed, driving through the intersection and pulling to the curb in front of the next street light. T.J.'s car parked behind her, and the other guy followed. Before she had time to cut the engine, she saw Leo in her rear-view mirror. He flung open his door and climbed from the car with his shoulders broad with menace. There wasn't an ounce of softness to his features as he turned his back and jogged to the stranger's car.

"Oh, shit." She watched in horror as he yanked the guy out by his shirt and thrust him against the side of the vehicle.

"Shay."

She screamed and then clasped a hand over her mouth. T.J. stood outside her car, one hand on the door handle while the other tapped on her window until she released the lock. He opened the door as she unclicked her seatbelt and then reached down to help her out.

"Come here."

She could hear Leo yelling as she went willingly into T.J.'s arms.

"It was just a misunderstanding," he cooed in her ear.

Misunderstanding?

She tilted her head, listening to Leo verbally abuse the man. "Well, you don't fucking chase after her. You drop the keys with the bouncers and let her figure out she's lost them. Why did you follow her into the parking lot anyway?"

Keys?

"Travis came to me in the club and said I freaked her out. I felt like shit and wanted to apologize." The man was almost talking too fast for her to understand, yet, all the awkward pieces began falling into place. "I gathered I was scaring her, so I stopped following, but she dropped her handbag and didn't pick up her keys. I'm sorry. It was my initial reaction to go after her."

Shay winced. "I'm such a tool."

"No, you're not." T.J. hugged her tight. "He should've known better than to go after you. You had every reason to be frightened."

She whimpered and closed her eyes, resting her head against his shoulder. The jingle of keys sounded and then a car door slammed. She closed her lids tighter as the stranger's car sped off and heavy footsteps approached.

When the crunch against the asphalt stopped, she held her breath in the silence. She couldn't look at Leo, couldn't take the anger in his eyes or the annoyance at her stupidity. Instead, she burrowed deeper into T.J., hoping he'd hold her a little longer, until she recovered enough from her embarrassment to drive home.

"I'll take it from here," Leo spoke softly.

Her lids fluttered open and her lips trembled with the need to protest as T.J. retreated a step. He gave a sad smile and stroked a lazy hand through her hair. "I'll head back to the club and close things up for the night. Call me if you need anything."

No. Don't leave me.

She stared wide-eyed, silently begging him not to bail on her. Especially when Leo didn't look like he was going anywhere. "I'll be fine," she croaked, hoping the two of them would leave together. "Thank you both." She kept her focus on T.J., no matter how hard Leo's gaze bore into the side of her face. "I'll see you both next week."

T.J. waited, scrutinizing her.

"I said I'd take care of it," Leo growled. "Just go."

A shiver ran down her spine at his command, and she twisted around to her car, ready to flee. She pulled open the door to the sound of T.J.'s retreating steps, then the air left her lungs as a heavy hand wove around her waist and slammed it shut again.

He was right behind her, his chest at her back, his breath in her hair. "I'll drive you home," he murmured, making her come undone, dragging the uncontrollable emotions higher up her throat.

She shook her head. They'd fought enough tonight. The battle scars still stung across her heart. Being around him now would make it ten times harder to stop the tears she despised from flowing. She wasn't a fucking crier. The last time she'd shed tears was years ago. And she'd be damned if she broke the achievement by blubbering over an enthusiastic masturbator and a case of mistaken intentions.

"I'm a big girl. I can drive myself home." She stood rigid, waiting for him to back off, hoping the warmth sinking under her skin would quickly vanish.

"Please, Shay."

His plea undid her. He didn't say another word, just continued to lean into her, his breath fanning her neck, his scent driving her crazy as T.J. pulled out from behind them. Leo placed his hand on her hip, sending a shudder through her stomach and higher to her nipples. She closed her eyes again, wishing the darkness would give her strength. But it didn't, it only gave her the image of him in her mind, the light dusting of stubble, the tempting lips she'd fall to her knees to taste.

She couldn't take it any longer, couldn't find the strength she hoped beyond hope to find. She turned in his arms, leaned against the cold metal of the car and stared up at him. Fragility stared back at her. His eyes were now a darker shade of blue, his forehead creased with a slight frown.

"I'm sorry," she whispered.

There, she'd apologized, so why did she still feel terrible?

"It's not your fault. Glenn knows better than to approach someone outside the club, no matter what the circumstances."

"No." She shook her head and lowered her gaze to the tanned skin exposed above the top button of his shirt. "I'm sorry for being such a bitch."

"Don't be." His response was immediate, without reservation.

Her guilt increased at his sudden acceptance of her apology.

"Your sexuality is none of my business," she continued. She deserved his wrath, and getting it over and done with now would make it easier to return to work next week.

"I kinda made it your business." The side of his lips tilted in a sly grin.

"It still doesn't excuse the way I acted."

"No, it doesn't." Seriousness entered his features. "But as your boss, I should've prepared you better. And—don't roll your eyes at me—because we're friends, I should've prepared you better. I'm not letting you get away with being a bitch. I'm just saying that I know you, and I should've expected the jabs at my ego. It's what you do when you're upset."

"You don't know me that well," she retorted. He didn't know her at all if he thought her side of their relationship was based on mere friendship. "I thought I knew you too..." She let the sentence hang.

"You do know me, Shay." He placed his hands on her hips, holding her tight, bringing them pelvis to hard, unyielding pelvis. "There's just one tiny aspect of my life you didn't know about."

"Tiny aspect?" She wanted to snort. A hidden tattoo equated to a tiny aspect. Owning and participating in a sex club was such an enormous part of his life that it deserved its own zip code.

"My sex life doesn't define me. I'm still the guy..."

She quirked a brow. Did he really not know how she felt? Or did saying it aloud make him uncomfortable?

"I fell in love with?" she answered for him. She was too tired for games, and maybe exposing how she felt would make him understand why Vault of Sin had rocked her foundations so hard. It wasn't all the cock swinging around, or all the screaming, squealing and grunting. It was the loss of love she now knew would never be returned.

Leo stared at her with narrowing eyes.

Yeah, asshole. Those overreactions were because of love, not my so-called normalness.

"I need to get home." She turned away from his scrutiny. "I'll drop you back at the club."

"No."

He grabbed her hand and led her to the other side of the car. She was helpless, her body craving his touch so much she didn't protest when he opened the passenger-side door and waited for her to climb in. As she clasped her belt, he loomed over her, his focus growing with intent.

"I'll get you home. Hopefully by then I'll have some semblance of mental capacity after the bomb you just dropped. Then I'll make us some coffee, 'cause we sure as shit aren't finished with this conversation."

CHAPTER SIX

*L*eo pulled into Shay's townhouse driveway, not entirely sure how he got there. He'd seen her home once before, at the end of a staff Christmas party. Tonight's trip had been done on autopilot. The drive had been silent, nothing but the churning of his brain to keep him company.

Love. Holy fuck.

Talk about a punch to the testicles. He didn't know whether to let excitement take hold, or if he should cut and run. Every woman he'd shown his true sexuality to had gutted him with their rapid rejection. And even though Shay had technically done the same, he couldn't fight the desire to let the grin pulling at his lips take hold. There was a glimmer of hope in this fucked-up mess. A glimmer he might be willing to explore, even though the pain from the past made him cautious.

Cutting the engine, he turned off the lights and sat in the darkened silence as she unbuckled her belt.

"I'm exhausted." Her fragile tone reaffirmed her words. "Can we talk about this another day? Or maybe never?"

Like hell. Love had never been within his grasp. He wouldn't let it go easily. "Sorry, little girl. We're doing this now."

Her head snapped around, her light-brown irises darkening as the side of her jaw flexed.

There you go. An added boost of adrenaline to keep you awake. He loved the way her eyes flared when he taunted her. He loved her sass. Fuck. He really did adore this woman.

She yanked her handbag from the floor, climbed from the car and slammed the door in a huff. He chuckled to himself while she stormed to the front of her home and began searching for her keys. The keys Glenn had picked up from the parking-lot asphalt and were now firmly sitting in Leo's trouser pocket.

After a few seconds of searching, she straightened and swung around to glare at him.

With a grin, he climbed from the car and jogged to her side.

"My keys?" She thrust out her palm. "*Please*."

He retrieved them from his pocket and placed them in her hand, touching her for longer than necessary. Her skin was soft, warm and too damn inviting after the anger he'd received from her earlier. As much as he liked teasing her, he hated her ire. Her lips were meant for smiling, not snarling. And he never wanted to see those light-brown irises peering up at him with anything other than lust and affection.

"Thank you," she muttered and then turned to open the door.

He followed her down a pitch-black hall and squinted when she flicked on a light to reveal an open kitchen, dining and living room area. She went to the fridge, retrieved a bottle of water and spun to him as she cracked open the lid.

"So...can we get this chat over with?" She raised a haughty brow. She was flustered, still the frightened lioness backed into a corner.

"No need to be aggressive. All I want to do is talk."

"Aggressive? No. I'm in shock. I'm disappointed. I'm probably overreacting a little, but I'm not aggressive. I just want to go to bed."

He quirked a brow, arrogantly suggesting he join her.

"Alone, Leo."

He held in a chuckle, yet he couldn't keep the side of his lips from tilting. Her vulnerability warmed his heart, made him yearn more to protect her. "Don't worry about next week. I'll find someone else to work the shift."

"Are you kidding?" She pushed from the counter and straightened her shoulders. "Working down there isn't the problem. I don't give a flying hoot what nameless, faceless people do in their spare time. This is about you blindsiding me when I'd made it clear I had feelings for you."

"I'm sorry." Even though her reactions had sparked an avalanche of bickering, this mess between them was his fault. He should've put his foot down when T.J. suggested she work in the Vault.

"You should've told me I had no chance."

"I tried." He moved forward slowly, not wanting to spook her into running. "After the time in the storeroom, I backed away."

She slumped against the counter and stared at the floor. "You know how women play hard to get because men like a challenge?"

He frowned. "Yeah."

"It works for women, too." She shrugged. "You only made me want you more."

"I should've known." He walked into the kitchen and rested his lower back against the counter opposite her. "I'm kinda irresistible. Sometimes I forget the effect I have on the opposite sex."

She glanced at him under thick eyelashes and released a huff of laughter. "You're a dick," she muttered, shaking her head and lowering her gaze back to the floor.

Silence fell between them, giving him the time to relive the mistakes he'd made. He never should've reciprocated her flirting. He sure as hell shouldn't have succumbed to temptation and followed her into the storeroom that day. In truth, he probably shouldn't have hired her when he realized he desired her the first day they met. Now she was fractured—her skin pale, her eyes empty, her smile hiding under layers of betrayal.

She raised her hands and stared blankly at her palms.

"You're shaking." He bridged the space between them in two strides and clasped her hands in his, ignoring the way she stiffened.

"It's been a long night."

She straightened the closer he inched forward, trying to maintain space between them. After a long shift at the club, she smelled like sin. Like hot, sweaty, entirely delectable sin.

Fuck his proclivities. Why couldn't he be happy to settle down in a normal relationship? It wasn't like he couldn't function without the thrill of exhibitionism. He'd lived without it before. He hadn't been happy, but then again, he hadn't had the right woman either.

Christ. Who was he kidding? He couldn't erase parts of his soul at will. If only. Life would be so much simpler. But he was finally confident with the harsh realities of his lifestyle. He'd earned his take-it-or-leave-it mentality. He owed it to himself not to revert back to being ashamed.

"I should call a cab." He let the words fall between them but didn't move. He couldn't. Her body was so warm against his, the lush curve of her breasts within his grasp, her soft lips tilted toward him.

"Yeah. You should." She didn't pull her hands away. Didn't slide out from between his body and the counter.

Listening to his libido would be a mistake. He'd get her into bed, make love to her until the sun rose, and they'd awaken to compounded problems that neither one of them wanted to face. Only he couldn't find the strength to step back.

"Want me to stay the night?"

Her throat worked over a heavy swallow. "You shouldn't."

She stood against him, her beautiful brown eyes darkening with lust, the swell of her breasts rising and falling with such innocent seduction that his balls tightened. He was stunned by her nearness. By the fact she knew his dirty little secret and still allowed him to be this close.

He released her hands, cupped her cheek and leaned his face close to hers. "I no longer give a shit about what we should and shouldn't do. I asked you what you wanted, Shay. Nothing else matters."

She ran a nervous swipe of her tongue over her bottom lip. "I…" She frowned and shook her head. "You know how I feel about you. But I'm not looking to sleep around. I'm after a relationship."

"Who says I'm not, too?" he asked, their mouths a mere inch apart.

"A monogamous relationship." She chuckled, but the humor didn't penetrate.

The heat of her breath brushed his lips, sending his rapidly beating heart into overdrive. At this moment, he'd vow to never sleep with another woman again if it meant getting between Shay's thighs. And he'd mean it, too.

"I can do monogamy." He'd always been faithful in relationships. Owning and participating in a sex club didn't mean he was an asshole. His desire to be watched and watch others had nothing to do with plowing the female playing field.

She quirked a brow, her mouth tilting at one side. "I find it hard to believe you'd be faithful with all that muff on display. I noticed the tent in your pants while you were guiding that couple tonight."

"That camping expedition was for you," he murmured against her lips.

She narrowed her gaze. "You didn't even know I was there."

"No. But I knew you weren't far away." He tilted his head, running the tip of his nose along the delicate skin of her cheek. "I wasn't watching Pamela and Jack. I was picturing you and me." He brushed his tongue along the side of her jaw and felt his cock pulse with her barely audible moan. "It was your petite little hands on my body." He nipped the skin below her ear and leaned his pelvis into her, giving his dick the friction it demanded. "It was your sassy mouth all over my cock."

She whimpered and clasped his shoulders. "We shouldn't do this."

"Why?" He had a myriad of reasons, yet none of them penetrated the intoxicating scent he continued to breathe into his lungs. His mouth found the sensitive spot at the base of her neck. He licked. He kissed. He sucked, until she was grinding against his thigh. "You want this. I want this."

She pulled back, blinking away the sexual haze in her eyes. "I want *us*."

She didn't need to add *and nobody else*. The words were already implied. He hung his head, fucking clueless at what to do. He wanted Shay, physically and emotionally, yet ditching one side of his life to obtain her wouldn't work. He'd tried changing himself for others. He'd gone down the vanilla path. Sex in bed with the blinds closed was fine to scratch an itch, but in the long run, he couldn't deny he would eventually want more.

He loved beautiful women, and he loved people watching him fuck beautiful women. It was art, a skill requiring technique and patience. The thrill at having others aroused by the way he touched a woman, making her come apart with his hands, his lips, his cock. Nothing could compare.

Shay was right. They shouldn't be doing this. Because once he laid her beautiful body down, he'd fuck her senseless. Today. Tomorrow. And every other day until the need to drag her to Vault of Sin and make love to her in front of an audience became too much.

"I'll call a cab."

She sucked in a ragged breath, stabbing him through the chest with her anguish. "Okay." Her hands fell from his neck and she slid out from between him and the counter. "Do you mind letting yourself out? I need to have a shower before I collapse."

He nodded, trying to let go of the sinking sensation telling him he was doing the wrong fucking thing. "No problem. I'll see you on Tuesday."

He walked away from her, each footstep harder than dragging his feet through cement. When he reached the door, he paused, his hand on the knob, his back rigid. He wanted to turn around, to give himself one last glance to make sure he was doing the right thing. But leaving was the only option.

One of them had to be willing to change, and from past experience, he knew it couldn't be him. And he sure as hell didn't want to be the one making someone else change their sexual proclivities when he'd fought so hard to be true to his own.

With an exasperated breath, he turned the handle and stepped into the darkness, whispering a silent farewell to the only chance at happiness he'd had in a long time.

CHAPTER SEVEN

Shay rested her hands against the bathroom tiles, letting the hot water rush down her back. She couldn't keep her eyes open, yet when she closed them, all she could see was the dejection in Leo's expression before he strode away from her.

Why was this so hard? It wasn't like she was batting away guys on a nightly basis...well, not decent ones anyway. She should listen to her hormones, enjoy a few hours of hot and dirty sex and then brush it away like any other one-night stand. There was no need for exclusivity.

Can you say delusional?

She wrinkled her nose. Her possessive side wasn't going to disappear overnight. If she went to bed with him, she'd want more. Maybe they could play around for a few weeks. With his experience, he could probably teach her a thing or two while getting the fucking out of their systems. Then finally she could move on.

Yeah, right.

She whimpered and raised her face to the water spray. She wanted Leo. Wanted him so much her chest hurt. Surely, if they decided to have fun together and things didn't work out, her loss wouldn't feel any less painful than what she was going through now, would it? It's better to have loved and lost, and all that sappy shit. Right?

"Oh, Christ." She knew this was going to be a mistake, and still she didn't care.

She turned off the water, slammed the shower door open and yanked a towel from the rack. Please don't be gone. She wrapped the plush material around her body, not bothering to dry herself before she secured it above her breasts, and ran from the bathroom.

With her wet hair dripping down her back, she hurried to the front door and flung it open. There was no time to contemplate the inevitable crash and burn as she rushed outside, taking the three steps to her front lawn while searching the darkness. "Leo?"

"Yeah." His voice drifted softly from the porch.

She spun around, finding him in the shadows, seated on her wooden deck chair, hunched over with his elbows on his knees, his head in his hands. He lifted his gaze, the wisps of loose hair framing his face as his soulful eyes stole her breath.

"Oh, good," she squeaked, suddenly feeling like a douche for running into the night in nothing but a towel. "I thought you might have left already."

"I haven't made the call, yet."

"Oh." Awkward. She'd run after him without weighing the consequences and now had no clue what to say.

"What did you want, Shay?"

You. She strolled back to the house, this time ascending the three steps leisurely, giving herself a moment to calm down.

"I thought maybe we could give this a try. Take things slow and see where it goes." She shrugged to lessen the impact of her statement and clung to the top of her towel.

"I don't like slow." His voice was smooth as velvet and deep enough to make her nipples tighten. "And you don't want to be with a perverted guy like me."

Her heart clenched. She'd been the cause of his current self-loathing. Her heartless insults from earlier were sinking in, her rejection of his lifestyle, too.

"You're not perverted, Leo. You're just different." She stood at the top of the steps, her bare feet bathed in the warm glow from the lounge room light.

He pushed from his chair, stalking toward her, his face devoid of emotion. "And you want to be different, too?"

She shrugged again. There was nothing blasé about her current emotions, yet she was determined not to show her fear. "I don't know what I want. But I'm willing to test my boundaries a bit."

He gave a derisive chuckle. "A bit?"

She stiffened at his animosity. His bitterness wasn't directed at her, she knew that, yet his scrutiny made her lose confidence.

"Drop the towel."

Oh, boy.

She bit back an anxious retort and raised her chin. He was pushing her away, trying to scare her with his ferocity. Only it had the opposite effect. She wanted to shock him enough to wipe the wicked sneer from his face. To make his eyes widen, his mouth drop. But could she release the towel, exposing herself to anyone who may happen to be awake at this early hour? This was her neighborhood. The place she had to come home to every day.

"See," he taunted, this time taking a step around her and heading for the stairs. "You couldn't handle the shit I'd make you do."

How much do you really want him?

She cursed her nerves and yanked at the towel, releasing the hold at her breasts. He paused as she let the material fall to the wooden floor, exposing herself to the world.

His nostrils flared, the tight grip on his restraint wavering before her eyes. She jutted her chin, waiting, her chest throbbing harder with each passing second. When the silence continued, she began to realize she wasn't good enough. He wanted a sexual goddess, someone capable of bending to his will in an instant. That change would take time, and with her stubborn streak, probably a lot of patience.

Breaking eye contact, she bent down to scoop up the towel. "Well, I guess there was no harm in trying." She swiveled on her toes and strode to the door. The urge to cover herself was cloying. Instead of succumbing, she remained strong, not giving him the excuse to claim she was scared.

She reached for the handle and paused at the sound of his footfalls pounding behind her. His body slammed against hers, making her gasp as he pushed her against the cold wood.

"Think twice." He gripped her upper arm and yanking her to face him. "Think about what I'll demand of you, and what you're willing to give."

His possession was a scorching balm against her wounded pride. The hardness of his cock pressed between her thighs. The stability of his hands held her tight. "That's all I've done for the past three hours."

He narrowed his gaze, his jaw harsh. "I won't stop this time."

"Well, hurry up and get start—"

He slammed his mouth against hers, pushing his tongue past her lips, searching. He devoured her, kissed her harder than she'd ever been kissed, turning her bones to mush, her strength to weakness. He ran greedy hands down her back, over her bottom and along the underside of her thighs, creating goose bumps in their wake. She gripped his shoulders as he lifted her leg, encouraging her to circle his hip.

"I'll ruin you," he growled into her mouth, thrusting his erection against her pubic bone. His gaze held her captive as her ass began to slam against the wooden door with each of his thrusts.

"You already have." She clawed at his shirt, willing the thin fabric to fall from his shoulders.

She kept her leg in place while he travelled his hand up the underside of her thigh and over her sex. He parted her folds with a finger, sliding it through the slickness of her arousal, and his accompanying throaty groan against her neck had her eyes closing in bliss. He teased her, relentlessly, dragging his finger back and forth, taking her mouth again and again. The slight breeze tickled her skin, an unwanted reminder of the exposure.

"Think of me," he whispered into her mouth. "Only of me."

She nodded. But as Leo's lips moved to her shoulder, her gaze couldn't help travelling to the darkened windows of the house across the street. A group of college kids lived there. They could be watching. Not that they could see much. Leo's bigger frame covered her completely, yet the light from her kitchen filtered through the glass panel beside the door, illuminating them like a flare in the desert.

"My hands, Shay."

She closed her eyes, concentrating on those hands, the way one continued to torment her greedy pussy. The other stroked her side, gently bringing all her nerve endings to life.

"My mouth." He sucked hard on her shoulder, bringing a bite of pain. "My tongue."

She shuddered and reached up to grab the band holding his hair together. She yanked it down and opened her eyes to watch the light-brown strands fall to span along the back of his neck.

"And eventually, my cock."

"Oh, Christ." She couldn't take anymore. She fumbled behind her for the door handle and turned the knob. Together, they stumbled into the house and he slammed the wood shut with the sole of his shoe.

He narrowed his gaze as she stepped back, her chest heaving, her sex throbbing. She could tell what he was thinking, that she couldn't hack being naked outside, and she supposed he was right. To him, being fucked in the open might be a daily ritual. To her, and surely to her neighbors, it wouldn't be so trivial.

"I have condoms in my bedside table," she said as an excuse.

"I have condoms in my pocket." His hair was loose around his cheeks, his dress shirt now untucked and crinkled.

She rolled her eyes, her breaths still coming out in harsh exhalations. "Of course you do."

He let his gaze rake her body. Gradually. Leaving a scorching trail all the way to her toes and up again. "Well, this is your domain now. So, what happens next?"

She sucked her bottom lip between her teeth, her heart a flutter at his raw masculinity.

"Shay, despite my statement earlier, this can go as fast or as slow as you like. There's no preconceptions on my end. If you want to stop, we stop. I just wanted to make sure you knew what you were doing."

"No." She shook her head. "No stopping."

His grin returned as he strode toward her and swept her off her feet. "I was hoping you'd say that."

She squealed—a little in delight, a little in pure adrenaline-filled nervousness. He carried her to the sofa and fell backward onto the cold leather upholstery with her on his lap.

"Straddle me."

She complied, placing her hands on his defined pecs while she spread her legs across either side of his thighs. Her breathing was labored, her heart a rapid pulse behind her ribs.

This was Leo, her boss, the man she'd been fantasizing about for a lifetime. Her dirty dream was finally a reality. Then his hands came to rest on her bare knees and he slowly slid them to her hips and time ceased.

He stared at her with adoration. There was no arrogance, no mildly annoying yet always attractive confidence. His gaze broke her, turning her lust into longing, her fear into anticipation. He was beautiful. His skin so smooth, so perfect. The darkened patch of stubble along his jaw too tempting not to reach out and brush her palm over the rough surface. No man had ever made her insides turn to butter, her brain into a mass of incoherent thoughts.

But nothing happened. He didn't make a move. Didn't speak. Didn't try and alleviate the mindlessness taking over her fluttering heart.

"Leo?"

He frowned. "I don't want to ruin this."

She pulled back at the underlying anger in his voice, unsure who it was directed at. "Umm."

"I don't want to push you or scare you away. Usually, I don't have to worry about what happens after I'm with a woman." His consuming ocean-blue irises made her come undone. "You're different, Shay. I've waited a lifetime for this. Fucking months spent immersed in thoughts of having you hot and ready for me. I've relived those moments in the storeroom over and over and fucking over again. And now that you're here, your pussy hovering over the hardest erection I've had since seventh grade, I'm worried about where to start."

Her cheeks lifted with a smile, one that grew until she was beaming back at him. She ran her hands from his stubble to the loose strands of his hair. "You start by kissing me senseless." She brushed her lips over his and moaned at the way he took possession of her mouth. He scorched her with ferocious licks of his tongue, bringing his hand up to palm the back of her head, to hold her tight.

Her nipples beaded to the point of pain, her sex becoming so hot she was sure she was leaving a wet patch on his trousers. As their tongues tangled, she trailed her hands down, back over his jawline, along his neck to the top button of his shirt. One by one, she undid the buttons and then pulled the shirt wide.

She wanted to look at him, to see the light dusting of hair she could feel beneath her fingers while she stroked his chest. She wanted to mark the skin with her nails, to see his eyes widen or maybe narrow with the pinch of pain. But she couldn't drag her mouth away from his, couldn't stop returning the strokes of tongue and mashing of lips that made her mind blank and her heart all the more attached to this gorgeous man.

"My pants." He spoke into her mouth. "Undo them."

She smiled against his lips. She'd never be a weak woman, easily snapping to comply with a man's demanding order, yet in this moment, with his hands holding her tight and his panted breaths mingling with hers, she could've easily seen herself falling to her knees in submission. Her fingers fumbled with his buckle, releasing the clasp and lowering his zipper.

"Touch me, Shay."

She whimpered, undone by his need. She ran her hand along his crotch, touching the heavy material of his pants and then the softness of silk before stilling on his thick erection. Closing her eyes, she dared not look, trying hard not to grin. The man had a lot to be confident about. He'd brought her undone with his fingers before, but this...this generous length of manliness was going to take her to heaven.

"What are you smirking at?" He tugged her hair until her eyes snapped open.

She giggled, she couldn't help it. The sound was girly and far too feminine, and fuck it, she didn't care. She was high, so damn delirious with lust that she could continue to sound like a virginal school girl and not give a shit.

She wanted the hardened length between her lips, pulsing in her mouth, his hands guiding her to take him deep until he shot down the back of her throat. Without answering, she tilted her head, moving until his hands fell to his sides. Then she backed off his lap, taking herself to the carpeted floor and kneeling between his feet.

His gaze followed her as she gripped the waistband of his pants and boxers, tugged at the material until he raised his ass and helped her lower them down his thighs. His cock stood proud from a patch of dark, trimmed curls, the length jerking toward her. Pre-come beaded his slit, the glistening moisture begging to be tasted. She leaned forward, hovering over him, and blew softly on the flesh she could already taste on her tongue.

"Tease me and I'll return the favor tenfold." He jutted his hips so the head of his shaft bumped her lips.

"That sounds like fun." She poked out her tongue and lightly lapped the salt of his flesh before retreating.

He groaned, the veins in his neck bulging as he threw his head back and gripped the sofa material near his knees. "I'll make sure it isn't." He lifted his head, pinning her with unadulterated lust. "I'll drive you insane. I'll tie you to the bed, bring you to the point of climax for hours on end until you're begging me to fuck you."

Shay pressed her lips together, trying not to smile at what he thought was a threat. If only he knew what she would give to be laid out for his pleasure for hours.

"Don't you like to beg?" She stretched out her tongue to flick the head of his shaft.

He cupped the side of her face, bringing her closer to his length. "This is me begging."

She opened her mouth, emboldened and empowered by the guttural way he growled.

"And when it comes to sex," he grated, "I like everything."

Shay raised a brow, running her tongue down his length and sucking him deep. She built his pleasure, feeling his dick pulse between her lips, ripping a moan from his throat, then she released him with a pop. "Care to elaborate?" She had too many questions when it came to his lifestyle. Only she still wasn't sure if she could handle the answers.

He guided her face back to his cock, encouraging her to take him again. "I've got other things on my mind right now." He smiled down at her, the blue-green of his irises darkening as she took him to the back of her mouth.

She worked the length with her lips and tongue, cupping his sac in her hands, stroking it gently with her fingers. Her sex clenched and the slickness of arousal dampened the inside of her thighs. Pleasure had never been this potent. Sex had never been this exciting. She didn't know if it stemmed from who she was with, how long she'd wanted this, or maybe it was the thrill of arousing a man who seemed to have an insatiable sexual appetite. Either way, her body was burning, craving his touch and aching in the most delicious places.

"Take me all the way in." He moved his other hand to the opposite side of her face. "I want to see those gorgeous lips stretched."

The need to please him was immense. She wanted to make an impact, to stand apart from all the women he'd slept with. Previously, she thought her competition was the unending line of beauties who rubbed up against him on the dance floor of Shot of Sin. Now she knew better. He had eager women at his disposal, ones he didn't have to chat up or flirt with. Women who strolled around in their underwear, who shared the same sexual disposition.

It made her all the more eager to control her breathing and take him as far as she could. Even after relaxing her throat, she still had at least two inches to go. Determination made her push past her gag reflex, taking his full length with eager strokes.

"*Fuck*, Shay." His hips began to buck, pistoning into her mouth, making her lips numb. "Jesus. You're driving me insane...stop."

She didn't listen, needing to make him mindless.

"Shay, *stop*." He grasped her arms, brought her to her feet and yanked her forward to straddle his lap. "Shooting down the back of your throat has been a fantasy of mine. But not tonight." He reached for his pocket and pulled out a condom. "Tonight, I want you riding my cock. I want to see your pretty mouth gasp in pleasure while I make you come."

He could make her orgasm with his dirty words alone. Already, her nipples throbbed and her clit tingled with heightened awareness. She bit her lip as he ripped open the silver packet and rolled the condom down his length. She was starved for him. Impatience clawed at her skin. Need pulsed through her veins. "Hurry the hell up."

Leo chuckled and grabbed the base of his covered shaft. "Ready and waiting, your feistiness."

She could already feel him inside her, could anticipate the delicious stretch of her muscles around him. Her hands were shaking, like a crack addict waiting for a fix. Grabbing his shoulders, she lifted and hovered her pussy above his cock. She closed her eyes, letting the engorged head swipe through her slick juices and across her clit before lowering in one exquisite motion.

Leo moaned as her walls contracted around him, sucking him deeper, holding him tight. He leaned in and rested his head against the side of hers, brushing his lips over the sensitive skin around her ear. "Fucking. Heaven."

She shuddered, taking his compliment to heart. Slowly, she began to undulate, grinding her hips back and forth, leisurely riding him. She set the pace, and Leo followed her lead, kissing her neck in the same soft motion, his hands relaxed and sensual as they explored her body.

Then his lips found hers. He trailed his palms to her breasts and the languid tempo flew out the window. She bucked against him, sucking his tongue into her mouth, delighting in his faint taste of alcohol. He tweaked her nipples and rubbed his calloused palms over the hardened flesh. When his hands grabbed her ass to set his own more punishing rhythm, she let go.

Her pussy clamped tight. Her breathing became erratic as her orgasm began to take over. With one hand, Leo lightly gripped the front of her neck, almost like a choke hold, and lifted her chin so all she could see was him.

She grasped for the top of the sofa behind his shoulders, arching her back while his gaze held her captive. His other hand continued to push her against his cock, the punishing movements making her sight darken in pleasure. She cried out in release, mewling, moaning, screaming to the heavens until the pulsing in her pussy subsided and she had the chance to watch Leo come undone.

His face contorted in lines of strain. He tightened his hand around her throat. "*Fuck.*" He roared and the sound reverberated around the room. He smashed his mouth against hers, and gradually, almost imperceptibly, his jolts slowed. The exquisite harshness of his kiss became a languorous mingling of tongues and lips. And when he pulled back, his face was filled with a softness she'd never been on the receiving end of.

"Shay?" His hand fell from her neck.

She quirked a brow and whimpered in reply, her head and eyelids now heavy with exhaustion.

"I think we're both in for a lot of trouble."

CHAPTER EIGHT

Leo pushed from the sofa, his softening dick still inside the sweetest pussy he'd ever plundered. Holy fuck, he was a lost man. Completely disoriented from the brilliance of her sexual appeal.

"Point me toward your room." He yanked up the waist of his pants so they didn't end up around his ankles.

Shay lifted her head from his shoulder and swung a lazy hand toward a darkened hall starting beside the kitchen. "Last door on the right."

She was a deadweight against his chest. Her arms were limp around his shoulders, her legs barely clinging around his waist. He carried her from the room, noticing the lack of frilly, girlie crap through the house. He'd always known her as a guy's girl. Someone more comfortable in a masculine environment, who had a low tolerance for bitchy drama. But tonight, he'd seen her fragile side.

She was still a feminine force to be reckoned with. Only now he'd seen the full picture instead of the layers of bravado she liked to strengthen herself behind. The realization made it harder for him to contemplate things between them not working.

"Fall asleep, baby girl. I'll get you to bed." He was enjoying holding the bundle of vulnerability in his arms. Shay had always been strong, confident, even a little pig-headed. He needed that—someone to keep him on his toes. Yet, he also needed a feminine presence. Someone he could protect. Someone with defenseless moments.

Shay was the brilliant mix of everything he desired. He just needed to figure out a way to remove the petrified look in her eyes every time they discussed Vault of Sin and replace it with something that didn't resemble a brick wall.

"You know I hate when you call me little girl or baby girl, right?" she mumbled against his shoulder. "If you hadn't sucked the life right outta me, I'd smack you."

He smiled, holding back a smart retort. He didn't want to rile her again. The sun would be rising in less than an hour, and she needed rest. And he had to take a clarifying step back. He was falling, way too fast, and at the moment he couldn't find the self-preserving pessimism to make himself stop.

Turning into the last room on the right, he inhaled the heady scent of Shay and held in a moan. The intoxicating mix of vanilla and strawberry would forever remind him of the woman in his arms. The sassy wench who smelled like nirvana. He laid her down, resting her head on a pillow before retreating.

"I'll be back in a sec." He went in search of her bathroom to clean himself up. Minutes later, he was standing at her bedroom door, leaning against the frame, simply watching her.

She lay on her side, her dark silken hair falling over her shoulder. Her breathing was gentle, her lips slightly parted, the faint hint of a contented smile tilting her lips.

"How long are you going to stand there?" she asked, her dark lashes resting against the tops of her smooth cheeks.

Forever. "I should go."

Her eyelids fluttered open and she sucked in a lazy breath. "What if I asked you to stay?"

Ask me, Shay. Grant me one last glimpse of your vulnerability before your mask of strength returns in the morning. "Is that what you want?"

"Yes." She pulled the sheet up to her chin. "I have questions."

He padded to the other side of her bed, shucked his loosened pants and climbed under the covers. "Ask all you want after you get some sleep."

She shook her head and turned to face him. "No. As tired as I am, I won't rest until we talk."

The dreaded *talk* didn't seem repulsive when discussed from the lips of this gorgeous woman. He slid across to the middle of the bed and rested on one elbow as he faced her. "Then ask."

He'd tell her everything, no matter how ugly the truth may be in her eyes. He'd learned long ago to never lie about his desires. He just needed to get over his own self-loathing.

"Why?" she whispered.

One word had enough meaning to tighten his lungs. He knew what she meant. No clarification necessary. He'd been asked the same thing numerous times, usually in a heated situation, where the word was an accusation, not a question.

"I'm not entirely sure." He shrugged. "It's an addiction of sorts."

Shit. Shay winced at his confession and he rushed to clarify. "Not to sex." He stroked a hand down her cheek. "I think I'm hooked on the rush of pride that follows a woman's orgasm at my hands. I love bringing pleasure. Making someone fall apart is a powerful thing. And having others watch only heightens the sensation."

She paid no attention to the stroke of his hand. She was emotionally detaching herself, taking a step back even in her almost comatose state. "So Vault of Sin is a part of your life you can't live without?"

He sucked in a silent breath, not wanting to push her away and not able to lie either. "A woman has the ability to change a man." He ran his finger under her chin, sliding his thumb along her lower lip.

"I don't want to change you." She frowned, clutching the sheet tighter to her chest.

"I know. And I appreciate that." He wanted so badly to sink his finger between her lips, to feel the rough surface of her tongue against his skin. To change the serious situation to something pleasurable. "I'm prepared to try, Shay. I think that's all that matters at the moment."

"Mmm." Her lids drifted shut. "I want to make you happy," she murmured. "I'm just not sure I can be the woman you need."

He remained quiet, listening to her breathing as it became heavier. Even in sleep she was alluring. He lay beside her, continuing to stroke her hair, pulling the sheet down a little to admire the flawless skin of her neck and shoulder. Things between them wouldn't be easy. Their hurdles were large and overbearing. But taking the chance would be worth it. He could risk rejection one last time. For her.

He just needed to make sure T.J. and Brute were onboard.

The club was a part of the three of them, something Shay probably hadn't realized, yet. They all spent time downstairs. They all watched. Leo only hoped he was nearby when she figured out being a part of his lifestyle also meant being a part of Brute and T.J.'s too.

CHAPTER NINE

Shay woke up on her stomach with a tickling sensation at the low of her back. She frowned, her eyes still closed, and wriggled in an attempt to make it stop.

"It's already past lunch time, gorgeous."

She moaned, tilting her head to the deep, smooth voice, and opened one eye a crack. Beside her was the rough-stubbled face of the sexiest man alive.

"Go away," she groaned and slammed the pillow over her head. Sexy as sin or not, nobody got away with waking her. It was bad enough on a night she'd slept soundly, but last night, or the early hours of today, it had been a constant struggle to stop her mind from churning.

"You sure you don't want to wake up?"

He smoothed his hand over her ass, delving between her crack to the heat of her pussy. He stroked her to life with two greedy fingers, making her wet within moments, tearing needy whimpers from her throat.

"Leo."

"Yeah." He pulled the sheet off her in a flourish and then the heavy weight of his body moved over hers. "You still want to go back to sleep?"

He ground his erection into her ass, the tip of his rubber-covered shaft teasing her until she had to bite the sheets to stop herself from moaning. His hips undulated, his cock inching lower, sinking to the place her body craved him to be. Then he was at her entrance, rubbing himself along her slit, sliding through her arousal.

"Your body may be asleep, but your pussy definitely isn't," he drawled with a chuckle.

She threw her pillow away and bucked, trying to get his self-righteous ass off her. "Don't be a jerk."

His weight became heavier against her back, the almost silent sound of his breathing brushing her ear. "Tell me to stop and I will. But I'll never apologize for craving your body."

Her heart fluttered as he stilled.

"Want me to get off, Shay?"

Her name on his lips was the most alluring sound she'd ever heard. It brought a smile to her mouth and a tingling throb to her muscles. "No." She tilted her ass so his cock head penetrated. Never.

He surged forward in a deep thrust, stealing her breath and replacing it with ecstasy. Her body welcomed him, squeezing around his length as he began to leisurely thrust.

"I've been watching you for hours," he murmured into her neck, blazing a trail of kisses along her shoulder.

She moaned, enjoying the delicious friction of skin against skin. His mouth hot and biting, his undulations smooth and languorous. "I was dreaming about you."

"Hmm? What was I doing?"

Shay closed her eyes, playing back the scene in her mind. They'd been at the club. Downstairs. In the darkened corner of one of the rooms. She was seated between Leo's thighs, her back to his chest, her hands on the hard muscle above his knees, while his fingers worked their way into her jeans and under the waistband of her panties.

They were watching a couple on the bed in the center of the room. The man was buff, blond, his face shadowed in the darkness while he fed his cock into an eager woman's mouth. Their movements were like a dance, melodic, hypnotizing and dream-time-Shay couldn't contain the slick arousal saturating Leo's fingers.

Now she wondered if watching another couple would be equally enjoyable in real life. Were her boundaries that easy to break?

"We were at work."

"In the storeroom? Being with you in there has haunted me for months. It killed me to walk away."

And to continue walking. She wanted to add. He'd never come back, not emotionally, not until last night anyway.

"No. We were at Vault of Sin. Watching."

She squeezed her muscles around his shaft and his answering groan sent a shiver down her spine.

"Please tell me you liked it."

Shay stopped, taking a moment to let the seriousness of his plea sink in. The club was a part of him. A place he would feel incomplete without. Even if he was willing to step away, even temporarily, it wouldn't change the fact he still yearned to go there.

Slowly, she nodded. "Yes. It was hot as hell."

He climbed off her, grabbed her hip and flipped her onto her back. She stared wide-eyed as he moved over her again, this time resting against her belly, his gaze narrowing on hers while his cock found its home. He entered her with care, gradually penetrating, letting every inch of him fill her while he watched the pleasure take hold. "What does that mean?"

Her focus waivered as he lowered his lips to her nipple and sucked the hardening peak into his mouth. Tingles ricocheted through her body, and she circled his hips with her thighs, needing more.

"I don't know," she murmured. "I think my subconscious is willing to see what happens."

He raised a brow, acknowledging the enormity of her statement. Instead of voicing the happiness she could see curving his lips, he merely moved to the other nipple to pay homage.

"I guess my subconscious is a dirty little whore," she added, slightly flustered by the ferocity in his eyes.

He chuckled and his puffed breaths brushed the sensitive skin of her breast. "Enjoying sex doesn't make you a whore." He thrust inside her, drawing a cry from her throat. "Watching others play doesn't make you dirty." His hips plunged harder. "I promise you, Shay, you'll never be left wanting if you're with me."

This time, his cock made her scream in delight.

Leo leaned in, stroking her lips apart with his tongue. "Just give me a chance."

She nodded, undone by his sincerity, captured by his raw plea. "I'll try," she whispered, raising her hips to meet his next slide home.

He burned her with his kiss, smashing his mouth against her with the same ferocity as his hips pounded. He drove her wild, he made her crazy, and all the while she could feel herself slipping more in love with him. With matched aggression, she clenched her thighs around him and dug her nails into the skin of his back.

"Wait." She broke their kiss, not wanting to come yet. Her pussy was already pulsing in anticipation, her limbs taut. She extended her neck, gasping for air. But he didn't quit, didn't stop thrusting into her, driving her pleasure higher. "I said stop. I don't want to come yet."

"You've got no say in the matter." He scraped his teeth up her neck. "I want to feel your pussy milking me. I want to see those pretty brown eyes roll back as you come undone."

"Leo," she warned, nudging closer and closer to the precipice with each undulation. Next Saturday was likely to break them, so she had to make now last forever.

"Fall apart for me, Shay."

His whisper against her ear was too much. She complied, her breathing coming in hard gasps as she tightened around his cock and rode the wave of orgasm. She drowned in the bliss, her hips continually reaching up to meet his thrusts until Leo swore and followed after her.

His lips continued to love her, his hands adoring with their gentle glide across her skin. As his movements came to a halt, her eyelids became droopy and she groaned with the need for sleep.

"You do wonders for a guy's self-esteem," he chuckled, sliding from her body.

"I try my best." She stretched, loving the delicious aches his lovemaking had left in her muscles.

The mattress dipped as he stood and strode for the bathroom, returning moments later with the smile she adored.

"Can I make you breakfast?" He waggled a brow. "Naked?"

She laughed, overcome by the dreamy warmth overtaking her chest. For too long, she'd been one of those women who'd believed men weren't a necessity in a strong woman's life. She was relatively successful. She paid her own bills. And her body would never be left unsatisfied with the big box of toys under her bed. But something about the way he looked at her made her feel empowered. His smile increased her confidence. His touch made her invincible. "I only have cereal."

"If you don't mind me driving your car, I can go pick something up."

"Naked?"

His smile widened. "Unfortunately, I don't think that's an option."

"Ahh, so you do have limits."

His humor gently faded. "I have many limits, Shay."

The quick slide into thoughts of Vault of Sin made the warmth inside her vanish. "Cereal it is." She climbed from the bed, and strode her naked ass to the walk-in closet, returning seconds later with a thin silk dressing gown.

"That's not going to happen." Leo eyed her clothing and crossed his arms over his chest. "Take it off."

Annoyance, or was that anticipation, shot up her spine. She raised a brow, coming to stand in front of him. "Is this where any normal woman would whimper and obey?"

His lip curled, predatory and too damn sexy for her to ignore. "This is where you take that off or I'll do it for you."

Her nipples hardened, already yearning for more of his touch. She grinned, shrugged and then made a move to walk around him, because that's what stubborn women do.

In a flash, she was spun back around. In seconds, rough hands stripped her naked. Then, in a few erratic beats of her heart, the sash was yanked from her dressing gown and Leo grabbed her, tying her hands behind her back.

She stood, shocked and silent in her hallway, wondering what the hell had just happened.

"Thank you," he taunted. "I actually enjoy doing things the hard way."

By the look of his growing erection, he wasn't lying. "Point taken. You can untie me now." She tried to purr, to be the seductive princess who would woo him with her charm, but he didn't succumb. Instead, he grinned the sly, arrogant grin that annoyed her and made her melt all at once.

"Nice try." He strode forward, grabbed the tie at her joined wrists and guided her forward. "It's time for breakfast."

CHAPTER TEN

*L*eo raised the toast to Shay's mouth, enjoying the way her naked chest delicately rose and fell as she ate. He should be thankful she denied him the choice to spoon-feed her cereal. The exercise would've ended in him *accidentally* pouring milk down her cleavage, watching the trail fall between those gorgeous breasts before finally licking it off when it came close to reaching the heat of her pussy.

He needed to keep his hands off her. To make her understand this thing between them wasn't based on sex. And to also give her time to think. He admired her strength and confidence above all else. So seeing her skittish at the mere mention of the Vault was something he needed to focus on resolving.

"Juice?" He placed the half-eaten piece of jam covered toast back on the plate in front of her.

She nodded. "Thank you."

He settled the glass against her lips, taking care to tip it at the right pace. He enjoyed caring for her, being the one making sure her needs were met. If he had more restraint, he'd stick around all day, keeping her hands tied as he catered to her every need. But it was only a matter of time before his dick took control.

"More toast?" He lowered the glass to the table and fought the need to kiss the juice from her mouth.

"No. I'm good." She nibbled her bottom lip. "But you can untie me."

"Soon." He cleaned away their cups and plates and stacked them in the dishwasher as Shay watched from the stool behind the kitchen counter. "I like having you defenseless for once."

She scoffed. "I'm always defenseless around you."

He copied her, scoffing louder. "The only time you've shown any vulnerability..." apart from what he'd witnessed in the last twelve hours, "...was the first night you worked the bar in Taste of Sin." Or maybe the days after he'd pleasured her in the storeroom.

She cringed, the tops of her cheeks turning the slightest shade of pink. "You remember that?"

He'd remembered every moment since she'd handed in her employment application. "I recall with vivid clarity, T.J. remarking on how cute you were at the start of your shift. He thought you were sweet and innocent." He closed the dishwasher and brushed the crumbs off his palms into her sink. "It didn't take long for him to determine those deep brown eyes were hiding a little minx."

She hit him with a dazzling smile. "Once the doors closed for the night, the three of you took pleasure in testing me. You barked off drink orders, making sure I knew how to prepare everything from memory."

He inclined his head. He'd never laughed harder in his life. One by one, Leo, Brute and T.J. had thrown names of cocktails at her, until finally T.J. requested a Crouching Tiger shot and they'd all been too drunk to notice she'd placed a mix of Sambuca, Tequila and Tabasco sauce in front of them instead.

"T.J. hadn't known what hit him."

"For a second, I thought he was going to die, he was choking so hard." She started to laugh, making those tempting breasts bounce. "I was glad you guys didn't fire me."

He ignored the way his cock jerked and made his way back to her side. It was time to leave. He wanted this moment to stick with him until Tuesday—her beautiful smile, the lush curve of her breasts, the way her hair fell like silk against her smooth skin.

"That was never an option." He untied the material at her wrists and helped her to her feet. "You fit in perfectly."

A little too perfectly at times. The three of them held a soft spot for Shay. She may have a temper, but her few bad days had never come close to outweighing the good. She always made them smile, either with her over-exaggerated annoyances or with her sassy, flirting banter.

"I'm glad you think so." She fell into him, resting her arms on his chest as she stared up at him.

He was falling—into desire, under her spell. "It's time for me to go."

Her brow furrowed the slightest bit and she stepped back. "You don't want to stay?"

"If I thought it was the right thing to do, I wouldn't leave until we had to go back to work on Tuesday." He grabbed her hand, entwined their fingers and tried to ease the dejection in her eyes. "But I bailed out on Travis last night. I need to call him and make sure Vault of Sin was closed without drama."

~

Vault of Sin—three innocent words potent enough to make Shay's stomach flutter. She nodded, trying not to let the passing seconds daunt her. She'd been in the zone, tied up like a little love slave waiting to be satisfied. And now he was leaving.

Look out toys, here I come.

"Are you sure you're comfortable working down there next Saturday?" Concern tainted his voice. "There's no pressure if you don't. I'll work the bar myself if I have to."

And be surrounded by voluptuous women vowing for his attention? "No. I can do it."

In the future, working her usual shift at Shot of Sin would be painful, knowing what Leo would be experiencing downstairs. Her imagination would be the death of her. She needed to face her fears head on, while also keeping him in her sights.

"You'll see me in the restaurant during the week and my shift at the club bar on Friday, so there's plenty of time to grill me beforehand. On Saturday, I can arrive early to check things out properly. You know, without all that cock staring me in the face."

It was meant as a joke, but Leo stiffened. "If you're uncomfortable—"

"I'm fine." She groaned. "Please, stop asking."

He leaned into her, moving to eye level. "Shay..."

"Don't." She pushed at his muscled chest and glanced away. She was intimidated, jealous, and yeah, maybe at the top of the nervous scale, but it didn't mean she was a chicken shit. "I said I'd try. This is me trying. I don't need you treating me like a little girl."

"Okay," his voice softened. "But if you change your mind all you have to do is tell me."

She nodded. "I need to get dressed."

They both knew it was a dismissal of the conversation. She didn't care. She was sick of worrying about it. Sick of thinking about it. Turning on her heel, she hastened down the hall in search of her dressing gown.

"I'll also need to show you the back entrance to the club, so make sure you remind me on Friday." Leo strode behind her, following her into her bedroom.

"Back entrance?" She peered over her shoulder, immediately engrossed by the flexing muscles of his arms as he reached for his clothes on the floor.

He glanced up from beneath thick, dark lashes and grinned. "I think I told you it was the delivery entrance when you first started."

Lying little bastard. "Anything else you've lied about?" She raised a brow and the humor died from his features.

"I've only ever lied to keep the club safe. Legally, it shouldn't be running within the walls of Shot of Sin." He pulled on his shirt, doing up the buttons as his gaze scrutinized her. "If we asked for government approval for a sex club, the local public would be notified. The anonymity of members would be breached, and I'm sure you could imagine the shit fight we'd have on our hands from do-gooders and religious groups." He straightened his collar and then yanked on his pants. "But now you know there's no need for secrecy between us. I won't lie to you. Even if the truth is brutal, I'll take a leaf out of Brute's book and let you have it straight." He stalked toward her and came to a stop at her feet.

Leo stroked a hand through her sleep-tangled hair. "I stayed away from you for a long time, wanting to ensure I didn't hurt you. So, whatever it takes, please know I have your best interest at heart."

Shay inhaled deeply and let it out on a sigh.

Okay, so maybe she was a little fragile. The thought of rejection sat like a lead balloon beneath her ribs. She was a grown woman, confident in every aspect of her life...up until this moment. Now she had to question if she was adventurous enough for Vault of Sin.

Only time would tell. All she knew was that being intimate with Leo and then going back to a platonic relationship wasn't an option her heart could handle. She was risking a lot with the hasty decisions she'd made during the early hours of the morning. And now it was too late to go back.

He leaned in, tilting her chin, bringing them a breath apart. "The only truth I have for you right now is that I want you. Any way I can." His eyes searched hers, focusing with heated intent so potent her body flushed. "Let's see where it takes us."

Shay bit her lip, fighting the need to wrap her hands around his neck and drag him back onto the bed. "I'll see you Tuesday then."

"Yeah. You will." He brushed his mouth over hers and then stepped back. "Just try and keep your wanton hands off me in front of the other staff, okay?" He grinned and headed for the door.

"You're an arrogant jerk," she called, her gaze trained on his sexy ass as he strutted from the room.

"A jerk you're now stuck with."

His steps retreated, each soft footfall making her want to yell for him to come back. She was hooked. Not just to his charm or the way he worked her body, but to the thought of them being together. The image of them holding hands had her turning all girlie with the yearning to squee.

Now all they had to do was get over their myriad of issues.

CHAPTER ELEVEN

*T*uesday morning took forever to arrive. Leo stood behind the Taste of Sin bar, waiting for the lunch staff to show up for work. One in particular. He'd spent the last two days distracting himself from calling, texting, emailing or even sending flowers to Shay.

The harder he tried to occupy his mind, the more potent his memories of her delicious body became. He'd thrashed himself at the gym, replied to a full inbox of work-related crap and even cleaned out his fridge. All before Sunday night arrived.

Now he couldn't wait for the next thirty minutes to tick by until she showed up for her shift. He wasn't just pussy-whipped, he was wrangled, tangled and tied to the bed waiting to be decimated.

He felt like a kid at an amusement park, all giddy excitement and nervous anticipation. Reality hadn't left the building. He still knew they had a shitload of problems to discuss and resolve, but finding a woman like Shay and having her stick around after learning his sordid secrets was an opportunity worthy of a little crazy optimism.

The first hurdle had been the hardest, and they'd sailed over the fucker with the grace of an Olympic champion. Okay, maybe his hindsight was skimming the Saturday night drama. He couldn't help it. His enthusiasm was out of control.

They both needed time. Flipping from a work relationship to lovers wasn't easy in a normal business environment. When a sex club was brought into the mix, it was like walking through a minefield. But instead of explosives, they were contending with jealousy, spite, judgments and lies.

He needed to make sure they avoided each detonation.

Every other woman had balked at his lifestyle choices. And he understood why. It wasn't common to share the person you cared for, and stripping in the middle of a crowded room wasn't on everyone's bucket list. Yet, Shay was still sticking around. She'd made him crazy with her curves, driven his desire to insatiable heights, and now he couldn't quit thinking about ways to make this work.

The front door swooshed open, stealing his attention, and there she was, in tight black pants, a white-collared shirt and the glow of the sun surrounding her in a halo.

"Morning." His gaze was glued to her, drinking her in as if he hadn't seen her in years.

"Morning." She grinned. "How were your days off?"

Unending. "Fine. You?" He strode around the bar and met her in the middle of the room filled with tables and chairs.

"Fine."

He stepped into her, wove his arm around her waist and tugged her softness against him. She'd arrived early and no other bar staff or waitresses were here. Apart from the chefs hidden in the kitchen out the back, they were alone. It gave him the perfect opportunity to take the edge off his craving.

"I missed you." His mouth found hers, kissing, nipping, licking until they both had to come up for air.

"I thought I was meant to keep my hands off you."

"You were." He pecked her lips. "You're not doing a very good job."

Her eyes twinkled, desire and sass staring back at him. "For such an accomplished man, you have very little restraint."

"And for such a flirty woman, you're doing a great job of brushing me off."

"I'm not brushing you off." She had the gall to gape at him with mock outrage. "It's just that my boss is a hard-ass and I don't want to get in trouble."

"Sometimes getting in trouble is the best part."

He'd never get enough of her quick-witted charm. Even the subtle changes in her expression added to her potent mix of confidence and sexuality. She knew how to work him. Hell, she probably knew how to work every man. But he didn't care. Shay was his now.

"True." She pressed her lips together, the corners of her mouth tilting in barely contained laughter.

He leaned in for another kiss, already tasting her on his tongue when she tilted her head away.

"Not here," she whispered, practically castrating him with the rejection.

She'd broken him, made him weak and lust-crazed in the one place he demanded control. All he wanted to do is strip her bare and sink into her over and over. Right now, he didn't care if the timid restaurant staff caught them. He didn't give a shit if his club secrets were exposed. His desire for her had already tightened his balls, making his shaft thicken with anticipation. His brain was deprived of blood flow and all the fucks he should've given about being caught were nowhere to be found. "Did you even think about me?"

"Of course." She smiled up at him, this time with genuine admiration. "I couldn't stop."

"And what about the Vault?" Regret hit him the same moment she stiffened in his arms. He should've stopped before curiosity got the better of him. Now the playfulness had left her features, replaced with discomfort.

"The jury's still out on that one."

"There's no rush. I can wait." He wasn't going to push or pry. He shouldn't have opened his mouth in the first place. Patience was the only option if this was going to work. He just needed to pull his dick into line.

She pushed gently at his chest, disentangling herself from his arms. "I need to get ready, otherwise my arrogant boss might fire my ass."

He groaned, long and low. Today would be torture, tomorrow too, and every other fucking day until he could get his fill of this beautiful woman. "Meet me in the storeroom in ten minutes." He was joking. At least he thought he was.

Shay's chuckle filled the room and she shook her head as the front door opened again. "I don't think those duties are in my job description."

He wanted to chase her, to stalk her into the nearest corner and show her exactly what duties he required of her. Only problem was they couldn't be caught together. He needed to explain the situation to T.J. and Brute first, and the two of them wouldn't turn up until later.

Staff and management relationships weren't forbidden. They'd worked together long enough to trust one another to make the right judgments, but when Vault of Sin was involved, they all second-guessed every decision they made. Because of the privacy issues and the lurid nature of what happened downstairs, they had to tread carefully. Shay was a liability now she knew their secret, and none of them liked any type of vulnerability when it came to their private club.

"We'll discuss this later," he called, and then growled when she replied with a girlie finger wave over her shoulder.

The lunch rush came and went, with Shay acting oblivious to his constant stare. He was sure she was deliberately teasing him. Torturing him. Making him so fucking crazy he ended up approaching her while serving a customer and asked her to meet him in the storeroom for a private discussion.

"I'll be there in a minute."

He stalked away and closed the storeroom door behind him to wait in peace. Time ticked by, hours, minutes...probably seconds, he couldn't tell the difference anymore. Then she opened the door and closed it quietly behind her before launching herself at him.

He stumbled back, hitting the stacked shelves, making the rows of bottles clang. They paused, making eye contact as the noise lessened, waiting for the all-clear to go ahead. Then Shay's gaze snapped to the shelf behind him and she frantically reached her arm out before a loud smash filled the room.

"Shit." She slid away from him.

As the heat of her fled his body, his heart rate quickened. He didn't give a fuck about the bottle, or the mess, or whatever the cost of the alcohol. His mind was only focused on one thing.

"I'll clean it up later." He grabbed her arms and pulled her back against his chest.

Passion flared in her eyes and she clung to him as he lowered his hands to the delicious curve of her ass. He kissed her, hard, while she relaxed into the grip of his hold and began wrapping her legs around his waist, climbing him, her hands everywhere. He smiled against her mouth, loving every breath of sweet-scented perfume, every soft whimper, every clench of her thighs around him.

"You're killing me," she rasped. "How am I meant to work with you watching my every move? I can't concentrate."

He yanked at her waistband, unbuckled the belt, flicked open the button. "You looked fine to me."

She clawed his shirt, sliding her hands under the material to run her fingernails against his skin. "I had to re-do three orders."

"I had to leave the service area to readjust my cock fifteen times."

She chuckled into his mouth, charming his tongue with hers, while her fingers glided through his hair. "I love knowing you're—"

The click of the door handle made him freeze and Shay stiffened against him. He didn't have time to move before the door flung open and a faint gasp had him closing his eyes with a wince.

Fuck. He glanced over his shoulder, finding the pale complexion of one of their female chefs. Her eyes were wide, her mouth agape. She shook her head, blinking away the shock and stepped back into the hall.

"Ahh..." Her gaze travelled between him and Shay, the high of her cheeks darkening. "I didn't mean to... I'm...ahh...sorry." She slammed the door shut, leaving them in silence to listen to the quickening pace of her shoes thumping down the hall.

Damn it.

Leo remained still, letting his idiocy sink in as he held Shay against him. He was the boss. He couldn't be pulling this crap at work. At least not upstairs where fucking in public wasn't expected.

"I'm sorry." Shay climbed off him and straightened her shirt.

"Not your fault." He righted his clothes and helped smooth out her tangled hair. He had no clue what he looked like, but Shay's blouse was crumpled and her hair well and truly mussed. She practically had *storeroom-fucker* tattooed on her forehead. If only they'd crossed the finish line to make it worthwhile.

"Do I look okay?" She glanced up at him, her pupils wide with concern.

"Umm."

She winced. "I look ridiculous, don't I?"

"You look like a woman who was caught rutting in the storeroom."

"Great." With one hand, she combed her fingers through her hair while the other pulled a hair tie from her pocket.

No, not great. He hadn't found the right moment to speak to T.J. and Brute yet, and he needed to get to them before the gossip mill.

"Shay, I'm sorry, but I've gotta speak to the guys before they find out what's going on from someone else." He kissed her temple and gripped her shoulders. "Will you be okay?"

She pulled a face, half funny, half awkward. "Yeah. Go."

"I'll meet you at your car when you finish your shift." Outside. Alone. Where they wouldn't be caught acting like secretive teenagers.

She nodded. "I'll clean up the mess."

He eyed the pool of alcohol and glass on the floor at the end of the shelves. "Damn it." He'd forgotten about the broken bottle. "I'll make it up to you. Promise." He gave her one last kiss and then stalked to the door, turned the handle and yanked it open to find Brute staring back at him. His friend was leaning against the wall, arms crossed over his chest, a fucked-off expression etched across his face.

Could this moment get worse?

"We need to talk," Brute growled.

Yes, apparently, it could.

CHAPTER TWELVE

Leo gave Brute ten minutes to cool his temper before he strode into the empty Shot of Sin night club.

"Speak of the devil."

He lifted his gaze as he approached the main bar and found T.J. swiveling around on his bar stool.

"About time." Brute turned from stocking chip packets behind the counter.

Leo ignored the jab and took a seat beside T.J. The three of them needed to talk, only the look on Brute's face said there wouldn't be a lot of civility involved.

"T.J. just finished filling me in on the stalker drama of Saturday night." Brute leaned against the counter on the other side of the bar, his gaze scrutinizing. "Please tell me you didn't sleep with her."

Leo winced.

"Fucking hell, man. Are you kidding me?" Brute's voice rose with each word, sparking Leo's anger.

"My free time is none of your business." It was a lie, a vain attempt to gain some ground over Brute's holier-than-thou attitude. Leo knew he was in the wrong. He should've told them about Shay as soon as they arrived. Better yet, he should've called them Sunday morning. But sometimes Brute's asshole attitude robbed him of his ability to think clearly, and all he could do was come back swinging.

"It is when you're shoveling your dick into one of our employees during business hours."

True, yet Leo didn't need a lecture. And Brute rarely listened to reason. For once, Leo wanted to be happy. To hold a tiny piece of merriment in his long-frozen chest and hope for the best. He slid from the stool and stepped back, ready to cut and run.

"Wait." T.J. grabbed Leo's upper arm. "You both need to calm down so we can discuss this."

Leo jerked off the hold and returned Brute's glare. "Then talk instead of being a fuckin' jerk."

A pregnant pause followed, nothing but the clang of pans echoing into the empty room from their adjoining restaurant.

"You know this can't end well," Brute finally muttered.

"Fucking this up isn't inevitable." It was highly likely, just not inevitable. "We're both taking it slow. Shay is willing to learn more about the lifestyle, so we're going to see where this takes us."

"Banging her in the storeroom is slow?" Brute shook his head and scoffed "And besides, Shay's been drooling over your ass for months. I'm pretty sure she'd do anything for a bone."

"Watch yourself." Leo pointed a furious finger across the bar. "I know the risks. I've been through this before."

"And obviously you didn't learn a thing. Does she realize what your lifestyle involves? Have you thoroughly discussed it? Because a few hours working in the Vault doesn't even scratch the surface of what goes on down there."

Fuck you.

Leo ground his teeth and turned his back to stare across the vacant dance floor. This was not what he expected from his friends. Yes, they'd all endured the same bullshit and broken relationships due to the club, but it didn't mean they had to ditch the idea of ever having a stable partner. Shay was his one chance to turn things around.

"Leo, it's not our business to dictate what you do. Or who you do," T.J. started. "But you're putting us all at risk. I didn't realize how much until Brute pointed it out."

"Of course he pointed it out." Leo swung back to face them. "Making others miserable is his M.O."

"That's not what this is about." The anger in Brute's gaze softened and he let out a huff. "We have a lot to lose."

"I'm aware."

Shay would no longer be able to work for them if this thing between them blew up in their faces. She'd have to walk, leaving them short staffed and Leo nursing another busted ego.

"Really?" Brute asked. "So you've thought about how much of a bullheaded spitfire she is? You fuck her over and she's going to fight back first and ask questions later."

Leo froze, swallowing over the ache tightening his throat. Shay was quick to lash out in armament, but she was professional...most of the time. "She wouldn't do anything stupid."

"And you're willing to put Vault of Sin on the line with that assumption?" Brute gave a derisive laugh. "For a smart guy, you're acting pretty fucking dumb."

"You two were the ones who forced this. Not me." His chest pounded with fury. None of this would've happened if they hadn't encouraged her to work downstairs. "I didn't want her down there in the first place."

"She was meant to work the bar, not your cock," Brute bit back.

"Calm down." T.J.'s demand reverberated off the walls. "For fuck's sake, take a breath, both of you."

Leo's nostrils flared as he tried to settle his rampant breathing. It wasn't only fury at Brute being an unsympathetic bastard making him hyperventilate. It was the fact his business partner was right about Shay's temperament. She was stubborn, and her initial reaction when hurt was to bite back. If Leo ran the business by himself and the risk of backlash only fell on his shoulders, maybe it wouldn't be so bad. But moving forward was dangerous to T.J., Brute, Vault of Sin and all the patrons who felt at home within its walls.

Fuck.

His mind had rested solely on the outcome of losing Shay as a friend and bartender. God knew his experience with backstabbing women was first-class. He should've contemplated every direction this relationship could turn instead of letting himself concentrate on the carnality.

"I'll print out a non-disclosure statement," T.J. broke the silence. "Exactly the same as the one we made Travis and Tracy sign. Then Shay will know the legal ramifications of exposing the Vault."

"Go ahead." Brute grunted. "But we all know it won't do shit when the club is running illegally."

Leo tried not to crumple under the weight of guilt pressing down on his chest and ran a weary hand over his face. Lack of sleep wasn't helping his ability to figure this shit out. He'd been too overcome by lust and the hope he'd finally found someone to accept his desires to be able to get more than a few hours' sleep over the last two nights.

This had to work. Somehow. He needed Shay, but he also needed the club and his friends by his side. "What should I do?" He grimaced when his voice waivered.

Brute sucked in a heavy breath. "Stay away from her."

"No." Leo shook his head, not in anger, not in defiance, but in resignation. He couldn't stay away. Today had proven he wasn't strong enough.

"I don't mean forever. Just a week or two. Let her think things over and make up her own mind without your sleazy pheromones playing havoc with her judgment. If she turns up to her shift at Vault of Sin this Saturday, at least we'll know she's taken the first step by herself."

"It'll also give us time to see if she can separate work and play," T.J. added. "Having you in the office doing the books isn't uncommon. Keep your distance. At least for a little while."

Leo gave a defeated laugh. "And you think Shay's going to be okay with being ignored? She'll be pissed." She'd be fucking furious.

"If this is about commitment and not just sex, she'll wait."

T.J. nodded. "I'm sorry, but I think it's necessary. I know I joked about you being with her, but we all risked a lot to open Vault of Sin. I'd feel better if I knew how serious she was taking this."

"We'll keep an eye on her for you." Brute lowered his voice, the hostility finally leaving his tone. "Unfortunately, with the way things have gone in the past, I think we need to be extra careful. None of us want to see another crash and burn."

"Yeah. I get it." Leo rubbed the tension from the back of his neck and let his last ounce of excitement fade away.

He owed T.J. and Brute peace of mind. Hell, if one of them were shacking up with a staff member, Leo would probably feel the same apprehension. Each of them had a cross to bear in relation to their desires. Brute had been open and honest about his sexual activities, not holding back with his friends and family when they found out. He'd taken their disapproval in his stride, closing himself off to each and every one of them, becoming more heartless with every lost tie and no longer giving a shit about who he offended.

While T.J. had done the opposite and run before he could inflict pain on himself or others. He'd left a beautiful wife and a promising future because he couldn't stand to taint the woman he loved. And neither Leo nor Brute blamed him. People had strong beliefs when it came to sex. Many of which couldn't be swayed. Only he couldn't walk away from Shay with no explanation and expect her to be waiting for him at the end of the week.

"I need to warn her first." He already dreaded the conversation. "I'll catch her in the parking lot before she leaves tonight."

"Do what you need to do."

"Just be mindful of all the players involved," Brute added.

Right. Leo turned on his heel and made his way back toward the Shot of Sin entrance.

"It'll work out for the best," T.J. called.

Leo scoffed. Women never wanted to be pushed away, and he'd already seen firsthand how Shay reacted to rejection. Too bad for him, he'd used all his luck on her over the weekend. What he needed now was a miracle.

CHAPTER THIRTEEN

Shay sauntered across the parking lot, smothering her elated grin at the sight of Leo leaning against the side of her car. The sun was fading, the birds chirping, and there he stood, a sight to behold in his suit pants and business shirt.

Wakey, wakey, uncontrollable hormones.

She'd been worried earlier, not knowing how Brute and T.J. would react to the storeroom issue or their relationship in general. But Leo hadn't come back to speak to her, so she assumed everything had worked out for the best. Good thing too, because she didn't know how they were going to hide this connection between them when they couldn't even keep their hands off each other.

"I hope you weren't waiting long."

The idea of him waiting at all made her belly flutter. Never before had she been a giddy girlfriend...or lover...or whatever the hell this was. The mere sight of Leo had her body on high alert.

"No."

She ignored his gruff tone and sidled up to him, yanking her handbag strap onto her shoulder. They'd only spent one night together, yet he'd instilled enough confidence in their future for her to wrap her hands around his neck and press her body into his. "Do you want to come back to my place tonight?"

Her stomach dropped when he stiffened, his lips thinning to a tight line. He looked straight through her. There was no heat or passion in his expression. Nothing. Only cold disengagement.

"Leo?" When he remained silent, she dropped her hands and stepped back. "What's going on?"

"Sorry." He blinked the light back into his eyes and reached for her. "Nothing's wrong. I just need to discuss a few things with you."

She brushed away his touch and remained out of reach. "That sounds delightfully ominous."

"It isn't." His words lacked the enthusiasm to back up the statement.

"Well, spill." She crossed her hands over her chest and it didn't skip her attention that he ignored the intentional plumping of her breasts. Something was wrong. Big time.

"I'm going to be in the office all week, so we probably won't get a chance to see each other."

She frowned, fixing him with a what-the-fuck expression. "That's it?"

He shrugged. "Yeah. I told you it was nothing." The indifference in his voice said otherwise. "I doubt if I'll get the chance to see you until Saturday night. I need to plow through a heap of book work."

And I won't be plowing you at all. "Right. So, in other words, Brute and T.J. are pissed." Alarm bells started to ring when he broke eye contact. "Or maybe this is you backtracking. Again."

"No." His tone was harsh as their gazes met. "I'm not backtracking. I just need to figure some shit out."

He reached for her, and this time she went willingly into his arms, needing his touch. She didn't want to lose him this time. Even though her own emotions had her threatening to run at the thought of Vault of Sin, she didn't want to be rejected by him again. Not when she knew they could be great together.

"I'm serious about us. But T.J. and Brute made me realize there's a lot to lose if this doesn't work. We both need to appreciate what's at stake."

She could understand the need for caution. Hell, she had already come to terms with resigning from her job if things turned sour. What clenched her heart was his waning enthusiasm. After this afternoon, she'd expected to move forward with increased flirting and maybe more heated moments in more secluded areas. Not the cold shoulder currently being shoved down her throat.

"I understand what's at stake."

He inclined his head. "Well, then take the time to contemplate what will happen in Vault of Sin. Not only as an employee, but how you will feel when you finally let me take you down there as my partner."

She shuddered at the image. The internet research she'd done on sex clubs during her days off hadn't bettered her opinion of the erotic scene. Every site had a different outlook, and none sat favorably. One even claimed most clubs ran like brothels, with all single females in attendance being paid sex workers to heighten the chance of men getting their money's worth. Distaste had accompanied her Google search. It hadn't stopped her fingers tapping the keys though. She spent hours reading through lurid information, searching for a place like Vault of Sin. Leo, Travis and even the woman who'd approached her in the bathroom had spoken of a respectful environment. One Shay could probably grow to enjoy. Yet, all the pages she found contained sleazy information more focused on male bragging rights.

"I know it won't happen for a while." Leo ran a hand through her loose hair and focused his gaze on her lips. "But it's better for you to determine you don't want to be part of the lifestyle now instead of becoming disgusted with yourself, or me, later."

She gave a jerky nod, wishing she could argue or rally against him and confidently say she was happy to move forward. Only her anxiety over sex in that sort of environment still plagued her. "Okay. So, the plan is to ignore each other until Saturday?"

"Like I said, I'll be in my office concentrating on orders and tax bullshit. I won't be ignoring you, but I doubt I'll see you either."

Another nod. She was the weaker party in this duo and the realization didn't sit favorably. Men usually fawned over her, clinging to every opportunity to smother her. Leo's ability to brush her away so easily was like a kick in her overly sensitized ovaries. The grass definitely didn't seem so crisp on this side of the fence.

Time apart might be a good thing, though. It would give her space to strengthen herself against his appeal. It could even work in her favor, if he began to miss her. All she could do was hope he succumbed to the memory of her charms and came running for her before she did it first.

"No problem," she lied and retreated from his embrace. "I guess I'll see you Saturday then."

"Yeah."

She smiled through the disappointment and unlocked her car. "Bye."

He grabbed her hand as she made to leave and pulled her back into his arms. She had a second to catch her breath before his lips brushed hers, delicately sweeping and disappearing just as quickly.

She inwardly cursed her need to take things further, to run her hands under his shirt and mark his skin with her nails. Instead, she strode the remaining steps to her car, not bothering to wait for another farewell as she ignored the devil on her shoulder who chanted she'd just been ditched by Leo.

Again.

CHAPTER FOURTEEN

Shay spent days *realizing what was at stake*. She thought getting through Tuesday to Thursday had been harrowing. Her body no longer ached from the sex high of the weekend. And the hours spent away from Leo, when he was only mere yards away, gave her doubts time to multiply. Yet, Friday night was worse.

She was working the main Shot of Sin bar, as usual, passing the time by trying to send Leo telepathic messages to come see her. Only he didn't. Not in the four hours since the club opened, or any other time during the past three days.

Her aggression had grown to a fever pitch. She was pissed off to the point of shaking, and no matter how hard she tried, she couldn't stop the ache in her chest demanding her to go in search of her damn annoying boss.

She didn't need space. She needed encouragement. Grounding. Maybe a little attention to relieve her apprehension. Now, after almost a week spent on the razor's edge of trepidation, she wasn't sure how she'd hold back her frustration when they finally did come face to face.

"Raspberry and vodka in a tall glass, please."

You've got to be fucking kidding me.

She ground her teeth at the same loner who came to her bar every damn week. He needed to learn that pretty pink drinks were never going to get him laid. Breathing deep, she grabbed a short glass from the tray, filled it and slid it toward him with a scowl.

"This isn't what I ordered." He frowned, raising his voice over the heavy bass music.

"No, it's not." Shay pointed to the scotch and dry in front of him. "This is what us bartenders like to call a man's drink." She paused, waiting for his ire. When none came, she smiled—all teeth and no charm. "That's all I'll be serving you from now on. So, drink up or find someone else to fill your order."

A scowl marred his usually smooth brow, yet he still handed over payment.

His inability to stick up for himself pissed her off even more. She was beyond frustrated. At the loner. At herself. And most of all, at Leo. He'd wrecked her, turning her into a pathetic, weak and second-guessing Nancy.

Her heart thumped in her chest. The strain from the previous week hit her with full force.

"I'm not finished." The words spilled out without her control. "You're also going to undo the top button of your straight-laced shirt, ruffle the fuck outta your nerdy hair, and for the love of God, walk around with a little pride. Stop sulking like you're handing over your balls every time you ask a woman if she wants a drink. You hear me?"

Her throat dried and her hands shook as she tried in vain to pull herself together. This was all Leo's fault. He was ignoring her. Flicking her away like a used candy wrapper. Not even sparing a moment to call, or send a freaking text message.

"Fucking asshole," she muttered and cringed when the customer's now angry gaze drifted past her shoulder.

"Shay."

She stiffened at the authoritative tone. *Christ.* The last thing she needed was Brute and all his heartless arrogance.

"Storeroom. Now," he growled.

She straightened her shoulders and swung around, not bothering to acknowledge her boss's existence before trudging away. As soon as they were alone in the small room, she began to crumple, her eyes burning with despised weakness.

"What's your problem?" he asked without inflection.

She didn't know how he contained himself. How he held all his feelings inside, never to be seen. Clearly, she didn't have his strength.

"Nothing."

He raised a brow. That was all it took, a haughty, impatient brow telling her to hurry up and spill.

"You know I slept with Leo." There, she'd admitted it. Now she didn't have to pretend like her emotions weren't on the spin cycle anymore. Professionalism be damned, she was a woman with a bruised ego, everyone prepare for hysterics.

"Yeah, I know."

She waited, for something, anything, only he continued to stand there with his haughty brow.

"Well, he's avoiding me." She threw her hands up in frustration. "I'm introduced to all the secrecy downstairs, he comes to my rescue when some guy follows my car, he takes me home and fucks me silly, vowing he wants to be with me. Then all of a sudden, I don't exist."

She paused, hoping for comfort she knew better than to expect. The longer Brute remained quiet, the more worthless she felt.

"If he made a mistake, fine," she lowered her voice in defeat. "He just needs to tell me. Not to keep dragging me along for days. Man up and let me have it."

"I told him to give you space."

"You what?"

His gaze hardened, piercing her with annoyance. "I warned you a long time ago to stay away from Leo. You didn't listen, now you need to step back and realize what will happen when this doesn't work out."

When, not if.

"I'm aware I'll lose my job."

"Yeah. You will," he said without regret. "But what about Leo? What about Vault of Sin?"

She frowned, suddenly defensive. "What about it?"

"You're strong, Shay, but you're also a temperamental bitch at times, and quick to fly off the handle. If you leave here in a snit, how do we know you won't blab our secrets to the world?"

She jerked back as if he'd slapped her. "I wouldn't do that."

"Maybe not." He shrugged. "I'm not convinced you'd leave amicably though. Then there's Leo. He'll drop the ball at work, and T.J. and I will have to pick up the slack. It'll increase the popularity downstairs because he'll start plowing through the women like he's on death row, but it won't make my job easier."

Her heart shot to her throat at the image of Leo surrounded by a sea of naked women, all of them vying for his attention. "You're such a bastard."

"Just proving my point, sweetheart. You're the jealous type. And I think knowing he's currently downstairs at a private party would be enough to spark you into a rage."

The heart in her throat stopped beating and plummeted to the base of her stomach. "You're lying."

What had she done to deserve this from Brute? She'd always respected him, had even gone to him for advice because he didn't disguise the truth with bullshit. Finding out their friendship was a one-way street was another kick in the teeth.

"Why would I bother?" The lack of sentiment in his eyes told her he was telling the truth. "It's an intimate party and the host specifically requested Leo to be the overseer. Apparently, I'm not chummy enough with the patrons." He smirked, showing pride in his asshole reputation. "And T.J. isn't known for his participation."

Shay clenched her stomach to stop herself from doubling over. "He should've told me," she whispered. Leo had promised fidelity, and she would take him at his word, but picturing him surrounded by temptation and easy offerings made her second-guess everything—her confidence, her job, even their future together.

"He can't start asking you for permission to do his job."

She gulped in a breath and nodded. He was right. It didn't stop her feeling betrayed though. Leo had told her last week that she could never go downstairs without him. Would the demand ever run both ways?

"Shay." Brute softened his tone. "It's not too late to change your mind. Go home. Think things through. If you decide you don't want to be with him, then we'll shuffle the shifts around so you don't have to work together for a while. It'll blow over in no time, and work can go back to the way it's always been." He pinned her with his stare. "Things won't be as easy once the two of you become close."

"And what if I can't walk away?"

Brute looked at her with sympathy, the first heartfelt emotion she'd ever seen cross his face. "Then we all take it a day at a time."

She gave a derisive chuckle. "This isn't a group relationship."

He stood silent for a long moment, the heavy beat of bass echoing the thump of her heart. "You haven't thought this through, because you're not seeing the bigger picture. I don't think you realize what a life with Leo will mean."

"I'm sure I don't." He'd surprised her enough already. "But isn't my willingness to try a good indication of where my heart's at?"

"Go home, Shay. Picture your future with him from every angle." He stepped forward and briefly squeezed her shoulder. "And don't worry if you aren't ready for tomorrow night. If you don't show up, I'll know you need more time."

She rolled her eyes, trying to lessen the tension in the room. "You're just driving me away so you get to spend more time downstairs with the ladies."

"Sure am." He smirked, yet the jubilation quickly faded. "We don't want to lose you."

The sorrow in his voice cut deep, and finally she understood how a woman could've broken him so badly. "It's because of Vault of Sin, isn't it?" she spoke almost to herself. His harshness, the reaction to her being with Leo, it was all because of the way one of his previous lovers had treated him.

"What do you mean?" His voice regained its emotionless tone.

Shay gazed up into his blue eyes, noticing for the first time the tiny gray flecks around his pupils. She wanted to run a hand through the blond, chin-length hair combed back from his face and gently glide her palm along the light beard covering his chiseled jaw.

Without the damaged soul, he could be a gorgeous man. Only he wore his hatred like a shield, rarely smiling or softening the bitterness from his features. It would take a strong woman to heal him, and she hoped one day he would find her.

"Nothing."

He shrugged. "Okay. I'll let the rest of the staff know you're knocking off early."

She nodded as he turned to the door and slid it open. "Hey, Brute..."

He paused and glanced over his shoulder.

"You're not as heartless as you want us all to believe."

He laughed without humor. "Think what you like, sweetheart. But I assure you, I'm only looking out for myself."

Then he was gone, leaving Shay to shrink under the weight of her thoughts.

CHAPTER FIFTEEN

*L*eo was pacing. Well, in reality he was sitting at the empty Vault bar, rubbing his forehead, wishing away his headache. But in his mind, he was climbing the walls. He couldn't stop. He was mentally exhausted, his body not equipped to handle this relationship bullshit.

Why did fucking someone on a regular basis have to be so complicated? He released a bark of laughter. If only this thing with Shay was mere fucking. But no, he had to go and get his emotions involved. He had to fall for her.

The last four days had been a nightmare. He'd sequestered himself in the back office, thinking the distance from the bar would make it easier for him to stay away. And it had been...until he'd remembered all the video feeds from the club could be accessed from his laptop. Then his working week had been shot to hell.

He'd watched her. For hours.

When the call for the private party had come through, he'd jumped at the opportunity to get away from his computer. Then he'd spent every hour downstairs wishing he was back behind his desk. Nothing took his mind off Shay, and now Saturday night had arrived, he wasn't sure how it would end.

A click sounded behind him, and he tilted his head to better hear the door opening from the main staircase. His heart beat in a crescendo, building with force until his chest pounded. He listened for the footfalls, hoping to hear the soft steps of Shay. He even held his breath, until the thudded stride informed him it wasn't the person he wanted.

"She's not here yet?" Brute asked.

Leo sighed and ran a hand down his face. "No. She's still got time though."

Last week, she'd said she'd arrive early, yet the seconds were ticking by. It was only forty-five minutes before guests would start to arrive.

Brute slid onto the stool beside him and stared straight ahead. "Don't hold your breath, buddy."

"Why?" Leo turned. "Do you know something I don't?"

"She snapped last night and took her anger out on one of the customers. I ended up sending her home early."

"Why wasn't I told?" He tried unsuccessfully to curb the steel in his tone.

"You were busy down here...which she didn't appreciate either."

Leo turned back to the bar, slowly counting the liquor bottles to stop himself from snapping. "You told her where I was?"

"Was I meant to lie?"

He lowered his head into his hands and sighed. "No. I just..." *Should've been the one to tell her.* "I want to see her." *I need her to show up.*

Christ. He had to shuffle on the stool to make sure he still had a dick between his thighs. He'd never cared this much for a woman. Not outside the bedroom, anyway.

"Look, man, I know you want this to work out, and so do I, but she doesn't have a clue about what to expect down here. I don't think she's even contemplated T.J. or my involvement."

"We were meant to be taking things slow. I didn't want to scare her off."

"Well, she'll be fucking frightened once she sees me naked. Ain't no woman gonna forget a package that big in a hurry."

Leo shook his head and grinned. "Too bad you don't know what to do with it."

"Sounds like jealousy, bro." Brute wiggled his fingers in Leo's ponytail.

"Fuck off." He slapped the hand away with a chuckle, yet the humor faded as fast as it arrived. His buddy was trying his best to cheer him up, and Leo appreciated it, only he'd been stuck in this sullen mood all week. Now time was running out, and his gut told him Shay wasn't going to show.

"I know I've been tough on you about this," Brute murmured into the quiet. "But I like Shay."

The hair on Leo's neck stiffened. His friend didn't admit to feelings. Ever. He didn't share or express affection. His admiration of women was only ever shown in the way his gaze raked their body, or how he went to great efforts to bring them pleasure. No words were ever spoken, because then they could be held against him.

"Stop bristling, lover boy. I'm not after your woman. I just wanted to keep an eye out for her. You strutted around the restaurant on Tuesday with your dick leading the way. I was hoping the days apart would give you both time to think clearly."

Leo released a painful breath. "My thoughts are as clear as they're gonna get, so can you let me take it from here now?"

"Sure thing." Brute slid from the stool. "I didn't push the issue about the non-disclosure during the week. So I'll bring it down later in the hopes she turns up."

Leo nodded, not convinced she would. "Thanks."

"Keep your head up." Brute began to walk from the main room. "You look like a pussy when you mope."

∼

Shay had been standing in the dim light above the back entrance to Vault of Sin for over ten minutes. She wasn't going to back out. Getting in the car to drive here had been the hard part. Only she wasn't entirely sure how to convince her finger to ring the bell on the control panel beside the door.

"This is work," she muttered to herself. "Nothing more."

Delusional much?

She may still be pissed off. Still angry as fuck at holding the weaker hand in whatever sexed-up game they were playing. But she was here for Leo. Plain and simple. Her cloying feelings for him were too strong to ignore.

No matter how many times she contemplated the worst-case-scenario outcome—the loss of her job, the hit to her confidence and the possible risk of utter humiliation—her heart continued to thump in a yearning beat. She needed Leo, and she was here to take a chance on any possible future with him. No matter how freakishly scary it was.

"Now you just have to press the goddamn button." She raised a shaky hand, held her breath and rammed her fingertip into the bell.

She ignored the small camera panel above the button and lowered her gaze to the shiny black heels she wore. Inwardly, she cursed herself for getting dressed up for tonight's shift. Her bartender uniform consisted of a Shot of Sin tank, which she currently wore. But instead of the three-quarter casual pants or jeans she normally donned, she was wearing a fucking skirt and her finest underwear. It had taken a truckload of chocolate to pull the lacy shit up her legs, and even more to clasp the Wonderbra behind her back. And she'd done it for him—the guy who'd ignored her all week.

The thick, steel-plated door creaked open, making her heart stop, and Leo came into view in his black pristine pants and another freshly ironed shirt. His lips were a thin line, lacking emotion, yet his eyes blazed with something she didn't want to determine. If he was angry she was a little late, he would have to deal with it.

He stood in silence, his gaze slowly raking her from head to toe and back again. Memories of last weekend heated her cheeks and she dulled the sudden spark of arousal with annoyance.

"Nice to see you again," she spoke over the lump in her throat.

His jaw stiffened, his nostrils flared, and right when she thought he was about to put her in her place, he grabbed her wrist and yanked her inside, pushing her against the wall as he slammed the door shut with his fist.

"Leo—"

He cut off her protest with his lips, devouring her mouth, claiming her before the darkened staircase. After a week without him, she couldn't maintain her anger. Her defenses crumpled, and she clung to him, kissing him back with equal fervor. His tongue entered her mouth, sliding against hers, drawing a moan from her throat.

This was what she wanted. Leo. Nothing else. No complications or expectations. Just him and her, together, enjoying one another. Then reality overcame her hormones and she remembered the distance he placed between them after every time they were intimate. She whimpered as she mustered the strength to nudge him away.

"Don't." She touched her lips with the tips of her fingers to stop them tingling.

"Shay." He reached for her with anguish etched across his features.

"You've been ignoring me."

He sighed and ran a rough hand through his hair, loosening the ponytail. "I told you, I was giving you time. And I owed it to T.J. and Brute to take this seriously. A lot is at stake."

"And what was I owed?" She'd never sounded so fragile, her voice had never been so weak, yet she couldn't strengthen her tone.

"The time to make up your own mind without me clouding your judgment." He leaned against the opposite wall, his focus never leaving hers. "I don't want to hurt you."

"You were hurting me all week."

"That wasn't deliberate. I've fucking missed you, Shay." He pushed from the wall and bridged the distance between them to rest his pelvis against hers. "If you knew how hard this week has been for me, you wouldn't still be shooting daggers my way."

"You set the distance rule, so you kinda deserve it." She softened her stare and gave him a weak smile. "Look, I know this will never be a conservative relationship. I've spent days coming to terms with that. But I'm here aren't I?" She wriggled out from underneath him and took the first few steps backward, needing space to remain clearheaded.

"They want you to sign a non-disclosure." He spoke as if it was the end of the world, waiting for her to become offended.

"Of course."

He narrowed his gaze and followed her. "You're unpredictable, you know that?"

She slid farther along the wall, sensing the heat radiating off him. "I aim to please."

His predatory focus honed in on her eyes as he closed in on her, leaning her into the cold plaster. "And you deliberately wore a skirt to tempt me, didn't you?"

Yes. "No. Not at all."

He laughed softly against her neck. "You're a seductress." He pulled back and rested his head against hers. "If you walk away, I'll respect your wishes. I won't chase you. But as long as you're here, I'm not going to be able to keep my hands off you."

She sucked in a breath at his raw possession. She itched to run her fingers under his shirt, to grind against the hardness in his pants. But the slightest touch would spark a fire she couldn't sate, and she didn't need to lose focus now. Not when she was meant to be working. "You need to increase your bipolar meds."

The side of his lips quirked as he pressed his erection into her abdomen. "You need to tame that sassy mouth."

"Or maybe you need to do it for me." She bit her lip, wishing she hadn't taunted him. "Come on. You need to show me around." This was going to be a tough night if she was the one who had to push away his advances. All week it had been the opposite, and she had no clue which dynamic she preferred. Chasing a gorgeous man was common sense. Pushing him away was plain idiocy.

She ducked under his arm and continued down the hall, around the corner and came out at the side of the bar. The empty room seemed different in the harsh fluorescent light and the scent of sex no longer permeated the air.

Leo groaned behind her and followed her into the open space. "Fine. But just so you know, I plan on following you home again tonight."

Shay kept her back to him, hiding her smile.

"We'll start over here."

She glanced over her shoulder and then turned to follow him into the first room along the side wall. She remembered it from last Saturday. The one with the large bed center stage.

Leo flicked on the light switch, and the tiny bulbs above the focal point twinkled to life. "My favorite room."

She remembered the threesome from last week with vivid clarity. The way the men had caressed the woman with loving affection. Shay could still see them on the mattress, their legs tangled, their smiles bright.

"You obviously already know about the bathrooms." He strode forward, pushed open the ladies door and reached inside to flick on the lights. Then he did the same with the males. "We've got cleaners who change the linens and restock supplies. If you ever work down here again, all you have to do is adjust all the lighting. But either myself, T.J. or Brute will always be down here to help." He strode past her to click on the bedside-table lamps.

"And what's your role down here," she asked.

He paused as he opened a drawer, and glanced over his shoulder.

"Supervisor. Confidant. Sometimes instigator. Our role is to make sure everyone is comfortable and that no issues arise." He raised a brow, waiting for her response.

Instead of voicing her opinion, she nodded and focused on the items in the drawer.

"The bedside tables are filled with necessities, too—restraints, vibrators, lube. Condoms are used on the toys for hygiene reasons, but they're also sterilized after every party."

Shay winced and withheld a shudder.

He slammed the drawer shut and walked to her. "Come on. You don't need to see the rest. I'll help you set up behind the bar before everyone arrives." He grabbed her hand in a gentle grip and led her back into the main room. He rubbed his thumb along her skin as they walked in silence, and her heart galloped at the simple gesture from a man more accustomed to sexual moves than sweet ones.

"You still good with this?" He flicked off the fluorescent light beside the entrance to the bar and turning on the mood lighting.

"I'm good." Her voice was too chipper, too unrealistic.

He slowed to a stop, turned to face her and backed her into the counter behind the bar. His lips tilted, his eyes dancing in the darkness. "You're shitting yourself."

She rolled her eyes at his attempt to put her at ease. "Well, not literally."

"There's the sass I was looking for."

"I thought you wanted me to leash my sassiness?" She raised a brow in defiance.

He leaned closer, licking his bottom lip. "It's endearing in an annoying sort of way."

"I could say the same about you."

His grin continued to grow as he bridged the distance between them and brushed his mouth against hers. "That fucking perfume is driving me wild."

Score one to Calvin Klein.

His lips were forceful as his tongue entered her mouth. He played with her, coaxing her into murmurs of lust, making her clench her thighs together. He grasped her hips, lifted her onto the counter beside the beer taps and spread her knees apart. Then he slid his hands up her thighs, under her skirt and lowered her lace G-string.

It was too much. Too quick. Lust suffused her veins. Heat invaded her limbs.

"*Leo.*" She pulled back to brace her hands on the cool counter top as she sucked in ragged breaths.

"We're alone." He bent to untangle the underwear now at her feet and threw them onto the bar. "No one will walk in."

He lowered his zipper and raised her blood pressure at the same time. She peered down at the enthusiasm tenting his boxers and bit her lip. He was impressive. More than impressive. He was orgasmic. And she was already wet for him, the tingling sensation between her thighs growing with every second.

"Come here." He grabbed her ass, pulling her to hover on the counter edge. He riffled through his pocket and pulled out a condom.

"Do you always have those on standby?"

"I will when I'm around you."

"Good answer." She watched him sheath himself, all that delicious male cock covered in dark blue and ready for her.

"Fast and hard, Shay. You ready?" He inched her off the bar, holding her in mid-air.

A grin tilted her lips. She loved the way he took charge. "Uh huh."

She clung to his shoulders and stifled a moan when he sunk home, just the way he promised. Quick and harsh. Needy and determined. Her core stretched around him with the slightest pleasure-filled ache.

It was forceful loving. Or fucking. She didn't know the difference, but he drove into her with powerful thrusts, the veins in his neck protruding, the muscles under her hands tightening.

He fucked her against the bar, consuming her with his efficiency, each movement hitting the exact spot necessary to nudge her pleasure into uncharted territory. The sound of skin slapping against skin filled the empty room, followed by her commands for more and his mindless groans. She wrapped her legs around his hips, demanding more, pulling him deeper until her throat went dry and her breasts ached to be touched.

"Fuck. You feel…" He closed his eyes and his nostrils flared as he panted.

Was he equally mindless? It didn't seem possible. He was experienced. Controlled. In contrast, she'd never had sex in a public place. Had only ever been touched by him in a storeroom.

The thought of being caught sent a wicked thrill down her spine, along each nerve, to throb in her pussy. This was all new. All pure fulfillment. She didn't want to let him go. Couldn't contemplate the thought of this ending. Yet, her core began to pulse with a building storm she'd never experienced so quickly.

"Holy shit." She was going to come and she'd barely kissed the man.

"You with me?" He opened his eyes, resting his head against hers as he continued to grind into her.

"God, yes." She was close enough to see black spots in her vision.

He leaned her against the bar, a hand grasping the back of her neck, his other arm holding her close. He started to move in rhythm. Thrust after deep-seated thrust, until she was digging her nails into his flesh, her mouth begging to be kissed.

He fulfilled her wish, taking her lips with harsh pressure, making her chest fire into a ball of uncontainable lust. She began to cry out in climax and he growled in response, following her over the edge.

Her back fought with the bar, her thighs clenched around his waist, her heart beat in a frantic pace of love, lust and fascination. Every part of her was consumed with him. Tuned to him. Hooked to only him.

The heavy slapping sounds lessened, the pounding rhythm died into a gentle embrace. She leaned back, meeting his stare and wondered how it had taken them so long to find something so natural.

Leo was what she needed.

He was the man to give her excitement, passion and pleasure.

He was the one who could keep her on her toes.

All she had to do now was convince herself this could work.

CHAPTER SIXTEEN

"Don't stare at me like that," Leo whispered, the dark ruby of her lips making him want her all over again.

"Like what?" She loosened her grip on his shoulders and stroked the side of his face with a finger. For someone so tough and opinionated, she had a soft heart.

"Like you're offering me your soul." Her brown irises were still dark with lust, her mouth tilted toward his, willing, waiting. "I'll take it, Shay. And I'll never give it back."

Her lips curved, a delicate, almost embarrassed smile hitting him full force. They were on the same wavelength, held the same desire. In the end, passion would win. He knew it would.

"You can—" She gasped at the click of an opening door behind them. "Shit."

She shoved at his chest, pushing him until she had room to slide off the counter. Heavy footfalls came from the entry, while Shay rushed to straighten her skirt and untangle her hair.

"It's only T.J. or Brute." He took his time disposing of the used condom. "Nobody else is allowed down here yet."

She shot him a look of incredulity. "*Exactly*."

His heart changed from the desire-ridden thump to something rough, something uncomfortable. They had so many things to discuss, and no time to do it. Later, once the club was closed and he'd taken her home to sate their lust, they'd talk. And they wouldn't stop until all cards were on the table.

She needed to understand his sex life was intertwined with T.J. and Brute's. They weren't gay, had never even glanced down that path, but they shared a lot of sexual moments, and many, many women. It was like an additional partnership added to their business relationship. The three of them knew how to work together, to make a woman wild and replete. Even though T.J. didn't participate physically, he still played an integral role, and contemplating the conclusion of this part of Leo's life was like a stab through his gut.

Shay was strong and he could sense her curiosity for Vault of Sin. But no matter how much she lessened the tight hold on her inhibitions, Leo doubted she would ever be able to participate with all her bosses around to enjoy the show.

Brute strode into the room, clearing his throat in a less than subtle manner. "Catch you at a bad time?" he drawled, hitting Leo with an unapologetic smirk. A silent message of congratulation passed between them, one that Leo acknowledged with a slight tip of his head.

Shay's back stiffened and she spun around to face the interloper. "Just setting up for the night."

Leo tried not to laugh at her high-pitched tone and placed a strong hand at the low of her back. "Chill," he whispered in her ear.

"Right." Brute raised a brow as he slid across a stool and stretched his arm over the bar. "You might need these then." He retrieved her lace G-string from the counter and held it up on his pointed finger.

She sucked in a breath, the back of her neck and sides of her cheeks turning pink. If it had been any other woman, Leo would've assumed she was embarrassed, only Shay's balled fists below the counter said otherwise.

"Thanks," she gritted through clenched teeth and snatched her underwear from Brute's hold. "I'm going to freshen up." She strode around the counter, head held high, spine straight, and left the room without another word.

Leo waited until she was out of view before he turned to Brute. "Was that necessary?"

"Yeah. Kinda." The smug fucker still flashed a tiny grin. "Thanks for the show. Obviously, you didn't hear me open the door the first time. I had to go back and pretend I was coming in again."

Leo narrowed his gaze. Normally, Brute wouldn't have given a shit about interrupting. He would've pulled up a stool and watched without remorse. "It's not like you to walk away from me putting on a show."

"It's not you I watch, asshole. My focus is always on the women, and this is different. This is Shay."

Shit. Had he fucked up by assuming his friends wouldn't mind her involvement in Vault of Sin? They hadn't brought it up, but neither had they discussed it. "And you don't want to watch her?"

"If I had a problem with her participating down here, I would've spoke up sooner. I just thought you guys were still on shaky ground and I didn't want to rock the boat."

Leo released the breath tightening his lungs. "Thanks."

"Relax. She turned up. That was the hardest part." The arrogance returned to Brute's face. "And for future reference, I'd watch her all damn day. In fact, I'd be happy to show her what she's missing not being with a real man."

Leo rolled his eyes. "No point baiting me. I'm wound too tight to snap back. You're more likely to score a fist to the throat."

"I actually thought Shay might've done the same when I was swinging around her panties." Brute chuckled. "That woman is going to keep you on your toes."

Damn straight. "Yeah. If this works out, she'll send me gray before my time." Leo couldn't wait.

"And what will it take for this to work? She was pretty freaked when I walked in. Are you willing to change your extra-curricular activities to keep her?"

Leo glanced toward the door Shay had disappeared into and rubbed a hand along the stubble of his chin. "I don't know. I'm going to try whatever necessary, and she's trying, too. It's a hell of a lot further than any of us have traveled with this fucked up lifestyle."

A bitter tinge entered Brute's gaze. "True. Just remember the higher you get, the harder you fall."

"I don't plan to fall."

"Good." Brute slid from his stool. "I'm happy for you both." He reached behind his back and pulled a folded piece of paper from his pocket. "The non-disclosure." He handed it over. "Make sure she reads it before you shove your dick into her again. We don't want her claiming she had to sign under duress."

The faint squeak of the bathroom door sounded as Leo snatched the paper. "If you walked in on us before, you'd know there was no duress. Just a gorgeous woman who happens to enjoy my handiwork."

Brute scoffed. "Yeah. Too bad for her, your personality isn't as endearing."

"As endearing as what?" Shay strolled toward them, one eyebrow raised.

"Nothin'." Leo strode around the bar, fighting the need to surge forward and claim her again. "Brute was just leaving."

CHAPTER SEVENTEEN

Shay was proud she'd kept her cool for most of her shift. She served partially dressed patrons with ease, even fought the impulse to stare at the appendages of the entirely naked ones, and she no longer felt the cloying discomfort whenever her gaze brushed past sex scenes in the main room.

In fact, she was beginning to enjoy watching, a little too much. Her G-string was uncomfortably soaked, and every time Leo walked into view, she cursed the way her nipples tingled. It was worse when he came to check on her. She ached to grab his shirt collar and drag him into the storeroom.

But that wasn't how things worked down here. Everything was about exhibitionism, not hiding in storage closets and making out in the dark. More importantly, it wasn't what Leo desired. As the minutes ticked by, her motivation to give him what he wanted increased. So did the nervousness.

"Can I order a juice, please?"

Shay smiled at the petite brunette and nodded. "Sure."

Another thing she loved was the professional manner in which everyone interacted. The cost of entry downstairs included free alcohol, yet none of them rushed to get their money's worth. Everyone played it cool, keeping level-headed. The perception of a seedy sex club was entirely different from the reality of Vault of Sin.

Shay handed over the juice and tingled with the brush of someone's gaze on her skin. She turned her head and found Leo watching her, his eyes glazed with lust. Her focus lowered to his crotch and she shuffled uncomfortably at the thickness pressed against his zipper.

Whore.

She smiled to herself. Yep, her thoughts were those of a bona fide slut, and she didn't give a rat's ass. She'd never been so aroused in her life. And right now, she didn't care what was turning Leo on. All she wanted was to sate their cravings.

As she continued to serve polite patrons, she watched him mingle in the main room. He put those who appeared nervous at ease. Always remaining the professional host with his confident posture and commanding stare, all the while glancing at her every few minutes with irises that never ceased making her burn.

To stop herself from escaping to the bathroom for her own private play session, she turned her back to the room and began wiping down the shelf filled with high-class liquor bottles.

"Leo."

The purred feminine call had Shay snapping round on her heels. The petite brunette she'd served earlier was now draped around Leo, both arms wrapped around his neck with a familiarity that flicked Shay's jealous-bitch switch.

The only thing between the attractive woman and the boner Shay wanted to grapple was two thin layers of clothing. *Keep calm. You can't stab people.* She swung back around, trying to curb her inner bitch by keeping busy, and accidentally nudged a bottle of lime-flavored syrup off the counter.

Fanfuckingtastic.

"Shay, are you all right?" Leo called, his voice more authoritative than concerned.

"Peachy." She chanced one last look at him and the leech hanging from his neck before she grabbed a dust pan from under the counter and began cleaning the sticky mess.

So much for her keeping her cool. Her eyes were burning and palms sweating with the need to start her first cat fight.

Just imagine what it will be like next week when you're working back upstairs and unable to keep an eye on him. Shay growled. Was it always going to be like this—peaks of arousal followed by consuming lows depressing enough to make her needy and weak?

"This sucks."

Surely there was something she could do to turn the tables. It wasn't about claiming him in front of a crowd. It was about feeling secure and confident again. It was about regaining her strength. She just wasn't sure how.

~

*E*very muscle in Leo's body was tense as he tried to keep his erect cock from rubbing against Grace. There was only one woman causing the current pubescent reaction to his body, and the sassy little wench was probably muttering a curse under her breath, hoping his eager appendage would fall off. Yet, he couldn't bring himself to ditch the woman before him just to sate Shay's unease.

It was a tough line to draw, but this was life in the Vault of Sin. He would never dishonor a monogamy vow. Ever. However, in the past he'd been intimate with more than one of the women participating tonight, and he wouldn't alienate them by brushing them aside.

It was still his job to make everyone comfortable within these sordid walls, and as long as he wasn't reciprocating any sexual advances, he wasn't doing anything wrong.

"You're stiff," Grace murmured.

No shit. He was hard as stone.

Grace giggled to herself. "I mean your posture. What's wrong?" She released her arms from his neck and met his gaze.

"I'm fine. Just a little out of sorts tonight." He glanced toward the bar. Shay rose to her feet with the dustpan in hand and shot him a scowl before breaking eye contact.

"Ouch." Grace followed his line of sight. "Your new bartender doesn't look happy."

He released a grunt of frustration and shook his head. Shay looked like she wanted to flay him alive.

"She's gorgeous though."

"Yeah." There was no denying it. "She is."

"Oh, damn." Grace took a step back and tilted her head to meet his line of vision. "Did I cause that? Are you two together?"

Leo struggled to paste on a smile and met Grace's gaze. "It's okay. I don't think either of us know what we're doing at the moment."

"She's not into girls, is she?" Grace grinned and waggled her brows.

Fuck. His dick pulsed, fighting with the zipper of his pants. He'd been down here too many times to have a hair-trigger cock, only the thought of Shay and Grace made his blood surge south. "She's not into the lifestyle."

His own words resonated, penetrating his cloud of arousal. This wasn't her scene. He was pushing her to change her ways. The exact thing he'd hated other women trying to do to him.

"Give her time. Apart from glaring at you with contempt, she doesn't seem to have an aversion to the club itself."

He nodded, gaining some comfort from the possibility of truth in her words. "Yeah. I'm trying." Only he didn't know how long he could stand back and let Shay move at her own pace. He was too eager to have her splayed before a crowd. To have others watch as her beautiful face contorted with release. To see her luscious breasts, smooth stomach and tight pink pussy moving in a dance to set them all on fire.

Yet, he'd drive himself insane with lust before he pushed her.

"Go to her." Grace jerked her head in the direction of the bar. "Give her my apologies. And if she's ever into a bit of girl-on-girl action, I call first dibs." She strode around him, slapping his ass hard enough to make him take a step forward.

Perfect timing. Shay hadn't missed the friendly tap. She stood tall with one hand tightly fisted around a mop handle. Her eyes were glittering and her cheeks flushed with spite. And he couldn't help acknowledging with a grin that she looked hotter than he'd ever seen.

Her nostrils flared as he made his way to the bar, instinctively staying on the customers' side so he didn't get a mop head to the balls. "I'd ask you how you're doing, but your facial expression says it all."

"I estimate you can see about a tenth of the emotion I currently feel." She scrunched her nose and sashayed her angry ass to the small storage room behind the bar.

He strode after her, the first time he'd ever chased a woman. Thankfully, she ditched the mop and made an attempt to push her way back to the bar., but he blocked the doorway with his body.

"Let it out." He blocked the doorway with his body. "Tell me what's making you want to claw my eyes out."

"Isn't it obvious?" She scowled. "I don't appreciate other women touching you. It's not something I think will ever change. And definitely not a scenario I want to imagine every time you're down here without me."

"You mean you can never get used to me rejecting attractive women so I can be with you? Because that's the way I see it." He stepped into her, grabbing her around the waist. "It will take time for everyone to know I'm no longer open to play. I'm not going to send out a fucking memo. So to some extent, you need to get over it."

She released a derisive laugh and shook her head in frustration.

"This isn't going to be the reason you walk away from me," he demanded. "This is the reason you're going to stick around. Because you'll soon realize you have what every other woman in here wants. Me."

"Arrogant much?"

He smirked and shrugged a shoulder. "Is it really arrogance if it's true?"

"*Yes.*"

He softened his features and brushed his lips against hers before she could pull away. "Grace told me to apologize to you. She realized why you were giving us the evil eye."

"Great." She stepped out of his embrace. "Now I'll be known as the jealous bar bitch."

"You play the part well."

Her eyes flared and he caught her wrist when she tried to slap his chest.

"Look." He chuckled. "I told her I was taken and she backed off. You should be happy. Even more so, that she then became more interested in seeing if you were into girl-on-girl action."

"What?" Her eyes widened.

"You heard me." He bridged the distance between them again, pushing them farther into the darkened storeroom, not giving a shit if patrons were waiting for bar service. "So should I be jealous?" He backed her into a wall, and leaned his body into hers. "Because I'm not. I'm hard as hell thinking about another woman going down between your pretty thighs."

CHAPTER EIGHTEEN

A strangled noise escaped Shay's throat. Yet again, she was struggling to gain her footing.

Girl-on-girl action? Holy shit. She'd thought her days of experimenting had died with her teen years. Muff diving had never been on her fantasy list. Yeah, she'd shared a drunken kiss or two with friends, but that had been a lifetime ago. Only now, knowing she'd excite Leo by diddling another woman made another thrill shoot through her body.

"I need to get back to work," she rasped.

He chuckled, fucking chuckled in her ear before stepping back to let her leave. "I'll be calling last drinks soon. You should start worrying about what will happen once we get back to your place. I've got a week's worth of attention to dish out."

She increased her pace from the storeroom, needing space so her nipples didn't bore a hole through her bra. She'd wanted to be more sure of herself before she left Vault of Sin tonight. Because walking out of here would be easy, but coming back as a participant would be a nervous nightmare. And after a lifetime of being confident in herself, she was damn sick of the apprehension.

She'd thought turning up tonight had been difficult, yet all her appearance had done was voice her willingness to be in a relationship with Leo. What she really needed to do was make a choice. Decide right here, right now, if she could be a part of this lifestyle. No fucking around for days. Or second-guessing what might or might not be. She couldn't wait around for a set of balls to miraculously appear between her thighs, she had to pull up those soggy, sexy lady underwear and bite the bullet. She didn't want to change the man she'd fallen for, so the question was, did she want to be with Leo on his terms, in his environment? Or say to hell with all the angst and take the easiest option for all of them, T.J. and Brute included, and simply walk away.

She sucked in a breath and ignored the stone settling in her chest. She adored Leo, always had, only things were much deeper now, and a great deal scarier. What if she gave Vault of Sin a try and her family found out? What if she choked, literally, and made a fool of herself? What if she wasn't good enough?

In reality, he was asking her to be a performer in the rawest way. And yeah, she owned her shit, but spreading her thighs to the world required a set of brass balls...and she didn't even own a plastic pair.

Leo strode past the bar, confident as always as he played the supervisor role. He was at home here in a club most people would cringe at. She was proud he owned his proclivities. Last week, she'd made a fool of herself by judging him without reason. Because glancing around the room, all she could see were happy faces. Everyone was having fun. Even those who sat in groups chatting, no orgasms required. The crowd was different from her previous visit. A completely new mass of faces, yet the atmosphere was the same.

Friends or strangers, they all seemed to be brought together by a familiar bond. They didn't snigger or walk off in small groups to pass judgment on others. It was a quaint group of friends having a party. Only instead of playing cards and getting drunk, people got naked and played with each other.

The lifestyle here wasn't seedy or sleazy. There were no men lurking in the corners, or women playing mind games. It was sex in a safe environment. Simple as that.

"Last drinks," Leo raised his voice to vibrate through all the rooms.

"Oh, shit." Shay felt the color drain from her face.

This was it. She had two options. One would test her limits and may even break her, but the chance of happiness would accompany the journey. While the other road was easy, only she'd walk the smooth, stone path alone.

"Bloody hell," she muttered to herself. There was no way she could find the answer tonight. Not without hard liquor. And there was no chance of getting up close and personal with Mr. Grey Goose while working and having to drive home later.

Fate had got her this far...along with a little stubbornness. It looked like a flip of the coin would have to do.

∽

*L*eo had called last drinks a few minutes early because Shay's complexion was becoming paler with every passing moment. He didn't want to contemplate the look in her eyes or what she planned on telling him the next time they were alone. So he kept himself busy and said farewell to the patrons who began to leave.

T.J. and Brute would've already closed Shot of Sin and be in the process of packing up for the night. He just hoped to fuck they didn't make their way downstairs looking to play while Shay was still around.

He knew she was slowly coming to terms with strangers fornicating around her, but he doubted she had grasped the concept of T.J. and Brute being involved. Or maybe she had in the last hour and that was why all the color had vanished from her skin.

"Good luck with your bartender." Grace came up to him, now dressed in a tight black cocktail dress with a purse clutched in one hand and a set of keys jangling in the other. She leaned in and placed a gentle kiss on his cheek. "Give her time. I know you haven't had the best experience with the ladies, but go easy on her. Adapting to new sexual experiences is more emotional for women. We tend to hold tight to our bad choices and analyze things to the point of insanity."

"Thanks," he muttered and then cringed at his rudeness. "I might see you next week," he lied. It was highly doubtful with the way things were heading with Shay. If he had to make a prediction, he'd say his time in the Vault was drawing to an end, at least for a while.

He walked away, heading for the entrance to turn off the large flat-screen. All he wanted was to get out of here. Which was fucking ironic, because all his problems with Shay stemmed from his need to be in Vault of Sin in the first place.

When he strode back into the main room, only three guys and two women remained, finishing their drinks as they lounged on one of the king-sized beds. His gaze sought Shay's, but she was gone. His head snapped around to do a quick visual sweep of the area—not in the bar, the storeroom door was closed and he doubted she was in any of the private rooms.

Shit.

He'd made a mistake earlier. He promised he wouldn't chase her if she ran. Hell. He didn't even know if she'd left and already he was fighting the need to kick everyone out so he could find her. His palms began to sweat as he pounded out the steps to the bar. Once he was behind the counter, he rushed to the cabinets under the sink and huffed out a relieved breath. Her handbag was there. She hadn't run. Not yet.

He climbed to his feet and checked the storeroom. Empty. He locked it behind him and went to the first private room filled with numerous beds. Again, no sign of her, so he flicked off the light and shut the door.

That only left one place to check, unless she was upstairs. He stood in the doorway of his favorite room and stared at the mattress bathed in light. Yesterday, he would've given anything to see Shay lying atop the black sheets. Now, he'd give anything to have her in his arms, simply holding her in the quiet of his apartment. Could he forego his current need to participate and live a life without Vault of Sin? Maybe. He would at least try. For Shay.

He flicked off the light, killing his fantasy with a sharp click and turned his attention to the ladies bathroom door as it squeaked open.

"Shay?"

She came to him with her head held high. In the dim light emanating from the main room, he could see the uncertainty in her eyes, right before she reached on her toes to kiss him. It was soft, sweet, entirely opposite to the ball-busting woman he knew, and his heart ached all the more for her.

His hands found her hips and he slid his tongue into her willing mouth as her warmth filled his chest. When she pulled back, he was no longer uncertain. He knew what he needed in his sex life and it wasn't other peoples' lust. It was Shay.

Only Shay.

She met his gaze with a half-smile, half-wince marring her face. Slowly, she raised her hands to the hem of her shirt and, with a deep, unsettling breath, raised the material over her head and let it fall to the floor.

Fuck me.

"There's people still out there." He glanced over his shoulder to make sure they were alone.

She gave a shaky nod and lowered her skirt to pool at her feet. "I know." She stood before him in black lace, the firm mounds of her breasts plumped and begging to be touched.

"*Shay.*" He swallowed over the dryness in his throat. She needed to put her clothes back on and walk from the room. Now. He didn't have the restraint to maintain the distance between them for too much longer. "What's this about?"

She sucked in a strengthening breath and climbed onto the bed, laying her delicious curves down in the middle of the mattress. "This is me, risking humiliation, to give myself to you."

He held back from pouncing, from taking what he wanted and instead rubbed a hand over the rough stubble at his jaw. Grace's words repeated in his mind. *"Adapting to new sexual experiences is more emotional for women. We tend to hold tight to our bad choices and analyze things to the point of insanity."*

This was too quick for Shay.

"Don't get me wrong, but why now? You're not ready for this."

Her face was shadowed in the darkness as she rested back on her elbows. "I'm taking a leap. I don't want to spend weeks stressing over what will happen. I want to do this now and have my answer straight away."

He stepped forward and rested his knees against the side of the bed. "What's the question?"

She paused, leaving them in heated silence for long moments. "I want to know if I can be enough for you."

His nostrils flared with a sudden burst of anger. He wanted to spank her ass and prove to her in many pleasurable ways just how compatible they were. "You're enough," he growled. No other woman had set his heart racing like she did.

"Then show me." She sat up and moved toward him on her knees. "Do with me what you will, and if we both make it through to the other side, maybe we'll have a chance of taking this further."

His body tensed from his chest to his toes as she ran her hands over his pecs to grab the collar of his shirt. She tugged him forward and he followed her onto the mattress, crawling between her parted thighs as she scooted back to the top of the bed.

She loosened his ponytail with a hand through his hair, making the chin length strands curtain their faces. "You're quiet," she whispered against his lips, her breath heating every inch of him.

"I'm worried."

She pulled back into the pillows and frowned up at him. "But I thought—"

"There's only two possible outcomes to this. Either we'll be perfect for each other..."

"Or I'll have to quit my job if things go wrong."

He nodded. Shay was a passionate woman with a mean jealous streak. Working together after a botched relationship wouldn't be an option. And as much as his dick was willing to take the chance, a dull throb behind his ribs made him proceed with caution. "We can save this for another day."

She remained still beneath him, her chest rising and falling against his. When her hand fell from his hair, he anticipated her moving out from beneath him, to leave and rethink her decision. Then she swept her fingertips over his jaw, his chin and finally his lower lip before her mouth brushed his.

"I'm willing to risk it."

∼

Shay waited with her heart in her throat and her confidence slowly fading. Leo continued to stare at her in the dim light, his quiet breathing the only thing she heard over the murmured voices in the next room.

People were out there, sipping drinks without a care while she lay in her underwear beneath a man she began to pray would say something.

"If we do this, I won't be quiet, and I won't allow you to hold in your pleasure," he warned. "We'll have an audience before my clothes hit the floor."

She swallowed. "I know."

He went silent again, and finally she appreciated the time he took to take the next step. His cock was hard between them, the thick length pressing against her pubic bone. He wanted her, yet he was proceeding with caution. Weighing up the pros and cons like she had for so long.

"I'll push you, Shay." He leaned in to gently slide his tongue along her bottom lip and his hand down her side to brush the curve of her breast. "I don't know any other way in here."

"I know." She shuddered, part of her wanting to be pushed while the other hoped adrenaline would see her through to the end without fleeing.

"Then take off your clothes." He pushed one cup of her bra up to expose her breast and leaned down to lap her nipple with his tongue. "I want every inch of you at my disposal."

She arched her back and swung her arms behind her to unclasp the hooks of her bra. As she slid the straps down, he lavished her with attention, licking one and then the other until her inhalations became labored and her skin tingled with sensitivity.

"Tell me you want me."

"I want you," she whispered, thrusting her breast into the heat of his mouth, dying under the touch of his fingers as they travelled along her waist.

"Louder."

Her heart thumped beneath her chest. "I want you." Her voice rose with each word, her adrenaline spiking with it.

He chuckled and pulled back to look her in the eye. "That meek voice does shit for my ego. Tell me you want me like you mean it. Like the tough girl I know you are."

She bit her lip, staring him down in determination, her nostrils flaring in spite. He raised a brow and skidded his fingers over her abdomen, slipping under the waistband of her G-string.

"Giving up already?" He flicked her clit, making her jolt.

"No. Just give me a second to prepare myself."

"No more thinking," he growled. "Say it." He parted her folds with his fingers and penetrated her in one delicious thrust. "Say it now."

"Jesus Christ," she wailed. "I want you, Leo."

He flashed her a predatory smile before sliding his touch from her body. "That's better." He gripped her G-string on either side of her hips and yanked the flimsy material down her legs.

She hoped the blood rushing through her ears was the only reason the soft murmuring in the next room had stopped. Not that they had fallen quiet to listen. Either way, she was determined to ignore any stranger who wanted to catch an eye full. This was her time to prove herself to the man she'd been dreaming about, and she definitely needed to lift her game.

She reached for his shirt and began to undo his buttons, unable to pull her gaze away from the skin she continued to expose. His chest was covered in a light dusting of hair, his pecs defined, his abs smooth and taut. She ached to run her hands along the lines of sinew, to bite into his flesh and make him flinch. She wanted to make him mindless, to repay him for the way he'd made her feel for too damn long.

With a rough hand, he pushed apart her thighs, exposing her, making her more vulnerable than ever before. She was on display, at his mercy, and her body had never felt more alive.

"You'll always be open for me. You understand?"

Her legs trembled as she undid his last button with shaky hands. "Yes," she murmured. "Always."

"And you will only ever give yourself to me."

She lowered her hands to her sides and raised a brow. "As long as the same rules apply to you."

"Always." He grinned, boosting her confidence even though the threat of other beautiful women from Vault of Sin hovered in the back of her mind.

"This is mine." He glided his hand over her abdomen and then lower. She pressed her lips together to fight a mewl when he slid two fingers through her dripping sex. He leaned over her, his hand still on her pussy while the other palmed her breast. "These are mine."

She whimpered, thrusting her chest into his hand. "Yes." She moved her hands to the bedhead and gripped the wooden frame, digging her nails into the timber. "Please, Leo."

He held her gaze, slowly gliding his fingers into her sheath as she released a long, deep moan. He withdrew just as languorously and wiped a trail of her juices around her clit, flicking the bundle of nerves back and forth. Movement came into her periphery and she froze, sensing more than one person hovering in the doorway.

"Focus on me," Leo demanded.

She tried. Really, she did, but the pleasure in her body began to ebb and all she could see were the shadows of onlookers darkening her lover's features.

"Me, Shay."

He yanked off his shirt and threw it to the mattress beside her. The hard, unyielding flesh was enough to distract her for a fleeting moment. Then her gaze drifted, moving to the couple standing close together against the wall, then to the two familiar faces in the open doorway.

"Holy shit." She grabbed Leo's shirt to cover her exposed breasts as she squeezed her eyes shut.

T.J. and Brute were there, watching her like a fucking porn show, their focus harsh enough to burn a lasting impression on her retinas.

"Close the door," Leo ordered, making her wince at the disappointment in his tone.

She'd wanted to impress him, to wipe away every memory he had of other women, and replace them with the crazy passion she had to share. How the heck had T.J. and Brute skipped her attention? Travis had mentioned staff participating after last drinks, yet the important point hadn't crossed her mind. She shook her head at herself as shuffled footsteps drifted into the distance and the door closed with a click.

Then the back of her eyelids were illuminated with the overhead lights and her eyes burst open.

Don't panic. Don't freak out...any more than you already have.

"Aren't they meant to be on the other side of the door?" She clung tighter to the shirt, as T.J. and Brute approach the bed.

"Calm down."

Calm down? She was crazy with panic. Hadn't they just discussed remaining faithful, albeit vaguely? Now T.J. stood to the left of the bed, his somber smile focused her way as if he was about to face a firing squad instead of a naked woman. Then there was Brute. His usual scowl had deepened, his eyes harsh with disapproval.

"Yeah, calm the fuck down, Shay," she muttered. "How the hell am I meant to do that with him glaring at me?" She flicked her gaze to Brute before swallowing over the emotion building in her throat and then focused on the black cotton sheets.

This was a fuck up of epic proportions.

"I suppose now would be an inappropriate time to ask for a glowing reference."

"I'm not letting you run," Leo spoke softly. "Look at me."

When she didn't, he made a move to climb off her. On instinct, she gripped him around the neck and yanked him back down.

"I'm naked," she ground through clenched teeth. "Move off me and die."

"I won't, if you look at me." He settled between her thighs and leaned on one elbow to peer down at her.

Fine. She raised her gaze, coming face-to-face with penetrating ocean eyes.

"You wanted to jump in the deep end, Shay. Don't forget how to swim now that you're here."

His words repeated in a continuous loop. Taking the plunge wasn't meant to be easy…it also wasn't meant to be this confronting, but if she walked away now, there was no way she would come back.

"I'm not in this for anyone else," she whispered. "All I wanted was you."

Her gaze drifted away, over the sheets to the dark blue jeans T.J. was wearing. He stood still, not uttering a word while Leo ran a finger along her jaw, regaining her attention.

"All you're getting is me. For however long you want me." He narrowed his gaze, hitting her hard with his sincerity. "Playing with others would only be for your pleasure. And that doesn't have to happen now, or tomorrow, or ever. You got that?"

She nodded, slightly relieved at his statement.

"But my ego needs to be fed." The corner of his lips lifted, making her chest pound with his sexy confident smirk. "I want them to see your beautiful body. I want them to take notes on how fucking amazing I make you feel. I want their gaze on your face as you come undone by my hands, or my mouth, or my cock. I want them delirious with the need to have you."

She shuddered, feeling the exposed skin all over her body break out in shivering gooseflesh.

"Do you trust me?" he asked.

She bit her tongue to fight back the hell no. "Not when you're smirking like the cat that got the cream."

"But I do have the cream, gorgeous." His grin increased as he slid a hand between them, spreading her slick, sensitive flesh. "I just need you to trust me so I can get the chance to taste it."

Her breath hitched as he sunk his fingers deeper, gliding his thumb over her clit. "Okay," she gasped. "Okay." Okay, okay, okay. She nodded and licked her lips, dying for more. One touch was all she required to make her succumb. One touch and one wickedly sexy grin and she was all his.

"That's my girl."

He leaned in for a demanding kiss. His tongue penetrated her mouth with the same delicious rhythm of his fingers in her pussy. She clung to him, one hand around his neck, the other on his biceps, and let sensation take away her insecurities.

When he pulled back, she was panting, rocking her hips in need for more.

"T.J., get the cuffs."

"What?" Her gaze shot to T.J. at the bedside table to her left, then over to Brute who took a seat on the mattress to her right, before snapping back to Leo. "Cuffs aren't necessary." She shook her head, pleading with her gaze. She had too much pride to plead aloud. If they were alone it would be different, but she had to regain some level of backbone to prove to the others she was worthy.

"They are until you lose that frightened look in your eyes."

"I assure you, cuffs won't help."

T.J. softly chuckled and the impact of the sound stunned her. She glanced over to him, to the sweet gentleness in his wistful smile and knew she was safe. He had yearning in his eyes, just like Leo, and she supposed Brute had it somewhere too, under all those layers of brutality. They'd lost hope in finding the women to complete them and needed hope to move forward. She was that hope.

Silently, she raised her arm to T.J., letting the gentle touch of his hand work the cold metal around her wrist. He held her gaze as he locked it in place and then lightly ran his fingers from her wrist to her elbow before backing away to throw the other set of cuffs to Brute.

She didn't want to turn her gaze to the smug bastard. He'd had his fun with her underwear earlier. She could imagine how he would torment her once this moment was over. So instead of looking at him, she raised her arm in his direction and stared at Leo as an unfamiliar touch worked its way around her skin. Fingers tickled her wrist, working higher over her palm, spreading her fingers before moving back down again.

"He needs you to acknowledge his presence," Leo murmured.

Too bad. She raised her chin and worked her lower lip between her teeth, waiting for the delicate touch to end. Brute was her friend, a great guy hiding behind an asshole persona. One glance could ruin the connection they had and she was already risking enough with Leo.

Leo chuckled. "Well, just so you know, he won't stop until he gets what he wants."

Her eyes widened as Brute's fingers continued to travel along her arm, from the tingling flesh around her elbow, to her biceps and finally her shoulder. She held her breath, wrapping her legs around Leo's waist for grounding, willing herself not to break.

Her skin burned in the wake of Brute's touch along her neckline, slowly down her sternum. She began to pant, caught between enjoying the lust wracking her body and the determination not to break so their relationship wasn't catapulted into another turbulent atmosphere.

"Shay," Brute's deep voice called.

She shook her head, fighting hard to calm herself.

"Shay." This time his voice was louder, and he drifted his fingers to the tingling flesh below her breast. "Look at me."

"Why?" She directed her frown at Leo. "You don't want me here." The truth escaped her lips. He'd warned her away from Leo when she was first employed and again last night. Subconsciously, his rejection had already cut deep.

"No." He let the force of his word sink in before he continued. "I don't want you hurt in here."

She looked at him then, at the way his scowl had softened into something like regret.

"I don't want to see you walk away like every other woman each of us have cared about."

That's not what their conversations had been about. Or was it? She scrutinized him, seeing the honesty in his features. Had his disapproval been out of protection for her?

"I'm a big girl."

He inclined his head. "I know, and that's why seeing you so shaken is hard to take." His touch travelled over her ribs and then dropped from her side. "I'm here to protect you. To make sure this guy doesn't fuck up, okay?"

Her lips tilted. "Okay."

"I won't fuck up," Leo interrupted and pulled back from her body.

She winced at the exposure, sensing the weight of three heated gazes rake her from head to toe. Leo stood at the foot of the bed, devouring her with his eyes as he unclasped the button at his waistband, lowered his zipper and pushed his pants to the floor.

His erection tented the front of his boxers, making her mouth salivate, her restrained hands clench. He lowered the last piece of material covering his body and let his cock bob against his abdomen as he shucked his underwear.

"Time for the cat to get the cream," he drawled.

He fucking drawled at her with smooth male arrogance and then crawled back onto the mattress and parted her thighs. He had no inhibitions, no shyness, no doubt. He was in his element, his eyes alight with determination.

"Jesus Christ, you're beautiful." He sat back on his haunches, staring down at her exposed flesh.

She pulled against her restraints and winced at the bite of pain to her wrists. In an instant, she had Leo's attention, and T.J. and Brute were at her cuffs, easing the skin around her holdings.

"I'm fine." She looked at each of them in turn. She'd never been adored before, never been fawned over or taken care of like this. "I'm not going to break."

"Good. Because I'm just getting started." Leo lowered between her thighs, placing his mouth an inch away from her pussy, letting the brush of his breath tickle her skin. "Wrap your legs around my shoulders."

She did as instructed, as fast as she could, hoping he wouldn't hold back from sinking his tongue between her folds. The first stroke down her core sent her back arching off the bed, her hands pulling at the restraints again. Caress after slow, sweeping caress, he tasted her, making her pant and wish she could run her hands through his hair and hold him in place.

"More," she pleaded. "Please." Her embarrassment at the compulsion to beg disappeared. She'd grovel for deeper penetration if she had to. She just wanted more. She tugged at the restraints in annoyance, not caring at the pain it caused her wrists. It provided a much needed relief from the torture Leo was lavishing on her body.

"Release her hands," Leo demanded. "She's going to hurt herself."

She straightened in relief, eager to touch every hard inch of his flesh. T.J. and Brute did as instructed, yet the restriction on her arms remained. T.J. entwined his fingers with hers and pressed down on her left hand while Brute held tight to her right. They climbed on the bed at her sides, watching in silence as Leo went back to devouring her pussy.

She squeezed T.J.'s fingers the closer she came to orgasm. Never would she have thought she'd be relieved to have all three of her bosses around to share the most sensual experience of her life. Without them it would still be profound—her taking a chance and giving herself to Leo— but now her pleasure was heightened, and more importantly, she felt at home around these men.

Each time Leo's fingers entered her, her gaze glanced from one man to the next. All their focus was dedicated to her body, to the way she began to writhe her hips. Their attention was addictive. She ground her pelvis harder, moaned a little louder every time Leo hit that perfect spot, and enjoyed the buzz of exhilaration that came with the flare of a nostril, the narrowing of a gaze or the tensing of a jaw.

Brute moved closer, leaning into her neck. The brush of his light beard was enough to escalate her lust and bring her closer to the edge.

"I knew you'd be like this," he murmured in her ear. "Receptive. Sensitive. And a fucking treasure to behold."

Oh God. She gasped. Dirty talk would send her over the edge and she didn't want to fly just yet. Leo's touch was enough, the brush of his fingers moving in and out, the suction of his mouth settling over her clit. She couldn't breathe, couldn't think with the delicious words flittering into her mind, Brute's breath tickling her neck.

"What I wouldn't give to be between those thighs, lapping your cream, nipping your skin." He nuzzled the sensitive skin below her ear with the tip of his nose. "Leo's a lucky son of a bitch."

She whimpered. Leo wasn't the lucky one. With her thighs tense with pleasure, her wrists held down by two drool-worthy men and her sex on the brink of detonation, she was the one getting the better end of the deal.

"I want to watch you come all over his mouth."

Fuck... The world faded, light turned to black, and she screamed as her orgasm hit hard. They held her down, Leo placing pressure on her hips, and T.J. and Brute at her wrists. She bucked, her core clenching out of control while her legs squeezed tight and her eyes clamped shut. Her breasts were on fire, her heart full and rapidly beating.

Leo didn't stop as her pleasure simmered, the heavy bursts of climax receding to a lesser tingling sensation. Her legs fell limp around him, her arms no longer fighting her restraint and then finally he backed away. She lazily opened her eyes, a smile tilting her lips, and found him on his haunches staring down at her. He didn't speak, didn't move, just continued to gaze at her with an emotion she couldn't pinpoint.

The pressure on her wrists vanished, allowing her to sit up on her elbows. "What's wrong?"

He inhaled deep and remained quiet.

"Petrova lost for words." Brute smirked. "It must be love."

Shay glanced at Brute in surprise and then straight back to Leo. His chin was jutted, his shoulders straight as she stared at him in disbelief.

"No." She shook her head. He didn't love her. He had feelings for her, lusted after her, but not love. Not yet.

Leo raised a brow, his glistening lips parting ever so slightly.

Speak to me. She needed an answer, wouldn't breathe until she had one. "You don't." *Do you?*

He leaned down, circled her waist and pulled her to his lap. She ignored the hardness pressing against her pubic bone and scrutinized the intensity in his eyes. "Leo?"

"Hmm?" He blinked as if awoken from a daze. "What, gorgeous?"

"You don't love me."

The side of his lips tilted. "Are you asking, or telling?"

"I don't know."

He licked his lips, casually stroked a lock of hair behind her ear and smiled. "Why are you so nervous at the thought of me loving you?"

Because you're Leo Petrova, the man of my dreams and creator of fantasies.

"Shay?"

Her focus turned to the door as it closed with a click. They were alone. T.J. and Brute had wordlessly left them in privacy.

"Shay?" Leo gripped her chin and turned her back to those penetrating blue-green eyes. "Are you scared that I love you?"

She snapped a hand over her mouth, covering a gasp. She'd never been here before, not only the sex club or a private room alone with three men, but having her feelings reciprocated. It was always a needy guy chasing her or her lusting over someone out of her league. Now she was in the arms of the man she'd given her heart to long ago, and he was returning it with his own.

"Hey." He gently pushed her hand away and ran a delicate thumb over her bottom lip. "The Shay I know wouldn't cry over a guy."

"I'm not crying." She was just trying to hide her hyperventilated breaths.

His smile grew the longer he gazed into her eyes. "I believe you."

For long moments, they sat in comfortable silence, gazing at one another, her heart growing fuller with each passing second. She'd always known Leo Petrova was a special man. Now she knew why. He was hers.

He lowered his hands from her face and gripped her around the waist. The instant the head of his cock nudged her entrance, the warmth of love suffusing her body turned into burning desire.

"Ready for your turn?" Shay gave him a wicked grin.

"I'll always be hard for you, but this isn't about turns." He reached back, picked up the row of condoms from the mattress and sheathed himself. "I'd be happy to bring you pleasure for the rest of my life without getting it in return."

She relaxed into him and hovered her lips a bare inch from his. "I call bullshit."

He chuckled. "Okay. So maybe I'm a little delusional. But that's your fault. You've made me crazy with the need to make you happy."

"I've been crazy for you for too long to remember."

"A stubborn woman like you?" He raised a brow. "You just wanted to get into my pants."

He leaned forward, laying her softly on the bed.

"Your heart, too," she murmured, then bit her lip waiting for his reaction. Even after his declaration, she still didn't feel comfortable sharing her feelings. He seemed too good to be true. Like a mirage about to disappear the closer they became.

He rolled her to her side and moved in behind her, settling the hardness of his body against her back. His hand found her hip and he delicately stroked the sensitive skin as he nuzzled her hair.

"You're there, Shay. You're mine, and no matter how scared you get, we'll work through it together." His shaft glided through the slick arousal of her pussy, nudging into her in tiny, teasing increments.

"I won't let either of us run." He slid home, ramming into her in a harsh, deep thrust.

They moaned in unison, and she craned her neck, allowing Leo to take her mouth in an equally strong kiss. This time, their connection was lazy and romantic. The pleasure building because of devotion and adoration. He treasured her, kissing her shoulder, slowly stroking her clit. They made love like a couple with a future, not two people expecting to be torn apart at any given moment.

"I can't believe this is happening." Her heart fluttered, her limbs were alive with arousal. Relief washed through her at the way the early morning had turned out. She'd jumped from the cliff and come out soaring.

"Believe it, gorgeous." He nuzzled her neck, never stopping the delicious sweep of his hips. "Because I never let go of what's mine."

CHAPTER NINETEEN

*L*eo reached for Shay's hand as they made their way from the bathroom and strolled into the main room of Vault of Sin. T.J. and Brute were seated at the bar, waiting, watching them approach. They hadn't stuck around to shoot the breeze. They were here for Shay, to make sure she was all right. And Leo was happy they'd had the balls to do so. It took a lot for any of them to show weakness toward a woman, and that was exactly what they were doing—showing Shay they cared.

"We cool?" Brute took a sip from his scotch glass.

Leo glanced at Shay and raised a brow.

"What?" she whispered.

"He's askin' you, gorgeous."

"Oh."

The tops of her cheeks darkened, making his cock stir to life again. Shay wasn't the embarrassed type, and seeing her flustered was like a shot of adrenaline to his dick.

"Yeah." She gave a breathy chuckle. "We're cool."

"You did good, Shay," Brute offered.

"Oh, thanks." She gave a derisive laugh. "I didn't realize my participation was a casting call."

"Don't get that tiny lace G-string of yours in a twist. I was just letting you know I'm happy for you both." Brute moved around the counter and placed his empty glass in the dishwasher. "Well, I'm heading off for the night. I need to catch some Z's. You need a lift, T?"

T.J. kept his gaze on the glass in his hands, the ice clinking against the sides as he tilted it back and forth. "Nope. I'm going to have one more." He reached for the Grey Goose bottle on the bar and poured himself another finger.

"Make sure you get a ride with Leo then. You're already over the limit."

"I'll be fine."

Brute met Leo's gaze, expressing a silent request to keep an eye on T.J.

"I'm happy to hang around and lock up," Leo offered. "If he needs a lift home, I'll drive him."

Brute came back around the bar and stopped beside Shay. "Call me if you need anything."

Leo could see the adoration in his friend's eyes and ignored the pang of jealousy expanding in his chest. "She's got me if she's in need." He tried to curb the slight annoyance in his tone.

"Yeah, but sometimes you're an ass." Brute slung his arm around her neck and kissed her temple.

"Pot. Kettle." Shay chuckled. "But thank you. I appreciate the offer."

Brute shrugged and headed for the door. "I've got reason to be the way I am. Leo no longer does." He gave a lazy salute and disappeared behind the back of the bar. "Catch you all next week."

Heavy footsteps faded into the distance, followed by the opening and closing of the back entrance door. Then it was quiet. Too quiet. Leo wanted to get Shay home, to snuggle, to talk, to fall asleep with her in his arms. Only something was up with T.J., and Leo wouldn't leave him alone like this.

"You okay?" Shay slid across the stool next to his friend and tilted her head to look at his downcast face.

"Yeah, sweetheart, just tired."

It was more than exhaustion weakening T.J.'s tone. Leo had watched him slide along the scale of self-pity for months now. Each day away from his wife hit harder for the guy who wore his heart on his sleeve.

"Are you sure." Shay met Leo's gaze with concern in her eyes. "Did I do something wrong?"

"No." Both Leo and T.J. spoke at once.

"It's family stuff," T.J. added. "The unending crap that goes along with my marriage."

Shay's eyes widened. "You're married? How did I not know that?"

"We've all got our secrets," Leo murmured, trying to take some of the heat. T.J.'s demons revolved around his wife. He loved her with every breath and every heartbeat. But their marriage had changed over the years, leading to their separation. Each day away from the woman of his dreams had taken a heavy toll, and Leo wasn't sure if the two of them would ever regain the relationship they'd once had.

"Really?" she drawled. "And what secrets do you have?"

Leo narrowed his gaze, wanting to slap her ass for being so sassy. "You already know mine, so stop looking at me like that."

She inclined her head as if to say touché and then turned back to T.J. "Is there anything I can do?"

"Nah." T.J. threw back the remainder of his vodka and slammed the glass down on the bar. "Just continue to make this guy happy." He slid from the stool, released a deep breath and plastered on a fake smile. "Wish me luck handing over the divorce papers."

Leo opened his mouth but silence remained. He had nothing—no words of advice or comfort. His friend had been married for six years. Six happy years. And now he was going to end it all. He hadn't even known his friend had been speaking to a divorce lawyer.

"You can't drive home." Shay slid off the stool and rushed around the bar to grab her handbag.

"I'm fine." T.J. copied Brute's farewell, sidling up to Shay, hugging her around the neck and placing a kiss on her temple.

There was no jealousy this time. All Leo felt was a gaping hole in his chest for the guy who had a bigger heart than Leo and Brute combined. A divorce wasn't the answer. Surely it couldn't be the answer. T.J. loved his wife, and from all their previous discussions, his wife loved him back.

"Are you sure about this?" Leo palmed his keys, ready to leave.

"Drop it. I've only had a few drinks. I'm right to drive."

"No." Leo shook his head. "I'm talking about the divorce. Why don't you give counselling a try?"

T.J. laughed. "Yeah, buddy, counselling. That'd be a hoot."

"I'm serious."

"And I'm done." T.J. shrugged. "I can't spend every night thinking about her, knowing I'm holding her back from the rest of her life. My own selfishness has dragged it this far. I couldn't stand the thought of her being with anyone else. But I've gotta let her go. She deserves better."

"Better than you?" Shay asked, her voice fragile. She climbed back onto a stool and then higher still to sit on the bar. "I don't understand."

"You don't need to, sweetheart." T.J. patted her thigh and made to leave. "I'll see you both next week."

"Wait." Leo jerked his head for Shay to follow. "I'll drop you off." T.J. wasn't drunk, but he was high on emotion. And in Leo's mind, that was a dangerous mix after a few drinks.

"Don't do this." T.J. swung to face him and held up a hand for Shay to stop her progression off her perch on the bar. "Tonight is about the two of you. Let me go. I'm safe to drive."

Leo scrutinized the lines of devastation on his friend's face and the concern in Shay's eyes. Talk about a rock and a hard place. Guys didn't do emotional bullshit. If T.J. wanted to be alone, so be it. He wasn't going to hold T.J.'s hand and spoon feed him ice cream. "Are you sure?"

T.J. rolled his eyes. "Fucking positive." He gave a lazy wave to Shay and headed for the back door. "Don't get into too much mischief over the next two days."

Shay met Leo's gaze, her lips slowly lifting at the edges. "We won't," she called over her shoulder and waited for the back door to close. "Is he really okay to drive?"

"He knows his limits. He'll be fine." T.J. was the responsible one, and the roads were deserted at this time of the morning. Leo was more concerned about the additional alcohol T.J. would consume once he stepped foot inside his apartment.

"That's it? You're his best friend and all you've got is I guess?"

Leo shrugged. Nothing he did would change the shit T.J. was going through. The guy was solid, he always bounced back. He just had a heart bigger than most. "Pretty much. And besides, he's not your concern." He stalked toward her and spread her thighs with a rough hand.

"Oh." She cocked her head in defiance. "And what is?"

"Me," he growled, pulling her off the bar. Her legs circled his waist, clinging tight as he strode for the exit. "Me and only me, for the rest of eternity."

"How poetic from a man who has probably never known monogamy."

He grinned at her, knowing she was going to keep him on his toes for a damn long time. "Not poetic, gorgeous." He placed a lingering kiss on her lips before opening his eyes to the passionate pull of her brown irises. "I've just been waiting for the right female to take me off the market. And now that I've found her, no other woman will ever exist."

EPILOGUE

"You're concocting a plan, I can tell."

Shay grinned down at Leo, ignoring his precise assumption. She was seated on the Vault of Sin bar, her favorite perch to see every inch of the now-vacant main room and glimpse inside the open doorways to the more private areas. "I'm pondering."

Brute groaned, striding around the bar to the sink. "Shut her down, Leo. You know the shit she comes up with is usually a pain in the ass."

"What?" She gasped in mock outrage and frowned at him over her shoulder. "My ideas for upstairs have been nothing but fabulous."

"Nothing but trouble," he countered.

She shook her head, turning back to Leo, who was chuckling from his position between her thighs. He sat on the stool in front of her, peering up at her with his piercing ocean stare. "I don't know, I think I'd like to hear what she has to say."

A ball of pins and needles rolled around in her belly. After a few weeks together, she still hadn't overcome the shock of being with such a gorgeous man. He was perfect. Attentive. Attuned to her needs and desires. The only downer was his reluctance to participate downstairs. He'd told her he wanted to wait for her to gain an understanding of what the club was all about.

Fair enough, she supposed. But it didn't lessen the arousal making her want to double over every time she thought about the possibilities.

She'd worked every available shift behind the bar of the sex club, building up her appreciation for the lifestyle. The more she watched, the more she enjoyed. And now she was at the point where she didn't think she could appreciate the sexual setting much more without grappling Leo in front of the patrons.

That's why she'd turned her focus toward club improvements. Vault of Sin required a woman's touch. A little femininity to mix things up. There were unlimited possibilities and opportunities. All she had to do was convince three stubborn-headed men to give her a chance.

"I was just thinking about ways we could make the Vault more exciting for guests."

"Shay," Brute warned. "If the men get more excited, the women won't enjoy themselves."

If Mr. Grumpy Ass thought he was funny, he was sadly mistaken. She ignored him, focusing on the sexy hunk of man in front of her. "Why don't you organize theme nights? Or even a costume party?"

Leo winced, and she tried to ignore that, too.

"Maybe because this is a sex club for adults," Brute drawled. "Not a birthday party for five-year-olds."

Shay shot him the bird over her shoulder. "I'm serious." She used her best doe eyes to implore Leo. The ploy worked in the bedroom, surely it could work here. "You could hold a masquerade party. Newbies are more likely to want to attend if they know their first experience can be hidden behind a mask. It would be less daunting."

Leo's brows drew together. "I kinda like the idea."

Score.

"You would *kinda like* any of her ideas," Brute muttered. "Because you're a fuckin' pussy."

Leo chuckled off the insult. "Speaking of pussy." He leaned forward, placing his hands on her knees to spread her legs wider. Her short skirt gave him an unrestricted view of her underwear, and he made no effort to hide his visual inspection.

"Leo, I'm serious." She swallowed over her suddenly dry throat. "I think a masquerade theme would work well."

He slid his palms up her thighs, releasing the floodgates of her arousal. She gripped the edge of the bar, not for stability, but to stop herself from jumping him and tearing his clothes off. Brute be damned.

"I know you are." His touch traveled higher, under her skirt to the edge of her panties. "A masquerade theme could work. It would help to maintain anonymity for those who aren't entirely sure they want to take the plunge int—"

"Just a heads up," Brute interrupted from over her shoulder. "I'm sick of watching you two. From now on, I'll be a fully-fledged participant if you get your fuck on in front of me."

Shay bit her lip, waiting for Leo's reaction. She was prepared to take his lead, no matter what path he chose. She trusted him and the decisions he made regarding their sexual relationship. Sharing is caring definitely hadn't become her motto, but Leo already knew she was willing to let him take the lead on their time downstairs.

Leo stared up at her under thick lashes. "Sorry, champ. I've become a little obsessed with keeping this lovely lady to myself."

She grinned, her ego overinflated. This man knew how to make her pulse race in the most delicious sort of way. He hooked a finger around the crotch of her panties, finding her slick arousal, making her burn. She whimpered, straightening her back, ensuring she didn't lose control. He played with her, holding her gaze the entire time he ran his finger up and down her entrance.

"You're naughty," she silently mouthed, struggling to keep her breathing under control. She was always hot for him. Always ready. Always waiting. Her appetite was insatiable, and she didn't anticipate it ever changing. No matter who was in their presence.

Kicking off one of her shoes, she placed her toes gently on the crotch of his pants, traced the outline of the hardness underneath and then lower to brush his balls. He seemed immune. In control. She loved that most about him—even though the length of his erection was hard beneath her, he didn't react. No matter where they were or what they did, he continued to remain level-headed. At least on the outside.

He became stronger the more time they spent together. He knew how to draw out the best orgasms. How to make her scream, or gasp, or giggle. They were a perfect fit—his sexual expertise and her unruly lust.

"Get your fucking hand out of her honey pot," Brute snapped. "Because, I swear, if you make me go home with wood again, I'll fucking kill you."

Leo grinned without remorse and snaked his fingers out of her underwear. "I don't condone violence."

No. No, no, no.

Shay groaned with the loss of his touch, not caring that he placed a forgiving kiss on the inside of her knee to soften the blow. Her pussy wanted to kick him in the balls. Brute too. Leo could take whatever stand he wanted on violence, but she sure as hell didn't condone cock blocking.

"We'll finish this later," he whispered against her skin.

Hell, yeah. She was definitely going to return the favor. It would begin with teasing him for unending moments. Drawing out his pleasure until he was hard and hot and willing to yell with the need for relief. Then she'd go make herself a fucking coffee and see how he liked to be denied.

She snapped her legs shut, almost ramming Leo's nose in the process. And still, the bastard chose to laugh. This wasn't funny. The dampness in her panties wasn't something to chuckle about, and getting home was going to be a humorless affair, too. She wasn't sure how the heck she was going to drive when her mind was obsessed with being driven by Leo.

"Well." She pushed off the bar and landed on her bare foot. "I want to plan a masquerade party." She retrieved her shoe from the floor and pointed it at Brute with a glare. "It doesn't have to be on a regular night, it could be a Thursday or even a Sunday."

"Well, I want you to put your pretty pink lips around my cock and blow me. But neither of us are going to get what we want. Are we?" Brute came around the bar, a scowl cemented into his features. The bulge straining the zipper of his jeans announced he wasn't lying about the blow job either. "We can't make plans without T.J."

Shay's heart clenched at the reminder of the third member of the masculine trio. T.J. hadn't returned to work since he dropped the news of his impending divorce. And yet, after everything he was going through, he'd still spared the time to message her and ask how she was recovering emotionally from her time in Vault of Sin.

He seemed encouraged by her feelings toward Leo. But when she'd asked about his wellbeing, he'd ignored her. She'd even tried calling him, but he wouldn't answer.

"I don't think T.J. will mind if we do the research and figure out the specifics." Leo stood and came to her side, daring to place a hand around her waist.

She stiffened beside him. Her nipples tingled against the delicate material of her bra and her goddamn panties were still soaked. The last thing she needed was more attention without the hope of a climax.

"Better yet, do up a proposal." Brute went to the light switch at the side of the bar and flicked on the houselights. "That way, when T.J. comes back, we can have a management meeting and discuss it without Romeo's dick playing a part in the decision process."

Leo leaned toward her ear, holding her tighter around the waist. "What he doesn't know," he whispered, "is that my dick plays an integral part in every decision that involves you."

"Not tonight it won't." She nudged him in the ribs to reiterate the rejection.

His huff of laughter heated her neck and his protective hold kept her strong, even though her body was weak for him. She could picture his smile in her mind, the one that lifted his cheeks and brightened his eyes. There was no way to deny him. No way to refute the attraction making her heart swell.

She trusted him, respected, and adored him. Her lust knew no bounds. Their time away from Shot of Sin was filled with laughter, and their working hours were even better. Although their relationship went against the grain of normality, they'd found happiness, and nobody could take that away from them.

She loved this man, dirty parts and all. And no hurdle, big, small, lurid or tame would change that...unless he didn't hurry up and give her a damn orgasm.

"Okay." She nodded. "One Masquerade plan coming right up."

MASQUERADE OF SIN

Masquerade of Sin

Dear Sinner,
 You are invited to attend our first, and quite possibly the only, Masquerade Party at Vault of Sin.
 The rules and entrance process are still the same. You will need to submit an application to attend and gain approval before you pass the sacred doors. However, this time, bringing a like-minded friend is encouraged. Any newbies will be vetted under the same process, but this special occasion will allow them the anonymity to hide their wicked fantasies under the veil of a mask for one night only.
 In the future, we hope to increase the number of nights you can sin in our presence, and inviting more members to our club is an integral part of achieving our aim.
 So, if you have a wicked friend, invite them along. It will be a night to remember, filled with pleasure you will never forget.

Kind regards,
 Vault of Sin.

UNION OF SIN

DEDICATION

To those naughty readers who came back for more after their first shot of sin. This one's for you.

CHAPTER ONE

𝒯.J. sat in his car, transfixed with a sight so familiar it brought a piercing ache to his sternum—his wife. Cassie's blonde hair gleamed from the early morning kiss of the sun. Her full-length dress clung to her every curve. With one glimpse, she made everything else cease to exist. It was only him and her. The two of them. No road too long or river too wide to stop him from claiming her.

At least that's how it had been...before he'd left. Now the few yards separating them, from his car to her position at the neighborhood park swing set, was as vast as the Atlantic.

This morning was his final farewell. His silent thank you to the heavens for giving him the few years of paradise he'd shared with this beautiful woman. Their time together was nothing short of a fairy tale—love at first sight, wedded bliss and the promise of a perfect future.

But they'd never received their happily ever after. He'd fucked up. Not once, many times. He just hadn't realized the extent until it was too late. Until he was separated from her, away from the mesmerizing spell of her love.

He'd almost destroyed this woman. He still could if he hung around.

Neither of them had seen it coming. They'd been consumed by happiness. The drug of euphoria had blinded them from reality.

Not anymore.

T.J. watched as Cassie guided her niece from the swing set and they began to walk from the playground hand in hand. Essentially, he was stalking her. He knew she took the little girl to the park every other Saturday morning. He also knew as soon as she returned the child to her mother, she would walk the two blocks to T.J.'s home.

Their home.

He followed her, inching the car forward with each of her steps. He made sure to lurk behind the street corners until she was out of sight before he'd move farther. When Cassie reached the road to their house, his stomach hollowed. A car was waiting in their driveway. A car he'd arranged to be there.

Her footsteps faltered as she approached, and when a man dressed in a tailored black suit slid from the car, she stopped abruptly. There was an exchange of words, but he was too far away to read lips. He didn't need to though. The envelope in the guy's hand said it all. The resulting anguish on his wife's stunning face cemented what had just happened.

The divorce papers were now firmly in her grasp. He couldn't help inching forward, taking her suffering head-on. He deserved her pain. Her spite. He wanted to feel it. To suffer as much as possible.

She wouldn't realize this was necessary. She probably never would. And that was okay. He could live with the responsibility. He already had for months.

The black Mercedes reversed from his driveway, pulled onto the road and disappeared into the distance. All he could do was stare. And suck in the pain he could see ebbing from his wife in tidal waves. She was shaking, clasping the envelope tightly, her gaze fixed on the green grass at her feet.

He inched the car forward, consoling himself with her proximity. She was so close. He could almost feel the delicate strands of her hair through his fingers. Could almost smell the perfume he'd bought her for their last wedding anniversary.

He'd kill to touch her again. To soothe the sorrow from her eyes with his kiss. With his passion.

But that would never happen. Not once. Not ever.

He focused over her shoulder, needing a distraction, and settled his gaze on the home they'd built with their bare hands. From the foundation to the curtains, the landscaping to the damn mailbox. All of it had been created with hard work, determination and love. Lots of love.

Cheesy, yes, but it had been one of those moments in life where he'd thought he'd actually achieved greatness. He'd had a wife he adored, a brand-new home to shelter the family they planned to create, and their German shepherd, Bear, to complete the package.

It seemed like yesterday they were arguing about the color to paint the internal walls. He'd remained adamant about his choice up until the moment they'd begun the arduous chore. Then, like always, the gorgeous smile Cassie had greeted him with as he'd opened the paint can had made her crappy selection worthwhile.

That smile undid him. Or it had. It felt like years had passed since she'd dazzled him with her happiness. A day without her resembled an eternity. So, the pain of the months spent separated couldn't be described.

He missed sweeping her off her feet—physically and emotionally. He missed the way she squealed when he tickled her ankles. Most of all, he missed feeling the softness of her curves against his body as he fell asleep.

He'd never get back to that place.

What they had was gone. Dead and buried. He'd killed all hope for a future. He'd wasted her time and ruined her life. He couldn't do it anymore. It had to stop.

He slammed his palms against the steering wheel and squeezed his eyes shut to fight the burn. Soon it would be over. Their court appearance was in less than a month. The documents in her hand explained all the assets he was giving her—the car, the house, their dog. She would continue to be financially stable if she retained her job. She would be safe and secure. And maybe, one day, happy.

The next twenty-seven days were going to kill him, though. Every other day afterward, too. But they could both start over after the heartache eased. Cassie could focus on working up the ranks in her hotel administration position. Maybe she'd find a new man. Someone else to love her. To hold her. To see those achingly brilliant smiles and wipe away her tears.

"*Shit.*" He needed to get out of here before he crumpled completely.

He opened his eyes, blinked to clear his vision and stared at the flawless woman as she squinted directly at his car. *Oh, fuck.*

The envelope dropped to the ground as her hands fell to her sides.

She stood there, lower lip trembling, chest convulsing, as her misery hit him tenfold.

"*Divorce papers?*" Her voice cracked as she yelled.

Jesus. He'd pushed her too far. Cassie was quiet, composed and polite, at least for every other day of their marriage. Right now, she was causing a scene, alerting their nosy neighbors to her imminent breakdown.

He shouldn't have come. He should've gone to Shot of Sin, drowned in a bottle of something expensive and relied on Leo and Brute to get him home. Instead, he was cutting the ignition and sliding from the car, unable to stand her misery.

He strode for her, determined to explain that life would be better this way. It had to be better. *She* had to be better. He couldn't exist if she wasn't.

"You're a coward, Tate Jackson." She didn't move, didn't budge as her lips trembled. "A weak, pathetic coward who can't even spare his wife the dignity of telling her he wants a divorce. You had to get some stranger to inform me."

He increased his pace up the drive. "Lower your voice."

Her eyes widened, her mouth parted slightly. Then she slowly raised her chin. "*No.*" Her voice was a breath. "That tone has no effect on me anymore. Those papers make it so." She waved a hand in the direction of the envelope on the grass. "How could you?"

He stopped in front of her, rested his hand against her upper arm and tried to lead her inside, away from prying eyes.

"Don't you dare." She slid away from him, her gentle features contorting into a glare. She'd never looked at him like this before. It was foreign. Hard to take.

He would give his soul to drag her forward into his chest and comfort her in his arms until the harsh reality faded. He missed her. God, how he missed her. Her scent lingered in the air, tempting his restraint. And those lips... He released a huff of frustration. The way she kissed would never be comparable. Her loving heart would forever be a part of him.

Cassie sucked in a breath, straightened her shoulders and met his gaze head-on. "Don't do this to us, T.J." Her light blue eyes pleaded more than her words ever could. "*Please.* I still love you. I'll *always* love you."

He was thankful for the rapid scampering of nails against cement, then the loud bark of Bear as he voiced his greeting from the side gate. They remained silent through the echoing noise, his focus unable to leave her face. Time stopped, and the understanding of why he was doing this became blurry.

She was still the most mesmerizing woman he'd ever seen. The dress she wore clung to all her delicious curves, outlining breasts and hips that had tormented his dreams. The nipples beading against the thin cotton made his mouth dry, and he wished like hell he hadn't noticed. But it was her eyes, the sky-blue depths welling with unshed tears that tore him apart.

"T.J." Her voice barely registered over the throbbing in his ears. Her hand came up between them, her palm creeping toward his chest.

He stepped back, sensing the burn her contact would ignite. Her delicate touch would undo him. It would send him spiraling with a one-way ticket to the courthouse to cancel the divorce proceedings.

She was his heart. The one woman who brought out his darkest desires and forged a sexual appetite he couldn't ignore. She allowed him the freedom to become the man he always wanted to be, yet at the same time made him wish he was someone else entirely. Someone better. Someone worthy of a woman so forgiving and sweet.

She dropped her hand slowly to her side and Bear quietened.

Her gaze lowered, her light lashes fluttering down toward her blushed cheeks. "I can't live without you, Tate."

Fucking hell. She was gutting him, slicing open his chest and letting his insides fall to the ground. How could he walk away? How could he leave her, knowing this time he'd never return?

"It's for the best," he lied.

For Cassie, it would be the truth, but from this moment on, he'd forever be less of a man for losing this woman from his life.

~

Cassie held her breath, agonizing over the resolution in her husband's tight features. He was adamant. Confident in his decision. For the life of her, she couldn't understand why.

She pressed her lips together, vowing not to shed another tear, at least not in front of him. *Goddamnit.* She wanted to shake him. To slap him out of whatever spell he was under and make him remember the happiness they'd once shared. She'd been content. Their honeymoon phase had never faded. It had only morphed into a deeper connection where T.J. had showed her a whole new side of herself.

He awakened her to life. To love. To pleasure. And although it had hurt when he'd packed his bags and told her he needed time apart, she'd known, without doubt, that their commitment to one another couldn't be extinguished by a few months' separation.

Love like theirs was a gift. One she couldn't go without.

"The divorce can't be legal. I won't agree to it."

"I don't need your consent, Cass, the court date has already been set."

"That's impossible." The blood drained from her face, making her dizzy. She shook her head, in disbelief or defiance, she wasn't sure. There was no way their separation fulfilled the legal requirements for what he was doing. "You moved out six months ago. I'm sure we need to be apart for twelve before you can file for divorce."

His gaze softened, his brown eyes filling with pity. "I stopped sleeping in your bed a year ago. That's enough for the courts."

Her heart stopped, and pain ricocheted through her ribs, growing with intensity. She pressed a hand to her chest, trying to alleviate the agony that wouldn't lessen. It continued to evolve, moving to her limbs, weakening her knees.

"Why?" The word skittered from her trembling lips.

The answer was clear without him having to voice it. His warped sense of masculine protection had taken its toll, leaving him a slave to the guilt he had no right to feel.

"Is this still about that stupid club?" The one fateful night where their excitement to experiment had gone too far.

"This is about me." His tone was low. Unwavering. "Nobody else."

"Liar." She knew the truth. They'd had one bad experience. One testing, heartbreaking experience, and now he was ready to quit. "You still haven't let go of what happened."

"You're right." He inclined his head. "I can't. I never will. But the divorce is about much more than that."

In her mind, she was screaming, clawing at the beautiful eyes she'd gazed into on her wedding day, the same ones she'd imagined would peer down at their first child with intense adoration if they were ever blessed with a baby.

"I'm sorry." He pressed his lips tight.

Sorry? He hadn't even given her the opportunity to repair what was broken. He hadn't even tried.

"Sorry doesn't cut it." She shook her head again, vehement this time.

Twelve months ago, he'd started sleeping on the sofa, breaking her heart with his need for space—for clarity she couldn't give. Six months later, he'd strode from their house needing more distance.

At the time, she'd thought it was best to adhere to his wishes. His love for her was still evident in his eyes, his words, his touch. So, she'd let him go, giving him what he needed. Months and months of space where she cried herself to sleep for nights on end, not once pushing him to return.

Now she wasn't so stupid. She wouldn't succumb to his requests again.

The pain in her chest morphed into anger, red-hot and all consuming. Every inch of her was filled with determination, every nerve thrumming with the need to win this battle.

"I'll fight it. I'll tell the judge we haven't been separated that long." Her voice rose. "I'll do whatever necessary."

His jaw ticked. "We both know you won't lie under oath."

Maybe not. He knew her too well.

"We never went to counseling. I'll tell the court I want to try that first." There had to be another way. A different option.

"You didn't go, Cass, but I did." He hung his head, hammering another nail into the coffin of their marriage.

"You went to counseling without me?" Her words barely registered. This didn't make sense. They were perfect together. They'd shared everything from explicit sexual fantasies to their greatest fears and everything in between. His actions didn't compute. They'd only made one wrong decision. One mistake, and now she was meant to give up on their future. There had to be more.

"Is there another woman?" Nausea edged up her throat. "Is that what this is about? You've found someone else?"

She died a thousand deaths waiting for his reply. Her mind went on a psychotic bender, picturing him cheating with beautiful women. Skinny, flawless women. Ones with slight curves and perky breasts.

She sucked in a breath. "That's it, isn't it? You've been unfaithful."

"No." The word was emphatic as he glanced at her through the loose strands of dark-brown hair falling around his chocolate eyes.

Her body sagged, and she clasped her hands to stop them from shaking. She believed him. She had no clue why, but she clung to the sincerity in his gaze. She had to.

"Then why, T.J.? You can't leave me because of one mistake."

"Cassie." Her name was a plea.

"Don't *Cassie* me. You need to explain how you can walk away so easily. It doesn't make sense." She no longer cared for the heartache etched in his features. All her sympathy had washed away under her own pain. She needed answers. Now.

His features crumpled as he turned his focus back to his car parked yards down the road. "This is about me wanting the best for you." He ran a rough hand through his hair and clutched the back of his head. "You deserve better."

"*Bullshit.* This is about one night, and one night only. Can't you see how ridiculous that is?"

"Lower your voice."

His commanding growl sent a myriad of heated memories to the forefront. She loved that dominant voice. But she'd never obey him again. Not unless they remained husband and wife.

"I didn't mean for this to happen." He stepped back, placing agonizing distance between them. "Hurting you is the last thing I want to do."

"Then stop."

"I have. That's what the divorce is all about. After you pick yourself up, you'll realize this is the best path for your future."

"The best path?" She glared. "No. The best path for me will always lead to my husband."

He raised his chin, met her gaze. "Trust me on this."

She stared at him, noticing the added lines of strain around his eyes, the downward turn of heavenly lips she was too used to seeing curved in the opposite direction.

"There is no more trust." She tried not to let his retreating steps make her want to buckle under the weight of loss.

T.J. acknowledged her bitter words with a nod and turned on his heels. He thought he was walking out of her life. Out of her heart. Yet, he could never leave. Even when he'd stopped sleeping in their bed, she'd still felt him beside her. And when he'd left their home, she'd clung to the thought of him, waiting for his return.

She would never lose faith in their marriage, no matter what lay ahead. The only problem was, after twelve months of despair, she didn't know how much fight she had left in her to battle for what they both deserved.

CHAPTER TWO

"Nice to see you, stranger."

T.J. swung around to face the playful voice he barely recognized over the heavy dance music. "Hey, sassy. Long time no see."

"Sassy?" Shay raised a brow and quirked her lips. "First time you've called me that."

"If the shoe fits." He nudged her arm and continued walking toward the guarded doorway leading to the private area downstairs. A Shot of Sin, the dance club he owned with his two best friends, Leo and Brute, was too noisy for him tonight. He was still adrift after seeing Cassie this morning. He needed grounding, and he wasn't going to get it from working behind a bustling bar. The only other option, now that their Taste of Sin restaurant was closed for the evening, was Vault of Sin.

Shay shrugged. "True." Her smile was genuine, full of the mischief he'd grown to enjoy. "So, what's with the request to work downstairs? Leo told me that part of the business wasn't your forte."

And so the inquisition began.

He came to a stop in front of the security guard situated at the entry to the staircase leading downstairs and gave a nod of appreciation as the man opened the door. The Vault, hidden below the main floor of Shot of Sin, was a private club where members had no intention of dancing and every motivation to get naked and participate in more carnal exercise.

The sex club had never been his favorite place to work because of his commitment to Cassie. She knew what happened behind the closed doors, and although he'd sensed her discomfort, she'd never stipulated he couldn't fulfill this part of his ownership duties.

He'd taken it upon himself to distance his time from the sexually explicit Vault of Sin. He did it as a mark of respect to the woman he adored, especially since they'd never had the opportunity to enjoy the area together. Their problems had started before the sex-club part of his business had been established. And once the doors had opened, he hadn't been able to bring himself to invite her in.

Now his presence didn't seem to matter so much.

"It's quieter down here," he murmured.

Shay followed him into the dimly lit staircase and the guard closed the door behind them. Together they descended, passing pictures of couples on the walls, naked bodies entwined in different sexual positions that only endeavored to remind him of his wife.

"It's quieter at the moment because nobody is down here. But it won't be for long." Shay chuckled. "Some of the clientele are noisy fuckers, and I mean that literally."

He withheld a groan. "I knew what you meant."

Her smile grew as they reached the basement floor. "Do you want to get the lights while I set up the adult entertainment? The first guests will arrive soon."

"Sure." He entered the pin code securing the door at the end of the hall and held the heavy wood open for her to proceed him into Vault of Sin. While Shay played with the television set in the newbie lounge, he dragged his feet to the main room and flicked the switches on the wall beside the bar. Florescent lights off, mood lighting on.

Truth be told, Cassie would've loved it down here. He supposed that was one of their problems in the first place. He'd shaped her to like what he liked. To adore the depravity he adored. She hadn't been that type of woman when they'd met. She was innocent. Almost pure. He'd shown her the far reaches of sexual desire, not once realizing he was molding her into someone else until it was too late.

A click sounded in the next room, followed by hearty moans and guttural groans from the large television screen Shay was setting up. The noise was far more prevalent than it would be once guests arrived and created the sexual sounds for themselves. The mental image should've awakened his arousal. Instead, he felt dirty. Depraved. A cheat.

He doubted the latter would ever fade.

When he did finally move on, it wouldn't be pretty. He'd always be emotionally committed to Cassie, and he knew his self-respect would be at an all-time low if he shared himself with another.

In his pitiful delusions, he'd even pondered the idea of paying a high-class escort to be the first. Emotions wouldn't be involved that way. It would be a job—for him to get over his wife and for his escort to pay the bills. Win-win. He even had a business card in his wallet. A constant reminder that moving on was a phone call away. Only he couldn't bring himself to dial the number.

"You okay, big guy?" Shay came up behind him.

"All good," he lied. He was dying inside, sinking into purgatory.

He seated himself at the bar, refrained from reaching for a bottle of Grey Goose and zoned out while Shay polished glasses and checked the beer taps to see if they were in working order. Time moved without him, the world not caring he was falling apart with each second that ticked by.

Patrons arrived in perfectly choreographed intervals. As the night dragged on, people came, literally, and went. He didn't know who or when. He scoped the rooms once or twice, shuffling his feet as he made sure all participation was above board and consensual. But nobody infiltrated his consciousness. Nothing invaded his thoughts. Nothing except Cassie.

"I love you," someone said behind him.

He winced, pushing through the heartache as he remembered the first time his wife uttered those words. He'd fallen for her long before that. Weeks, maybe even months prior to her declaration. He'd kept his adoration to himself, not willing to project his feelings onto her when he wasn't entirely sure she felt the same way.

She had though.

In the sweetest possible way, she'd whispered those words to him. "I love you, Tate. We were made for each other."

"And always will be," he mouthed the words he'd spoken, seeing her image in his mind.

She'd smiled, her cheeks lifting, tiny dimples showing. The sun rose and set in those features. If only he could go back. Change the path. Tweak their outcome.

"Make love to me. Show me you love me, too."

Her words had filled him with determination. He'd do anything for her, including making the world around them vanish as he devoted his mind, body and soul to her. "I don't know how I lived without you."

Sappy dialogue had never been his calling card. Yes, he prided himself on being a gentleman, but it wasn't until Cassie that he'd truly understood the power words yielded. Over time, the memory of his touch would fade. He could only hope she'd never lose the recollection of the softly uttered endearments he gifted to her.

"You didn't," she'd murmured. "You existed. Life didn't start until there was you and me."

T.J. brushed his lips over hers, sliding his hands under her shirt. The softness of her body undid him. He liked curves, and Cassie had them in abundance. He lifted her, cradling her in his arms as he strode to their bedroom.

He placed her on her feet and undid the buttons of his shirt. "There's a present for you in my top drawer."

Her gaze narrowed, her angelic eyes reading him as her lips curved in awareness. He'd done this before—placed items in his bedside table for her. Always of a sexual nature. Vibrators, dildos, nipple stimulators, anything and everything to improve her enjoyment.

She turned, slid out his top drawer and frowned. "What is it?"

"Take it out and have a look." Her innocence did funny things to him. He always got a kick out of introducing her to new pleasures, testing her boundaries, awakening her to something different. It was the reason their sexuality had gone too far, too fast. He couldn't help himself.

"What am I meant to do with it?" She picked up the C-shaped toy between her thumb and forefinger and examined it with a frown.

"The smaller end goes inside you, against your G-spot. The thicker part curls around your pubic bone to rest on your clit."

She shot him a look, her lips curved in a smirk. "Sounds like a lot of fun for me. Where do you come into all this?"

"I'll come. Don't worry about that." He stepped forward, lifting the flimsy material of her shirt over her head, revealing her sensuous breasts contained in a white lace bra. She lowered her skirt to the ground, gifting him with the exposure of matching panties while her heated gaze ate him up.

"Take off your underwear."

She inclined her head, lowering her focus in submission. Elegant fingers gripped her waistband, baring more tempting flesh—the trimmed strip of hair at her mound, the glimpse of pussy lips, her thighs, her generous ass.

"The bra, too."

She raised her brows. "I'm getting there." Her hands wove around her back, working the clasp before the material fell free and drifted to the floor. "Is that better?"

"You should never wear clothes," he uttered the truth. Cassie was made for a nudist colony. For the admiring glances from men and women alike.

She hugged her stomach, succumbing to doubt.

"Don't ever cover yourself." With a gentle finger, he tapped her wrists in a silent command. "I want this inside you." He motioned to the toy in her hand and gripped the narrow, thinner end. Slowly, he guided the rounded tip down her body, over her abdomen, straight to the apex of her thighs. "I want to watch you take it from here."

The tops of her cheeks darkened to the most precious shade of pink. "How do I turn it on?"

"You don't, my love." He was confident calling her that now. And always would be. She was his love. His one and only. "Just put it inside that gorgeous pussy of yours and I'll do the rest."

She nodded, the slight, almost nervous movement making the protective part of him explode in the need to bring confidence to her actions. She was style. She was grace. She was everything and anything a man like him could wish for. Her inability to see her value or strut around showing it off astounded him.

With her hand still clutching the toy, she crawled onto the bed and rested on her back. He couldn't tear his gaze away—didn't want to, never would—as she closed her eyes briefly and slipped the black object into her pussy.

"Perfect." The word was a whisper through his drying mouth.

"I *do* try my best."

There it was, the brief spark, the tiny glimmer of sexual confidence that drove him to madness. She was at home in his bed.

He pulled his phone from the back pocket of his pants and scrolled to the most recently downloaded app. The software that had come with the product allowed him to control the device remotely. From her side, to another state, or even another country, he could initiate her pleasure with the touch of a button. All he had to do was decide whether he wanted to stimulate her G-spot, her clit, or both at once, and at what ferocity.

"Let's take our time, shall we." He wasn't one to rush. He enjoyed building her arousal, stoking her into a craze before allowing her to succumb to bliss. With a quick double-tap, the external stimulator hummed to life, wrenching a gasp from her throat.

"Jesus." Her eyes widened.

He chuckled as he shucked his pants, leaving them in a heap at his feet. "You like?"

"As always." The shock left her features, replaced with a sultry, dreamy gleam in her eye. "I still don't get how you're going to benefit from this."

"Your pleasure is my pleasure." He'd play the selfless card a little longer, until he couldn't take it anymore. Then he'd inform her the toy and his cock could both easily be accommodated inside her body. He'd make sure of it.

He tapped his phone screen again, twice more on the external stimulation and once for the vibrations to start against her G-spot.

"Oh, holy hell, T.J." She grasped at the quilt, arching her back, closing her eyes.

One day, he wanted to lay all his gifts out on the bed—the cuffs, the massage oils, the fetish restrains, the anal plug and vibrators. One by one, he'd use them all, sating her to the point of exhaustion before finally taking his own pleasure inside her breathtaking body.

"T.J.?" Cassie began to writhe, her tone foreign. Distorted with lust.

"Hmm?" He smiled down at her, sensing her apprehension, feeling it spur to life underneath his ribcage, because just like her pleasure, her worry was his to own as well.

"T.J.?"

Her voice became distant, her image darkening. Fading. He squinted, blinked and tried to focus back on the heaven before him as it continued to drift away.

"*T.J.*"

Shit. He snapped out of the memory and frowned up at Shay. She stood beside the light switch, her hair more frazzled than it was moments ago, her brown eyes tired. "Can you help me pack up?"

He shot a glance over his shoulder to the now empty room. Seconds ago, naked bodies had writhed in wanton abandon behind him. The sex swing had been in use, the space filled with chatter and sexual delirium.

He was losing his goddamn mind.

"Yeah." He cleared his throat and slid from the stool, thankful for the bar that currently hid the dying bulge in his pants. "What needs to be done?"

Shay looked at him, *really* looked at him. Her brow was furrowed, her mouth set in a tight line. "Where the hell have you been the last three hours?"

He broke eye contact, the uncomfortable shiver of exposure drifting down his spine. "I guess I got caught up in my thoughts."

"About your wife?" She grabbed a yellow cloth from the counter and began polishing the bar.

"About life in general. I've got a lot on my mind."

He strode for the first private area and flicked on the fluorescent light, not in the mood to talk. The large bed in the middle of the room was mussed, the cushions scattered in varying positions on the mattress and floor. One by one, he picked them up, removing their cloth covers and throwing the material toward the doorway. He didn't usually partake in cleaning. The contracted business they paid handsomely for privacy's sake would be here in a matter of hours. He just needed an excuse to keep away from Shay and her questions.

The woman was a pit bull. A beautiful, sassy pit bull who should have her hands full with her new boyfriend Leo, instead of trying to ride T.J.'s ass about his divorce.

"Leo and Brute are on the way down," she called from the main area. "They want to speak to you before you leave."

He withheld a sigh and scrubbed both hands down his face. "About?"

"Don't worry, it's nothing intrusive." Her slight frame filled the doorway. "It's business. My business, actually. I came up with a few ideas for the Vault and they want to speak to you privately about it."

Damn it. It was God knows when in the early hours of the morning. He didn't have the brain capacity to think of anything but Cassie. All his mind revolved around were blue eyes, soft curves and a gorgeous smile.

Shay cocked her hip against the door frame. "Can I ask you something?"

No. *Hell no.* He didn't want to talk. Not about work or life. Especially not about love. "I'm tired. Can we do this later?"

"I'm worried about you." Her soft footfalls brushed against the carpet as she strode toward him. "I didn't realize you were stuck in a bad marriage."

"I wasn't stuck." The need to defend Cassie was instantaneous. Painfully so. "It wasn't bad either."

"Then why?" She frowned. "I don't understand."

Neither did Leo or Brute, and that was okay. Their perception of his relationship wasn't important. They were his closest friends, but in contrast, Cassie was his world. The problems that had led to their divorce were private. He wouldn't betray her, even now when they weren't together anymore.

"It's complicated." He bided his time, yanking the fitted sheet off the bed and balling it before launching it toward the pile of cushion covers near the door.

"*That* I can understand. Especially when I assume sexuality played an integral role." She strolled for the bedside table and flicked off the lamp. "But if it wasn't bad, why the divorce?"

"Presuming anything in this lifestyle and working environment is dangerous, Shay." His tone was authoritative. Annoyed. Something he didn't show often. "Misconceptions and thoughtlessness can get you in a lot of trouble." He knew from experience.

"Okay..." She pulled back in offense and strode for the door. "Point taken."

Great. Now, he not only felt like shit, he felt like an asshole, too. "Shay, wait." He jogged after her. "I appreciate your concern, but I'm good. Promise."

She raised a brow and crossed her arms over her chest. "I was only trying to help."

The door from the entry creaked open, burying the conversation. At least he hoped so. The sound of heavy footsteps reached them moments before Leo and Brute strode into the main Vault of Sin room.

"Is this a bad time?" Leo asked, his jaw tight, his gaze locked on Shay.

"No. We're good." Her tone said otherwise as she sidled up to Leo and placed a kiss on his lips. "I'll go upstairs so the three of you can talk." Without another word, she sauntered from the room, closing the door behind her with a harsh clunk.

"Why did she look pissed off?" Leo asked.

"Doesn't she always look like that?" T.J. rested his hip against the side of the tan leather sofa in the middle of the room.

Brute gave a halfhearted snicker. "Yep. She's either pissed or up to something. Neither look is comforting."

"Maybe if you quit giving her hell, she'd quit sharpening her claws." Leo leaned against the back of the sofa. "Just admit you love riling her."

"You know what I'd love?" Brute flashed his teeth in a vicious smile. "I'd love to see you and Shay interact without your dick involved. Get a room. Go on vacation. Just keep your lily-white ass outta my face."

"Jealous much?"

"Fuck y—"

"Come on, guys." T.J. was too tired for this. "Shay said you have something to speak to me about."

Leo smirked, claiming victory over the argument.

"Don't preen like a peacock," Brute demanded. "Now you've gotta explain your crazy girlfriend's fucked-up ideas for our damn sex club."

T.J. closed his eyes, letting exhaustion take hold. He didn't have the strength to participate in this bullshit tonight. He didn't even have the will to smile.

"Relax." Leo nudged his shoulder. "It's not that bad."

Brute cleared his throat. "Depends on your perspective."

"Just spit it out." T.J. scrubbed a hand along his jaw, across the harsh stubble that reminded him he hadn't shaved in two days. "What is Shay up to?"

"She had a few ideas to increase attendance in the Vault."

"The main idea being a dress-up party," Brute drawled.

"What?" T.J. loved Shay, but people dressing up as Fred Flintstone or Superman was not the type of professional image he wanted for their club. Having girlfriends or lovers involved in the decision-making process of their business wasn't something he approved of either. That's why Cassie had always been a silent partner.

"It's a fucking masquerade party, you idiot." Leo shot Brute the bird. "It'll give those who are interested in playing but reluctant to be seen in this type of environment a chance to remain anonymous."

"I'm listening." T.J.'s tiredness abated somewhat. The idea could have merit. Maybe. He jerked his chin in Brute's direction and was immediately pinned by his friend's scowl. "I gather you're against the idea."

"The club has never been about games or *playing* to me. It's a lifestyle choice. Either own up to your proclivities, or fuck off and go to another club—one that doesn't pride itself on integrity and the privacy of all our members."

The reminder of other clubs made cement solidify in T.J.'s gut. He'd been there, done that. It hadn't been pretty. "Just because you're out and proud doesn't mean everyone else has to be. Some of the people interested in the lifestyle aren't willing to risk losing family or friends if they're caught." He knew that all too well. "And others have their religion and employment to think about."

"Don't get me started on religion."

"Or anything else that doesn't gain your approval," Leo muttered.

"So, you *are* against the idea?" T.J. asked. Brute wasn't pro anything. He was the glass-half-empty kind of guy. The one who took pleasure in making others fail. He was brutal, thus the nickname.

"He's fucking fine with it." Leo spoke through a laugh. "He already gave the go-ahead. He's just being his typical moody self."

Brute shrugged. "Your girlfriend is a hard woman to deny."

"*My* girlfriend being the operative words."

It was Brute's turn to chuckle. "Yes, *currently*, she is."

Leo growled and straightened, crossing his arms over his chest.

"Come on, guys." T.J. was going to have to crash on one of the Vault beds if they didn't get this conversation done with. He didn't want to drive to his apartment when he couldn't keep his eyes open. "I guess we all agree about the masquerade party. So where do we go from here?"

Brute laughed. "I'll let Leo answer that one, too."

"Actually..." Leo drew the word out. "Shay's arranged for the first trial run to take place next Thursday night."

T.J. struggled to ignore the nudge of betrayal filling his chest. "Right..." They'd planned it without him.

"We weren't sure when you were going to return to work." Leo held up his hands in surrender. "You've—"

"Doesn't take much to pick up the phone. Or text." He'd never felt more alone. Cassie was gone. The club was moving on without him, evolving, when every part of his soul was crumpling to shit.

"Yeah, well, that's a two-way street." Brute raised an accusatory brow. "You could've given us a heads-up about when you were returning. Or that you planned to bail on us in the first place. This is a business. We rely on you."

Ouch. It wouldn't hurt so much if they weren't right.

"I couldn't deal," he admitted. With work. With the world. With life in general. He'd had no choice. Finding the strength to hand over the divorce papers hadn't been easy. Reflection and determination had taken time.

"We know." Leo nudged his shoulder. "It's no big deal. So, about this masquerade thing..."

"I guess I'll just sit back and let you guys run the show, seeing as you've already started the project." He kept the resentment from his voice the best he could.

Brute smirked. "Don't look at me. This is all on Lothario. He couldn't say no because Shay has his balls in the palm of her hand."

"Shay prefers my balls in her mouth, asshole," Leo snarled. "And to be honest, I always thought it was a good idea. I would've shut her down otherwise."

Brute snorted and received a middle-finger salute in return.

"The entry and dress codes will all remain the same," Leo continued. "We're still obtaining non-disclosures before they arrive, proof of identification and photos. The only difference is that patrons can maintain their anonymity from other guests once they arrive. Brute will know who they are from the online registration."

"Okay." He shrugged. He didn't have the energy to protest even if he did disagree. "Has there been much interest?"

An arrogant smile brightened Leo's features. "We're almost at full capacity."

CHAPTER THREE

Cassie increased the volume on her earphones, trying to drown out her thoughts. It didn't help that she was sitting at the dining room table, her gaze glued to the website causing the pain in her veins to increase.

Vault of Sin.

She was on their mailing list. Had been since the club opened a year ago. Today, she'd finally had the strength to enter back into the real world—showering, cooking, cleaning the house, and lastly, checking her email.

It was a sign. A blatant nudge from fate. The Vault was holding its first masquerade party. A private, anonymous event. Cassie's heart was racing over the notification. Something churned in her belly, telling her she had to be there. Yeah, it could be indigestion, but she chose to ignore that train of thought.

It was the perfect opportunity to insert herself back into T.J.'s life. Gradually. Without him even knowing. Without *anyone* knowing.

This email acknowledged all her fears and set them at ease. With a disguise, she could attend the event at the Vault and see if T.J. was already moving on. Determine his mindset about the divorce. And hopefully gain a better plan to reconnect. All she had to do was overcome all the obstacles stopping her from getting through the front doors.

She'd never stepped foot in the private part of the business. No matter how intrigued she was by the mere thought of her husband's sex club, there hadn't been time to visit. Not since her relationship with T.J. had hit rocky ground around the same time the establishment had opened. Beforehand, he'd spoken to her at length about his involvement, obtaining her understanding over the duties he would be required to perform. She'd trusted him. Unequivocally. The only unmanageable emotion she had felt had been excitement, knowing the club would eventually become a part of their sexual journey.

That part of their future had never eventuated.

Now, the place readily available for sex and seduction was constantly on her mind. Not only because it was a significant threat to losing her husband to another woman, it was also the perfect location to try and win him back.

"Cassie," a female voice called behind her, followed by a loud knock that startled her to her feet, the earplugs painfully yanking from her ears as her chair fell to the floor.

"It's just me." Jan, her friend from across the street, held up her hands from the other side of the glass sliding door. "I didn't mean to scare you."

"Well, you failed miserably." Cassie breathed deeply, working hard to calm the rapid beat of her heart. Six months hadn't been enough time to get used to living without a man in the house. She still found it hard sleeping alone, without T.J. to protect her.

Obviously, Bear wasn't the best guard dog either. He currently sat at Jan's side, his large tail wagging, his eyes bright with playfulness.

Cassie unlocked the door and slid it open. "What are you doing here?" *Again.*

Jan shrugged. "Just dropping by before I hit the sack."

"I've told you—" *a hundred times*, "—that isn't necessary. I swear, I'm fine." Or she would be. One day. In the unforeseeable future. Depending on the outcome of her marriage.

"Sweetie, you lost your husband."

"I didn't *lose* him." She knew exactly where he was. "He's just stubborn, that's all. He'll be back before you know it."

Jan gave her a placating smile. "Are you sure? He doesn't seem the type of man to make mistakes. Especially big ones."

There was a first for everything. T.J. was a man that owned everything he did—his attitude, his strength, his determination. Most importantly, his love for her. He just hid his confidence under a gentlemanly façade, not needing to prove himself to anyone. It was only a matter of time before she convinced him to return. But there was no point arguing with Jan. She would never understand. Nobody would.

Jan's gaze drifted to Cassie's laptop screen, her brow furrowing. "What are you looking at?"

Oh, Christ. Cassie lunged toward the laptop and slammed the screen closed to cut off the sordid images that set the scene on the Vault's website. "Nothing."

Jan's lip twitched. "Did I interrupt something?"

"*No.* Of course not."

"You sure you weren't watching porn?" Jan raised a brow. "Did I fuck with your motion of the ocean?"

"Oh, my God." Heat burned in her cheeks. "No." The last thing her body was capable of was arousal.

"So, what were you looking at?"

"Nothing."

Jan cocked her hip, settling into a comfortable position that wordlessly announced she wasn't going anywhere without an answer.

"Fine." Cassie huffed and crossed her arms over her chest. "I'm working out a plan to get T.J. back."

"With the help of porn?" Jan's expression turned bleak.

"It's not *goddamn* porn."

"Okay, okay." Jan balked. "Then explain."

Cassie didn't want to. There were things in life that should be kept between husband and wife. Their reason for divorce was one of them. So was the plan for trying to get him back. Even though Jan was older and more open-minded than the friends Cassie had grown up with, it still didn't seem like a conversation they should be having. "I can't. It would feel like I was betraying him."

"Cass..." Jan pulled out a chair and took a seat. "You don't owe him anything. He already wants to move on."

Damn. The truth stung. "There's other reasons, too."

"Like?"

"Like I don't want you to judge him. Or us as a couple. Our relationship wasn't normal by society's standards."

"Right..." Jan raised a haughty brow. "I'm going to pretend I'm not offended by your assumption, and remind you I'm a single forty-two-year-old that has never had a prudish bone in my body."

Although Jan had become her closest confidant in the months since T.J. had moved out, Cassie hadn't shared private information. Only heartache and fear for the future. The secrets she kept with her husband were a gift only the two of them shared. They'd never been the type to crave attention. T.J. guarded the intimate parts of his life. They both did. He'd learned through the mistakes of his friends that people were too quick to judge decisions that were none of their business.

"If you can't tell me—" Jan reached for the laptop, "—show me what you were looking at."

Cassie warred with herself, caught between needing to talk and having to remain true to her husband. She still didn't believe T.J. wanted to move on. She could change his mind. She knew she could. It was loneliness that pushed her to share her pain.

"Please keep an open mind." She spared her friend a brief glance before she lifted the laptop screen and swiped her fingers over the mouse pad. The Vault website burst to life as Jan scooted closer in her chair.

"What am I looking at?"

The inside of Cassie's wildest fantasies. "An invitation to a sex club."

Jan's eyes widened as she began to nod, slowly, not taking her focus from the page before her.

"T.J. is going to be there." At least she thought he would be. His name adorned the bottom of the invitation after all.

"He's been cheating on you?" Jan screeched. She glanced over her shoulder, her face a mask of fury. "He told you that?"

"No." Cassie shook her head, clutching the back of the wooden chair in front of her. "It's not like that. He's not there to have sex." As far as she knew. "This club is part of the business he owns with his friends. Very few people know of its existence."

"Right." Jan chuckled, the sound almost delirious. "I guess it's true—the quiet ones are always the freakiest in the sack."

Cassie gave a halfhearted smile. "He was definitely talented in that department."

"So how does this club work in with winning him back? Or can't you tell me that either?"

Cassie sagged under the weight of hopelessness. She hadn't told anyone the real reason T.J. had asked for a divorce. Not even the blatant lie of *incompatibility* stated on the legal documentation. It was too private. Being vague was her only option.

"T.J. isn't like most guys. He cherished me. He was a protector. A provider—in every sense of the word. He continuously worked at maintaining our perfect marriage and prided himself on his dedication to me."

"He placed you on a pedestal."

Exactly. "Yes. He did that, too. His love was infallible."

"But?"

Cassie sighed. "He placed too much onus on his responsibility in our relationship. It was almost an obsession to keep me happy, and I completely adored the attention. If I was sick, he nurtured me to health. If I was sad, he figured out a way to brighten my mood. My contentment was everything to him."

"Until?"

Cassie shrugged. "Everything went to hell a year ago. I placed myself in a bad position. A *really* bad position. I was hurt, and he blames himself. He always blames himself."

Jan shook her head with a disbelieving furrow of her brow. "How come you never told me any of this?"

"The circumstances aren't..." Socially acceptable? Morally adequate? "Favorable."

"Okay, I get that you want to keep the details close to your chest. So, let's return the convo to the fuck club. What's that got to do with getting him back?"

Fuck club?

Cassie smiled. "We've been emotionally disconnected for twelve months. I want to get to know him again—his strengths and weaknesses. I need to be close to him, maybe then things will be clearer."

"Then go. Do it. Get your kink on, you naughty little girl."

Cassie couldn't contain her laugh. "It's not that easy. Although the night in question will be their first masquerade party, there's a line of hoops I need to jump through to gain entry. One of them being proof of identification."

"And..."

"And I know the person who handles applications. If he sees my name, he won't let me in." Brute was a hard-ass. A man who couldn't be swayed or easily fooled.

"So, what you're saying is that you need a new identity?"

"What I need is a new name, face, body—everything." It was useless. Cassie leaned over the back of the chair and scrolled to the page on the Vault of Sin website which listed entry requirements. "There." She pointed to the screen. "I need a recent photo, plus a copy of my driver's license."

"Is that all?" Jan focused on the website, her eyes squinted.

Is that all? "I don't think you understand. I can't get in with my current license. They'll recognize me straightaway."

"What if you used someone else's? Maybe someone that looks similar to you."

"No." Cassie shook her head. "That would mean telling more people, and that's not something I'm willing to do."

"We need a fake ID."

"Yeah," Cassie spoke with derision. In her reality, obtaining illegal documents was as likely as robbing a bank. "I'll just ask one of the criminal mastermind friends of mine to whip one up for me."

"Don't give me sass, girlie. I'm sure we can sort something out."

The dull beat of Cassie's heart began to thud with earnest. The slightest glimmer of hope sparked a fire under her ribs. "We can?"

"Yeah. Maybe. I dunno." Jan turned to face her. "I can give you a makeover. We'll concentrate on being the opposite of how you are now—fake nails, salon tan, bright makeup, ostentatious clothes. And with the right wig, you could look completely different."

"It still leaves the problem of identification." Fooling Brute wouldn't be easy, yet her appearance was the least difficult part of the plan.

"That's where my brother may be able to help." Jan pushed from her seat. "You may not know any criminal masterminds, but I'm sure he does."

"Isn't he a cop?" Cassie closed her gaping mouth. This was crazy. "I don't want to get arrested."

Jan waved her comment away. "You'll be fine. As long as you still want to go ahead with your plan."

Shady police. Lies. Illegal activity. Was it worth it? "Yes. I do."

"Then leave it to me. How much time do I have?"

"Four days until the party, but I need to submit my application as soon as possible."

Jan winced. "Okay. First thing tomorrow, you need to get to work on changing your appearance. Leave the ID to me."

Christ. This was really happening. She was going to walk into an unfamiliar sex club, dressed in a disguise, and try to win back her husband. She was even prepared to break the law. *Ha*. The level of devotion was crazy. But for T.J., it was all worth it.

CHAPTER FOUR

The days leading to the fateful night were a whirlwind. Cassie didn't sleep, barely ate and her boss didn't cut her any slack when he found out about the impending divorce. Not that she'd expected him to. The dictator of the hotel she worked at was a ballbuster who didn't hide his disapproval over her new fake tan and plum polish highlighting longer-than-normal nails.

"This is the driveway, right?" Jan asked from the driver's seat.

"Yeah, go through to the parking lot out back." They slowly glided past the large building with impeccably clean windows giving a look into the interior of Taste of Sin. Beside the door to the restaurant was the darkened entry to Shot of Sin. It was currently abandoned. The dance club wasn't open on Thursday nights.

"Are you ready?"

Nope. "Yes." Cassie's voice was filled with panic, her heart a rampant beat in her chest.

The twenty-minute journey to T.J.'s business had been done in nerve-filled silence. She had no clue what would happen once she arrived. She didn't even know if she'd get inside. After submitting her application, she was sure a rejection would soon follow. She'd even stalked her email, unsure if it would be better emotionally to gain approval to see her husband, or take it as a sign if her request was denied.

Days had gone by and she still didn't know if this was the right idea.

Jan pulled into one of the parking spaces at the back of Shot of Sin and cut the ignition. "Now, remember, call me at any time to come pick you up. I'll be waiting."

Oh, Christ. This was really happening.

"Stop fretting." Jan placed a hand on Cassie's shoulder and squeezed. "No man is going to want to squish your titties when you look like you're about to vomit."

"I'm not going to vomit." Her conviction was a lie. She was light-headed. Scared. And she wasn't sure what worried her most—entering a sex club she wasn't familiar with or the possibility of finding another woman in her husband's arms.

"I'm just not sure if I can do this." The admission was painful. As if she were giving up. Admitting defeat.

"No problem. I'll drive us home." Jan started the ignition.

"*Wait.*" Damn it. "You and your damn reverse psychology."

Jan smirked. "It worked, didn't it?"

Cassie growled and fought the need to scratch under the wig itching her scalp. "You're so mean to me." She grasped for her handbag and unclicked her seat belt. "I need a few minutes to prepare."

Jan rolled her eyes. "You already said that when I wanted to get started on your hair. Then again when I attempted to do your makeup. *And* when I tried to get you in the car. Not to mention the three laps around the block you made me do."

"I'm walking into a sex club, not a Seven-Eleven."

"Your husband is down there. You'll be fine."

"I *think* my husband is down there." Cassie shoved the car door open with force. "I have no confirmation of that."

"Then think of it as an adventure. Even if you don't participate, you're about to see more action than I have in years."

Cassie grabbed her clutch and shoved from the car. "Still not comforting."

"Don't forget about your mask," Jan cooed. "I love you, you naughty little minx."

Still hidden behind the car, Cassie pulled her mask into place. "Thanks," she drawled and closed the door on her friend's laughter.

As Jan's car drove from the parking lot, Cassie began to shake. She was on her own. Vulnerable. Looking like a whore and feeling like a clown in all her fake attire. The dark blue dress sculpting her curves was unlike anything she'd usually wear. It was tight. Too tight. And it was only there to save her thinly veiled modesty during the short walk to the back entrance of the sex club. Once inside, she would need to remove it and reveal the skimpy slip she wore underneath to fit the clubs scantily clad dress code.

Everything adorning her body was new, and the exact opposite of what she would normally wear. Her shiny heels were stiletto thin, the color perfectly matching the dark purple of her nails and the lace outlining her mask. There was no turning back. Not unless she wanted to strut her hooker-heels to the curb and call Jan to pick her up.

She glanced toward the back entrance of the club, to the couple standing at the door getting their ID checked by two men. They were tall, broad, burly males who seemed ominous under the dim glow of the outside light yards above their heads.

Their faces came into focus as she approached, her footsteps crunching against the asphalt. One guard was dressed in navy slacks and a white-collared shirt. His expression was friendly, comforting. The man beside him was not. His stare was lethal, his features tight as he scrutinized the people before him. Typical Brute. She'd never forget his critical stare, the one that hid the caring man underneath. Deep, deep underneath. His gaze wasn't even upon her, yet she already felt the weight of it. Grueling, criticizing. *Shit.* She shouldn't be doing this.

He was going to recognize her no matter how she'd tried to hide her identity. Her long blonde hair was now short and black, thanks to the excessively itchy wig. Her light blue eyes were dark brown from the contacts she'd purchased from her optometrist. And her lips, usually adorned with gentle colors, were bright red and glossy, standing out like a beacon in the dead of night. The only solace she gained was from the mask that covered most of her forehead, the area around her eyes and down to her cheek bones, giving her a sense of anonymity.

What if she had to take it off to prove her identity?

Hell. Heart in her throat, she came to stand at the end of the line and smiled at the woman who turned to greet her with a flash of perfect teeth. The bright pink mask she wore was covered in glitter with some of the shimmering glow resting on her cheeks.

"This your first time?" The woman's gaze fell to the red band around Cassie's wrist.

"Yes." Her voice faltered, not only from nerves. She couldn't fail at this. Brute couldn't turn her away. She wouldn't know what to do if he did.

"You'll have fun, I promise." The woman turned to her companion and stepped forward, offering Brute their identification.

Cassie's throat tightened. Blood rushed through her ears in a painful thrum she was sure the whole world could hear. Then the couple disappeared, moving forward, out of sight, leaving her to stand face-to-face with Brute, his hand outstretched as she convinced herself not to run.

"ID," he grunted.

She placed her fake driver's license in his hand and hoped he didn't notice the tremor in her fingers. She was sweating. The back of her neck tingled. Her scalp itched.

"Name?" he muttered.

Oh, no. He already had her identification. Her name was clearly written on it. He was testing her.

"Tanya Johnson." Her voice broke. This wouldn't work. Not in her meek, frightened state of mind. She had to place this in perspective. Her marriage was on the line. Her happiness. Everything that had ever mattered to her was dependent on reconnecting with T.J.

She raised her chin, cleared her throat and met Brute's stare as he palmed a small electronic tablet in his hand.

"First-timer." His gaze lowered over her chest, her stomach, then came to rest on her arm. "Make sure you don't remove the wristband."

"I won't."

He grunted, making her increasingly aware he hadn't outgrown his arrogant attitude in the months since she'd seen him last.

"We have strict rules here, Tanya."

"I know."

Brute's position at the entry was deliberate. Not only to check identification, but to give an unspoken warning to everyone who passed through the doors. If word got out about Vault of Sin, he would deal with it. Harshly. He was the brutality protecting the carnal pleasure beneath the Shot of Sin dance floor.

"Be sure to adhere to them and you'll have a great time." His lethal tone implied otherwise. "If you have any problems or concerns, there's staff members dressed in full attire to help you—Leo, T.J. and Travis."

The sound of her husband's name sent a barb of fire through her chest. He was here. In a sex club. No longer needing to remain a voyeur as he would soon be single.

"And if you'd prefer to discuss any issues with a female member of staff," Brute continued, "let me know and I'll arrange it."

She inclined her head and broke eye contact, unable to hold his lethal stare. "Thank you."

He moved to the side, allowing her stomach to drop to the tips of her toes as she started forward into the darkness. A cement staircase came into view, the couple before her barely visible as they reached the bottom landing and turned left.

She focused on the path before her, trying not to let past experience taint this moment. T.J. would never align himself with sleaziness. She had to trust her memory of him. She had to trust the Vault of Sin. It was a mantra. A comforting acknowledgement she had to repeat over and over again to keep her feet progressing to the start of the stairs.

"Oh, boy." Dizzying nerves, stiletto heels and a rapid descent. Not a great combination.

The sound of sex, chatter and clinking glassware entered her ears as she progressed at a snail's pace, not allowing nausea to creep in.

"You'll be fine," a female voice spoke over her shoulder.

Cassie reached out a hand to grip the wall. She glanced behind her to the smile almost covered by the green feathers bordering the blonde's mask, the color almost perfectly matching her eyes.

"Don't panic." The woman's gaze lowered, her lips curving sweetly when she spied the red band adorning Cassie's wrist. "The first time is always the worst. Just stay away from the bukkake ritual."

Holy shit. Was she serious?

"I'm joking. I'm joking." The woman chuckled and grabbed the crook of Cassie's elbow. "I should know better than to tease."

"It's okay," Cassie croaked. Sure it was. She just couldn't get the image of a group of men poised over her kneeling body as they prepared to spray her face with their release. *Shudder.* "I'm a little nervous, that's all." And apprehensive. And nauseous. And scared.

"You came alone?"

They began to descend together, the woman's gentle touch still resting on Cassie's arm. "Yeah. Stupid, right?"

"Not at all. My first Vault experience was on my own."

Cassie's concern began to ebb under the woman's comforting voice.

There was no sexual inclination to her touch. Cassie's intuition told her to trust this woman. To believe her friendship was genuine. Then again, her intuition had been nowhere in sight for the last twelve months, so what the hell did she know?

They reached the bottom step and the calming grip on her arm disappeared. The sound of sex and excited conversation had grown. Loud enough to ring in her ears. With trepidation, she turned on the tips of her sexy shoes and came face-to-face with her first glimpse of the Vault of Sin.

"*Holy smokes.*" Her words were a whispered breath.

She could only see the corner of what she assumed was a large room. And in that corner was a sex swing. An *occupied* sex swing. The woman was reclined on her back, her torso encased in black straps, her legs wrapped around a Greek god as he sank into her. Over and over again. Her dark hair hung in the air behind her, the glossy strands swaying with each thrust.

It was glorious. Stupefying in its perfection. They paid no attention to her fascination, or the other people within view who were also watching. It was as if they were alone. Immersed in their own bubble of pleasure.

"Are swings your thing?" The woman beside her asked.

Cassie shook her head, still unable to drag her focus away from the live porn before her. "I've never tried one."

"Tonight might be your lucky night."

Cassie coughed to smother a laugh. "No. Not tonight."

There would be no sex for her, even though the tingle of arousal was already pulsing between her thighs. This was about getting to know T.J. again. Finding out where he was at. What he was thinking. Maybe she would reveal herself to him, maybe she wouldn't. But sex wasn't in the equation as far as she was concerned.

"You never know." The woman chuckled. "I'm Zoe by the way."

"Cas—" *Shit.* Cassie snapped her attention from the fornicating couple and pasted on a fake smile. "I'm Tanya."

Zoe's smile faltered, suspicion growing heavy in the narrowing of her framed eyes. "Come on, Tanya. I'll escort you to the change rooms."

Cassie wasn't sure if her slip up had been a close call or the other woman had no curiosity to pry. Either way, she released a silent sigh of relief. Zoe strode from the darkened hall, her shoulders back, her head high with grace and dignity. Cassie tried to mimic the confidence, failing miserably with the awe assailing her as the full room came into view.

A crowd of people mingled along a long stretch of bar. They were all in different stages of undress. Some women were in corsets, others in bras and panties. A few were topless. The men on the other hand were in boxer briefs—Calvin Klein, Emporio Armani, Tommy John.

The area screamed with invigorating debauchery. There were chaises, a bed, maybe more than one. She couldn't see much over the people constricting her view. Two doors were open to her left, with the shadows of people inside. And an archway was to the far end of the room.

It was different from what she'd experienced in the only other club she'd been to. The ambiance, although dripping with seduction, was classy. Everything was red and black—sheets, lamp shades, furniture.

The people surrounding her were young, fit and attractive. Complete contrasts to the old, overweight men who'd lined the walls of the previous club she'd run from. She turned in a circle, amazed and more than a little proud at the perfection of the atmosphere.

"It's this way." Zoe raised her voice and didn't acknowledge the loud cry of, "Oh yes, oh yes, fuck me harder," from the woman in the sex swing.

"I'm right behind you." She was following, no matter how stunted her steps.

Curiosity had her enthralled, but there was something that began to concern her. She'd memorized every inch of the main room, taken a glimpse into the two private areas, and not once had she caught sight of her husband.

~

"Are you coming down to the party?"

T.J. squeezed his eyes shut and massaged his lids, ignoring the question for as long as he could. Shay wouldn't leave him alone. She hovered. Everywhere. All the time. No matter where he went, she was in his tracks with a friendly smile and a comforting pat on his back. He loathed it. The old Shay, the one who'd talked smack and given him hell, was the woman he needed. Not this highly attuned, feminine ball of emotional support that kept him on edge.

"I'll get down there when I'm ready." The growl of his voice echoed through the empty Shot of Sin dance club. He liked the peace and quiet. And he deserved the loneliness.

"Did you think about what I said in the restaurant yesterday?"

He couldn't forget. Shay's idea of getting over his wife was to move on. Hop on the bike again, so to speak. Take a new woman for a test drive. Brute concurred, ever the heartless bastard.

The thought made him sick.

"Why don't we talk about you for a change?" He dropped his hand from his face and straightened at the sight of her. She was adorned in a see-through black dress, her shiny red bra and panties visible beneath to match her glossy high heels. She wore a swatch of black lace over her eyes. Simple yet elegant. *Beautiful.*

"How are things with you and Leo?" He spoke to hide his discomfort. Seeing Shay like this wasn't something he could get used to overnight. She'd been his friend for a long time. His employee even longer. Now he'd have to watch as she strutted her gorgeous body around the Vault on her nights off.

She rolled her pretty brown eyes. "You know, you could just tell me you don't want to talk."

Perfect. "I don't want to talk about it, Shayna." His glare was far harsher than his tone. He couldn't help it. He was tired—his heart, his body and his mind. Enough was enough.

"No problem." She raised her chin, the defiance of the woman he used to know coming back in full force.

"So how about you and Leo? What did I miss while I was away?"

She waggled her brows. "A lot of debauchery."

No way. Leo was taking it slow, unwilling to risk scaring her away from the lifestyle. "Are you fucking with me?"

"Yes." Her smile was bright. "We're taking our relationship day by day."

"But you're enjoying yourself." He could see it in the undiluted happiness of her features. She was no longer opposed to the Vault. The realization stung. Why couldn't it have turned out this way for him and Cass? Why did he have to ruin what they could've been?

Because he couldn't help fucking up.

"I'm glad the two of you are working things out." He hadn't been able to do the same with his wife. The guilt was too heavy, the weight of regret a constant punishment. Everything else that followed was like an avalanche burying the happiness he'd once had. "I suppose I better get downstairs and show Leo and Brute I'm not slacking off."

He pushed from the stool and strode to her. "I hope you're right about this masquerade party."

She flashed him a confident smile. "I am."

He followed her down the stairs to the Vault. They passed people in the hall, couples, singles, some dressed in evening attire, others already in lingerie and making their way back into the main part of the club. All of them wore masks to partially or completely hide their faces.

"Hey, Zoe," Shay called out.

Zoe James, one of their regulars, sauntered toward them. "I'm loving this masquerade idea."

She wore a flattering shimmery dress, her sexy attire matching her equally appealing personality. However, it was her companion, the dark-haired woman lingering behind her, that caught his attention.

Her inability to hold his gaze confirmed her club virginity before his focus had a chance to rest on her wristband. The poor woman was distraught, her wringing hands another indication of her anxiety.

If it were any other day, maybe he would've tried to offer support. A welcoming smile or an indication for Shay to show her around. But there was something about her that put him on edge. She was *too* nervous, her gaze lowering almost as if in submission as he scrutinized her.

Did he know her? Something inside him sparked familiarity, yet he couldn't place her features. He usually noticed the blondes. Ones who didn't need to bolster their confidence behind a mask of bright lipstick and dark eye makeup. This woman was a poser. The type to boost her esteem through a fake façade.

So why was he suddenly comparing her features to his wife? *Fuck.* He needed to ditch the matrimonial titles and remember Cassie was destined to be his ex.

A new wave of hurt hit him as he tore his gaze away and massaged his forehead to fight the lingering thoughts. "I gotta get going." He maneuvered around them, not chancing another glance at the woman. "I'll see you all inside."

This was what it had been like all week. All month. Every woman reminded him of Cassie. Every shadow was hers. She was already haunting him, and there was nothing he could do about it. Not that he wanted to rid himself of her presence. The memories, although painful, were also a blessing. Without her, he was nothing.

He entered a four-digit code into the panel at the closed door at the end of the hall and yanked the heavy wood open. Pleasure bombarded him. Not his own, unfortunately. The fulfillment of others surrounded him as he strode through the newbie area and into the main room of Vault of Sin.

He inclined his head at guests, recognizing some and completely oblivious to the identity of others as he maneuvered around patrons. Beds were already in use, their occupants participating in varying degrees of flirtation, foreplay and sex.

Leo was behind the bar, dressed the same as T.J. in a suit and tie—standard attire for Vault staff.

Leo jerked his head in greeting. "I'm glad you came."

"Was there ever any doubt?"

He hated the diminished respect Leo and Brute had tried to hide due to his time off. Since returning, they tiptoed around him, treating him like a casual part of the ownership team instead of an equal partner.

"Maybe a little."

T.J. winced. "Well, I'm here. What do you need me to do?"

"Want to take over helping Travis while I do a walk-around? Brute will be finished assisting security at the door soon. Then I think the two of us should relax and take the night off." A smirk curled the corner of Leo's lips. "You never know, you might find someone willing to occupy your time."

"Yeah, whatever." He ignored yet another hint to move on from his wife. *His ex*. He'd never get used to calling Cassie that.

They didn't understand. If you fell off a bike and skinned your knee, you got straight back on to fight the childish fear. If you shattered your marriage, devastating not only your own life, but also the future of the one person who would forever hold your heart, you didn't slide straight back into the dating pool. You waited for the burn to heal. You waited for the shattered parts of your soul to return from wherever the fuck they'd fled to, so you could finally sleep at night and gain some perspective that wasn't tarnished by the psychotic ramblings of insomnia.

Or maybe you didn't. Maybe you cut and run. How the hell did he know? Was it best to take a shot of cement, harden the hell up and build that damn bridge straightaway? *Fuck*. Nothing made sense. Nothing mattered. There was no longer a paved road toward the perfect future.

He was in limbo.

In the past, sex had always had healing qualities. The rush of release, the boost of endorphins. Hooking up with a random woman and starting the transition could be the best thing for him.

Doubtful.

He was so damn sick of the confusion. The warring emotions. It was bad enough making the decision to leave Cassie in the first place. Moving on seemed harder. Permanent. A divorce only ruined the piece of paper that made them husband and wife. Sleeping with someone else would finalize the process. Never to be rekindled.

He needed to sort his shit out. Now. Before he lost any more respect and entitlement.

So, who was he? The bastard in need of closure? Or the man who'd vowed to forever remain true to Cassie, even after divorce tore them apart?

Hell. He didn't have a clue, but by the end of the night, he had a feeling he would.

CHAPTER FIVE

With shaky hands, Cassie placed her dress in the locker. Her skin was still on fire from the run-in with T.J. in the hall. It may be delusional or wishful thinking, but she could've sworn there'd been a spark of recognition in his eyes. Pain, too.

"Are you meeting anyone here tonight?" Zoe asked. "Maybe your husband…"

Cassie looked down at herself, making sure her slip covered all her important parts. Her breasts had barely fit into the cups, their volume overflowing and creating a mass of cleavage. She didn't have the courage to expose her stomach. The vulnerability of showing her thighs was hard enough with the material barely reaching the bottom of her matching panties. The more skin she covered, the better—for her confidence and T.J.'s inability to recognize her.

"I'm not married." Cassie closed the locker door. She didn't want to go into the details of her failed love life. The less connection she had to T.J., the smaller the chance of getting caught.

Zoe raised her chin and focused on Cassie's hands. "Your rings say otherwise."

"Oh, *shit*." She turned her body away, frantically working the jewelry from her wedding finger. "It's not what you think."

The room filled with silence, the comforting aura Zoe had bathed her in washed away. Cassie worked the rings off and hastened to enter the security pin into the electronic locker keypad before anyone else spied the telling jewelry. "I'm not married," she blurted. "Or I soon won't be."

How could she have forgotten her rings? They'd been a constant symbol of love and affection, more so since T.J. had abandoned her. They were the lifeline she gazed upon for fortitude. One glimpse at the diamonds adorning her finger would've been enough for her husband to recognize her.

"It's not my business." Zoe's voice was low. "If cheating is your thing, so be it. I just think you should know that you'll be booted if the owners find out. They don't need the drama that will arise from a jealous lover."

Cassie closed the locker door again, keeping her palm against the cool metal. "Please..." She didn't know what to ask for. Help? Privacy? A hug? "My husband is meant to be here."

There was no reason to trust this woman. None other than instinct. Yet, Cassie did anyway. There was something in the woman's demeanor. The way she held her head high, her shoulders straight, with comfort shining bright in her eyes.

"My husband *is* here," Cassie repeated, stronger this time. "He wants a divorce, and I'm here to win him back."

Silence.

They were alone in the room, the chattering voices from people in the hall echoing from outside. Cassie glanced to the side and met Zoe's gaze. There was no longer friendship in her features. There was concern. Uncertainty... Pity.

"Do you need help?" she asked, although the pained tone announced she was out of her depth.

"No." Cassie straightened. "All I need is a minute to myself to figure out what the hell I'm doing before I go in there."

Zoe nodded, her brief glimpse of skin above her mask announcing her frown. "If you need someone, please find me. I'm usually in the first private room closest to the parking-lot entrance."

Cassie gave a halfhearted smile in thanks. She was doing this all wrong. She wanted to show T.J. she was strong. Capable. For him, she could be fearless, facing the pain of the past, all for him. *Them.*

Zoe sauntered toward the door and paused inside the frame. "Make sure you find me if you need me." Then she was gone, allowing silence to sink back into the small space.

Cassie rested her back on the locker and let her head clang against the metal. What was she doing? She was half-dressed, in a sex club, hiding under a disguise in an attempt to...what? She could be a voyeur and merely watch to see if he was moving on. Or maybe seduce him, proving he was drawn to her even when her identity was cloaked.

Butterflies crept into her stomach, growing with every second she remained immobile. There'd been nothing to lose by entering the Vault. Apart from her dignity, and that was currently veiled. Nobody needed to know of her desperation to win T.J. back. She needed to stop succumbing to nerves and get this over and done with. She was running out of time and didn't have the luxury to second-guess herself.

She pushed from the lockers and strode for the door. She followed after another couple, thankful they'd remembered the code to get into the main part of the club because she couldn't remember the digits she'd been assigned in her approval letter.

Inside, there were more people than earlier. She passed two softly murmuring couples in the newbie lounge, their conversation unhindered by the large screen of porn playing beside them.

Her scalp itched as she dawdled through the rooms, getting to know her surroundings. People greeted her with smiles, others didn't notice her existence because they were balls-deep in pussy or throat-deep in cock.

One of the private rooms contained numerous pieces of furniture. Almost like a maze of chaises, ottomans and silk-lined single mattresses. Most of which were occupied. There was a mass of mingling bodies, all of them glistening with the slight sheen of pleasure-induced sweat.

The second room was where she found Zoe, caught between two gorgeous men on the bed, aglow from lights in the ceiling. Both males were naked and paying homage to the woman's lingerie-covered body, their attention transfixed. It was another exquisite scene where adoration played a vital role. There was no cockiness. No superiority. The three of them admired one another in scrapes of teeth and gentle swipes of fingers.

"Beautiful, isn't it?"

Cassie glanced over her shoulder to the woman who had greeted Zoe when they'd first arrived—Shay—an employee her husband had spoken about many times.

"Very beautiful." Cassie turned her attention to the main room to shield her face. "In fact, they've made me quite thirsty. Please excuse me while I get a drink."

"No problem."

Cassie walked away, discretely eying T.J.'s employee as she placed distance between them. Sometimes women were more perceptive than men. She didn't want to risk Shay sensing her apprehension and informing management. At least not before she had a chance to speak to her husband.

She entered the main area and came to a halt at the bar, her heart kicking up in pace at the man who sat at the far end. The short wisps of his brown hair hung around his forehead as he sipped from the scotch glass in his hand. He was more familiar than her own body. His image more necessary to her senses than the need to breathe.

From the side, he seemed gaunt. Defeated. The desire to soothe him was painful. But at least he wasn't happy, she supposed. His acceptance of their separation would've hurt more.

She drifted toward him, her feet moving of their own accord, her gaze glued to his frame. The stool beside him was taken, the man in her periphery barely visible because her vision was only attuned to one person. Had only ever been.

"Would you like a seat?" The guy beside T.J. stood, his hand gently clutching hers to guide her forward.

"Thank you." She didn't divert her attention from her husband.

She was so close. Their arms would almost touch if she placed them on the bar. That's all it would take, a brush of skin, a graze of appreciation. He was lost. So was she. But they were side by side and could find their way home together. All she had to do was open her mouth. Start a conversation. Give him hope and love.

She leaned in, her chest pounding the closer she moved, the more potent the scent of his deep, woody aftershave became. Her throat tightened. Memories of the past assailed her. She loved this man so much. It wasn't the typical love found between a man and woman—the jovial smiles and regularly scheduled affection. They were much more than that. Their relationship had been a constant barrage of devotion. Each day growing more intense than the last. Every memory was bathed in happiness that would never be tainted.

She breathed deep of his aftershave, gaining strength from the well-known scent.

"Hi," she murmured.

CHAPTER SIX

T.J. sipped his scotch, unable to lift his game to help out with his own business.

He should be greeting guests, making them feel welcome and at home. Especially when there were more newbies than usual tonight. The party was a success. He just couldn't bring himself to be happy about the influx of fresh patrons.

He missed Cassie. All the more now because he knew it was over. The divorce was in motion, unable to be stopped. At least not by her.

"Hi."

He straightened at the sound of her voice and snapped his gaze to the woman settled on the stool beside him. *Fuck.* The delusions had returned. Not in a vision this time, but her tone.

"Did I startle you?" She edged back, apprehension filling her brown eyes.

"No." His voice was gruff. Unforgiving. "You just sound like someone I know."

Her ruby lips parted, working up and down in a blatant show of unease. What the hell was he thinking? The woman was nothing like his wife. The eyes, framed by a concealing mask, were dark, not the inviting shade of light blue he'd fallen in love with. She had a short, black bob haircut instead of the long locks he'd adored tangling his fingers in. Fuck-me lips that resembled those of his wife, but Cassie's mouth had always been soft and sweet with warm inviting shades, instead of tawdry colors.

"I'm sorry." He focused back on his drink. "I didn't mean to be rude."

The woman cleared her throat. "It's okay."

Her voice was different now, sultrier. Nothing like Cassie's voice. It merely proved his insanity. He needed to move on. To focus on something other than the perfect gift he'd thrown away.

"Do you want a drink?" It was a lame attempt at an apology, but it was the best he could do under the circumstances.

"I'd love one."

"What can I get you?"

"Umm..."

He glanced at her from the corner of his eye. She was biting her lip in an excruciatingly familiar way. He couldn't stop seeing his wife reflected back at him, the way her teeth worked in deep concentration. He needed to get a grip.

"Malibu and lemonade, please."

She met his gaze and her fake eyelashes flickered in an alluring message he chose to ignore.

"Travis?" He jutted his chin at the bartender and waited for the man's attention. "Malibu and lemonade for the lady, and another scotch for me."

"Sure thing." Travis began fixing their order.

"Where's your mask?" the woman uttered. "And why are you still dressed?"

"I'm working." He fought to curb the agitation in his tone. It wasn't her fault he was losing his mind. If someone with completely opposite features to his wife was driving him crazy with recognition, he needed help.

"Doesn't look like it to me."

He followed her gaze to the fresh glass Travis slid into his hand. No, it didn't look like it to him either. But he wouldn't be able to move until he overcame the ache in his chest. Another drink would do it. Maybe two.

"I'm taking a short break."

She smiled, stealing the air from his lungs with her beauty. *Fuck.* What the hell was happening to him? She was his wife. His fantasy. The same bone structure, the same body frame. Yet, everything else didn't align.

"Is this your first time?" *Shit.* He already knew the answer. He'd seen her wristband earlier when she'd been with Zoe.

"Yeah." She raised her arm and showed the red plastic strip around her wrist. "First time here, but not to this type of establishment."

Right. He needed to quit this conversation and put a stop to the hallucinations. His interest in the woman was a betrayal to his marriage—a marriage that would soon be over. He stared straight ahead, his gaze forsaking his brain to go in search of her reflection in the mirror behind the bar. He couldn't look away. There was something about her. Something he recognized yet couldn't put his finger on.

"Would you mind showing me around?"

There was more than one question in her gravel-rich words. But could he take her up on it? Even for a brief moment to innocently show her around?

"Please." She met his stare in the mirror, her sultry lips tilting at the sides. "It's all a bit daunting."

His heart thumped in his chest, and he wasn't sure if it was from apprehension or anticipation. Without thought, he was on his feet, his body moving of its own volition. She was teasing him. Seducing him. And he was powerless under her spell...or maybe his heart just yearned for something other than alcohol to occupy his mind.

She wasn't his type, that was for sure. He'd always preferred blondes. Women that didn't rely on fake nails and the slightly unnatural glow of a salon tan to boost their appeal. She may remind him of Cassie, yet his dick remained true to his wife.

He outstretched a hand, wordlessly asking her to proceed him through the crowd. He fell back, trying to work out what it was that sparked his interest.

"This way?" she asked over her shoulder.

"Yeah." He jerked his head toward the room farthest from the bar. The one that didn't have a crowd hovering around the door. No doubt Zoe was doing her exhibitionist thing in the other private area, putting on a show with her men. "This room will soon be revamped."

At the moment, it was filled with furniture. A heap of different comfortable surfaces to rest upon. Last he'd heard, Leo and Brute wanted to turn it into a room with a more specific agenda. Restraints maybe. Role-play. They'd even spoken of development nights where they could hire people qualified to teach courses on sex and sensuality, even BDSM.

"And what type of things do people do in here?" the woman asked.

He closed his eyes, imagining it was Cassie beside him, her voice so familiar. "Whatever the hell they want, sweetheart. As long as it's consensual."

She stepped closer, the heat from her body thrumming from her in waves. "And what have you done in here?" she cooed.

Not a damn thing. "I watch," he grated. "That's it." He opened his eyes and caught sight of her lips pursed in a conniving smile.

"Would you like to watch *me?*" she whispered.

Fuck. His nostrils flared and a burst of adrenaline shot down his spine. She was a temptation, but more for the need to quash his preoccupation with Cassie than a sexual desire. He wouldn't enjoy her show, no matter what she did. Although his cock did stir at the image. The first sign of interest his dick had given the world in months.

"Not tonight." He eased a hand through her hair, trying to soften the rejection. The coarse texture ran over his palm, nothing like the silky blonde strands he'd spent years filtering his fingers through.

He turned to walk away and then froze when she grabbed his hand. He stiffened, his spine rigid as she came up behind him, hovering at his shoulder. Gentle hands encased his waist, the pleasant slide of her fingertips moved over his stomach, the softness of a womanly body melted against his back. Over the scent of sex and foreplay in the air, he could smell her, not this stranger, but his wife.

She was here. In his head. Under his skin.

"Don't be so quick to walk away." The woman sounded more like Cassie with every heartbeat. "What harm can come from watching?"

CHAPTER SEVEN

Cassie wasn't prone to crazy outbursts. At least she hadn't been. Until now, apparently. She didn't even know what the innuendo in her own words meant. There was no plan. No strategy. Just an invitation to put on a show she didn't have the faintest clue how to perform. The only thing she knew was that she couldn't let him go. His back against her chest was too comforting, and watching him walk away again wasn't an option.

At first, she'd sat next to him at the bar, hoping to witness the level of his suffering. His emotional struggle had been clear to see. But it wasn't enough. She yearned for something else. Something she had no clue of. That's when she'd asked for a tour.

A part of her wanted to be rejected. She already knew her way around. The request was a test. An indicator. She'd held her breath, waiting for him to shoo her away, to show no interest in the appeal of a woman that he didn't know was his wife.

Then he'd caved, too easily, and a part of her heart had shattered. At the same time, the pounding in her chest had intensified, yearning for more of the ferocity in his eyes. She'd became seduced by his proximity. After the months apart, she would kill to have his hands on her. To feel his passion and adoration.

He was hooked.

To her.

He turned in her embrace, his jaw set in a stubborn line. "Let me go."

No. Not now, not ever. She did loosen her grip, though. "Don't newbies get special treatment?" Still, she had no clue where her words were coming from. This wasn't her.

She dug her teeth into her lower lip and batted her fake lashes. "You don't have to touch. You don't even have to speak. Just watch. Your eyes will tell me everything I need to know."

His discomfort gave her confidence. Too much. Because now she was backtracking to the empty single bed, hiding the grief of losing his body heat as she scooted onto the mattress. A feast, not only for his eyes, but for the numerous other patrons in the room.

He was interested in her for one reason—she was his wife. His soul mate. Nobody else here tonight could've evoked interest from him. His attraction was subconscious. She knew it was and wouldn't allow herself to believe otherwise.

She crooked a finger at him and slid farther back. This was crazy. The actions of a love-starved woman. But he was also her husband. She could do insane things for him. Anything for him.

She nestled onto the cushions, parting her thighs while she licked her lower lip in a coy taunt. Her stomach was filled with butterflies. Her heart was pounding in her throat. And despite the nerves, her nipples hardened to painful peaks and the sweet spot between her thighs began to tingle.

T.J. lifted his chin and clenched his hands at his sides once...twice. The internal struggle was etched across his tight features. He was fighting the attraction, denying he wanted another woman. When all along it was his wife he still desired.

Slowly, she raised a hand, trailing it over the material of her slip, along her sternum, her neck, to her lips. T.J. watched the progression, his focus riveted, his hands still clenched. She sucked the finger into her mouth, all the way to the knuckle, and then released it with a pop.

She'd never been so blatant. That had always been his job. He'd taught her everything she knew about sex. His desires had shaped her own. She'd been the young, inexperienced woman about to reach her twenties when T.J. had strode into her life and ruined her for all other men.

He'd taken his time, getting to know her leisurely. Intimately. More thoroughly than she'd known herself. The sex between them had gone from casual to exploratory. By the time they'd married, she'd been willing and eager to try anything and everything.

In the past, the awe in his eyes had given her the confidence to find herself sexually. Right now, that same look gave her the ability to be on a foreign bed, observed by strangers as her finger lowered to the hem of her tiny dress and underneath to the waistband of her panties. She couldn't tear her gaze away from him. Like a hawk, she scrutinized his expression, gaining evidence of his arousal from the flaring of his nostrils and the rapid rise and fall of his chest.

"Do you want a taste?" It was a bittersweet question. Dismissal would bathe her in rejection. Acquiescence would mean he was ready to move on from their marriage. So she was thankful he didn't answer.

Still unsure what she was doing, or why, she continued the charade. She slid her hand under the lace of her underwear, the tingles of awareness igniting all over the newly skimmed flesh. She grazed the rough patch of curls at the apex of her thighs and held her breath as she drowned in the darkness of his eyes. She was on display, alone, confused, yet her body was burning with the need to be sated.

By him. Only him.

Her husband inched forward, his large frame a menacing force at the end of the bed. He was riveted with her, his jaw tight, his hands still clenched, yet those deep irises were enthralled with her alluring display. Hypnotized.

She crept her hand lower, closing her eyes briefly when her fingertips found her clit. The tiny bundle of nerves was throbbing. Begging. Pleading with every rush of blood and pound of her heart to be sated beyond her wildest imagination. Here. In front of all these people.

Pleasure took over, her fingers moved of their own accord as they rubbed back and forth, tearing a gasp from her throat.

"You should stop." His words barely penetrated the pounding heartbeat echoing in her ears. "I need to get back to work."

She quirked a brow when he didn't leave. Rejection would soon be upon her. It was inevitable. But her mask would hide the humiliation. It was already shielding her from the intensity of numerous people who had stopped their own play sessions to see if she would succeed in seducing this glorious man.

With a dramatic sigh, she slid her hand from her panties and crawled toward him. He backtracked, cautiously leaving space between them as if she were a predator ready to pounce. The contrasting dynamic was unnerving. T.J. had always been the dominant force. He never backed away. He always inspired the need to please him. The desire to succumb. She thrived on the way her heart, mind and body submitted wholeheartedly to his instructions. Now she was in the lead and wasn't sure what to do with the power.

She stood, allowing a few brief seconds for her jelly legs to strengthen before she sauntered toward him on her heels. Her gaze held his as she approached. The room fell silent, and the pressure of anticipation pressed hard against her skin. There was a breath of space between them when she planted her feet and peered up at him with a coy smile.

"Touch me." Her heart hammered behind her ribs. It was becoming harder to disguise her voice. Everything inside her urged her to stop pretending. To quit hiding.

"I can't." His fierce tone was almost inaudible. "I've gotta go." Again, he didn't move. He held his chin high. His shoulders were broad and eyes intense as he frowned. "I just don't understand."

"Understand what, T.J.?" She raised a hand, her touch almost reaching his cheek when he lifted his arm in a flash and a heavy force gripped her wrist.

"Understand your familiarity," he growled. His gaze narrowed, the softness she'd always seen in the brown depths now harsh and unforgiving. "How do you know my name?"

Oh, heck. Her lips worked as she struggled to figure out her answer, his grip unyielding. "You work here." She managed a fake grin. "The man at the door told me your name."

He jerked back, his eyes clouding with confusion as he released his hold. "I'm...sorry."

"Don't be." She bridged the distance between them again and rested her palms on his hard chest. She missed this expanse of skin. The hard muscle that used to keep her protected at night. "Sometimes attraction can be confusing." She glided her hands higher, over his shoulders, around his neck. "Sometimes it can be clarifying, too, like the world is sending you a sign."

She was going to tell him. As soon as her heart stopped pounding, she was going to remove her wig and prove he would always be attracted to her. "You want me," she whispered.

He sucked in a breath, the rampant beat of his chest echoing into hers as she leaned into him.

"You want me just as bad as I want you." Her stomach was overcome with excitement. With passion. In her mind, she wasn't wearing a mask, or a wig, or fake nails. She was the normal Cassie, whispering words of endearment to a husband who had lost faith. It was just the two of them. No sex club. No witnesses.

She pushed up on the tips of her toes and pressed her mouth against his, kissing love back between them. He stiffened, dropping his hands to her hips. She wasn't sure if he was poised to pull her closer or ready to push her away, but she didn't care. She gripped him tighter as she parted his lips with her tongue, unable to deny herself even a second of his confused acquiescence.

Don't let me go.

She clung to him, kissing him harder, pressing her breasts into him as she reveled in the only physical affection he'd given her in over twelve months. This was her home—in his arms. This was her life—striving for more of his love.

She stepped closer, moving one thigh between his, brushing her pelvis against the thickness of his erection. The comforting feel of his arousal rekindled hope. Their bodies were meant to be like this. Brushing. Touching. Always connected. She tilted her pelvis, rubbing her pubic bone against the hardness of his leg. Her pussy was begging for him. Soaking her panties. Every inch of her wanted to be consumed. She was merely waiting for him to take over. For her husband to find his usual dominance and use it against her.

Her excitement grew, the pleasure inside her morphing into a need more necessary than breath. She loved this man. So much it hurt and healed, all at once. But it was his hands, the relaxation of his grip against her hips, his surrender to the affection, that washed away the desire and filled her with nauseating clarity.

She was kissing her husband. Reuniting passion. Yet *he* was kissing a stranger. Extinguishing the memory of their marriage and moving on.

The truth filled her with agony. Their connection becoming bittersweet.

With every brush of his tongue, he was leaving her. And she'd been the one to help him take the first step.

CHAPTER EIGHT

T.J. closed his eyes at the taste of her lips. It was like coming home, her mouth achingly familiar and yet punishingly different. This woman kissed like Cassie, with slow sweeps of her tongue and tiny whimpers of yearning.

He sank into the well-known sensation. Devouring it. Savoring her taste, her essence. Even breathing deep of the perfume he remembered she loved so much. It was his wife. He was kissing Cassie. At least that's what he imagined he was doing.

His tongue tangled with hers, unable to get enough. No longer willing to hold back. He gave her everything he had. He showed his devotion with the trail of his hands over her back. He displayed his attraction by the grinding of his erection against her abdomen.

He was delirious with the need to have her again. Just one more night. One more kiss before the divorce was final.

"T.J.," she whispered into his mouth.

"Cassie."

She stiffened at the name. *Hell.* This wasn't his wife—his love. This was no one. A stranger. Some stray woman who'd dissolved his commitment to his marriage with barely a blink of her fake lashes. He stumbled back, his lips burning, his chest hollow.

What the fuck had happened?

One minute he'd been at the bar drowning his sorrows, the next he was betraying everything he held dear. It didn't make sense. This woman, although not his type, could have any man. Yet she'd come to him.

"Why did they tell you my name?" His voice was accusatory. "Why would anyone tell you who I was?"

Leo had admitted earlier they weren't sure he was going to show up tonight. They thought he was fragile. Incapable of working. So why would they point him out to new members? Why would they try penetrating his grief bubble unless they were attempting to burst it?

She stepped into him, her palm landing on his clothed chest, scorching the skin underneath. "You intrigued me. From the moment I walked in, I wanted to get to know you."

Liar. He'd acted like a drunken bum all night—sitting at the bar, sulking into a glass of scotch. Unless she was a glutton for rejection, she was hiding something. And he was certain he knew what it was.

They'd set him up—Leo, Brute, Shay. There was no other reason for her to know who he was. His business partners—his *friends*—had gone against his wishes and calculated a plan to get his mind off the divorce and his body craving the addictive release of sex.

They had no right to do this to him. He hadn't consciously made the choice to find another lover. Moving on had turned into a mess of indecision that had been taken out of his hands. The last thing he wanted was to hurt Cassie. But he just had. Even if she never found out.

He grazed a rough hand over his lips, wiping away the woman's taste. The guilt of betrayal weighed on his shoulders as anger built in his chest. Tonight was a mistake. He couldn't move on. At least not now. Not until the divorce was final. Maybe longer—weeks, months. Hell, if he didn't kiss another woman in the years to come, it'd be too soon.

"You don't think I know what you're up to?" he seethed. Somewhere, deep down, he knew it wasn't her fault. He'd succumbed on his own. Had become too entangled in delusions and the need for comfort that he'd strayed. "I know exactly why you're here. And let me tell you, honey, it ain't gonna work. You need to leave."

This wasn't Cassie. She was nothing like the woman he loved with her cheap nails and tawdry red lips. *Jesus.* He rubbed the back of his neck and struggled for calm. He wanted to vomit. To fall to his knees and never get up. At least not until the bitterness washed away.

The woman's cheeks paled, her eyes widening in horror. "But...T.J."

There she went with his name again.

"You don't think I worked it out?" His voice grew louder, the anger seeping through his words. "That I don't know who you are?" He still wasn't sure if she was a paid escort or an interested clubber with the desire for a challenge, but she was playing him nonetheless. That was enough for him. "Leave before I get security to kick you out."

She stepped away from him, as if finally realizing she'd been caught in her little game of lies. "But...I..." Her focus flew to the door, to the crowd of people gathering.

"Tanya?" Zoe pushed through the bodies crowding the entrance to the room, followed close behind by Shay. "What's going on?"

Tanya. He'd never forget that name, or the rage it solicited. "Get her out of here." Their hovering presence only cemented the betrayal. He wouldn't be surprised if they'd been watching, waiting for the deed to be done.

He shot the woman a glare, letting his disgust become evident before turning to Shay. "I don't want to see her down here again." The crowd parted as he stormed forward, coming face-to-face with Brute.

"You causing trouble?" His friend's voice was a threat.

T.J. shouldered past him, seething as he headed for the bathroom. He was in mourning. Senseless from stupidity. If he didn't find space to be alone, he'd lose himself.

His footsteps echoed in his ears as he bypassed the small crowd of underwear-clad patrons and made his way into the next private room. Zoe's companions were on the bed, both their faces filled with concern as T.J. continued forward, shoving past the bathroom door and into the calm, cool silence.

He had a few seconds, barely even time to take a deep breath or utter a greeting to the two men at the sink, before Brute stormed into the small space, followed by Leo.

"*Out.*" Brute jerked a thumb over his shoulder, not sparing their paying customers any pleasantries in his request for privacy. "If you stand watch at the door, I'll comp your next entrance fee."

The men nodded, wordlessly leaving the room, the door swinging shut behind them.

The bathroom became quiet, allowing the pounding in T.J.'s head to grow louder. Deafening. His business was meant to be where his future lay. It was meant to be the distraction from the agony. The solace from the guilt.

"Care to explain?" Leo crossed his arms over his chest.

T.J. gave a derisive laugh and strode for the basin counter. He clutched the cold marble in his hands, letting his head fall. Breath after breath soaked his lungs, as he tried to wipe the memory of the kiss from his mind and the burn still marring his lips.

"You'd want to start talking." Brute's tone was lethal. "You fucked up in front of paying clients. You better have a good reason."

T.J. closed his eyes. Was this the end? Not only of his marriage, but his friendship with Leo and Brute? They'd crossed the line. He wasn't sure if he could come back from that. There was no trust. No understanding. *Fuck.* He was losing his mind.

"I was already getting sick to death of your moping," Brute continued. "But I won't stand for outbursts in the club. And I sure as hell won't allow you to upset patrons."

T.J.'s vision darkened and his knuckles pulsed to the point of pain, his grip tightening against the counter. "I don't care how sick of my moping you are—" he swung around, his chest heaving, "—you don't pay a fucking hooker in the hopes I'll miraculously get over my wife."

Brute didn't retreat, didn't show any sign of concern. The only reaction he gave was the contortion of his features that transformed into a look of incredulity. "What the hell are you talking about?"

T.J. clenched his jaw and spoke through gritted teeth. "Don't patronize me. Did you really think I wouldn't work it out? That I was that stupid?"

Brute gave Leo a questioning look. "Do you know what he's rambling about?"

Leo shook his head. "I'm lost."

"That woman," T.J. sneered. "The one you paid to seduce me. You'll be happy to know she did her job. Although, maybe not to the extent you wanted."

"Paid?" Leo ran a hand through his loose hair. "Why would we pay someone to fuck you when half the women down here would happily do it for free?"

Semantics. "The woman you propositioned then." The perplexed way they blinked back at him drove his anger to new heights. He didn't expect Brute to understand how momentous their betrayal was. The guy had a heart for one reason, and it had nothing to do with emotion and everything to do with blood flow. But Leo was different. He understood love and the inability to control it.

"I'm still clueless." Leo shrugged.

T.J. closed his eyes and leaned back against the counter, trying to stop the room from spinning. This didn't add up. Brute was a heartless asshole. Most importantly, he was an *honest* heartless asshole. He wouldn't continue with a charade this long.

"There was a woman," he grated. "She wanted to sleep with me."

Brute's laugh was harsh. Humorless. "Man, you're so far outta the game you have no clue."

T.J. opened his eyes, glaring. "What does that mean?"

"A woman wanted to fuck you and you blame me?" Brute scoffed. "Jesus. Do you think I give a shit about your sex life?"

"So, you deny having anything to do with it?" He straightened and pinned Brute and then Leo with a stare. "It must've been Shay. Your girlfriend is poking her nose where it doesn't belong."

"No, she isn't." Leo squared his shoulders and stepped forward. "Apart from holding an unfavorable amount of concern for you, she hasn't done anything wrong."

"Even if one of us did, what's the big deal?" Brute stepped forward, scowling. "You're single."

Single in title only. His heart was still taken. His soul, too.

"Forget it." He was stupid to think they'd understand. Neither of them had a clue what it was like to love unequivocally. Undeniably. They were virgins when it came to devotion.

"No." Brute loomed closer, his emotionless façade faltering under the anger in his eyes. "You've caused a shit fight out there and I want to know why."

"Get outta my face." T.J. shoved Brute's chest, unwilling to be the stand-up guy this time. They'd pushed his kindness too far. He was entitled to his own slice of brutality.

Brute's eyes widened with the assault, then in a blink, the shock disappeared, replaced with fury. He lunged forward, swinging T.J. around until his back was up against the wall with a tight hand around his throat. "Answer me."

T.J. smirked, itching for a fight. They'd never expect it from him. He was the level-headed neutral party. He broke up brawls and dissolved arguments. He was the damn A-class citizen who made up for his dirty proclivities by being a stand-up guy, every single day of his goddamn life.

Not tonight.

"*Brute*," Leo warned.

"Answer me."

The hand around T.J.'s neck tightened and he enjoyed the panic that cleared his mind of heartache. "Go to hell."

Brute gave a feral smile. "I've been there for years, my friend. It's nice for you to finally come for a visit."

The tight grip loosened, allowing T.J. to rest his head against the cool tile. Life was never meant to be this hard. He'd been kind to everyone—his friends, his staff, his family. He was the gentleman. The comforter. He didn't deserve this. He was sacrificing his marriage for Cassie's happiness after all. This was for her future.

"I still fucking love her, okay?" He didn't move. Didn't open his eyes. He couldn't. "I don't want to live without her. I never did. But it's the only option. For her sake, I have to give her up."

"Why?" Brute's tone was murderous as his hand fell away.

"It's a long story."

"We've got time," Brute grated through clenched teeth.

T.J. released the air tightening his lungs, hoping it would lessen the pain in his chest. "Because love isn't a good enough reason to destroy someone." He opened his eyes and wished the two men staring back at him with curiosity could understand. "And that's exactly what will happen if we stay together."

CHAPTER NINE

Cassie was trembling—her arms, her legs, her chest. She couldn't breathe. Everyone was staring at her, their pity shrouding her like a dirty blanket as T.J. stormed from the room.

She hung her head and covered her face with her hands, fighting back the need to cry.

"Come with me."

A feminine hand came to rest on Cassie's back and she raised her gaze to find Shay standing beside her.

"It's going to be okay." Zoe approached. "We'll sort this out."

No. She shook her head. It wouldn't be okay. It wouldn't get sorted out. T.J. had made it perfectly clear he no longer wanted her. He'd seen through her disguise, humiliated her and demanded she leave.

"Trust me." Shay placed pressure on Cassie's back, guiding her forward. "Let's go upstairs where it's quiet."

All Cassie wanted to do was go home. But her house was filled with loneliness and despair. There was nobody there to comfort her. With a silent nod, she allowed them to lead her into the main room, bypassing the curious stares of patrons and straight past the secured door. The change rooms were a blur. The staircase upstairs was taken with no memory at all. They reached the deserted Shot of Sin bar and wordlessly guided her onto a stool.

"Do you want to talk about it?" Zoe asked, rubbing her warm palm in circles over the nakedness of Cassie's upper back.

"Come on, honey." Shay slid a glass of water over the bar, the swatch of lace over her eyes still perfectly in place. "You can tell us."

The burn of humiliation heated Cassie's cheeks. These were the last people she should tell. The thought of even explaining to Jan when she got home stung more than she could bear.

"I know I don't look suitably dressed," Shay continued. "But I've worked here for a while. I'm sure whatever happened with T.J. was a misunderstanding. Usually, he's a really nice guy. He's just going through a rough patch at the moment."

Rough patch? It was demeaning that the destruction of Cassie's marriage could be described in such simple terms. "I know." She met the sympathy in the bartender's expression. "I also know who you are, Shay."

The woman frowned and ceased pouring the glass of wine she'd been preparing. "I'm sorry," she spoke with a cautionary tone and slipped the strip of lace covering her eyes to her forehead, scrutinizing Cassie, "but I can't place your face under the disguise."

"We've never actually met." Cassie grasped the bottom of her mask and sighed as she lifted the covering from her face. She shouldn't be doing this. These were T.J.'s friends. *His* support network. Not hers.

"I've heard a lot about you through my husband." She raised the mask over her head and met the bartenders gaze. "I'm T.J.'s wife, Cassie."

Shay's eyes widened, but it was Zoe's gasp that made Cassie swivel on her stool. "I'm sorry I lied about my name. I didn't want to risk being thrown out."

Zoe shook her head, her lips gaping. "I'm not offended. I'm shocked T.J.'s married. He's never made it known to guests. I always assumed he was single."

He hadn't made his marriage known. In a sex club, surrounded by women and men grasping for carnality and pleasure, he hadn't told the members he was taken. Nobody knew of their love. Why did that knowledge fill her with horror?

"Don't panic." Zoe reached out a hand and squeezed Cassie's shoulder. "I've never seen him with anyone. I rarely see him downstairs at all. It was merely an assumption."

Cassie played with the elastic band on her mask, occupying her hands because she had no control over her mind.

"I didn't know until recently either," Shay added. "I think he's far too much of a gentleman to share his personal details in a work environment."

Yes, maybe that was it. He'd admitted long ago that he didn't want her being a part of the sex club. Not until they had measures in place to safeguard the identity of everyone involved.

"He's protective." Cassie lowered her gaze to her lap, threading the elastic through her fingers. "I used to attend work functions years ago. But once they started chatting about opening Vault of Sin, T.J. wanted me as far away from the business as possible. He didn't want to risk my involvement if the privacy of the club was ever breached."

"Hold up." Shay leaned forward, into Cassie's periphery. "If he's so protective, why did he let you in tonight? What was the fight about?"

Cassie met the woman's gaze with a wince. "He didn't let me in. I used a fake ID."

"Oh, shit. Brute is gonna be pissed that you slipped past him."

"Not as pissed as T.J. was when he found out he was kissing his wife instead of a stranger."

Shay's mouth gaped. "He didn't know?"

Cassie shook her head and grabbed the front of her hairpiece. "I went to a lot of effort to make myself unrecognizable." She pulled the wig off her head and placed it on the bar. "I'm blonde." She mussed her hair, trying to form some semblance of normality from the plastered-down strands she could see in the mirror behind the bar. "Everything about me is different. Apart from the weight. Although, I have dropped a dress size since my husband informed me of the divorce."

"Was this retaliation?" Zoe asked, sliding onto a stool.

"God, no."

"Then what?" Zoe's tone was gentle, the soft lilt filled with comfort and concern. "Why turn up at his sex club and pretend you're someone else?"

"Because I love him." Cassie hung her head. "I don't want a divorce, and with every part of me, I know T.J. doesn't either."

"Then why would he request it?"

"It's complicated." She gave a derisive laugh. "Yet simplistic, too. We both made a mistake that he takes full credit for. He thinks he let me down. He's too defensive when it comes to my wellbeing."

"Okay." Shay cleared her throat. "You're going to have to go into more depth than that. I need deets."

Tension built in Cassie's chest, the need to bare her soul itched to break free. Nobody in her day-to-day life would understand. These women were the closest she would get to a knowledgeable sounding board, and she needed to rid herself of the guilt from the past. "My marriage with T.J. was nothing but flawless—"

"Really?" Shay drawled in disbelief.

"Let me finish. We rarely fought. We meshed perfectly. He gave me everything I needed from a lover and a friend, and I tried to give him the same in return." The women were staring at her, clinging to her every word. "I learned a lot about myself because of him. Sexually speaking, I mean."

She cleared the discomfort from her throat. "As a new couple, we tried everything and anything. As time went on, we began pushing boundaries. I had limited experience when we first met, and T.J. opened my eyes to the possibilities. He made me feel comfortable fantasizing about things that aren't society's standard of normal."

"Like?"

Cassie shrugged. "It started off simple, with sex toys and classy porn."

"Classy porn?" Zoe raised a brow, a smile brightening her features. "Is that even a thing?"

"Well, there's dirty porn and there's the stuff with the faintest hint of a romantic storyline. Neither have good acting."

Zoe chuckled. "Okay. Carry on."

"That evolved into light BDSM, but apart from T.J.'s usual dominance, it wasn't our scene. We started talking about other topics like voyeurism and exhibitionism. It was around the same time the Vault was being discussed as a possible form of revenue for the business." Cassie waved the conversation away. "I'm rambling. You guys don't want to hear all this."

"Of course we do." Shay grabbed a bottle of wine from the fridge underneath the far side of the bar. "I'll even provide refreshments."

The verbal purge didn't seem to be lessening the tight hold on Cassie's heart. It wasn't helping. Yet neither would going home to a lonely house. "To cut a long story relatively short, the reason T.J. is leaving me is because we decided to go to our first sex club about a year ago. It was out of the blue. Unplanned. In fact, we were out of town, staying in Brute's Tampa apartment. In Florida, people are open to much more than they are here. So, we went to a club on a whim... The worst whim of my life."

"You didn't like it?" Shay paused in the middle of pouring the first of three wine glasses on the bar.

"I don't think the first time is ever easy," Zoe added. "Even more so when you're in an established relationship and have to consider the possibility of how it could affect your future together."

"It was a disaster." Cassie sucked in a breath, held it until the pain took over the nerves in her belly, then released it in a rush. "It was the biggest mistake of my life."

Shay cringed. "It's not for everyone. Hell, even I was disgusted to begin with."

"That wasn't the half of it." She wrung her hands together in her lap, wiping the sweat from her palms. "For starters, I'd glamorized the thought of a sex club. I anticipated seduction and passion. Fine furnishings and men who cherished their women like T.J. cherished me. The place we went to was cold, dank and sleazy."

"That's not good." Shay slid a glass of wine toward Cassie and another in front of Zoe.

"T.J. wanted to leave straightaway. I could sense his annoyance. But the surprising conditions didn't curb my curiosity. We were out of town, finally in a place where I wouldn't feel nervous about my friends and family finding out about our sexual tendencies." Cassie placed the mask on the bar beside the wig and grabbed for the wine glass. "We'd been talking about going to a club for so long...work had already started on the Vault. And even though the scene was far from erotic, I wanted to understand what a sex club was all about. There had to be a reason why women were there, right? So, I begged T.J. to hang around, just for one drink."

She sipped her wine, the sweet taste exploding over her tongue in complete contrast to the liquid she remembered consuming that night in Tampa. The bartender—dressed in a frayed wife-beater and ill-fitting silk boxers—had leered at her as he handed over the soda glass filled with cheap wine. He was just one of many men who'd eyed her like a dish they were determined to taste.

"T.J. didn't drink. He stayed at my side, his hand always protectively placed on my hip as we watched men rut like dogs in heat. There was no seduction. No interest in pleasuring anyone but themselves. The women were merely a vessel to be used."

"Drugged?" Shay asked.

Zoe swiveled in the stool, her knee grazing Cassie's thigh. "Paid escorts, I'd assume."

"Yeah." Cassie gave Zoe a nod. "Apparently, it's not uncommon. T.J. had murmured in my ear that some clubs who can't obtain willing female clientele actually pay escorts to attend. So, in retrospect, I was like the rainbow unicorn—the one willing female who had turned up to this sleazy place without monetary compensation." She shrugged off the stupidity, because she hadn't even broached the worst part. "I made a vain attempt to salvage the night. I ignored our surroundings and tried my hardest to feel sexy as I stripped to my underwear. But my halfhearted attempt to get T.J. in the mood didn't work."

The humiliation of going down on a husband that couldn't get hard was just as potent as how naïve she'd felt walking into an environment she had no right being in. "After twenty minutes inside that place, I'd lost all hope of exploring this part of our sexuality."

"Oh, sweetie." Zoe placed a hand on Cassie's shoulder. "You can't judge the lifestyle by one seedy club."

Cassie ran her finger mindlessly through the ring of condensation left on the bar from her glass. Time hadn't dimmed the memory of that night. It was the first regretful moment of her married life. One that had sparked a continuous tally of devastation.

"It gets worse," she uttered. "Our apartment was a half-hour drive away, so I decided to use the bathroom before we left. T.J. did the same. It was the first time he'd strayed from my side, and he wasn't happy about it either. He told me he'd be waiting right outside the bathroom door once he finished, and that I shouldn't speak to anyone while we were separated."

She stared at the polished bar, seeing the memory replay in her mind. T.J. had been pale with concern, extinguishing the adrenaline in her veins and replacing it with fear. He'd clutched her biceps, reiterating that she wasn't to speak to anyone. Not even the women.

She'd nodded, and done as he requested, entering the empty bathroom and using the facilities as quickly as possible. She'd been poised to flush the toilet when the swing of the bathroom door had announced someone else had entered. As she'd clutched her handbag to her waist, she'd opened the stall door, prepared to keep her head low while she washed her hands and then get straight back to T.J.'s side.

"A man followed me into the bathroom." He'd been one of the younger men, somewhere in his late twenties, she guessed. Tall and scrawny with the glaze of a drug-fueled high in his eyes. "At first, I thought maybe he was disoriented. That he'd picked the wrong bathroom. But he showed no shock at seeing me walk from the stall. He'd known I was in there."

The recollection was vivid. He'd had oily blond hair and a sharp, bird-like nose. His eyes had been devoid of emotion, light blue and feral. There'd been no defining scars, only a permanent frown on his forehead. But his boxer briefs were what she remembered most. Probably because the image of his erection pressing against the crotch still made nausea creep up her throat.

"I smiled, somewhat nervously, as I approached the basin to wash my hands. I joked about him being in the wrong bathroom. Although something inside me was screaming to run, I didn't want to act like a fool in case he'd made a genuine mistake." Her ears filled with silence, her mind consumed with memories. "He made no move to leave. Instead, he approached me. And again, I did nothing. I kept denying what was clearly happening. I didn't think that a man would ever try to hurt me in a public place with my husband in the bathroom next door."

It had been too blatant to be real. Nobody could be that stupid. But apparently, she had been. "He started talking, his words slurred as he asked what my plans were for the night. He wanted to know why I was there. If I was unsatisfied with my current lover since it was obvious T.J. wasn't in the mood."

She'd washed her hands, tracking him in the mirror as he continued to approach. "He'd been watching us. *Me.* And my pathetic attempts to try and go down on T.J." It made her feel dirty, but there still hadn't been any confirmed threat, nothing apart from intuition screaming at her to leave. "I assured him I was there out of curiosity, and that I'd decided this was no longer a lifestyle choice I was interested in. I began to walk for the door when he stepped in front of me, blocking my path."

He'd seemed to ponder her words as his gaze raked her body in a way she'd never experienced before. He was sizing her up, determining something she couldn't or didn't want to understand. "I didn't want to scream. I had already started blaming myself. If I hadn't gone there, this man wouldn't have had the wrong impression of me. He thought I was an easy lay, and I wasn't. I tried to talk him down, assuring him I wouldn't be going back into the main room."

His eyes had been vacant, icy-blue irises that reflected an empty soul. The first step he'd taken toward her had made her realize she needed to act. It finally sank in. He was a threat and she needed to get out of there. "I'm not interested." She'd raised her chin and glared at him as her head had begun to pound with too many thoughts to comprehend what to do. Did she try to hurt him? Did she run? Was T.J. right outside the door like he'd promised, or had something happened to him too? "I'll scream."

"Hey." Zoe's hand came to rest on Cassie's back again, rubbing in soothing circles. "You're safe now."

Cassie tried to shake away the nightmare, but he kept approaching. "It didn't go much further." She didn't want to relive the way his hand had lashed out, climbing under her loose skirt to tear away her G-string before she could scream. "I called for help, and T.J. was there in an instant. My husband was unrecognizable, his expression contorted in anguish and rage as he threw the guy to the floor and started pounding his fists into the man's face. Again and again and again. More people entered the room as the bastard on the floor stopped fighting back."

Cassie met the distraught features of each woman in turn, both of them riveted by her story. "They had to drag T.J. off him." He'd been rabid. Crazed. "He was yelling as they hauled him from the building. His voice was so loud, demanding they let go, shouting for them to get their hands off me as they yanked me along after him. Their greedy palms touching me in places I wish I could forget."

She didn't remember how they arrived back at the apartment, and the memories after that were like photographs. Snapshots. She'd sat on the shower floor, hugging her knees to her chest as the water cascaded over her body. The darkness of the room as she lay in bed, while the sound of T.J. vomiting carried from the bathroom. The muted plane ride home. And the silence they'd both shared for the weeks that followed.

"He wanted to call the police. That night, he even drove to a nearby police station. But I couldn't do it." She squeezed her eyes shut briefly. "There were too many reasons to keep my mouth shut. I'd placed myself in that position. I'd been stupid. I know it doesn't excuse what happened. I just couldn't risk public scrutiny either. My family would've been devastated. I would've lost my job or been pressured to quit from the nastiness of others. But the determining factor was Vault of Sin. T.J., Leo and Brute are loyal men. I didn't want them to contemplate abandoning their plans for the private part of the club to spare my dignity. So, I told T.J. I didn't want anyone knowing. Not the police, not family and definitely not our business partners."

They'd never discussed what happened with anyone. T.J. had barely mentioned the night in the last twelve months. Yet, she refused to feel guilty about opening her mouth now. If it meant saving her marriage, she'd disclose every last detail, her pride and reputation be damned.

"That asshole deserves to be shot," Shay seethed.

Cassie inclined her head. "Yeah. It wasn't the best experience I've ever had. Then again, I was lucky T.J. saved me. It just wasn't enough for him. He blames himself, and I think what happened destroyed him more than me. I never truly got him back after that night."

He hadn't been able to look at her for weeks. He couldn't touch her without his eyes glazing as he lost himself to hindsight. In his mind, the blame over not researching the club rested solely on his shoulders, with him unwilling to let her take any responsibility. He considered it his own weakness for succumbing to the temptation of exposing her to something new. He thrived on broadening her sex life and wouldn't forgive himself for rushing in unprepared.

"A month passed before he started sleeping on the couch, claiming he didn't want to keep me awake with his restlessness. That night turned into every night until I started noticing the spare bed was being slept in. Six months later, he moved out."

"I need to clear my head. Just a few days. Maybe a week."

He'd been exceptionally agitated the day he'd walked from their home. As if the months of guilt had collided, and she'd had no desire to hurt him more by making him stay.

"I don't know what to say," Shay whispered.

Cassie met her gaze and winced at the sorrow shining back at her. "There's nothing *to* say. I didn't want to believe he was serious about the divorce, but after tonight, I think it's clear he can't get over the past. He's never looked at me in anger before."

She sipped her wine, uncomfortable in the silence with these women who were practically strangers. The chatter of people in the distance was all she could hear until footsteps echoed up the Vault staircase, the pounding getting louder.

"Quick," Shay blurted. "Put the wig back on. The mask, too."

Cassie's heart throttled to high speed. Although T.J. knew she was here, she didn't want anyone else to find out.

As Shay straightened and Zoe turned to face the stairway, Cassie hitched the fake hair back into position and slid the mask into place. She was still straightening the stray strands of hair sticking out at odd angles when the footsteps stopped.

"Ladies." Leo's honeyed tone filled her belly with nerves. "There seems to be a misunderstanding that I need to get to the bottom of." The pounding of his shoes against the floor sounded again, getting closer and closer. "T.J. is under the impression someone paid an escort to seduce him."

What? Cassie's gaze snapped to Shay, hoping to gain some understanding while she kept her back to her business partner.

"I thought you said he knew you were here," Zoe muttered under her breath.

He did. T.J. had whispered her name as they'd kissed. Right before he'd demanded she leave.

"Shay." The name was a deeply masculine growl. "Please tell me you don't know anything about this. I assured T.J. my adorably sweet girlfriend wouldn't be stupid enough to risk her job by getting involved."

Shay released a nervous chuckle. "Honey, you say the nicest things, but your tone implies you don't think I'm that sweet."

"Yeah," he grated. "I should work on that."

Shay strode around the bar and sauntered toward Leo. Cassie swiveled in her stool, keeping her face shadowed by her hair as Shay stopped in front of her boyfriend and leaned to whisper something in his ear.

As the faint hint of her words drifted forward, Leo's scrutinizing gaze snapped to Cassie. His frown deepened, the wrinkles increasing with each passing second until Shay stepped back.

"What's going on here?" Leo approached, shoving his hands in his pockets in a vain attempt to appear nonchalant.

Zoe scooted to the side of her stool, turning her knees into Cassie. "If you want to leave right now, no questions asked, just tell me. I'll escort you out. You don't need to speak to him. We can go somewhere else and talk about this."

We. Such a simple word, yet the friendship behind it brought an explosion of warmth through Cassie's body. "Thank you, but I think he deserves to know why I caused the scene downstairs."

Zoe inclined her head. "It's up to you."

Cassie removed her mask and checked her reflection in the mirror across the bar. There wouldn't be any beauty awards heading her way in the near future, and even without the mask, she was still barely recognizable.

She pushed from the stool and straightened her shoulders as she faced Leo, a man she'd met numerous times but didn't claim to know well enough to anticipate how he'd react. She gave him a sad smile and pulled off her wig, exposing the blonde hair beneath.

He squinted at her, his gaze raking her face, then lower, all the way to her high-heel-covered toes.

"Fake nails." She placed the wig on the bar and wiggled her fingers. "Fake tan." She indicated her body with a wave of her hand. "Contact lenses." She pointed to her eyes. "All of it's fake."

"Oh, shit." His voice was barely audible. "Cassie? Is that really you?"

She gave a regretful nod. "Hi, Leo."

"*Jesus Christ.*" He massaged his forehead and began to pace. "I need to tell him."

"No." Cassie scooted forward, her heels tapping frantically along the floor. "Wait." She grabbed his arm as he turned to leave. "What did you mean when you said T.J. thinks someone paid an escort?"

"I mean exactly that, Cass. He's down there, almost coming to blows with Brute because he thinks the woman he was making out with was a hooker."

Cassie shook her head. "He said my name. He knew it was me."

Leo peered down at her, seeming to read her thoughts when she couldn't even understand them herself. "You can interpret it however you like, but he's down there thinking he cheated on his wife. He has no clue you're here."

"He doesn't?" She felt like a parrot, repeating the words in her head over and over again. But if he didn't know she was here, why had he said her name? "He must have been thinking about me." A smile tilted her lips. A weak, almost useless smile that filled her aching heart with hope.

Then whiplash had her straightening. He may have been *thinking* about her. However, to his knowledge, he'd been kissing someone else. He'd cheated on her...*with* her.

"Cassie, I'm sorry, I know you're hurting." Leo stroked her cheek with his knuckles. "But you have to leave. I can't be a part of this, not only because he's my business partner. He's my friend above all else."

"And he's my husband." She swallowed over the dryness in her throat and dropped her hold on his arm. "I'll do anything to get him back."

"We'll figure out another plan together," Shay offered.

"Shay," Leo warned. "I don't want to hear this."

"Then run along, sweetheart."

His ocean-blue irises darkened with contempt. "You don't understand. T.J. is going out of his mind. He's beside himself. I've never seen him so distraught."

"That can only work in Cassie's favor." The sound of Zoe's footsteps approached. "If there's still emotional attachment, surely there has to be a way to stop the divorce."

"You both need to stay out of it," Leo grated. "We won't stand for drama in the club. No matter who's involved. Tonight has been bad enough. The only saving grace for you, Cass, is that he has no clue it was you."

Drama hadn't been her intent. She hadn't even planned to seduce him. That was a bonus. One that would've kicked her in the balls if she had any. "I'm sorry for the stress I caused. I just can't let him go. I know he still loves me."

Leo inclined his head. "I know that, too."

Wait. What? "You do?"

"Yes." His tone was comforting even though a scowl creased his forehead. "You don't understand what's going on downstairs. I've just spent the last ten minutes holed up in the bathroom with him. He's spilling secrets and losing his shit. It's obvious he loves you."

This was the first true glimmer of hope. Doubt had started to whittle away the certainty of T.J.'s affection. Now her confidence was renewed. "He told you about the other club." It wasn't a question. She could see understanding in his eyes.

He nodded and gave her a somber smile. "He mentioned it. Among other things. And to be honest, I understand his reasons for the divorce. Maybe it's for the best."

The meager glimpse of hope shattered, leaving her chest hollow. It wasn't Leo's words. It was the pity in his expression. The complete lack of belief for any happiness in her future.

"How?" Shay accused. "One bad decision shouldn't end a marriage. How could he leave her after what had happened? If anything, he should be ashamed for not sticking by her. He'd walked out when she needed him the most."

Leo inclined his head. "He has a lot of regret. But this isn't about one mistake. There are ongoing issues that led to his decision."

"Ongoing issues?" Cassie reached out a hand, needing grounding, needing something. Anything. Then she let her arm fall back to her side. "Tell me. If there's more, I deserve to know."

"I'm not willing to get involved. Not any more than I already have." He held up his hands in surrender. "I won't."

Searing pain seeped into Cassie's heart. The harder she pushed for answers, the less clarity came. There couldn't be more reasons to the divorce. She refused to believe that. They'd been happy. Hadn't they? Or had she taken steps along the contented path on her own?

"Well, maybe there are things I'm no longer willing to do for you either," Shay cooed.

Leo turned to his girlfriend, hitting her with a confident stare that spoke of his disbelief. "You need to stay out of it."

Shay crossed her arms over her chest. "While I'm staying out of it, there's something you'll be staying out of, too." A feral smirk tilted her lips. "My pussy."

"Thanks for the clarification, sweetheart. I wouldn't have figured out what you meant otherwise." He rolled his eyes and turned back to Cassie with a shrug. "Look, this is your life and your marriage. I'm not going to dictate what you should do. But I need to respect T.J.'s decision." He grabbed her hand, kissed her knuckles and released his hold just as quickly. "I hope you can work it out."

He walked away, his heavy steps echoing through the club before he disappeared behind the door leading downstairs.

"So, where do we go from here?" Shay stepped into Cassie's vision, shattering her concentration.

"*We* don't go anywhere." These women were lovely. Without encouragement, they'd befriended her and helped to pick her up after the humiliation downstairs. "Thank you both for being so kind to me. I appreciate it."

It was time to leave. Her mind was filled with fog, her heart torn in two from the emotional blows too numerous to recall. She needed to get home and lick her wounds. To see if she could pick herself back up and return to the battlefield when she now had no clue who or what her enemy was.

"Don't listen to him." Shay waved a hand toward the doorway Leo had fled behind. "Whatever happens, he'll get over it."

"Shay, maybe you *should* stay out of it." Zoe came to stand beside Cassie. "I can help where possible."

"No." Cassie strode for the bar and snatched the wig off the counter. She tugged it back on and stared at her reflection in the mirror, instantly wanting to scratch the itch from her scalp. "Both of you should stay out of it. The last thing I want to do is undermine T.J."

She turned and gave them a fake smile. "I'll be fine."

Zoe approached and helped position the wig back in place. "Do you have a plan?"

Cassie shook her head. She didn't have anything. Apparently, she didn't even have the real reason why T.J. wanted a divorce. "I have determination. And for now, that's all I need."

CHAPTER TEN

Three days later, Cassie was still numb as she drove home from the supermarket. She'd spent every waking moment trying to figure out what could've caused the need for a divorce if it hadn't been the assault in the sex club. There was no answer. Not even a clue. And even worse, she didn't have a plan to win T.J. back either.

At least she was eating again. Her lack of appetite had fallen prey to the need to binge, and she currently had a car full of junk food.

Soon she'd need to accept that her husband wasn't coming back. No matter how much he still loved her. His stubborn streak was going to win, and she was going to end up alone.

She turned onto her street and eased off the accelerator at the sight of an unfamiliar car parked in her driveway. She wasn't prone to fits of apprehension over foreign vehicles, but after T.J. had surprised her with the divorce, she was skeptical of any strangers that came to visit.

Her fingers skimmed the garage clicker and she pressed the button to open the door. As she passed the vehicle to her left, she glimpsed long dark hair. A woman. Great. Maybe today's surprise would be sponsored by a pregnant mistress or jealous girlfriend.

Pulling the car to a stop, she grabbed her handbag and yanked it to her side in a vain attempt for comfort. She fled the vehicle, her chin held high, her limbs heavy from exhaustion. As she pasted a smile on her lips, she came face-to-face with a gorgeous brunette at the trunk of her car.

The woman's features were shaded by the Sinner baseball cap she wore, her loose T-shirt and short shorts exposing an enviable figure.

"Shay?" Cassie squinted into the sun.

"I look different with my clothes on, don't I?" Shay smiled, resurrecting the comforting friendship from Thursday. "So do you."

"What are you doing here?"

"I'm not really here. I'm at the gym." Her smile widened. "I wanted to see how you were feeling after the other night."

Cassie winced through the painful reminder and chose to deflect. "Do you want to come inside for a coffee?"

"Love to."

Cassie ignored the bags of groceries on her backseat and ushered Shay into the house. The woman was gorgeous, her face brighter in the daylight. The gleam of mischief in her eyes sparked an unnerving sense of foreboding.

"What's the plan of attack?" Shay rubbed her hands together and rested back into the dining room chair.

"No plan." Not yet anyway, and she was running out of time. "I thought you weren't meant to get involved."

"It seems I have a problem with authority. Usually, when I'm told not to do something, it makes it impossible for me to stay away. And besides, making Leo angry is a major turn-on."

"Is he the one who told you where I live?" Having Leo on her side would be a step in the right direction. Whatever T.J. was going through, he needed his friends, and if those friends were supporting her endeavors to win him back, it would make her life easier.

"I can't divulge how I came about that information. Let's just say I'd be in a lot of trouble if your husband or my boyfriend found out."

Cassie nodded, trying to hide her disappointment.

"So where are you going from here? I thought I might see you back at the club on Saturday night."

"No. I wasn't interested in making the same mistake twice." She'd tried and failed in her first attempt to get close to her husband. "On Friday, I went in search of legal representative to help fight the divorce. Everyone I called was enthusiastic about taking my money to gain more assets in the settlement, but that's not what I'm after. I want my husband. I want my marriage. Nobody could understand that."

Cassie stared blankly into her coffee, seeing nothing but T.J. in her vision. "The only way I can stop the proceedings is to convince him to change his mind, and I'm no longer confident I can do that."

"Hey." Shay's voice was strong. Firm. Even a little angry. "You can't give up."

Cassie lifted her gaze and was hit with the determination in Shay's fierce brown eyes. "I don't want to give up. But at some point, I'm going to have to. I know he's making a mistake, and one day he'll realize it, too. I'm just not sure how long I'm willing to fight while I wait for him to figure it out. I've lost a year of my life anticipating the return of our perfect marriage." She swallowed over the tightness in her throat. "When am I allowed to give up?"

"Not yet, that's for sure. You need to try harder."

Cassie sighed. "I don't know if I can. It hurts too much." The worst of it came at night, when she was alone in her bed, nothing but blankets to comfort her.

"It'll hurt more once there's no hope. The divorce isn't final yet."

"No, but he kissed someone else. At least that's what he thinks. He's already moving on."

Shay leaned forward, demanding Cassie's full attention. "He's struggling. He won't talk to anyone. Whatever that kiss meant to him wasn't good, I assure you. I think he hates himself for it."

Cassie winced. She didn't want to take pleasure in his suffering, but a tiny part of her did. Something inside her burned to life with the knowledge he was as miserable as she was. "What can I do?"

A sly grin tilted Shay's lips. "You hinted the other night that you owned part of the business. That you were a partner. Is that true?"

Cassie shrugged slowly. "I'm a silent partner. T.J. and I share a third of the business. I kept my own full-time job because we weren't sure the club and restaurant were going to be successful."

"Are you legally required to remain a silent partner?"

"Not that I know of." Cassie drew out her words, uncertain where the conversation was heading. "It was never really discussed. Not between T.J. and I, anyway. I'm not sure what was said to Leo and Brute." A shiver ran down her spine as Shay's lips quirked into a conniving smile. "Why? What are you thinking?"

"T.J. is trying to shut himself off to any thoughts or memories of you. He hates being reminded of his marriage. I'm sure he's striving to get you out of his mind so he can move on."

"Awesome," Cassie drawled. The realization stung. She'd never be able to get him out of her mind. In time, she may be able to dull the hurt with a fling or two, but he would always be in her heart. He'd always be a major part of her life.

"Let me finish." Shay held up a hand. "Being part owner means you can claim your rightful place as a manager of the club. Tell him you no longer want to remain a silent partner. Demand a position within the business."

Cassie shook her head. "I can't. He's left me a substantial amount of assets in the divorce in return for my share. Soon, I'll have no right to be there at all."

"*Soon*. But not yet. The divorce isn't final. You still have a few weeks, right?"

"Yeah…" She refused to count down the days.

"You know, the economy isn't great at the moment. Unemployment is at an all-time high." Shay gave a theatrical gasp and covered a hand over her mouth. "Oh, my gosh, Cass, what would you do if you lost your job? There'd be no choice. You'd have to work with your husband, at least until you found another form of income."

"You want me to quit my job?" No way. No way in hell. She was consumed with the need to fix her marriage, but she wasn't this conniving.

Shay shrugged. "How badly do you want your husband back?"

Her phone trilled from the kitchen counter, announcing an incoming message…or maybe acknowledging a winning idea. She stood and dragged her feet toward the device to cradle it in her palm. "They'll refuse. Not only T.J., Brute and Leo, too. None of them will want me there. They'll fight to make sure I can't step foot inside their club."

"*Your* club," Shay clarified. "And leave Leo to me. I have ways of encouraging his compliance."

Cassie released a halfhearted laugh. "That still leaves two."

"Lucky for us, Brute's heartlessness runs both ways. If he thinks it's in T.J.'s best interest to stay married, he'll support you." Shay rolled her eyes. "Not that he'll go out of his way to show it. I just need to convince him that T.J. doesn't want a divorce. What he really needs is a kick in the ass."

Shay made it sound easy, and maybe, for a woman like her, it would be. Cassie wasn't as prone to making decisions that would hurt or annoy others. It was one thing to push T.J. out of his comfort zone in an effort to win him back. It was entirely another to turn his best friends against him and work her way into their business.

"I don't know..." She unlocked her phone, needing time to think, and held her breath at the sight of T.J.'s name on her screen.

"Can I come over today?"

"What is it?"

Cassie didn't realize she was smiling until she met Shay's gaze. "It's T.J. He wants to come over."

"Why?" Shay frowned.

"I don't know. I guess to talk. Maybe he's changed his mind." That was her first thought, and the one she'd cling to. Her heart was already aflutter, her belly filling with longing.

"Ask him." Shay stood and walked forward. "Don't make assumptions. Especially when the other possibilities could hurt. You need to stay in the game. Remain strong."

Cassie didn't want to think about the potential reasons for the message. She would remain positive. She had to. "So, what do I send back?"

"Give it here." Shay grabbed the phone from Cassie's hand and began typing. "There."

"*Wait.* Don't send anything." She snatched the device back and read the message Shay had already sent. *"Why? I'm kinda busy today and I thought you'd already gotten everything off your chest."*

Jesus Christ. "He'll know that didn't come from me. I've never spoken to him like that before." She wasn't a ballbuster like Shay.

"He needs to know you're not waiting around, spending every minute trying to work out ways to get him back. He's—"

"But I am." The last thing she wanted was for her husband to think she was moving on, giving him more of an excuse to do the same.

"What he doesn't know can only help our cause. Play hardball. If he thinks you're busy, he'll wonder who with. At least until we find out what he wants."

The phone vibrated in her hands seconds before the trill of the incoming message.

"It doesn't need to be today. I only want to pick up my stuff and get it out of your way."

"It's bad, isn't it?" Shay asked.

Bad. Horrifying. Devastating. Cassie swallowed, determined not to let the tingle in her nose turn into tears. "He's ready to move all his belongings out."

His shirts were what got her through the lonely nights. His scent still lingered in the threads. The soft cotton against her skin helped to create the fantasy he was still there. Still in their marriage bed. What would she do without the constant reminders?

"You're right," Cassie murmured. "I need to play dirty. At least until this is over."

"So, you're going to come to work at Shot of Sin."

Cassie raised her chin and met the mischief in Shay's eyes. "Yep. I'm going to quit my job."

CHAPTER ELEVEN

"Wasn't it a beautiful day today?"

T.J. raised a brow at Shay's uncharacteristic chipper voice. "Are you high?"

"Nope." She grinned. "Just happy to be alive."

Not high, but clearly up to no good. Nobody should be happy stuck at the Shot of Sin bar on a Thursday night when they'd usually be taking it easy, helping out at Taste of Sin. The two of them had been assigned to a private twenty-first birthday party for a spoiled brat with too much money. None of the kids had manners, and T.J. was certain none of them would be standing once the clock struck midnight. They would either be cut off because they couldn't handle their alcohol consumption or booted from the club for a misdemeanor.

"You know," she started, looking at him thoughtfully, "this place needs more of a woman's touch. There's only so much magic I can add to drown out all the uber-masculine feels."

"The club is fine, Shay." He handed over a raspberry and vodka to a woman who seemed far too young to be legal. "And so is downstairs, and the restaurant, too."

She shrugged. "It was just a thought."

If only she could keep her thoughts to herself, life would be sweet. Well, nowhere near saccharine, but a whole lot better than when she ran her mouth about his personal problems. "I'm going to check on the restaurant. I'll be back later."

He strode around the bar, moving into the small crowd and winced when her voice hit his ears.

"Aren't you meant to be having a meeting with Leo and Brute right about now?"

He turned back to her in confusion. She was focused on her watch, her forehead set in a frown.

"Yep." She met his gaze. "I'm sure Leo said nine pm."

"This is the first I've heard of it."

A firm slap landed on his shoulder before Brute strolled around him. "What's with the meeting? I see your ass too much already."

"Me?" T.J. frowned as Leo walked past on his other side. "I didn't ask for a meeting."

He glanced from Brute's scowl to Leo, who shrugged before diverting his attention to Shay. The bartender was wiping down the counter, pretending to ignore their conversation. He had a sinking feeling she knew more about what was going on than he did. "Shay?"

She raised her gaze, the confidence in her stare wavering as she opened her mouth. "Yeah?"

His hearing honed, blocking out the music of the D.J. and chattering drinkers to the sexy clap of heels approaching from behind him. Leo and Brute glanced over his shoulder, their attention landing on the same spot, their expressions tightening almost imperceptibly.

"Good evening, gentleman."

T.J closed his eyes at the sound of Cassie's voice. He didn't turn, didn't even bother to meet her gaze as her footsteps came to a stop beside him.

"Thank you for meeting me."

"You organized this?" Brute crossed his arms over his chest—his usual defensive stance.

"Oh." Cassie released a gasp and raised her voice to compete with the people dancing around them. "Didn't I write my name at the bottom of the email? Damn it, I could've sworn I did."

Feigning ignorance didn't suit her. She wasn't stupid, and they all knew it. He wanted to call her on it, only he couldn't open his mouth, not without spilling fractured words that would deny the adamant position he was trying to maintain with their divorce.

"I hope you didn't mind me using your email, T.J., I don't have a business account of my own and needed to get in contact with you all as soon as possible."

"Of course not," he ground out, still unable to look at her. He couldn't. He'd begun to live with the pain of being away from her. If he met her sweet stare, he'd have to start all over again. Ripping open barely healed wounds.

"What can we do for you, Cassie?" Leo asked.

She sighed, the feminine sound sinking into his ears and sending an ache through his chest.

"I've lost my job."

T.J.'s heart sank and he finally turned to her. She didn't seem distraught, not when her position at the hotel had been a former source of pride. Instead, she was beautiful, her blonde hair hanging over her shoulders, her black skirt exposing legs he loved entwining with his own. She had the glow of determination in her eyes and confidence showed in her perfect posture.

"With the divorce moving forward and my own income now non-existent, I've had to rethink my position as silent partner."

His heart was throbbing, pounding. His mind was a mass of thoughts, trying to figure out what was going to fall from her precious lips next.

"I've spent days thinking over my options, and every time I come to the same conclusion. I have no choice but to come work here. At least until I find another job."

Nobody spoke. He wasn't sure if his friends were stunned into silence or waiting for his restraint to crack so they could step in. Either way, he was in hot water, unable to let Cassie nudge her way back into his life, yet also incapable of turning away from her when she needed help.

"What a coincidence," Shay chuckled. "I was telling T.J. a few minutes ago how badly we need more of a feminine touch around here."

He glared at Shay, his blood pressure rising with the smug way she met his stare as she continued to serve people lined along the bar.

"Shay," Leo warned.

"It's not permanent." Cassie's voice was sweet and awkwardly comforting. "I'm already seeking other employment. Things are just slow in my line of work at the moment."

"I'll give you the money," T.J. grated. He'd give her anything, now and after the divorce, she only had to ask. What he couldn't give her was access to his life. Being around her, unable to touch or taste, would tear his already fractured restraint into pieces.

"No," she insisted. "I'm not going to take your money. I need to re-establish my independence."

He remained still. Unwilling to rake a hand through his hair to expose his trembling fingers.

"I think it's a great idea," Shay called from the bar, striding away to the opposite end to serve the birthday girl. "Welcome to the team."

T.J.'s nostrils flared. Leo wasn't happy either. He was glaring at his girlfriend, his jaw set in a stubborn line, while Brute carried his usual air of disinterest.

"When do you plan on starting?" Leo murmured.

"Actually, I came prepared to learn the ropes tonight. There's been a lot of changes to the club since I was last here, and I thought I could spend the next few hours familiarizing myself."

A tick formed under T.J.'s eye, the nervous twitch causing him to blink. He knew exactly where Cassie wanted to go, and he wouldn't allow it. Not if he couldn't be with her. The Vault of Sin was a place of pleasure, and he could never take her down there and leave her wanting.

It had been his sexual aspiration to introduce her to the club. To show the world how beautiful and responsive she was—the perfect wife. He didn't brag. He didn't boast. But he'd always envisaged the moment when he'd escort her downstairs and the patrons could see for themselves just how lucky he was.

"Maybe another time." Preferably when he was dead and buried. "Go home. Leave us to figure out how to address this."

"I'm afraid you don't understand." She turned to him. "This is my business, too. Anything you need to *figure out* should be done with my involvement."

Brute cleared his throat. "Let's not make this into an issue. I'll show her around. She can work the restaurant bar on slow nights, or help with the books. No big deal."

T.J. kept his gaze on her, wishing he could ignore the silent threat hidden beneath the innocent light blue of her eyes. "She's not going downstairs."

"There's no need to refer to me like I'm not here. We can both be adults about this."

"Can we?" He cocked a brow. She wasn't acting like herself. He'd first noticed it in the way she'd replied to his message on Sunday. He was unfamiliar with her spite. He was used to sweet, nurturing, breathtaking Cassie. The woman before him was someone different, with a smile carved of malice. "You won't go downstairs while you're here."

"This is my business, too. Where I go and what I do is none of your concern, as long as I do my job."

He released a caustic laugh. That's where she was wrong. She'd always be his concern—today, tomorrow and twenty years from now. That was the problem. He couldn't let her go. But he was trying. Every inch of him hurt, every single day, in an effort to let go. If she came to work here, he'd be consumed with the need to be around her. He'd lose his mind. No doubt about it.

He broke away from her gaze and focused on Brute and Leo in turn. "She's not to go down there. Hear me?"

He didn't wait for a reply. He turned and stalked from the Shot of Sin dance floor to head for the upstairs office, as far away from Cassie as possible. There were many things he was capable of right now—madness, mayhem, murder—what he couldn't do was keep pretending he didn't love her with all his heart.

She had too much to lose if they remained together. And even if she didn't know it, he would kill himself trying to make up for the mistakes of his past.

∼

*C*assie's cheeks ached from pasting the fake smile on her face for the last three hours. She was nervous. Nauseous from treating T.J. badly. Manipulation wasn't something she agreed with, and the only thing keeping her here was the knowledge she'd gotten under his skin.

"I'd like to see downstairs." She waited for her husband's head to jerk up.

She'd been standing at the door to the upstairs office for a few minutes, merely watching him as he sat at the thick oak table, a laptop in front of him. He was lost in thought, not having moved since she'd found his hiding place. His eyes barely blinked as he stared at the screen reflecting its glow back on his handsome face.

"Not tonight." His voice was low, barely reaching her ears.

"Why not? I'd like to see it." She stepped forward, entering the room. He was entirely perfect—his face clean-shaven, his hair styled as usual, his suit flawless. He'd recovered from his misstep on Thursday and was now taking the divorce in stride, when even breathing seemed hard for her. "Brute said he'd be happy to show me around."

His gaze gradually rose to meet hers, his eyes dark with anger. "This isn't up for negotiation."

She scoffed. Who was this man? He'd dictated the terms of their divorce, and even though they were largely made in her favor, she still resented his inability to discuss any of it with her first. Now he was telling her where she could and couldn't go?

"You're right." She kept her tone light, unwilling to let the frustration, pain, anger and grief take over. "I *am* going down there. It isn't up for negot—"

His chair shot back, the rough scrape along the wooden floorboards sending her heart into a rapid beat as he loomed over the desk. "Don't push me, Cassie." He strode for her, his chest rising and falling with labored breaths. "I've said no."

She was scared—that she was pushing him away instead of tugging him forward. That he was beginning to hate her instead of realizing how much he loved her. That the plan was going in the opposite direction and she was digging her own grave. But his anger was far more appealing than his disregard for her existence.

"Why are you against me going down there? That part of the club isn't even open tonight. It's vacant. It's not like I'm married and overseeing a sex club without the presence of my partner."

His jaw clenched, his fists, too. "You said you didn't have a problem with me working down there."

"And I didn't." Not until he'd blindsided her with the end of their marriage. "So, you have no right to say I can't go down there when it's currently unoccupied. When I can't even witness all those images you teased me with. Or experience all the pleasure you once promised. I'm going down there, T.J., whether you like it or not." The more he refused, the more she wanted to push him, hoping he'd break.

"Not now, Cassie."

The way he said her name, the raw savagery, made her throat constrict with sorrow. "Then when?"

Anguish flickered across his features, telling her there would never be a good time. She didn't know what his problem was. It was an empty sex club. Why was he adamant she couldn't enter the sacred walls? Could it be guilt? More misplaced protection? Or did he want to claim the club as his own, trying to keep the taint of his wife out of the sordid area so he could move on easier?

"I don't know."

She gave a sad smile and shrugged. "Well, I think now is the perfect time. And I'm sure I don't need to remind you I'm still part owner, so your permission isn't necessary." She turned and sauntered the few steps to the door. "I'll be going down there with Brute as soon as the private party is finished."

As she reached the threshold, he still hadn't responded, breaking her heart all over again because he'd stopped fighting so easily. He didn't make sense to her anymore. She couldn't read him. Couldn't predict his thoughts or actions, when once his love had been a reliable strength she could always count on.

She hung her head and entered the hall. No tears formed even though pain consumed her. She was all cried out. She was past waterworks. Tears didn't fix anything. People did. *She* did. So why the heck couldn't she figure out the man she knew better than she knew herself?

"Cass…"

She froze, straightening her shoulders as the muted thump of the downstairs music throbbed around her.

"Don't do this to me," he pleaded. "I've given you the car, the house, the dog. Leave me the Vault. Just give me this one thing."

Her throat tightened, the beat of her heart increasing until the rhythmic pounding became painful. "Don't do this to *you?*" She swung around, hoping the fury in her veins matched the expression on her face. "How dare you? You break my heart, turn my life upside down and expect me to do you favors? And over the same type of establishment that destroyed our marriage? Christ, T.J. Who the hell are you?"

He stood in the doorway, unable to meet her gaze as he opened his mouth to speak.

"No." She raised a hand, cutting him off. "Forget it. I'm going downstairs with Brute. You can have your damn club once the divorce is final. Until then, you better get used to me going wherever the hell I like."

Instead of fighting like she anticipated, he stepped backward, disappearing into the office and closing the door behind him.

Damn him.

The more they fought, the more she questioned what she was doing. His unfamiliar actions were making her second-guess the marriage they'd once had. Second-guess T.J. in general. Previously, she'd thought he could never taint the memories she had. Now, she wasn't so sure. He was dampening everything. Their love. Their happiness.

Shay was wrong. Being close to him hadn't given her the upper hand. It had resulted in the opposite. Because now she was beginning to believe the divorce may be exactly what they needed. Maybe they were better off alone.

CHAPTER TWELVE

Cassie finished stocking bottles of wine into the fridge under the bar and moved to her feet. Shay and Leo were escorting the last of the private party toward the club entrance, while Brute was beside her, clearing away dirty glasses along the counter.

"Are you ready?" she asked.

He didn't glance her way, didn't quit stacking glasses in a long tower to rest against his chest. "Where's T.J.?"

"Still upstairs."

He nodded and continued stacking. "We'll wait a minute."

Cassie frowned. "He's not coming, if that's what you're waiting for."

He cleaned the bar as he went, stacked glasses in one hand, damp cloth in the other, until he reached the dishwasher.

"Do you need a hand?"

"Nope. Leo and Shay can finish up when they come back. I'm just waiting for a minute."

"What are you waiting..." Her words trailed off as a thud sounded upstairs, then the heavy rhythmic pounding of angered footsteps.

"For that," Brute muttered. "Let's go." He closed the dishwasher and stalked around the bar, leading her toward the locked door at the far side of the club.

"Wait," T.J.'s shout shot down her spine, all the way to her toes.

Brute didn't pause, didn't even glance over his shoulder, so neither did she. T.J. wasn't going to stop her. This was her last hurrah. The final push until she walked away forever.

She sucked in deep breath after deep breath, calming herself as Brute unlocked the heavy padlock securing the entry to the staircase leading to the Vault of Sin.

"Wait," T.J. growled. "I'm coming, too."

Her head snapped around, her eyes greedily eating up the sight of her husband as he strode toward them. He was furious. All that anger and animosity directed right at her. If he was trying to intimidate her, he was failing miserably. Her body had the opposite reaction. Her nipples were pulsing, her throat tight, lips dry.

"Let's get this over with."

Her naïve heart fluttered. Her mind knew his acquiescence didn't mean a thing. It was merely a control measure. But anticipation filled her anyway. This was the first and maybe the last time she'd walk down these stairs with him. What once had been a fantasy was now a broken reality, and she'd take it nonetheless.

Brute swung the door open and waved out an arm for her to proceed. Before her was darkness. She could sense the staircase looming to her left because she knew it was there, yet she had no clue where the light switch was.

"Move," T.J. growled, pushing past her. He flicked on the light, illuminating the staircase she remembered from Thursday night.

Images lined the walls, the hedonistic pictures of sex and foreplay making her pussy throb. The scrape of her thighs against one another as she descended the stairs only made her arousal more potent and the slickness of her sex seep into her panties. She wondered if T.J. would care. Or how he'd react if she told him. Yet telling him scared her. Especially when she now struggled to recognize her husband.

His large frame was tense, his back ramrod straight as he led the way while Brute followed behind her. It could've been intimidating—her angered husband in front, a brutal man at her back—maybe that was their intent. Instead, it awakened fantasies, making her burn all the more to experience the Vault when it was at full capacity, this time without a disguise.

When T.J. reached the bottom step, he flung out his arm and flicked on another set of lights, bringing the entry area into view. She wasn't given a guided tour. T.J. didn't even acknowledge the doors leading to the locker or change rooms. He stormed ahead, moving to the keypad securing the entrance to Vault of Sin at the end of the hall.

He slammed his index finger against four numbers in quick succession and the panel let out a caustic beep. He did it again, slamming harder this time, and earned another beep in return.

"*Fuck.*"

His hand was shaking, his head now hung low with his hair curtaining his eyes. His fragility consumed her, washing away her arousal, replacing it with the need to console. He wasn't just filled with anger. She knew that. Underneath his resentment was pain.

"Want me to do it?" Brute asked.

"Fuck you." T.J. straightened and poised his finger over the panel again. This time, he entered the numbers slower, the same four digits she'd memorized since childhood—one, zero, one, six.

"My birthday," she whispered as the lock released with a click. He may be fighting to push her away now, but back when the club had opened, even after the assault in Tampa, she'd been the first thing on his mind when he'd chosen a security code for the sex club.

He flung the door wide and held it there, peering down at her without emotion as she strolled into the room fighting to hold back a grin. Her first glimpse was different from her recollection. The large screen previously playing porn was black. Silent. The room was bathed in sterile florescent light instead of the dimmer lamps to help set the mood. But it wasn't the Vault she was interested in. It was T.J.'s reaction. He was watching her, not in anger, not in spite, but in pained curiosity.

If only she could bathe him in the praise he deserved for creating such a respectful, reputable environment. She had no delusions that setting up this club had been difficult for him after what they'd gone through. Even though he hadn't been able to bring her down here, a part of her was in every piece of the Vault. She was in the heavy vetting process established to make sure participants were genuine and honest. She was in the classy furniture and clean sheets. She was in the heart of this club, and he'd never be able to take her out.

"This is where the fledglings stay until they feel comfortable playing with the big kids," Brute drawled, squeezing past her.

She inclined her head. "I like the idea."

She continued to watch T.J. from her periphery. His posture was taut, his discomfort visible even from a side glimpse. As she approached, he strode forward, leaving her and Brute alone in the small space.

"Why is he acting like this?" She turned to face Brute.

Her business partner raised a brow. "Maybe because he wants a divorce and you won't let him go."

She snapped her lips shut, refusing to bite back at his heartlessness. There was no empathy in his features. No kindness. No annoyance. Nothing. He was void of emotion.

"You raise a good point." She walked past him, into the main open room of Vault of Sin.

Everything was set out the same as the masquerade party. There was a corner lounge to her left, the bar up ahead with an entrance to the staircase leading to the parking lot hidden around the side. The sex swing still hung in the far corner. There was a king-size bed to her right, and every inch of the room screamed with debauchery, even though there were no writhing bodies.

She pretended to take in her surroundings, while her focus kept returning to T.J. with his back leaned against the bar in between two stools. He was watching her like a hawk. Scrutinizing her perusal, reigniting her arousal.

"I like the sex swing," she announced to no one in particular. "I assume staff get free entry." It was a joke. Her halfhearted chuckle announcing humor that nobody else returned.

T.J.'s nostrils flared, his arms crossing over his chest. "I'd die before I let you participate down here."

She sauntered toward the bar, bridging the space between them, smiling as she did so. "And will you pay me the same respect?" She raised a brow, trying to contain the snarl in her voice. "Or is it already too late?"

His face fell. Undiluted guilt filtered into his features. His eyes, previously harsh with annoyance, filled with devastation. Then, in a blink, it washed away. He schooled his features, straightened and shrugged. "As far as I'm concerned, you're free to do as you wish, Cassie. You just won't be doing it in here."

He met her gaze, her calm, gentle husband nowhere to be seen. Instead, she stared back at a man filled with torment she couldn't soothe. He'd been broken by something. If it wasn't the club in Tampa, she had no clue what. And it scared her to ponder the possibilities.

"Exactly what I thought," she muttered. "You didn't answer the question."

It was harsh to taunt him with guilt he shouldn't feel. Regret he hadn't earned. But she had very few cards up her sleeve, and the knowledge he'd made a mistake on Thursday was one of them.

"I guess I should be happy." She clutched the seats of the stools he stood between, her shoes almost touching his. "Once the divorce is final, I'll be able to get back to exploring all those things you promised me."

He broke eye contact, his jaw ticking. His chest began to rise and fall, his chin jutting to fight off her attack. She didn't move back, didn't leave his personal space. She couldn't. This harsh side of him did things to her belly, and places much lower. If only he'd succumb to his desire for her. She knew it was there, hidden under his fear.

"I wish you all the best with finding what you need." His words were like a steel blade—lethal, sterile, cold. Deep down, she knew he didn't mean it. He couldn't. But her strength to push wavered under his callousness.

They were playing a game. Each of them shoving at the other, waiting for the first one to crack. He would either succumb to his need for her and revoke the poor excuse for a divorce, or she would buckle under his heartlessness, too hurt to keep fighting him.

"Do you mind if we pause the tour so I can use the bathroom?" She couldn't maintain the strong façade much longer. She needed privacy. A few moments to regroup before she came back swinging.

"No problem." His focus narrowed on her, his curiosity seeing straight through her. He knew he was winning the war. And by the barely visible pity in Brute's eyes, he did, too.

∞

T.J. watched her disappear into the room leading to the bathrooms. He'd grown weak, his gaze tracking her every movement, his feelings for her shoving to the forefront again.

"She sure knows her way around for someone who's never been down here before," Brute drawled.

T.J. tore his attention from the doorway and scowled. "What do you mean?"

Brute shrugged, acting as if his words weren't a bombshell. "I sure as hell didn't show her where the bathrooms are."

Panic washed over him. "She couldn't..." It would have been impossible for her to get into the Vault. "You handle all entry information. How could she have been down here without you knowing?"

Brute narrowed his gaze. "Is that accusation I hear in your tone?"

No. It was fury. How the fuck had his wife gotten into Vault of Sin without his approval? The how, what, where and when assailed him. Was it recently? Had it been all those months ago when the Vault first opened? Or maybe a few nights ago at the masquerade party, hiding under a disguise to watch him disrespect their marriage vows.

"When?" he asked through clenched teeth. "How could this happen?"

His mouth dried as he tried to figure it out. The Vault was locked when not in use. Dead-bolted. On event nights, not only did the downstairs entrance have a digital alarm, the upstairs door and parking lot entrance were both manned by security guards. If she was callous enough to try and attend a night the Vault was open, she would've had to go through the approval process—photos, ID, approval at the door. It was impossible.

"Maybe she took a wild stab at where they were." He glanced at Brute in hope.

His friend raised a brow, not needing to back up his disbelief with anything other than his confident stare.

Fuck. "It had to be Shay." She'd been a pain in his ass since the news of his divorce.

Brute narrowed his focus to a glare. "Accusing Shay without evidence is going to land you in a world of hurt."

As if he wasn't there already. "For her sake, I hope I'm wrong."

Shay was a friend, but above all else, she was an employee. One that seemed more committed to gossip than her duties to their business. She'd asked one too many questions about his divorce. Had followed him around like gum stuck to his shoe. And when Cassie had showed up tonight, Shay hadn't been surprised at all, as if they'd planned the reunion together.

"Hold on a goddamn minute." He turned toward the room his wife had disappeared into. "Shay has never met Cassie before. Why the hell did they seem familiar with one another when Cassie turned up tonight?"

Brute's lips twitched slightly as he shrugged again.

Motherfucker. Something was going on, and it was about time T.J. put a stop to it.

"You better not be involved." He pointed a menacing finger toward Brute's chest and stormed away, hell-bent on finding the answers he couldn't live without.

CHAPTER THIRTEEN

Cassie was washing her hands in the basin when the bathroom door flung open, hitting the wall with a deafening crack. She turned, startled by a remembered sense of fear from a similar situation, and stared at the fury in T.J.'s eyes as he loomed in the doorway.

"You've been down here before."

She snapped her gaping mouth shut and schooled her expression. *Breathe.* She broke the words down in her mind, hoping to convince herself they were spoken in jealousy, not hatred. "I don't know what you're talking about."

His nostrils flared and his large frame inched forward, for the first time coming toward her with menace. "You gave yourself away."

She turned back toward the basin, lowering her head as she calmly grabbed the hand towel and dried her fingers. "I gave what away?"

He growled, the deep rumble of his chest caressing her ears. He came up behind her, grabbed the towel and threw it back onto the counter. "Look at me."

She swallowed, raising her focus to the mirror and the furious man staring back at her. For a second, she was scared, not of him, but of how their marriage was turning into more of a mangled wreck with each passing second. Soon it would be unsalvageable. Soon all hope would be lost.

He grabbed her wrist and spun her to face him. Although he was angry as hell, his grip was in contrast, a light caress, a loving brush of fingers. She turned to him, glimpsed the sadness in his eyes right before his gaze fell to where they touched, and he dropped his hold.

Emotions flickered across his features—heartache, yearning, confusion, before finally morphing back to anger. "Answer me," he snarled.

She scoffed. "From my understanding, all you've done is fling accusations at me. I've yet to be asked a question." She stepped into him and raised her chin so they were almost eye to eye. "And even if you were demanding answers from me, you have no right anymore. I'm no longer your concern."

"Don't play with me, Cass." He stepped into her, thigh to thigh, menacingly close.

She'd never been immune to his dominance. Outside of the bedroom, they were a regular couple. Scratch that. Outside of the bedroom, they were an enviable couple, their love evident to anyone who witnessed them together. Behind closed doors, the parallels of their relationship changed. He was no longer the protector. He was the predator. The man with an insatiable need for her, a passion so carnal she woke up in a sweat from mere dreams of it.

"I can't stand seeing you this way." His nose scrunched in distaste. "Spite doesn't look pretty on you."

Spite? *Spite*. Could he not see she was fighting for her life here? For his love?

"Yeah?" She raised a brow in defiance. "Well, being a coward doesn't look favorably on you either."

"I'm not a coward, Cass."

"Hmm?" She narrowed her gaze. "Then what would you call it? You're running away from a perfect marriage. You're hiding from something you can't even tell me about. If that's not cowardice, I don't know what is."

"There's a lot you don't know."

"Because you won't tell me." Her voice turned to a plea.

"It's better this way. I need you to come to terms with that."

"No. You need to come to terms with me not giving up on us." Her tone lacked conviction. Her heart, too. She couldn't take much more of this. Fighting for a man who no longer wanted to be fought for. Battling for a cause that had already been lost. "Until I have all the answers, I can't give up. I need closure." She stepped into him, resting her forearms against his chest. "Tell me why you need this divorce. Tell me what changed if it wasn't that night in Tampa."

She ran her tongue over her bottom lip, unable to stop herself when he was so close. Her mouth ached for him. All she needed was a kiss. A connection. She'd convince him to stay from the slightest contact.

"You still desire me." She didn't break their stare. "I think you always will."

"You're right. But my attraction to you was never in question."

She balked at his honesty. "Then what is it? Don't you love me anymore?"

Her fingers clung to his shirt, her gaze raking his features, scouring for answers. She was inching closer to where she needed to be. If she knew what she was fighting against, she could better equip herself. She'd no longer be battling in the dark.

"Tate, *please* tell me."

His gaze softened, his lips parted as if poised to speak. Then the shield went down, his forehead scrunched in annoyance, and he stepped back with a derisive laugh. "You almost had me."

He shook his head, ran a hand over the darkened stubble of his chin. "But let's get back to the real reason I'm in here, shall we?" Her heart dropped at the returned venom in his tone. "Tell me, Cassie. When did you come to the Vault without me?"

∼

Hell. How the fuck had this turned back to him? He couldn't think straight around her. She was confusing him. Changing the subject without him noticing. He hadn't come in here to succumb to the emotional plea in her eyes. He'd come for answers.

"How did you get in?" He attempted to act in control even though he was backtracking, stepping away from her.

She huffed. "I guess we both have questions that won't get answered."

The way she focused on him, intent, powerful, made him drown in the sparkling gorgeousness of her conviction. She had unending faith in them. In their love. And fuck, it was tearing him apart. He wanted to tell her, to announce the truth and let her know this divorce wasn't what he wanted.

It was what he needed—to protect her.

He'd changed her. Shaped a beautifully innocent woman into a skillful seductress because of his wants and desires. He'd driven her to be curious about a place like the filthy establishment in Tampa. But that was only half of his problem. The rest was out of his control. There was so much she didn't know, and telling her would only inflict more pain.

"I guess we're done here." She paused for a moment, waiting for words he couldn't find. With an overly dramatic flick of her hair over her shoulder, she turned on her heel and sauntered out of the bathroom, leaving him to sink into infatuation.

He couldn't help it. Couldn't fight it. No matter how much time they spent apart, he'd always want her. Need her. Beg to be between her heavenly thighs, tearing murmurs of adoration from her lips. Even just to hold her. To comfort. He'd give all their years together if they could start again. He had no control over his body's reaction to Cassie. His palms itched to touch, his lips ached at the thought of a kiss.

There had never been anything more mesmerizing than the love and affection he'd once glimpsed in her eyes. Yet here, now, the spark of determination he'd seen burning inside her was like a physical caress over his cock.

He all but jogged from the bathroom, yanking the door open with too much force. "How did you get down here?" His voice was loud, almost a yell. He still needed answers. Even more so, he needed her proximity.

She stopped at the foot of the large bed in the center of the room and slid a hand on her hip. "I followed you down here, remember?"

"You know I'm not talking about tonight." He lumbered toward her, clenching his fists at his sides to stop from reaching for her. "Tell me when you've been down here before."

"Or what?" She cocked a brow. "What are you going to do if I don't tell?"

He growled his frustration, the rumble burning from his chest all the way up his throat. "I already know the answer. I could tell by your lack of surprise when you walked in here tonight. I'd just been too distracted until now to pick up on it. There's no point denying the truth, Cass. I know you've been down here."

Her lips tilted in a seductive curve. "Maybe."

"Who let you in?"

The curve of her lips increased. "That's not your concern anymore, remember?"

Jealousy, thick and rich, pulsed through his veins. "Cassie." Her name vibrated from his lips in a lethal combination of anger and anguish.

"Tate," she mimicked.

"When?" The bed was right here. At his side. A taunting possibility that he could throw her on the mattress and tie her down until he'd sated himself inside her addictive body. "Did a staff member show you around? Was it Travis? Shay? Or was it during a party night?"

"Why do you want to know so badly?" She was enjoying this. The excitement was in her eyes, the kick of her lips. He was revealing his cards. Showing her he still cared. "Why, T.J.? You made it clear you no longer love me."

He squeezed his eyes shut, unwilling to fall into her trap. He wanted to deny it, to explain exactly how much her love meant to him. But he couldn't afford to take another retreating step tonight.

"You entered the club without my knowledge. I want to know how." He opened his eyes and peered down at her, taking the final step between them. She had a hold of him. Every limb, every breath. He could no longer stand the thought of her down here without him. The need to know burned through his veins. The images of her amongst the club patrons was torture.

"Please." He glided his fingers over her jaw, gently grabbed her chin and savored the way her eyes fluttered closed. "You're fucking gorgeous, Cassie. I can only imagine the impact you had on the regulars if you came down here while it was open."

He ran his thumb over her chin, grazing the sensitive skin just below her mouth. "Was it, sweetheart? Did you come here to play? Did Brute see you? Leo?"

She was falling under his spell, her lips parting in need. Problem was, he was equally consumed with desire. His cock was throbbing, pounding in an incessant beat to match his pulse.

He ran a hand through her loose hair and placed the other on her hip, ascending, climbing higher until his palm was almost at the curve of her breast. "Tell me," he whispered. "When were you down here?"

She shook her head, denying him her thoughts, but not her body. Her head leaned into his grasp, her chest into his, the warmth of her abdomen scorching his cock.

He was slipping out of lucidity, his head now filled with thoughts of pleasure, his body lost to the possibility of release. He leaned in, brushed his lips over the perfection of the smooth skin below her ear and breathed in her perfume.

"Tell me." He was no longer sure what he was asking for. Couldn't remember why he was even here, apart from the need to have her.

Her hands came to rest on his pecs. The greedy scratch of her nails above his shirt drove him insane with want. It had been over twelve months since he'd paid homage to her body. More than 365 days. An eternity.

His mind knew that was way too long. His cock did, too. It was his heart, the painful ache in his chest that tainted the moment, reminding him he'd made the choice to give up this pleasure. He couldn't succumb under the weight of attraction.

But he'd started this for a reason. He still needed answers. Sleeping at night wouldn't be an option if he didn't find out when she'd been here and what she'd done. He pulled back, waited until her eyes blinked open, before he wove her hair around his fist, making it impossible for her to move. "I need to know."

"And I need you." She trailed her fingertips down his chest, over his stomach to the crotch of his pants. Her hand palmed his cock, releasing a needy little moan as she did it.

He snarled, hating how weak she made him, fighting the burn of attraction as she nuzzled her nose against his. "*Tell me.*"

He didn't wait for an answer he knew wasn't coming. Instead, he smashed his mouth against hers and gripped the back of her head to hold her tightly. He parted her lips with his tongue and ground his erection into her.

He could feel her everywhere—against his chest, in his mind, through his soul.

"*Tell me*," he growled into her mouth.

She whimpered, her body going languid against him. Her lips were the most delicate silk, her scent an intoxicating blend of everything sweet and vulnerable in the world. She gripped his shirt and pulled it from his waistband, brushing her fingers against his skin like a branding iron.

His need for answers became lost in the urgency to have her. *Twelve months*, he kept repeating to himself. He'd done without this for twelve months. How had he lived? How had he breathed?

He lifted her, placed her on the clean sheets of the bed in the middle of the room and then strode for the door, slamming it shut with a hard shove of his trembling hand.

When he turned to her, she was on her back, resting against her elbows, her body a vision he'd been starved of. He wanted to make it right, to turn off the fluorescent lights and bathe her in the warm glow of the lamp, but this wasn't about setting a mood or deepening her already infallible appeal. This was about finding answers. It was. It really, really was.

If only he could focus.

He stormed for her, not stopping until his knees hit the mattress, jolting the bed frame. "Tell me," he demanded. "When were you here?"

She frowned, breaking the glazed look of arousal. "I guess this was a mistake." She pushed to a seated position, her body turning briefly to the opposite side of the bed in an attempt to flee.

Like hell. He lunged for her, caught her around the waist and dragged her back to the center of the mattress. When he released her this time, something new twinkled in her eyes. Something fierce and deliciously naughty. Something he'd never seen from Cass before.

He lunged for her again, this time her mouth, slamming his lips into hers with enough force to steal the breath from her lungs. She clung to him, digging her fingertips into his shoulders, running a hand through his hair. He was lost, delirious, inching closer to being sated.

He parted her legs with a shove of his knee and sank his body between her thighs, pinning her to the bed. She didn't protest, didn't deny him, yet when he pulled back, the look she gave him was lethal. A warning he was sure he'd regret not adhering to in the near future.

With his pelvis holding down her lower body, he reached for the bedside dresser and removed a scarf from the drawer. She licked her lips as he slanted over her, her gaze tracing his movements as he tied her left and then her right wrist to the wrought-iron bedhead.

She was a sight. Splayed for his gratification. A goddess at his mercy. *Exquisite.* All he needed was her clothes on the floor and her legs parted with restraints, then she would be perfect.

He cascaded one hand over her body—down her arm, over the

curves of her breasts to the softness of her waist. "I could touch you for hours."

She bucked her hips, pulsing her abdomen into him, making his fingers itch to go lower. "Yet you haven't in months."

He ignored her, unable to give her a response that wouldn't incite self-loathing. He'd vowed to stay away, to let her move on. More importantly, he'd promised himself not to succumb to his desires, not wanting to give her hope... And now look where he was.

Fuck. He needed to get out of here. *Now.* "When were you here, Cass?"

She whimpered, undulating her hips against his. "Kiss me." Her voice was breathy—a seductive plea.

He lowered his head to her neck, hiding his pain from view. There was no doubt she thought this was about lust, and, yes, he was burning to have her. But what kept him here was fear. The panic that she was curious enough to attend a sex club without him. That she could walk into another predator's trap in the future if he wasn't there to look after her. And it was jealousy, too. So much goddamn jealousy he wanted to cry out at the pain of it.

There was no other man for her. There couldn't be.

Not now. Not ever.

He brushed his mouth against her neck, her jaw, her cheek. Each touch resulted in a tiny whimper from her lips, and a harsh pulse of blood to his cock. "I suppose I can't blame you for your curiosity." He lavished her with delicate kisses. "I'm just disappointed I wasn't here to witness the first time you came to the Vault."

Devastated was more accurate.

Her eyes were closed, her hands gripping the scarf woven around her palms. He licked the seam of her lips, teased her tongue with his own. She was so receptive, her body rising to meet the glide of his hand as it travelled lower, over her thigh to the hem of her short skirt.

He didn't want to go this far. He'd die a million deaths getting over this. Only she felt too good. Too right.

"God, how I've missed this body." He hadn't meant to say it aloud. Her curves did crazy things to him. She was the perfect fit, a flawless woman in every sense of the word. He closed his eyes as the tips of his fingers reached her panties, the heat of her sex so close to his touch. "Tell me, gorgeous. Did you come here to see me?"

She whimpered again, this time tilting her head to demand a kiss he wouldn't give.

"You can tell me." He was struggling to find the strength to speak. The power to stop. He wanted to shuck his pants and drive into her, knowing full well her pussy would be dripping wet for him.

"Yes." She nodded, straining against her restraints. "I was here."

He froze, every nerve tense, every muscle taut. "When?" He spoke even though his throat threatened to close over.

"Does it matter?" she panted.

He growled, his frustration barely contained. The tips of his fingers ran through the brief patch of hair at the apex of her thighs, his touch stopping on the swollen nub just beneath. "Everything matters," he grated into her ear. "Tell me everything."

She shook her head, her hands pulling tighter against the scarf.

He flicked her clit, once, twice, gaining sadistic satisfaction every time she whimpered. The need for her ran heavy through his veins, pulsing with undeniable intent. He had to pleasure her. To bring her to climax like he had so many times before.

"I was here last week."

He stopped breathing. His vision blurred. "At the masquerade party?"

She mewled, nodding.

Vertigo assailed him, and he sank the arm he rested on deeper into the bed to keep him stable while his fingers clung to the sheet. He forced his other hand to continue stroking her clit, denying himself the need to flee before he knew every little detail.

"Were you with someone?"

She opened her eyes, the arousal flickering under the scrutiny of her narrowed gaze. "Yes." The word was emphatic, confident, shooting an arrow through his chest.

"Tell me who, Cass." He couldn't control the steel in his tone. He would kill the man. Maim him, at the very least. "Who were you with?"

Her features softened, the caring, sweet woman he knew came shining through. She leaned forward, then fell back and huffed in frustration over the restraints. She snaked out her tongue, moistening kiss-darkened lips. "I was with the man I love."

Fuck. Her words were like dynamite, blowing him to pieces. He slid back, moving from the bed, unwilling to believe what her words implied.

"I was with you," she continued.

"No." His heart pumped at the speed of a freight train. His mind flashed images with vivid clarity. The new member—the woman with black hair and brown eyes. *Jesus Christ.* She'd gone to a lot of trouble to trick him.

"Yes," she whispered. "You kissed *me*, T.J. You were attracted *to me.*"

Fucking hell. He'd died ten times over from guilt because of her. Yet he'd known. Somehow. There was no way he could've kissed someone else. His subconscious had known it was her. Even under the disguise.

"I knew you still loved me," she announced with conviction. "Thursday night was proof of that. You couldn't resist. Just like you can't now. We weren't meant to be apart, T.J."

He ignored her, wiping a hand down his face as he began to pace. "How did you get in?"

She tugged at her restraints and huffed. "Can you untie me?"

"*How*, Cassie?"

She flopped back against the pillows. "Fake ID."

He stopped pacing, nodded and succumbed to defeat. He'd received the answers he needed to sleep at night. He'd also received a reprieve from a small part of his guilt. Now it was time to leave.

He strode for the head of the bed, focusing on her restraints instead of the glimmer of hope in her eyes. He was a fucking bastard. A coward, like she'd accused earlier. He leaned down and kissed the smooth skin of her wrist, right above the scarf.

"I know you still love me." She reached for his face.

He pulled away, unable to withstand the affection in her touch. This was it. The final blow that would make her stop doubting that their marriage was over. He needed to convince her to move on. And unfortunately, he knew exactly how to do it.

"The affect you had was desire." He straightened to his full height, glancing down at her with what he hoped was a convincing look of pity. "Nothing more."

The lie stung, and each word he spoke crumpled her determined features into a mass of heart-wrenching anguish.

"I don't believe you."

A part of him cheered that she knew him so well. The rest of him died under the need to push harder. He shrugged, giving her a look that belied the guilt assailing him. "I'm not going to waste time mourning our marriage. I'm moving on. I suggest you do the same."

Her face paled, the final blow hitting its mark. He turned, unable to see her like this. Unable to withstand it when he was the one tearing her apart. He strode for the door, each step away from her bringing more agony.

She wouldn't recover from this. He knew it, because he wouldn't recover either.

CHAPTER FOURTEEN

"*T.J.*" Cassie screamed at the door her husband had closed behind him and sank back into the pillows. Humiliation assailed her, dragging tears from her eyes to trail down the side of her face.

He wasn't coming back to untie her.

She was alone. Sobbing. Trying in vain to fight herself free of the silk scarf he'd tied her hands in. Her skin already burned from the friction, and the pain came nowhere near what she felt inside her chest.

The far-off beat of footsteps approached, the click of a door releasing and the squeak as it was pushed open an inch.

"T.J.?"

"You decent?" *Brute*. Perfect. Her night couldn't get any worse.

"Not really," she muttered. Her nose was a running mess, her skirt raised to her hips, displaying her silken underwear. The only saving grace was the panties that covered her intimate parts...the same parts that still throbbed from her husband's touch.

He'd never had a problem arousing her. He'd always made it his mission to make her come before him. Usually, more than once. Walking away while she was wild with need was a sign she finally needed to sit back and listen to. Her husband was gone, and the man who'd taken his place wasn't afraid of making her feel worthless and dirty.

"Too bad." Brute shoved into the room, his features schooled, not showing shock or disgust at how she was tied to the bed, her cheeks tear-streaked, her clothes and hair disheveled. "Looks like you had fun."

She glared at him as he came to the side of the bed and untangled the scarf on her right wrist. "Yeah," she grated. "It's like fucking Disneyland in here."

He paused, at her uncharacteristically bad language or the crack in her voice, she wasn't sure. Her wrist fell free with the release of the material and she looked to the far side of the room, unable to stand his impassive scrutiny.

"You took a risk by pushing him." Brute made his way to the other side of the bed. "Unfortunately, it backfired."

She glared straight ahead, tugged down the hem of her skirt with one hand while he approached her other wrist.

"Are you going to give up now? I assume it would be better to maintain some sort of friendship, or whatever you normal people have, instead of being unable to communicate at all."

Neither option had been acceptable before she'd come downstairs. Now she wasn't sure if never seeing T.J. again was such a bad idea. He'd tainted memories she'd never thought could be spoiled. He was not only destroying their future, he was contaminating their past.

"I couldn't believe he'd give up on us." She wiggled her wrist free as he loosened the scarf. "I had to fight for what we had."

He inclined his head, his expression devoid of care. She would've denied he had compassion at all if it wasn't for the cotton handkerchief he pulled from his trouser pocket and thrust in her direction.

She blew her nose and dabbed at her cheeks. "I was here the night of the masquerade party. He kissed me."

"You think I didn't know you were here?" He gave a harsh laugh. "Nobody passes through those doors without me knowing. Although, you did a good job on the fake ID, I wasn't entirely convinced it was you until you showed up."

"You knew?" Her voice rose. "Why didn't you say something? Why didn't you tell T.J.?"

He shrugged. "It wasn't my place. You obviously went to great lengths to gain entry to the club, and I had no doubt it was to try to win him back. And besides, I wanted to see if you had the balls to show up. I never thought you were the devious type."

He settled onto the bed at her side, reached for her with a furrowed brow and swept the tear-soaked hair from her cheek, as if the gentle gesture was foreign. "He doesn't want to hurt you." The words were barely audible, barely believable from such a harsh man. "We all know that. This is his way of protecting you. Let him. That's all he has left."

She growled and pulled away from his touch. "Protecting me from what?"

"The past." His lips tilted. "The present." His grin increased. "The future."

"Is this a game to you?" she snapped, sliding from the bed.

"No." He stood, facing her from the far side of the mattress. "Kinda feels like I'm in an X-rated soap opera, though."

She scowled, seeing his actions for what they were—a diversion. He'd shown too much sympathy, and now he was making up for it by being an asshole. Hiding the softer side of himself in an effort to protect his vulnerability.

"I feel sorry for you." She did. She really did. He was cold. Heartless. Lacking the ability to step out on a limb because he was too scared to be hurt. "You must be lonely."

"Lonely? Why? I have everything I need—money, prestige and innumerable women at my disposal."

"You don't have love."

He scoffed. "Does it even exist?"

It was her turn to look at him with pity. "Sure it does. I should know. I experienced it with T.J. for years."

She gave him a sad smile in farewell and then strode for the door. Once she reached the threshold, she paused, realizing she was unable to leave without making her way back up those stairs toward her husband.

"Need me to get something for you?" Brute spoke over her shoulder.

She sagged and nodded. "Please." She needed to leave out the back entrance. To scamper away like the dirty vermin T.J. had turned her into. "My purse and keys are under the main bar."

Brute squeezed past her, doing her bidding without a falter in his step. He was probably happy to see the back of her, too. The secured door clunked in the distance, cocooning her in silence. She sucked in a breath, waiting, the minutes ticking by like slow, dreary days. She memorized her surroundings, strolling around the furniture, brushing her fingers along the sofa backs.

She refused to glance toward the mirror behind the bar. Her

reflection would tell her what her aching heart already knew—it was over. There was no more will to fight. All hope was lost.

In a few weeks, she would be single. Alone. Broken. As if she could shatter any more than she already had.

The swoosh of the door opening startled her, and she made her way toward the newbie area.

"This it?" Brute asked, holding out her purse and keys.

"Yeah." She nodded, taking her belongings from his hand before wrapping her arms around her chest. "I guess this is goodbye."

He pressed his lips together, the harshness of his features becoming more sterile as he frowned down at her. "I guess so."

She held in a caustic laugh and turned on her heel. A Shot of Sin had been a big part of her marriage when it first opened. Now it would be a memory. A brief flicker of remembrance.

"Cass, wait."

She glanced over her shoulder, to the steely expression that hadn't faltered. The only difference was Brute's stance, his arms were raised, held open in front of him.

She pivoted back to him, frowning.

"Come on," he growled. "This is more uncomfortable for me than it is for you."

His discomfort brought a brief smile to her lips. "You're a confusing man, Bryan."

He rolled his eyes and stepped forward, engulfing her in a hug. For a long time, they simply held each other, her head on his shoulder, his arms around her back.

"I've always admired T.J.," he spoke into her hair. "He puts himself last, no matter what the situation. And he's far too kind for his own good. He'd rather push you away and torture himself in the process than expose you to something hurtful. I envy his selflessness."

Cassie pushed back from Brute's chest and looked him in the eye. "Right now, I loathe it."

"Understandable." He inclined his head. "But even though he's acting this way, deep down I think he'd want you to know your pain is killing him."

"I thought you didn't get involved in personal matters." She gave a halfhearted grin, unable to keep it plastered on her face for longer than a few seconds.

"I guess I'm a sucker for a damsel in distress."

"No." She shook her head, sliding from his embrace. "You've got a big heart. You're just too afraid to show it."

"Nah. I really don't." He glanced toward the bar, denying her his gaze. "If you leave out the back door, I'll lock it behind you."

She wanted to laugh at the abrupt change in conversation. Instead, she thumped his shoulder with her purse, lightening the mood. "I'll see you around, big guy."

He nodded, his features returning to their emotionless state. "Look after yourself."

"Will do." She headed for the staircase leading to the parking lot, ignoring the impending breakdown she could feel pressing on her shoulders. The time had come to move on. No more second-guessing. No more trying to fight an unidentifiable opponent. Her marriage was over. And after tonight, she was determined to move on.

~

T.J. leaned against the wall beside the upstairs entrance to the Vault, waiting for Brute to return. As soon as the door opened, he straightened, watching as his business partner strode for the bar.

"Is she gone?" His voice echoed through the empty room, taunting him.

"Yep." Brute's tone was too blasé for T.J.'s liking. "For good."

Fuck. He ran a hand over his face and tilted his head to the ceiling. "Is she okay?"

"You don't want to hear how she is." Brute continued across the dance floor, heading for Shay and Leo who stood behind the bar.

"Yeah, I do." T.J. pushed off the wall. "Tell me."

Brute swung around. "She's fucked. Is that what you want to hear?" He threw his hands up in the air and let them drop to his sides. "You've broken her. She's done. Gone. Congratulations."

"Jesus," Shay whispered.

"You stay the fuck out of this." T.J. stormed for the bar, pointing a threatening finger in her direction as his mental stability splintered. "It's your fault she was here."

Shay balked at his vicious tone. "What—"

"Have I disrespected you in some way? Was this retaliation for something I've done? Or were you just being a heartless, nosy bitch, thinking you knew better because I'm merely a male and have no clue what it's like to feel?"

The words flowed from his mouth like he was stuck in an out-of-body experience. They were his thoughts that never should've been spoken. His torment that should've remained his own.

Her mouth opened, closed. She glanced to her left, to Leo at her side, before returning to face him. "It was neither. I—"

"You encouraged her to come tonight, didn't you?"

"I...I..." Her shoulders fell and she gave a brief nod. "I know you love her. I thought the two of you could work things out if you spent some time together."

"Fucking hell, Shay," Brute muttered.

"It's not her fault." Leo came around the bar. "Her heart was in the right place. She was only trying to help."

"Well, she didn't. She made me spit in the face of my marriage. And I want to know what the fuck you plan to do about it. She can't work here anymore. I want her gone."

"That's the pain talking," Leo growled. "Shay's far more than an employee to us, and you know it."

T.J. raised his chin, refusing to agree.

"Look, you're pissed. We know that." Brute strode around the back of the bar and pulled a can of Scotch and dry from the fridge. "But Cass is out of your hair now. She's moving on. You've got what you wanted. Don't go blaming anyone else for something you put into motion."

T.J. clenched his jaw, breathing heavily through his nose in an effort to keep the hateful words in his chest. It *was* his fault. He *was* to blame.

"What was I meant to do?" he asked. "I can't tell her the truth. It will kill her."

"What *is* the truth, T.J.?" Shay asked.

Leo winced and shook his head, but the silent protest wasn't enough to stop the words that inched up T.J.'s throat. "Six months ago, the man who assaulted her was charged with a brutal rape. The woman almost died."

Shay gasped. "Cassie doesn't know?"

"No," he grated. "And I don't plan on telling her either. She would blame herself when it isn't her fault."

It was his.

If only he hadn't taken her to that sex club. If only he would've listened to his gut and not allowed her to walk from his side to use the bathroom. She never would've been assaulted and he wouldn't have the guilt of two tortured women weighing down his shoulders.

"Then don't tell her...but you can't divorce her because of this either," Shay begged.

"You expect me to hide it from her for the rest of my life?" He glared. "I *love her*, Shay. I'd do anything for her. But what I won't do is create a marriage based on lies. She deserves more than me. She deserves more than a man who would put her in that sort of position."

He'd only found out about the charges because he'd employed an investigator to do some digging. Almost six months to the day after that night in the club, he'd received an email with images attached. A twenty-six-year-old, shy and beautiful, had been dragged into a car. She hadn't stood a chance.

"Cassie currently thinks this divorce is hard," he continued. "If she found out what this man could've done to her, or what could've been avoided if only we'd gone to the police, she won't recover. I can't do that to her."

He ground his teeth together and focused a lethal stare on Shay. "And I won't allow you to shove your nose into our business and risk her finding out just so you can push your own agenda."

"I'm sorry." Her face crumpled. "I didn't know."

"Sorry doesn't cut it." *Fucking hell.* The things he'd said to Cassie downstairs... The things he'd done. Even God couldn't forgive him for betraying her like that.

"The offer to fuck him up is still on the table." Brute drank from the can, not even bothering to focus his full attention on the way T.J.'s life was ending.

"No. Thank you," T.J. grated. "He was caught and prosecuted. Once he was sent to jail, the story died, and that's how I want it to stay."

"He deserves some form of retaliation."

T.J. inclined his head. "Yes, but at the risk of Cassie finding out? I'd prefer him to rot in his cell."

Shay turned to Leo. "You knew about this?"

"Yeah. Since the masquerade party."

"But, T.J., you love her so much." Her voice rose. "You can't leave her."

He'd spent months trying to determine if he could live a lie just to stay with Cassie. Counseling hadn't helped. He either had to tell the truth and watch her suffer through the consequences, knowing with each passing day that he was to blame. Or he could leave and allow her to find a brighter future with someone else.

"There's no other option."

Brute slammed his can on the counter and pulled another from the fridge. "I still think that bastard needs to suffer."

"And you think I don't? He's in jail. What's done is done." Cassie was gone. He'd pushed her to her breaking point and doubted she'd have the heart to fight back.

"Then I suggest we let it go." Leo crossed his arms over his chest. "Let *her* go."

Words were so easily spoken. It was the pain they inflicted that made it hard to breathe. "Yeah, just dust that shit off, right?"

As if it would ever be that easy.

Leo snarled. "Look, we're trying to be here for you, but you're making it fucking hard."

"*Leo*," Shay chastised and made her way onto the dance floor. "I made a huge mistake, and I'm incredibly sorry. I never would've placed Cassie in this situation if I knew. Please forgive me."

T.J. looked away. He didn't want to hurt her. It *was* the pain, the anger and the desperation making him volatile. "I can't even forgive myself right now."

She nodded. "Then tell me what I can do to help. I know you have to pick up your belongings on Sunday. Let me do that for you."

To hell with that. He'd do it himself. He was becoming accustomed to seeing his wife pained beyond recognition. Nobody else deserved to experience her anguish like he did. "No, it's okay."

Misguided or not, these people were his friends, and he was punishing them for something that was his fault. "This is my mistake. Let's just pretend like tonight didn't happen." And the years with Cassie were only a dream. "I'm going to go home. I'll see you all tomorrow."

Silence followed him as he walked from Shot of Sin. Silence and mourning. He'd done the right thing...maybe not in the right way, but protecting Cassie from the past had been his aim, and he'd achieved that. Now all he had to do was live with the consequences.

CHAPTER FIFTEEN

Cassie spent three days in hiding. She didn't answer the door when Jan came over, or pick up the phone when Shay called. She didn't even turn on the television to let the outside world in.

Instead, she packed T.J.'s things. Piece by piece, she placed her husband's belongings into empty boxes. She could've thrown them on the front lawn, giving him a taste of retaliation, but she wasn't convinced he'd even care anymore. She no longer knew how he would react, or if he was even going to show up to claim what she'd packed.

She hadn't spoken to him since she'd run from the club on Thursday night. Hours later, she'd started removing his things from her life. The process had been cathartic. Each item of clothing, pair of shoes and personal object had received a silent goodbye to the memories they held.

His wedding tux had been the hardest. She'd unzipped the clothing protector, flattened the familiar outfit on the bed and lain on top of it. With softly falling tears, she'd closed her eyes, wrapping her arms around the waist of the coat, pretending she was back there. On their special day. Speaking vows of love and commitment.

She was stronger now though. All that remained of T.J. were stacked boxes at her door. She'd blocked him from her mind. Pushed him from her heart. And would proceed to carry on with her chin held high.

But as Bear began to bark from the backyard, she wasn't sure who she'd been kidding. This was it. There was no reason for him to come back after today. There was nothing to keep him here.

She sucked in a deep breath and yanked the front door open.

"T.J.," she greeted.

He gave her an awkward smile. "Hi, Cass."

She broke eye contact, unable to stand the familiar man who acted like a stranger. "I've packed your things and stacked the boxes inside the door. There's a few more in the dining room."

"You didn't have to do that."

No, she didn't. She owed him nothing. "I'll leave you to it."

He inclined his head, his face solemn as he leaned inside and grabbed the first heavy box from the stack.

He walked away with too much ease. She didn't understand it. Couldn't contemplate how a man who'd once claimed to love her with all his heart could find it so easy to cut ties. But she wasn't going to think about that anymore. Nope. Not even once.

She strode for the back of the house, breathing through the pain overtaking her lungs. She refused to cry. Not after all the tears she'd shed. She was done. D-O-N-E. Or maybe it was spelled differently. More like D-A-M-A-G-E-D. She didn't know anymore. Everything felt like varying degrees of numbness.

She hid in the spare bedroom at the rear of the house for over an hour, nestled upon the corner of the bed, her feet tucked beneath her as she stared blankly out the window. This was the furthest point in the house from him, and still the scrape of cardboard taunted her as he slowly dragged boxes of memories from her life.

"Cassie?" His call floated softly down the hall.

She remained quiet, unwilling to see him again. She had no more time for his pity. Or the pain he inflicted.

"Cassie? I'm done."

She sighed. He was done. They were done. Everything was done.

"Okay," she called out, unmoving. "I guess I'll see you around."

She held her breath, waiting for the front door to close. When the sound of his footsteps approached, echoing up the hall, her heart climbed to her throat. She pushed from the bed, scooting to the window to pretend she'd been caught staring at something fascinating as his frame came to stand in the doorway.

"I'm leaving now."

She nodded again. Leaving here. Leaving her. "Good luck with everything." The words burned her throat.

"Are you okay?"

His tone mocked her. Their marriage, too. Of course she wasn't okay. He shouldn't be either.

"Peachy," she drawled.

He approached, his broad shoulders taking up her peripheral vision. "Is there anything you want me to do while I'm here?"

Hold me. Love me. Stay. "I think you've done enough."

The room fell silent, the cloying thickness of memories filling the small space. She wanted to open her mouth, to remind him of all the precious moments he'd ruined with his recent actions. He'd tainted it all. Nothing was left unscathed. She didn't even know if anything they shared was real.

"I never wanted it to end this way." He came to stand in front of her, cocking his hip against the windowsill. "I didn't want to hurt you."

"Really?" She turned her focus to him. "I've never been hurt more than what you've put me through in the last few weeks. Three nights ago, you used my love for you against me, tied me to a bed and left me there, humiliated and more devastated than the day you arranged for a stranger to give me the divorce papers."

"I know." His forehead creased into a mass of tension lines. "I hate myself for what I've done."

She hated him even more. And she still loved him all the same.

"Then why do it? Why tear apart everything we had?"

He glanced away, focusing out the window. He had something to say, she could see it in the strain of his features. Yet, his lips didn't move.

"I guess you can tell Leo and Brute," she seethed. "You just can't tell—"

"You deserve better," he growled.

She jerked back. "Do you think our relationship was that bad? That we couldn't have worked through whatever this problem is together?" It seemed a vivid black-and-white scenario to her—you talked through issues and resolved them, or you kept them bottled up and slowly drowned. "Did you have that little faith in us that you couldn't even discuss it with me?"

"No." His tone was sharp. "Being with you was everything to me. It always will be, Cass. I just can't risk hurting you anymore."

The tension in his features increased. He wasn't lying, she knew that much. "Then tell me. Explain." She stepped forward, unable to resist his sorrow. "I know our marriage is over. We're done. Just please tell me why."

He reached out a hand, stroked his calloused finger along her jawline. Her skin tingled along the trail of his touch, every nerve awakening while her heart ached for more.

"I shouldn't have come today." He streaked his other hand down her cheek, killing her with kindness. "Going to sleep at night, knowing you hate me is the worst feeling in the world. I knew once I saw you again I'd succumb to my own selfish need to touch you."

Cassie closed her eyes. *This* was her husband. *This* was the man she'd married. With his heart on his sleeve and his love pulsing from him in waves, he made her toes curl with his affection. "Go on," she whispered, opening her eyes to his dark gaze.

"You're right about me holding on to my guilt. I hated myself for not protecting you in Tampa. And I loathed myself even more for not being able to help you after."

"We could've gotten through it, if only you'd talked to me."

He inclined his head. "Maybe. But you never should've been there. My stupidity could've cost you everything."

"Could've, but it didn't." The words were a breathy exhale. She needed to know what haunted him, only the agony in his eyes made her second-guess if she really wanted to know. "You're still not going to tell me, are you?"

"No."

She winced, and scooted back to sit on the windowsill to space herself from the burn. His admission broke her heart. Collapsed her chest. "I need to know what you're going through, Tate. I need to know what's dragging you away."

Her nose began to burn, her vision blurred. She still refused to cry. There was nothing tears could do to stop the damage that had already occurred. But everything inside her ached with the unfairness of what had happened.

"I do love you, Cass. But our marriage is over."

The reminder of his love hurt more now than ever. They'd done so many things wrong. From the night of the club, to the way they reacted, to the underhanded way she'd first entered Vault of Sin, and everything in between. It was a tangled mess. One that would never unravel.

"But I..." She didn't know what to say. She wrapped her arms around herself, wishing she had more will to fight. "What if—"

"No." He gave a sad smile, announcing a myriad of emotions in one simple glance. "Please don't fight this anymore. I can't take it."

She tried to mimic his calm, and was sure she came up short. It wasn't easy when her insides were putty and the pounding in her veins felt like the world was going to end. She needed to touch him. Just once. To feel the strength under her palm and the heat to warm her frigid soul. She reached for him, running her fingers over his chest, sinking under the hypnotizing beat of his heart.

"I won't stop loving you." She continued to cling to his shirt, bowing her head to his shoulder. She closed her eyes, sinking into the rhythm of his heartbeat, wishing they were in another place and another time.

"I know. But will you ever forgive me?"

His whisper spread right through her, touching every nerve. She squeezed her eyes, gripping the material in her fists until her knuckles hurt. "I don't know."

There was so much to forgive—the way he'd shut her out for months after their trip to Tampa, the way he'd tied her to the bed in Vault of Sin and left her blanketed in humiliation, and most of all, the unanswered questions.

"I'm so sorry, Cass. I wish I knew how to explain my guilt so you would understand." His breath brushed her ear, his lips a delicate caress against her skin. "I never should've introduced you to all this. I should've been happy with what we had."

If only they hadn't pushed the boundaries. If only she hadn't enjoyed it enough to want more. If only they weren't lost to breathtaking, heart-palpitating love, none of this would've happened.

If only.

She pulled back, her fingers still tangled in his shirt. "Your lifestyle choices were what I chose for myself, too. I wanted everything you offered. I would've told you if I didn't."

He winced, the harshness crumpling his strong features into something heartbreakingly vulnerable. "I wish..." He sighed. "I should go."

He moved to pull away and she increased her grip. Yes, this was goodbye, but she couldn't lose his warmth just yet. She needed to hold him, to breathe deep of his scent so her memory never faded.

He was beautiful. His face a picture of torture and devotion. Grief and adoration. She loved this man. Always would. And now she had to let him go.

"Goodbye, Tate." She leaned into him, brushing her mouth over his. The delicate sweep scorched her all the way to the tips of her toes. It was exquisite in its softness. A purely instinctual glide of lips.

He returned her affection, sinking between her thighs, weaving a hand around her neck. She knew this was goodbye. The end. And still, she couldn't stop herself from deepening the connection, sliding her tongue into his mouth.

Her fingers gripped tighter on his shirt, her body unable to get close enough, her heart too far away. She adored this man. Always would. But they were over now. This was all they had left.

She moaned against his mouth, kissing him harder. The parts of her soul that had died when he'd walked from her life reawakened with the force of a million tiny nerve explosions. He was everywhere—in her mind, in her heart, his taste on her lips, his love in her veins.

She couldn't get enough.

He groaned and pulled back, snapping her from the pleasured daze. His eyes were filled with heat, his breath coming in short, shallow pants. He was on the brink, just like her. Wanting to take this further, yet needing to walk away.

"This is the end, Cass. I don't want to give you the wrong impression."

"I know," she spoke against his lips. "But I'm already dead inside. Make me feel alive again, one last time."

He closed his eyes, his forehead etched with lines of pain as he winced. When he looked at her again, she glimpsed determination. Desire. Passion so wild and unrestrained that it caught her off-guard when he slammed his lips back against hers.

He grabbed her hips and yanked her forward to the edge of the windowsill, his body sinking between her thighs. "God, I'll miss you."

She released his shirt, sinking her hands into the lengths of his hair like she'd done so many times before. "Make love to me, T.J."

He growled and shook his head.

"Please." She met his gaze, showing him the resignation she felt for their marriage. She knew it was over. He'd never let her jeopardize her future, even if she weighed up the risks and threw caution to the wind.

"I don't want you to think—"

"We're over, T.J." She kissed the side of his lips, his cheek, his earlobe. "Show me how much you love me before you leave."

He froze, his spine stiff as her pulse echoed in her ears. *Please don't walk away.*

"I'll love you forever." The clatter of his belt was a melodic frenzy, followed by the grate of his zipper.

She pulled at his shirt, tugged it over his head and let it fall to the floor. He was more defined than she remembered. His muscles were honed, his skin taut and inviting.

She grappled for the waistband of his boxer briefs and yanked them forward to expose the tip of the erection begging to be freed. Her mouth watered at the sight of it. The thick, bulbous head she wanted to get her mouth around.

"Cass..." He scrunched the material of her dress, tugging it up her thighs. "I haven't had sex in a long time. I haven't been with anyone but you."

She grinned, enjoying his pained lack of self-control.

"You think this is funny?" he taunted, hitching a finger under the crotch of her panties. "You seem just as defenseless, pretty lady."

She nodded, jolting her hips toward his touch, striving for the briefest glimpse of penetration to sooth the ache in her pussy. "I've never wanted you inside me as much as I do right now."

She lifted her dress over her head and threw the material aimlessly. She didn't care if the neighbors could see her in her underwear. Instead, she sank under the spell of lust and love her husband was bathing her in, refusing to believe this was the end.

"You're still the most beautiful woman I've ever seen."

Her heart fluttered. "I guess you still don't get out much."

"I get out just fine, thank you," he growled, reaching around her back to unclasp her bra.

Her breasts fell free, tingling under the admiration of his gaze. He descended upon her, taking her hardened nipple in his mouth, lavishing it with his tongue in an intricate pattern that tore a whimper from her lips.

"I need these off." He yanked her panties down as he moved to the other breast, paying it the same attention.

She lifted her ass off the windowsill, one hand on the frame, the other clutching his neck while he tugged the last item of clothing down her legs to fall to the floor.

"Spread your thighs," he demanded. "One foot up on the sill."

Her core clenched at his command. "I'm not as flexible as I used to be."

"Sure you are. You just need the temptation of an orgasm to test yourself."

There he was, the man who pushed her boundaries. The one who didn't take no for an answer when it came to pleasure. She tilted her hips and lifted one foot to let it rest on the windowsill, baring herself completely.

He stepped back, taking in the sight of her, his chest rising and falling with fevered breaths. "Jesus fucking Christ."

He sank to his knees, tearing a gasp from her throat as he roughly wove his arms around her legs and lowered his head between her thighs. He wasn't timid. He wasn't kind. He devoured her, his tongue lapping her sex and parting her pussy lips to taste her arousal.

She squeezed her eyes shut, focusing on the sweep of his mouth, the rough graze of stubble against her skin. His grip tightened, the dominant grasp of his hands on her thighs adding to the ease in which she submitted to him.

She was at his mercy. A mere leaf up against the harshest northern wind.

"T.J." She reached out a hand, searching for stability and grasping nothing but air. Her pussy was throbbing. Deep down inside her, every nerve was pulsing, poised, waiting for that next brief swipe of his tongue over her clit.

Then he stopped, leaving her panting, her lungs threatening to explode as he stood and shucked his jeans. The remains of his clothes fell to the floor at his feet. He was glorious. His chest heaving, his eyes feral. He appraised her again, taking his time while his cock pulsed against the slight patch of hair leading to his naval.

"Having second thoughts?" She cocked a brow and swallowed over the dryness in her throat.

"Actually." He cleared his throat. "I'm devoid of thought. Your beauty makes it hard to think."

She smiled and leaned forward, swinging her arm around his neck to pull him against her body. There was the briefest moment as he lowered to kiss her, mere seconds when their passion-filled gazes collided, that their connection flung her into the past.

This was perfection.

Bliss on every level, emotional and physical.

She kissed him, hard, and moaned at the taste of her pleasure on his lips. The sun beat down on her back, but it was his chest, the skin radiating with heat that warmed her from the inside out.

She needed more of him. She needed everything.

"I have to have you." Her ass was poised on the edge of the windowsill, his erection rubbing against her pussy.

He slid his hand between them, positioning his cock at her entrance. The briefest glide of his length over her sex made her whimper. The memories of what he could do to her already had her poised on the brink of orgasm.

He paused, no doubt trying to build anticipation she was already too aroused to appreciate, before he thrust into her, his shaft stretching muscles that hadn't been used in a long time.

"Jesus." His voice was guttural. "There'll never be anyone else for me. Nobody can compare—"

"Shh." She placed a finger on his mouth and savored the way he closed his eyes at her touch. With the tip of her finger, she rubbed his lower lip and sucked in a breath when he sank his teeth into her nail.

"Nobody." He blinked down at her, the rhythmic movement of his hips now demanding.

She nodded, becoming breathless as one of his large hands cradled her head, the other gripping her hip. He leaned his forehead against hers, holding her gaze as he continued to make love to her. With a rhythm perfected over time, he undulated inside her. Forward, back, forward, back, each thrust grinding harder.

Her pleasure spun out of control, building with intensity she couldn't deny. She clung to him, gripping his broad shoulder, clutching at his hair. A cry escaped her lungs as her orgasm hit—one of pleasure and despair. She was soaring, at the high of all highs, but on the other side was grief. She could already feel it seeping in—the anguish, the loneliness.

His thrusts became harsh, his guttural groan announcing his release. She would never forget the way he looked, his eyes riveted on hers, every flicker of his thoughts showing through the emotion in his features.

Goodbye, T.J.

She placed a palm against his stubbled cheek and rocked her pelvis harder, enjoying the last diluted pulse of euphoria before it was gone forever. Slowly, he stilled, his hips no longer moving, his length buried deep inside her.

She savored his scent, his beauty, and was thankful for this one last moment together. All that was left was to move forward.

"Thank you." She wasn't referring to the pleasure. Her appreciation was for how they would end this—with love instead of hate.

He nodded and slid his arms around her waist to hold her close.

She wanted to remain like this forever. To continue to fight for what they had.

If only she could. He'd never give her the option.

Unfortunately, she knew his mind was made up. There was no going back. She placed her forehead against his, rubbing the pad of her thumb over masculine skin she would never lose the need to touch.

"T.J." She cleared her throat and straightened her shoulders. "I think it's time for you to leave."

CHAPTER SIXTEEN

One week later.
Cassie was back to packing boxes. She'd found more of T.J.'s belongings in the cupboards of the spare bedroom. Then more in the home office. She hadn't thought to clean out his business files or disconnect his emails from the computer until now...when her mind was finally accepting her fate.

T.J. had already changed his email password. The software would no longer download new mail. But it didn't make the old messages disappear. There were still business emails in the inbox, a sent box full of his mail, along with messages in the deleted folder.

They needed to go. *Everything* needed to go.

With a glass of wine in hand, she delved through his past, making sure she wasn't deleting anything important before permanently removing them all one by one. She tried to pretend his name wasn't comforting. That the professional and gentlemanly way he responded to clients didn't make her heart ache. She pretended until her head was buzzing with alcohol and her stomach grumbled for food.

Business email—delete. Business email—delete. Spam—delete. Business email—delete. Sports subscription—delete. Private message... She clicked on the latter, the subject—*Private and Confidential*— piquing her interest.

Thank you for your email, Scott.

> I'm sorry it's taken hours to reply. I'll be entirely honest and say I feel responsible for the young woman's situation.
> I'd like to thank you for the files you prepared and the links you sent. I agree there is no longer a need for your services now that the man is in custody, however, before you send me the final invoice for the work completed, I'd like you to investigate whether or not I could financially compensate this woman without a trail leading back to me.
> I would be grateful for any information on this matter, and as usual, your discretion is appreciated.
> Tate Jackson

Cassie placed her wine glass on the table and stared blankly at the screen. A shiver of dread inched down her spine and she couldn't deny the jealousy pooling in her stomach. Was this the information she needed to prove there was another woman? Was the compensation for a child?

She scrolled lower, hoping to read Scott's original email below T.J.'s text. Nothing was there. *Shit.* She pressed print on the cryptic message and then searched for more mail sent to Scott's address. Nothing. If there was any other mail sent to that address, T.J. had done his best to hide it.

Her heart thumped harder, the buzz of intoxication dying under fear. She'd ended her relationship with T.J. on a bittersweet note. The only way she slept at night was knowing he still loved her. She could hold a tiny glimmer of hope that one day he would wake up and realize his mistake. Only now, his claims of guilt had a different context.

She navigated to the deleted folder, searched for Scott's name. Again, nothing. There were no more emails to or from this man.

"Damn it." She couldn't call T.J. and ask about it. They were done. Over. She had to find more information somewhere else.

Files and links.

There had to be an internet trail. Or documents on the computer somewhere. She opened an internet browser, clicked on *History* and scrolled all the way back to the date on the email.

Six months ago.

She straightened, her breaths coming hard and fast. This had something to do with T.J. moving out. She knew it did. There was no evidence yet, nothing to cement her assumption. It was the ache in her bones that told her the truth.

She clutched the wine glass, took sip after sip until the website links on screen aligned with the date in the email. There were only two, with the preview text on both linking to the same news site.

Her hand shook as she clicked the first website address. Then everything in her stomach threatened to revolt when a familiar man came on screen. Haunted blue eyes, a sharp nose and oil-slicked hair. The glass slid from her hand, the base connecting with the desk and then toppling to the floor.

She couldn't see straight. Couldn't think. There were only memories, vivid recollections, as she blinked her eyes to focus.

Serial Rapist Back Behind Bars.

She held her breath and skimmed the article, her gaze catching on caustic words like rape, brutal, hospitalized, forty-year sentence. She pushed from the chair, stumbled back and covered her mouth to fight the nausea creeping up her throat.

Nothing could stop the onslaught assailing her. Tears fell without her permission. Her chest threatened to explode. A woman had been raped. An innocent young woman had had her life ruined by the same man who'd assaulted Cassie, and it had happened only six months ago.

She stumbled from the room and ran down the hall. Her feet stumbled as she shoved past the bathroom door to lose the contents of her stomach in a violent purge.

T.J. had known. He'd known for over six months.

Six months. Since the day he left.

"Oh, God." She retched again and closed her eyes as the tears continued to fall.

The divorce made sense now. Everything made sense with torturous clarity. The devastation of their marriage was her fault. Not only that, but a woman had been raped because Cassie hadn't gone to the police.

She leaned back against the bathroom wall and let the sobs take over. Time passed in the measure of tears. She didn't know how long she sat there, wasn't sure when the sun set and darkness seeped in.

The phone had trilled its sterile call more than once. The television still mumbled from the main room, and everything inside her ached. She wasn't sure what made her more emotional—the woman whose rape could've been prevented, the years of marriage that could've been saved, or the secrets T.J. had kept from her.

"Cassie," his voice called in her mind.

She winced through the delirium and cried a little more. She didn't deny the madness. She deserved it, and so much more.

"*Cassie.*"

This time, she frowned and slowly moved to her feet. His voice wasn't a dream. He was here, unlocking her front door and stepping into her nightmare.

~

"*C*assie." T.J. shoved into the house, his heart pounding. He ran for the hall and pulled up short at the sight of her in the fading light. Her hair was a mess, her eyes bloodshot and skin pale. "What's wrong?"

She blinked up at him, her forehead creasing. "What are you doing here?"

"Jan called." He held out a hand, like he was creeping toward a frightened child. She looked fragile. Breakable. "She said she could hear you crying but you wouldn't answer the door."

Cassie blinked and shook her head. "I didn't hear it." Her voice wasn't even the same. It was lifeless. Numb.

"Cassie..." He took another step, needing to fix whatever was broken. After sleeping with her last week, he'd vowed to stay away, but as soon as Jan called, he'd been in the car, frantic as hell to get to her side. This was what he'd feared would happen, that he would walk away to protect her but not know how she coped while they lived separate lives. "Tell me what's wrong."

She frowned at him, anger creeping into her expression. "You knew." Her chest rose and fell with harsh breaths. "You knew and you didn't tell me." She stepped toward him, glaring. "You knew." She shoved at his chest. "And you kept me in the dark."

"Cassie." He retreated, bumping into the wall as he slid backward. "What did I know?"

She gave a delirious laugh. "Everything." She shoved again, and a tear fell down her pale cheek. "Why didn't you tell me?" Her voice was a plea. "I deserved to know what I'd done."

His throat closed over. "You haven't done anything, sweetheart."

Her face crumpled as she slammed her fists into his chest and sobbed. "I ruined all our lives." She sucked in a manic breath. "A woman was raped."

Everything inside him died. For a second, he stared at her. At the destruction he'd tried to avoid. At the pain he couldn't stand to inflict. He yanked her to his chest and closed his eyes to stem his own tears.

"It's okay," he whispered, holding her tightly while her body shook. "It's not your fault."

It was his. It had started years ago, when he'd began to push the boundaries. Love required spontaneity, but he'd gone too far. Their marriage had been perfect, and he'd ruined it with the continuous desire to strive for more excitement. He'd driven her to that club. He'd held her hand as they walked through the door. And he hadn't yanked her out of there when he'd discovered it was less than worthy of their attendance.

She'd been his responsibility, and in return, he was to blame for her suffering.

"Did you give money to the woman?" Her voice was barely a whisper.

"No." He'd tried hard to cover his tracks, to delete phone logs and emails, but Cassie must've found a message from the investigator. Yet another mistake he'd made. "I wanted to. But the possibility of upsetting her because she didn't know where the funds came from made me rethink the idea."

Her face contorted in pain and she sucked in a breath. "Is she okay though? I mean…is she…does she have people to support her?"

No. "Yes." Honestly, he had no clue. He couldn't bring himself to snoop. He wouldn't risk scaring her if she found out an investigator was following her. So, he'd made his final payment to Scott six months ago and tried to leave it behind him.

She pushed back from his chest, scrutinizing him. "Why don't I believe you?"

He winced. There were no words, only the confirmation in Cassie's eyes that told him she hated what he'd done.

"You should've told me." She shrugged off his touch and moved out of reach. "How could you keep this from me?"

"Because I didn't want to see you go through this."

"You withheld information of a rape, and the entire reason for our divorce, because you can't handle my tears?"

"No." He shook his head. "I mean you don't deserve this. This isn't your guilt to bear. It's mine."

"So, I wasn't responsible for telling the police of a crime this man committed?" Her words were filled with venom. "I couldn't have changed that woman's future if I'd pressed charges against her rapist well before she was raped? He could've been in jail sooner."

"You never would've been in that club if it wasn't for me." He got in her face, needing her to listen to the truth. "You wouldn't have been attacked, Cassie. There never would've been a cause for us to fall apart, and you wouldn't have even known of this man's existence. My decisions led to this. Not yours."

"You're wrong." She glared at him, her puffy eyes filled with contempt. "I want you to leave."

"I tried to save you from this, Cass."

"I'm a grown woman." Her voice rumbled off the walls. "I take responsibility for my own mistakes."

"Yes. But this mistake wasn't yours. It was *his* and mine."

"Get out." Her voice held less venom this time. "Just go, T.J." Her shoulders slumped, all the fight and fury vanishing.

"Cass, please. This isn't your fault. You aren't to blame."

"No?" She raised a brow. "Then why keep it from me? Why end our marriage if not because you're disgusted by my actions?"

"Why?" She knew so much, yet so little. "Because I no longer deserved to kiss you when there were secrets between us. I couldn't stand to look at you knowing I withheld the truth, and I couldn't sleep in our bed when I kept thinking that woman could've easily been you. I've told you all along, my guilt made it hard to be close to you."

"Well, your guilt is misguided. And to think you see me as someone weak and incapable of making my own decisions disgusts me." She glanced away and sighed. "I don't know who you see when you look at me, T.J., but it's definitely not the woman I am."

"I know you." He knew her better than himself. She was beautiful. Kind. Nurturing. Above all, she had a heart that felt the pain of others far worse than her own.

"You don't." She shook her head and walked away. "You don't believe in my strength. You don't think I'm capable of making my own decisions. So, I guess this divorce is for the best after all. I finally agree we're better apart."

"You don't mean that." She was in shock. Getting over this news would be the hardest struggle she'd had to endure, and he couldn't stand to let her face it on her own. "Let me stay with you a while."

"No." She stopped at the end of the hall, her breathtaking silhouette making his chest ache. "All those nights I wished you were here, holding me. Now I'm thankful I'm not stuck in a toxic marriage." She strode out of view, taking his heart with her. "Make sure you lock the door on the way out."

CHAPTER SEVENTEEN

T.J. was pacing. Again. It seemed that was all he did lately. Each day, he walked miles in the same spot, trying to drive away the image of Cassie. Not only was she haunting his dreams, she was now terrorizing his every waking breath.

"You summoned us," Leo drawled, his frame coming into view from the threshold of the Shot of Sin office.

"Again." Brute shouldered his way into the room.

Shit. His heart was in his throat, his pulse a rapid beat, his palms sweating. He couldn't stop the fear that throbbed through his veins, telling him he was making the wrong choice by continuing with the divorce. The apprehension increased with every passing second that neared the day he would legally sever himself from his wife.

"What's the reason for the meeting this time?" Brute scowled. "Apart from the need to re-carpet the office due to you wearing down the pile."

T.J. planted his feet, fighting the urge to keep moving. He'd kept track of Cassie every day since she'd found the lone email he should've deleted. Jan was keeping an eye on her, Shay too, and every spare second he had was spent doing drive-bys past his old house in an effort to feel close to her. He'd called a time or two, exchanged a few guilt-filled words, but she never wanted to talk. She was moving on, and doing a better job of it than he was.

"I think I'm making a mistake." He ran a shaky hand over his jaw. He hadn't been able to say the words aloud all week. Only the panic wouldn't stop. His chest was pounding with each tick of the clock.

"Which one?" Leo raised a superior brow and sank into the sofa opposite the office desk.

T.J. shook his head. This was a mistake. It was nerves. Indecision. Obviously, he'd have to experience some form of chaotic regret as the time dwindled to doomsday. What he was feeling was only natural... Right? "Just forget it, okay?"

He had less than forty-eight hours to get through. Relief would come once the divorce was final. Cassie would start to drift from his mind once they were legally separated. She had to.

"Spit it out," Brute grated. "I've got suppliers to call and wages to pay."

T.J. closed his eyes and rubbed the tension from his forehead. His friends were going to be pissed. They deserved to be after what he'd put them through.

"I think going ahead with the divorce is a mistake." He glanced at Brute, winced at his furious expression and then turned his focus to Leo. "She knows the truth now. There's nothing left to hide. It's only my guilt keeping me away, and I don't think that's enough anymore."

"Are you fucking serious?" Brute stared at him, deadpan.

"I don't know." It was the truth. He couldn't think straight anymore. His conscience was aware that leaving Cassie was the right option. But his heart? His soul? Every part of his chest that pounded all day long? They all told another story. They pushed him to go after her and make sure she was coping with the news.

"You're joking, right?" Leo asked. "You've already dragged her to hell and back, and now you want to do it again?"

"I don't know." That was the problem. He couldn't decide. "I don't know what to do. I'm not sure if this is cold feet, or if it's intuition telling me I need to change my mind before it's too late."

"It could be your menstrual cycle." Leo crossed his arms over his chest and sank back into the sofa. "You've been majorly moody lately."

"You're one to talk," Brute interrupted. "I seem to recall putting up with the same shit when you were having problems with Shay."

"Point taken." A grin stole across Leo's face. "So, what do you need from us?"

T.J. shrugged. "Just tell me I'm doing the right thing. Tell me I can't go back and beg her forgiveness."

"In *that* case..." Leo cringed. "I think you're right."

"*That* case?"

"If the aim is to stop her from hurting, I'd let her go. She's recovering better than you'd expected. She's going to counseling, and Shay is always over there doing girlie things. She's not dying without you."

But he was dying without her.

"You're wasting our time," Brute grated. "You don't want the truth. You want us to stroke your guilty conscience and make you feel better. You want us to placate you and come up with suggestions that will never be better than the option to cut and run."

True. All of it was true.

"But if you're looking to punish yourself, I'll give you my honest opinion." Brute's frown increased. "You're a fucking idiot for taking her to that club and leaving her alone. But most of all, you're a *fucking idiot* for letting her go. I know it, Leo knows it and so do you."

"She never asked for this lifestyle or the depravity that skirts the boundaries of what we do. And what if I hurt her again? What if I fuck up?"

"You're worried about making another mistake?" Brute scoffed. "Don't. If you fuck her over again doing some stupid, irresponsible shit, you won't have time to deal with her pain, because I'll fuck you up myself." Brute spoke without a hint of humor. Not even a glimpse.

His friend would do exactly as promised and not spare a thought.

"You fucked up once, give yourself a break," Leo added. "But if you fuck up twice, I won't save you from Shay. I promise she'll be more of a threat than Brute."

"I'll never hurt her again," he promised. He'd die before he caused her more tears.

"*No.*" Brute raised his voice. "Hurting her is inevitable. It's how relationships work. Don't even think you can go rekindle your marriage and treat her like glass. If you do go crawling back, do right by her. Treat her exactly the way she wants to be treated, not the way you think she deserves. Her fragility is your issue, asshole, not hers."

Asshole. That was as close to an endearment as T.J. would get from Brute.

"You both know I love her more than life," he murmured.

Brute smiled, all teeth, no charm. "And you know I'll gladly take her off your hands the next time you mess up."

T.J. rolled his eyes and focused on Leo. "Any more words of wisdom from you?"

"Yeah, you're running out of time."

"Don't you think I know that? Tomorrow's the last day before the divorce is finalized."

Leo winced. "Yeah, tomorrow's also the day Shay takes your wife out for a night in the city to help her move on."

Goddamn it. That kick-started his heart into next Tuesday. "Are you serious?"

Leo inclined his head. "Deadly serious. And from the look of the outfit Shay picked out for Cass, she won't be going home alone."

CHAPTER EIGHTEEN

"You look edible."

Cassie blushed at Shay's compliment and gave a halfhearted smile in thanks. The Bodycon dress was too tight, the material barely coming to her knees, accentuating every curve...and she had many.

"It isn't too much?" She pulled at the hem in a vain attempt to hide more skin. "Don't be silly. The aim of the game is to regain your confidence and put a smile back on your face. Now get in the damn car."

This wasn't a game, it was torture. Shay had spent days consoling her through grief and guilt. Along with Jan and a newly found counselor. Sleep was still illusive, and the pain wouldn't ebb, but for tonight, Cassie wanted to paste on a smile and pretend like her life wasn't going to be irrevocably changed tomorrow.

"Come on. Come on. Come on." Shay strutted toward her car parked in Cassie's driveway, swaying her perfect ass. "I'm dying for a drink."

It was already approaching nine o'clock when they slid into the small hatchback.

"So where are we going?" Shay hadn't given specifics. A club on Crockett Street had been mentioned once or twice. A club that was currently in the opposite direction to where they were headed.

"I made an executive decision and changed our plans."

Cassie sighed, now all too familiar with Shay's chipper tone that announced she was up to something. "You know what? Don't tell me, just turn the car around and drive me home. I always seem to get myself in trouble when I'm with you."

Shay snorted, ignoring her request. "And that's my fault?"

"Ah, yeah. I was trouble-free before we met."

"Sounds kinda boring," Shay said around a chuckle.

Boring but safe. There was no more desire for fun or depravity. Without T.J., none of it really mattered. Yeah, she planned on having a fling or two in the future…maybe…if she gained the courage to go home with a stranger. But that would take time, and determination she currently didn't have. "Why don't we go to my place and have a few drinks instead?"

Shay shook her head. "I know what you're doing, and I'm not going to let you. The first step is the hardest. Once tonight is over, you'll find it easier to go out next time. And then the time after that, and so on and so forth. The longer you put it off the harder it will be."

"Fine." Cassie sighed. "So where are we going? And don't think I haven't noticed that you distracted me for long enough to take me out of walking distance from my house."

"I can't slip anything by you, can I?" Shay shot her a grin.

"So?"

"So…we're going to the Vault."

Oh, no. *Hell*, no. "Forget it. Stop the car. *Right now*. I'm not going anywhere near there."

Shay waved away her protest. "Calm down. T.J. won't find out. And besides, you can't back out now. I arranged the whole night for you. Vault of Sin doesn't usually open on Thursday nights, so I've invited a few regulars. I picked them out specifically to ensure you have a great time."

The innuendo in Shay's tone turned Cassie's cheeks to flame, the heat expanding all the way to her chest. "I don't want to sleep with anyone—"

"You don't have to."

"I don't want to cause trouble the night before the divor—"

"You're not going to. T.J. doesn't work tonight. He won't even be there."

Damn it. This woman couldn't take no for an answer. "Leo and Brute wouldn't approve either."

"Actually," Shay drew out the word, giving her a pointed look. "Leo's the one who suggested it."

"*Bullshit.*"

Shay turned her focus back to the road and nodded. "I'm not lying. He's worried about you. If you're going to get laid, he'd prefer you do it at the club, with someone who has gone through the vetting process. It's a safe environment. You won't have to contemplate taking strangers back to your house, or be enticed to go home with someone."

"I've already said I don't want to get laid," Cassie grated. This was ridiculous.

"Believe me, I've heard you. But it's a woman's prerogative to change her mind. It's just an option. If you want to sit at the bar and talk all night, we can. There won't be loud music or sleazy guys annoying us. And if you start having fun and don't want to stop, I'm sure being in the Vault will be of some comfort to you."

Cassie kept her mouth shut, not willing to admit going to a quieter, more familiar club was reassuring. It was still the Vault—a place she'd been to twice, yet it held palpable memories she wasn't sure she wanted to be reminded of.

As they turned into Shot of Sin's street, her heart pounded. "If I want to leave, are you going to try and convince me to stay?"

Shay shrugged. "That depends."

"On?"

"If you want to leave as soon as we walk in the door. You need to give it time. At least three drinks minimum."

"Three drinks?" Cassie gaped. She hadn't had more than a drink or two in a damn long time. Shay knew it, too. Three would have her dancing on the bar. "How about two?"

Shay smirked and flicked her indicator to enter the club parking lot. "Four."

Damn her. "Three it is. But I won't promise to enjoy myself."

"Doesn't bother me, honey." Shay pulled into one of the few remaining parking spots and cut the ignition. "As long as I stay out long enough to work Leo into a jealous frenzy, I'll be happy."

"Stop pacing." T.J. wasn't comfortable telling someone else to stop doing what he'd been doing all week, but the way Leo huffed back and forth was filling the now empty Taste of Sin restaurant with cloying apprehension. "Why the hell are you pacing, anyway?"

"Just anxious." Leo checked a text message on his phone. "That's all."

"With good reason." Brute smirked.

"Do you mind filling me in on what's going on?" They'd been seated at the bar for an hour, yet T.J. felt like his friends had spent the whole time having a secret conversation without him.

Brute reached over the bar and poured himself another beer. "It's nothing."

Leo groaned and flung back the remaining bourbon in his glass. "Can't we just go? Shay and Cassie will be out by now."

"No." T.J. was adamant. He wanted Cassie to have a few hours to herself. Besides, alcohol would calm her nerves and make it easier for him to approach her later. He'd get her brutal honesty after she'd had a few drinks, and he didn't want to risk arriving early. Timing was everything. "We'll leave soon enough."

Leo pulled his cell from his back jeans pocket. "I might give Shay a call th—"

"Fuck off." Brute snatched the device from Leo's hand. "Don't you trust your woman?"

Leo scowled. "Of course I do. I just think it would be best if we get a move on."

"I'm not keeping you here." They were making him nervous with their bullshit attitudes. Leo didn't stress often. He did moody and irrational, but he didn't do anxiety. And Brute... Well, that fucker was smiling, which was an anomaly all on its own. "If you want us to meet you in the city, go ahead. It's no big deal."

"It's fine," Leo grated. "I'll stick around."

The large dining area fell silent. Brute continued to smirk to himself as he topped up his beer. Leo's fingers kept tap, tap, tapping against the bar, while T.J. tried to think of what he was going to say to make Cassie forgive him for all the heartache.

"You know what?" Leo shoved from his stool. "I've got something to say."

Brute swiveled in his stool, still smirking as he crossed his arms over his chest and looked at Leo. T.J. followed, leaving his scotch on the counter to turn and face the man who appeared ready to make a Hulk transformation.

"Before we find Cassie and Shay," Leo started. "I want you to know something."

"Is this the *something* that's had you jittering and snarling all night?"

Leo let out a bitter laugh. "*No.* We'll get to that next. What I want to discuss is how you got in this fucked situation in the first place."

T.J. raised his chin, trying to steel himself against the punch to his pride. "What of it?"

"It's about all the guilt you piled on yourself that could've been eased if only you'd spoken to us. It's about you, and your inability to let us help."

"I didn't think I needed it." Cassie was *his* wife. *His* love. *His* responsibility. He cleaned up his own messes…well, usually he did. Only this time, he'd left a trail in the form of an email.

"Yes, you did. You've just been kidding yourself for so long you started believing your own lies."

"Fuck you." T.J. slid to his feet. The last thing he needed was a guilt trip. He'd had enough guilt to last a lifetime.

"Don't get defensive. I'm just trying to tell you, you've gotta realize, no matter how much you want to, you won't always be able to protect her. Sometimes you'll need to rely on us to help. Sometimes she's going to be fine all by herself. And then there'll be other times when no matter what any of us do, she's still going to get hurt, and there's nothing you can do about it."

T.J. winced. This was what it all came down to. His issues. His guilt. "I know."

"Do you?" Leo raised a disbelieving brow. "Because you fucked up in Tampa and didn't bother telling us. How could you keep that a secret? How could you quit sleeping in your wife's bed for six months, killing yourself with guilt, and not breathe a word of it to either of us?"

"It wasn't something either Cassie or I wanted to share."

"Yeah, well, it says a lot about our friendship, doesn't it?"

Whoa.

"Hold up." T.J. raised his hands in surrender. "Cassie's everything to me. I didn't want to share information that would upset her."

"And if you had shared that information, I would've kicked your ass to next Tuesday. Brute, too. Aren't I right?" He jerked his chin in question.

"Yeah." The sadistic grin vanished from Brute's features. "Everything would've been out in the open. We would've made you pay for your mistakes and you would've moved on. None of this would've happened."

"It wouldn't have stopped the guilt." They didn't know what it was like to deal with the what-ifs.

"No, it wouldn't." Leo inclined his head in acknowledgement. "But we could've helped with that, too. It didn't have to be like this."

T.J.'s chest constricted, squeezing the air from his lungs. He couldn't look back now. He couldn't admit he'd done the wrong thing by her again. There was too much blame already. That night in Tampa had changed him. She'd been so scared. Her beautiful skin pale as a ghost when he'd slammed into that bathroom.

"It wasn't your mess." The shame at placing her in that position, the fear of it ever happening again, had been his burden to bear.

"It *fucking* was," Brute raised his voice. "That's what Leo is trying to tell you. You're like a brother to us. And you know what? You've always had Cassie, and now Leo has Shay, but I've only ever had you guys at my back. We're not meant to go through shit like this on our own. So, next time, quit being a fucking tool and ask for help."

T.J. swallowed over the dryness in his mouth. "I don't like relying on other people when it comes to Cassie."

"Why?" Leo slumped back onto his stool. "What's the big deal?"

T.J. shook his head and broke eye contact. "Cassie is everything," he murmured the painful truth. "She's perfect. I can't fault anything about her. Even the way she's handled this divorce—fighting for me, when deep down I always wanted her to, then giving up when I couldn't handle her anguish anymore. She's all I've ever wanted. And more than I'll ever deserve."

He stared at the scuff marks on his black shoes. "Doing this by myself was an attempt to make up for all my mistakes. I'd let her go and take the fall. I was happy to do it because then I'd never have to spend another night lying awake, wondering when I'd put her in another position where she'd get hurt. I deserved this mess." And he deserved a lot more. "I just can't go through with it. I love her too much."

They didn't respond. He sat there, silent, their gazes weighing heavy on his shoulders.

"See...I'm pathetic."

"That's not breaking news." Leo chuckled.

T.J. glanced at his friend from the corner of his eye and tried to laugh, but the sound came out halfhearted. He couldn't find humor in this. "What if I let her down again?"

"And what if you don't get the choice?" Leo cocked a brow. "I'd rather go in, guns blazing, full speed ahead, than not have a chance at happiness at all."

"You've sure changed your tune since hooking up with Shay."

"Yeah? Well, maybe you should do the same. You can't protect Cassie twenty-four-seven. You need to start trusting her to make the right decisions. To start believing Brute and I have your back, as well as hers. It's not rocket science. And besides, if you don't hurry up, the decision might be taken out of your hands. I'm not sure how long she'll be left alone in the Vault when she has Shay at her side, egging her on."

"The Vault?" T.J. scrutinized his friend, waiting for the punch line. "What have you done?"

Brute leaned over the bar again to place his empty glass in the sink. "We saved you the hassle of driving into the city."

"Wha—"

"Calm down, my friend. I did exactly what you would've done if you had the ability to think clearly." Leo released a long huff of breath and wiped a hand down his face. "Cass is somewhere safe, with men we know, also under the surveillance of Travis behind the bar."

"That's why you've been flustered all night?" *Fucking hell.* Cassie was in the goddamn Vault.

"Flustered isn't a word worthy of how I've felt the last two hours, knowing Shay has been in a sex club with your wife."

"Then why the hell—"

"It was better than the alternative of them going somewhere else." Brute snatched his wallet off the bar and shoved it in the back pocket of his dress pants. "It's not like I could warn every club-goer in Beaumont to keep their hands off your wife, like I can in our own club."

"You did that?" Brute's assurances did nothing to curb T.J.'s jealousy.

"Of course we did," Leo growled. "However, it doesn't mean my manipulative girlfriend won't talk anyone into testing my authority."

CHAPTER NINETEEN

"Was I right? Or was I right?"

Cassie rolled her eyes at Shay and chuckled. "You were right."

It helped that the three mandatory drinks had gone down in quick succession to fight her nerves, but it was also comforting to spend her last night as a married woman in a place she felt close to her husband.

She hadn't been able to stay mad at him. Once the tears faded, she'd understood why he'd kept the information to himself. She still didn't appreciate the way he coddled her, but there was forgiveness in her heart. And longing, too. Being back in his club didn't ease her tumultuous emotions.

The vibe tonight was different from the masquerade party. Most people were focused on drinking and foreplay instead of nudity and sex. No dress code was in force either, meaning most people were in evening attire instead of underwear.

It was laid-back. Sexy. With security at the back entrance and on-call for any issues that could arise. The guests Shay had invited to *play* were also happy to do their own thing, with the understanding Cassie was only available if words of consent were physically spoken.

Which would never happen. Not only because she wasn't ready, but because it would be disrespectful to T.J.

"Can I buy you ladies a drink?" The deep, unfamiliar voice drifted over Cassie's shoulder, making her tense.

"Not for me, thanks, Luke." Shay grinned. "I'm spoken for tonight."

Cassie swiveled in her stool, coming face-to-face with muscled beauty. The man was ripped, showing an expanse of gorgeously tanned skin from his shoulders all the way down to his silk boxers.

"How about you, beautiful?"

Cassie jerked back at the compliment. He was handsome as hell, half-naked and wanted to buy her a drink? No, thank you. She needed to cut her teeth on someone less perfect.

"She's with me tonight," Shay spoke for her.

The man's lips curved, exposing a glimpse of flawless white teeth. "With you? As in, the two of you together?" He raised a brow. "I have to admit, I'd love to see that."

"No." Shay rolled her eyes. "We're not together. Just friends sharing a few drinks."

"That's a shame." The man shrugged and began walking away. "Seeing the two of you all hot and heavy would've been the highlight of my year."

Cassie's eyes bugged as she turned back to the bar. "*Jesus Christ.* Is he serious?" She glanced at the bartender for confirmation, not trusting Shay for a truthful answer.

"Definitely." Travis had a smug expression on his handsome face. "We don't see a lot of girl-on-girl action down here." He grabbed her empty glass and placed it in a dishwasher rack on the sink. "It happens. Just not often, and probably not with women as lovely as the two of you."

"You're so smooth, Travis," Shay cooed.

"Yeah." Cassie had to agree. "He almost deserves a little show-and-tell for his efforts. Don't you think, Shay?"

The ease in which she slid back into the single mindset confronted her with the force of a punch to the stomach. Had she really just said that? *Christ.*

"Can I have another drink, please?" She tapped the bar and breathed out the ache in her lungs.

"Are you serious?" Shay asked, the corner of her lips twitching.

"About the drink?" Travis and Shay were both looking at her—her friend in humor, the bartender with a scowl.

"We don't joke in the Vault, Cass." Travis's tone was low. Her heart climbed into her throat. *Wait.* Was *he* joking? "Read the rules and regulations. We don't condone misrepresentation."

"Oh, fuck off, Travis." Shay swiveled on her stool to face Cassie. "It's all about keeping lines of communication open. If you're teasing, it gives false hope and mixed signals, which can be dangerous in a place like this. But ignore him, he's being overly dramatic."

Okay. He definitely wasn't joking, which kind of pissed her off. She had enough to deal with without her lame attempt at humor being taken out of hand.

"Then maybe I wasn't misrepresenting." She cocked a brow at Travis and swiveled her stool toward Shay. "I wouldn't want to be seen breaking the rules in my husband's club."

"Now I know that's the liquor talking." Shay snorted.

"Doesn't have to be." Cassie straightened her shoulders. She wasn't sure where the confidence was coming from...oh, wait, yes she did. Those three mandatory drinks her scheming friend made her have were kicking in nicely. "I'm single, remember?"

"But Shay isn't," Travis drawled.

"Mind your own damn business. I'm sure Leo would be satisfied with a blow-by-blow recount." Shay leaned forward, resting her palms on Cassie's thighs. "What do you think?"

Cassie's throat dried in an instant. Where was the liquid courage now? The corner of Shay's mouth quirked as she leaned in, brushing their cheeks together before resting her lips near Cassie's ear.

"I started flirting back because I thought you were joking," Shay whispered. "Now I'm kinda nervous because you might be serious."

Cassie closed her eyes, keeping up the façade as she nuzzled the side of her face into Shay's hair. "I *was* totally joking."

Was... Now she wasn't so sure. Shay's attention was nice. Soothing. The brush of another body against hers sparked a warmth inside her chest that she hadn't expected. When she opened her eyes, more than one gaze was upon them, the interest from club patrons making the lonely parts of Cassie feel adored again. "I thought uptight Travis and your friend Luke deserved a show."

"Hmm." Shay continued to brush her lips down Cassie's neck, each touch sparking a frenzy of heat in her veins. "So how far did you want to take this?"

"Mmm." Cassie arched her neck, half of her playing along with the pretense, the other half falling under the spell of arousal. "I hadn't thought that far."

Shay was so soft and unfamiliar. She was unlike anything Cassie had ever felt before. Her dating life had only ever consisted of men. And not many at that. But they had all been highly masculine partners, with rough skin and calloused hands. The attention from Shay was entirely different. Exquisite in its delicacy. Instead of dominant and demanding, it was tender and fragile.

The hands on her thighs were still, the fingertips rubbing in intricate patterns over her sensitive skin. She ran her fingers through Shay's hair, enjoying the brief slide out of loneliness. But it was the infrequent, slight hitches in the other woman's breathing that made Cassie's nipples harden to tight peaks.

They were both aroused, no matter what act they were trying to play.

"I've never kissed a woman before." The words whispered from her lips. Maybe it was a mistake. Maybe it wasn't. Honestly, she didn't care anymore. "I wonder what it would be like to kiss you."

Shay pulled back, a mischievous grin tilting her mouth. "I was thinking the same thing."

Travis cleared his throat from the other side of the bar. "Ladies."

Cassie grinned, ignoring the warning in Travis's tone. "What about Leo? Will he—"

"*Ladies,*" Travis growled. "You've got company."

Cassie pulled back, her hand still in Shay's hair as she met T.J.'s gaze from the other side of the main room. *Oh, God.* The nausea was instantaneous, pulsing up her throat as she slid off the stool.

"I'm sorry." She mouthed the words to him because she couldn't find her voice. His expression was unreadable, far less undecipherable than the impressed smirk from Leo and Brute at his sides.

"I've gotta go." She turned to Shay, being punished all over again from the understanding in her friend's features. "I'll speak to you later." On a cell she didn't have because it was sitting in a Vault locker.

She didn't know how she was going to pay a cab driver without her purse either. But she'd find a way. What she couldn't see herself through was a discussion with T.J. about why she'd come here tonight when they both knew it would hurt him. She couldn't bear for him to think this was retaliation.

With her head down, she strode for the end of the bar, then around the side to the darkened stairwell leading to the parking lot. The club had quieted, the drama she always seemed to bring with her setting in yet again.

All she could hear were footsteps—her own, soft footfalls of patrons and heavy thumping right behind her that could be her thunderous heartbeat echoing in her ears.

"Hey." A strong arm wrapped around her waist, pulling her back into a chiseled chest. "Don't run."

She squeezed her eyes shut and shrank into T.J.'s hold, ashamed and so damn sorry that she'd tainted the one place he'd wanted to remain his own. "Please forgive me. I had no intention of being with anyone tonight." Her voice was breaking. "We thought the Vault would be quieter than a dance club in the city. And—"

"We?"

There was no way she was going to blame Shay. Although coerced, Cassie had always had a choice. "Yes."

He gave a halfhearted chuckle, his warm breath brushing over her ear. "You and Shay have become close."

"I'm not going to blame her, if that's what you mean."

"No." He gripped her shoulder and turned her to face him. "That's definitely *not* what I meant. I expected to find you down here with a man, not a woman. Least of all Shay."

"I wouldn't do that to you, no matter what has happened between us." She frowned up at him, trying to understand what his words and the sad smile on his face meant. "I'd never be with another man in your club, and definitely not the night before our divorce."

He nodded, the movement slow and dreary. "I hoped as much."

Damn him. She didn't want to hear this. "I need to go." She pushed at his chest, feeling a wave of grief as he willingly let her walk away. "Again, I'm sorry."

"Cassie, wait."

Her feet planted of their own accord as she stared at the top of the staircase, wishing she was closer to freedom.

"There's something I want to talk to you about."

There was nothing left. Tomorrow their marriage would be over. She'd agreed to all his conditions. The paperwork to hand over her share of the business was prepared and ready to be signed. She'd spent weeks coming to terms with the dissolution of what they'd once had, and she was trying her best to finally embrace independence.

"I know I've dragged you to hell and back." His voice was gravel-rich. Filled with turmoil. "But I wanted to know if you'd forgive me if I changed my mind."

She frowned at the faint light coming in through the door at the staircase. "Changed your mind?"

"About the divorce."

The light faded. Everything in her body shut down. Her heart stopped, her knees threatened to buckle, her lungs wouldn't fill with air.

"I've made many mistakes, but I can't live without you."

The words were drifting through her ears, not penetrating. She was still stuck on those four words—I changed my mind.

"I want to make this right—" his soft footsteps approached and the heat of his chest settled into her back, "—I know you probably can't forgive me. All I'm asking is that you'll try."

Her chest tightened with the lack of oxygen, her face began to heat.

"I'm not a perfect man, Cass. I no longer believe I'm even a good man. I dragged you into a lifestyle you never should've been a part of. But I still hope you'll give me another chance to make it up to you. To set things right and get our marriage on track."

He pressed his lips to the back of her head, and she squeezed her eyes shut to stop tears from forming.

"Nothing has changed." Her words dripped with defiance. "Unless your guilt has suddenly disappeared, which I doubt. So nothing between us is different. Your excuse for breaking my heart is still there."

He held her tighter. "I'm different."

"This isn't fair," she whispered. "I'm not going to live with the thought of you leaving hanging over my head."

He couldn't dictate their future based on a whim. A whim was what had gotten them here in the first place—the thoughtless decision to go to an unknown sex club had started this chain reaction.

She turned to him, meeting the darkness of his stare in the shadowed hallway. "Am I meant to take you back and forget you kept things from me? That none of this would've happened if only you'd opened up to me?"

"I wanted to spare you the pain. But you know the truth now and I can't stand the thought of you dealing with it alone." He straightened, dropping his hands from her waist. "But, no, you don't have to take me back at all. I just want you to know I made a mistake. I made many. And if given the chance, I'll make it up to you."

"How?" She wasn't sure it was possible. The pain he'd put her through was beyond words. "I love you, T.J., but I can't come back to you when you click your fingers. I can't dust my hands of everything you've done in the past twelve months and pretend it never happened. Our problems started long before those secrets drove you from our house."

Nobody could deny her commitment to him. But at some point, she had to remember the commitment she had to herself. To self-preservation. He had to give her more.

"I don't blame you." He nodded and stepped back. "And I understand what you're trying to say."

"No, you don't." She bridged the space between them in two steps. "There were times when I thought I was going to die from the torment of losing you. Not just when you served me the divorce papers. It all started the night of the assault."

She scrutinized him, hoping for once he would understand what agony really meant. "If anyone had the right to walk away, it was me. You were hurting me because you couldn't handle your own pain. You punished me—"

"I know."

"—because you couldn't..." She frowned at him. "Wait...did you just agree with me?"

"Yes." He swallowed deep. "I was punishing you because I couldn't handle what happened that night. I thought it was guilt. But it was so much more. There was fear and failure. I'd always tried to do everything right by you, and in the blink of an eye, I ruined it all. It scared the hell out of me, Cass. It still does. And I'll never forgive myself."

"If you can't forgive yourself, how am I meant to?" She pressed closer, unwilling to let him off so easily, yet unable to stay away. They both knew where this was heading. It could only ever end in her heartfelt acquiescence. He had to earn it though.

"Your heart is much bigger than mine. You'll forgive me before I forgive myself." He cupped her cheek and caressed her skin with his thumb.

"Then my next question is how can I trust you to not react the same way if I make another bad judgment call in the future?" She raised her chin, their mouths so close she could feel their breath mingling over her lips.

"I'm going to make mistakes, T.J. I *want* to make mistakes. But you need to trust that I've weighed the risks and come to the conclusion on my own. This garbage about you dragging me into a lifestyle I was never meant to be a part of is insulting. I want to be here. Otherwise, I wouldn't have come tonight." She swallowed over the dryness in her throat. "Yes, I'll be smarter in the future, but I can't live with the fear of you leaving me again. I don't care if it's for my own good. I need to know you'll talk to me."

"I promise to try."

"Not good enough." She retreated a step.

He reached out his arm and dragged her back into his chest. "I'll do everything in my power to love you more than life itself."

"I've always had your love. What I want now is your trust. Have faith that I can take responsibility for my own mistakes, and be confident I can deal with the consequences."

He pressed his lips together, fighting the emotion taking over his face. "I promise."

"Really?"

"Cassie, I'm trying my hardest. I always will. But I'm not going to lie to you. Until something happens, I can only prepare myself to act better in the future."

She quirked a brow at him and wiggled from his arms. "Well, why don't I make something happen?"

CHAPTER TWENTY

T.J. watched Cassie saunter from the darkened hall and didn't let her walk out of view. He followed after her, his pulse increasing the more adamant her steps became.

"Are you okay?" Shay straightened from her position against the back of the sofa closest to the bar and didn't flinch when Cassie continued toward her, sliding against the other woman's body before brushing their lips together.

"Fuck me drunk." Leo's words rang heavy in the room. "What the hell did you say to her?"

T.J. ignored the question, too transfixed with the sight before him. Cassie glided her hand into Shay's hair, the long strands of dark silk brushing through his wife's delicate fingers. They were mesmerizing. Captivating. The two of them making out as if they were long-lost lovers, not women who were sharing their first kiss. At least he thought it was their first.

"Have they done this before?" T.J. slumped onto the stool next to Leo and pounded the bar. "Bourbon. Straight. Now."

"Make that two," Leo muttered. "And I fucking hope not. The way those two look together, I'm starting to think Shay might leave me for a better offer."

She wouldn't get the chance. T.J. grasped the glass Travis slid in to his hand and threw the liquid back in one gulp. Cassie had made her point. In her mind, she was testing boundaries and taking a chance. And no matter how inviting her so-called risk currently was, he'd had his fill for the night.

He needed her. To claim what he'd been missing for too damn long.

He slammed his glass down on the bar, giving his wife a warning before he strode for her. "That's enough, ladies." He moved in behind Cassie, slid an arm around her waist and flung her around to stand before him. "What was that all about?"

Her chest was rising and falling, her gorgeous lips kiss-stained. "I'm not going to return to a marriage where I'll be scared to take chances."

"That wasn't really taking a chance, my love." He prowled toward her, his dick pulsing at the way her pupils dilated.

She backtracked, bumped into the sofa and straightened as she kept distance between them, fleeing toward the back of the main room. "How was I to know she was going to kiss me back? She could've just as easily slapped me or pushed me away."

"Really?" He quirked a brow. "From what I witnessed earlier, it seemed more like you were finishing what you'd already started."

Her lips rose at the edges, and she snaked her tempting tongue out to moisten her lips. "Well, okay, maybe it wasn't much of a risk..." She beamed at him. "Baby steps, right?"

A growl formed in his chest, the warmest, richest sound he'd ever made without conscious thought. Behind him was loneliness and safety. Before him stood pain and pleasure. The sweetest mix of everything volatile and risky.

He'd obsessed over Cassie's protection and happiness—past, present and future. It was the way he measured his worth in the world. If this gorgeous woman was smiling due to his words, his touch, his love, he was a satisfied man. But he had to sever that addiction. He had to step back and let her find her own happiness. Make her secure her own safety.

"Does this mean you forgive me?" He was so close, yet so far. He could reach out a hand and touch her, to brush her smooth skin, to drag her against his body, only her smile faltered, piercing him in the chest with sorrow.

"You need to do more than growl at me to earn my forgiveness." Her grin returned, washing away the hurt and replacing it with hope.

"Make a list. Whatever you want is yours." He'd make it up to her somehow. With every day for the rest of their lives.

He continued for her, her retreating steps approaching the back wall. "How come you're running from me?"

"I have no clue." Her words were whispers. "You'd think I wouldn't be nervous after all the chasing I did to try and get you back."

"Nervous?" He stopped, unable to move another inch. "Well, why don't I start things off myself. You can come to me when you're ready?" He didn't want her apprehension. He needed excitement, love, passion and hope for their future. *Baby steps.*

She frowned, cocking her head in the cutest confused expression as he strode to the king-sized bed in the corner. He slid onto the mattress, resting his back against the headboard and crossed his feet at the ankles.

On the outside, he was relaxed. Calm. Inside was a different story. The pulse of his heart was heavy, a pounding ache in his chest. His hands were shaking, sweat slicking his palms, but his cock was the worst offender. He was hard as granite, the length of his shaft pressing against his zipper with incessant force.

Cassie sauntered forward, her steps measured and slow. Her gaze raked his body, focusing on the bulge at his crotch, then rising to his face.

He cleared his throat and wiggled his shoulders, settling into his position. "I haven't had a chance to ask you what you think of the club."

"It's more than I ever imagined." She glanced over her shoulder, taking in the room. "The bar, the rooms, the furnishings—it all fits together perfectly."

"We try and keep security to a maximum. Not only on function nights, but during the vetting process."

"I know." A smirk curved her lips and she broke their stare to focus on the bedsheet.

She was breathtaking. Her hair loose, her curves tightly caressed by the dress she wore. He wanted her legs wrapped around him, her high-heel-covered feet crossed around his back.

"Of course you do." He placed his hands behind his head, the picture of leisure. "You experienced the entry process for the masquerade party."

She nodded, still looking down at the sheet.

"Do you have any idea what the memories of that night do to me?" They were vivid. A crystal-clear recollection continuously playing in the back of his mind.

"I'd take a guess that the effect isn't nice," she murmured. "From the anger you showed toward me when I told you, I can only assume you're still horrified."

Far from it. "At first, yes. It was brutal. But when I got home and went over those moments with fresh eyes, knowing it was you instead of a stranger, it was the most erotic memory I'd ever had." He stared at her, mentally begging her to look at him. "You seducing me. Here. In front of all those people. I've been haunted by an insistent hard-on that can't be assuaged."

Her head shot up, the tops of her cheeks turning a light shade of pink as their gazes collided. "You're not mad anymore?"

Only at himself. He'd still cheated on his wife, and that was unforgivable. "Mad?" He chuckled. "Do you have any idea how many times I've had to jerk off to gain some semblance of relief?" His cock had been punishing him ever since. "I still remember your voice and the familiar way you said hi at the bar."

"I hadn't thought to school my tone." The nervousness in her features began to settle, the apprehension in her eyes softening with comfort. "Well, I had, but I was too flustered to remember. I even forgot to take off my wedding rings until Zoe asked me about them in the change rooms."

"I can't believe you had me fooled." Although, in hindsight, his eyes were the only things that had been misled. The rest of his senses had known—touch, taste, sound. Even her presence was familiar. The way he'd closed his eyes and pictured Cassie instead of the dark-haired, dark-eyed beauty. "But it was when you asked if I wanted to watch you that lust mixed with confusion. I didn't stand a chance."

She nestled on the foot of the bed, the dress slipping higher up her thigh.

"I guess I should return the favor," he murmured.

Her eyes widened, her brow furrowing in the sexiest way. "What do you mean?"

He grinned, breathing in her nervousness. Consuming it. "It's your turn to watch."

∼

Cassie swallowed and glanced over her shoulder, thankful that the few remaining people in the room weren't paying them attention.

"W-what do you mean?" She turned back to T.J., receiving her answer from the quirk in his lips.

He removed one hand from behind his head and lowered it to his waistband. "Watch," he reiterated, releasing the button on his pants and then lowering his zipper with torturing lethargy. "You scooted back onto that bed like a fucking dream."

He hitched his ass off the mattress and lowered the material to the tops of his thighs, still with one lazy hand behind his head. The hardness of his cock was clearly visible through the thin material of his boxer briefs. She could see every inch, could almost feel the remembered sensation of his shaft in her palm.

"And that finger you placed in your mouth." He groaned. "*Jesus,* that was hot."

Her heart was fluttering uncontrollably. She was reliving those moments with a new perspective. No longer feeling the desperate humiliation.

He slid his hand over his crotch and closed his eyes briefly. His arousal was seeping under her skin, making her ache for what was right before her. Making her wet for his length. She knew the pleasure he would bring her, could already feel it with the tightening of her pussy.

He stroked his cock through his underwear, holding her gaze as he did it. "I've come so many times since that night, but my hand never seems to be enough." He slipped his fingers under the elastic of his briefs and lowered the material as he gripped his bare shaft.

Saliva pooled in her mouth, the greedy need for him becoming overwhelming. Over a year had passed since she'd felt him at the back of her throat. She couldn't wait any longer. She needed a taste, a touch, anything to take her mind off the slickness in her panties and the way her core continuously convulsed, begging for penetration.

She inched forward on her hands and knees, spreading his legs with her weight as she sank between them. His cock was right there, a mere lick away. Pre-come seeped from his slit, taunting her while his fist continued to work the length, up and down, stealing a hiss from his lips.

She reached for him, wanting his grip to be hers, needing her fingers to be the ones bringing him pleasure.

"Not tonight." He lowered his hand from the headboard and delicately gripped her chin. "I want you too much, Cassie."

She nodded, sneaking her tongue out to moisten her lips. The throb in her chest became heavier, anticipation and nerves working side by side. This was her first proper experience in a sex club. The one they'd been daydreaming about for years. The masquerade party had been a job, a task to try and win her husband back. This was different. Right now was all about foreplay and arousal, heat and love.

"Come here." He held out his hand, silently asking for hers, and guided her to straddle his lap.

The material of her dress pulled uncomfortably tight around her thighs, the hem digging into her skin as she hovered over him.

"Can I hitch it up?" His words were soft, gentle, unlike the T.J. she was used to in the bedroom. "I know you're nervous. I am, too. There are a million thoughts running through my mind. About our past and our future. Where we are and the people watching. But I don't want to think about that. I just want to think about you."

He leaned forward, brushing his lips over hers. "Nobody else exists anymore. I'm done with the outside world."

She remained still, poised over his lap, staring into the truth in his eyes. "Hitch it up."

He slid the material higher, exposing the top of her thighs, coming to a stop when he exposed her black silk panties. T.J.'s brow furrowed, the briefest hint that he knew what she was thinking as he slid his hands around to her ass, digging his fingers into her skin with delicious ferocity.

"You're fucking gorgeous." He added pressure to his touch, guiding her down to nestle against the hardness of his erection. She withheld a groan at the blissful torture of his heated shaft. The only thing between them was one thin layer of material, which was currently soaked with her arousal. "And wet."

She nodded. "If we were at home right now, I'd beg you to fuck me."

"Do it anyway. What's stopping you?"

She held in a nervous laugh. "Maybe the fifteen to twenty people that would come rushing over to see the show."

His lips quirked, the unmistakable sign of arrogance she loved seeing in this man. "They know better than to stare. They'd steal a brief glimpse for now, and that's all. They know you're new down here."

"Are you trying to make me more nervous?"

He chuckled. "No. But the few people paying us attention are currently doing so because you're beautiful. You have a body built for pleasure. And it isn't hard to tell what they're thinking."

"Hmm?" She didn't want to ask. Her lips wouldn't move to voice the words. The fact they were watching at all had adrenaline pulsing through her veins.

He leaned into her, nuzzled her neck, running his lips along her skin. "They want to fuck you, Cassie." He nipped at her. "Almost as much as I do."

She moaned, arching her neck to give him better access. Her nerves were on fire, every inch of her tingling with sensations.

"They want to tie you up. To fuck you until you scream. They'd fight to have you, if I let them."

Her nipples hardened at his words. She didn't want anyone else. Never would. Yet, the admiration of strangers made her body ignite in the most delirious sort of way.

"They want you in the swing, your body completely naked apart from the straps holding you up. They want your thighs tight around their waist. Your pussy at their mercy."

She closed her eyes and began rocking against his erection, unable to deny the friction her clit was demanding.

"They want you riding them. Just like you're riding me, teasing my cock with that sweet heat of yours."

She whimpered. *Oh, God.* She needed relief. Half her body had lost sensation, while the other half—the half that consisted of her thighs, abdomen and sex—were all pulsing, throbbing, tingling with a mass of intensity she couldn't control.

He slid his fingers between them, and she snapped her eyes open to witness him gripping the crotch of her panties, pulling them to the side.

"I'm dying to be inside you."

She was dying for him to be there, for the torment to be over and the pleasure to take hold. She hovered above him, her hands gripping his shoulders as he rubbed his cock down her opening, his fingers still holding her panties out of the way.

Fuck it. "I'll take them off." She scampered, twisting and turning, wiggling and shimmying until the panties were off. Then she was back straddling him, her ass still covered by the dress, but her sex clearly visible between them.

"You're a dream, Cassie. A fantasy." He ran a hand through her hair and palmed her nape, dragged her to his lips. "I'm one lucky son of a bitch."

She smiled against his mouth. "Your mother wouldn't appreciate that."

"Don't go killing the buzz, my love."

She chuckled and closed her eyes, sinking down on to him, the hardness of his cock tearing a moan from her throat.

"Fuck, you're wet."

"Fuck, you're hard." He was so thick, so absolutely perfect that her pussy was already threatening to become overwhelmed. Her hips rocked of their own accord, their bodies already familiar with passion.

He gripped her ass in one hand, grinding into her, giving her clit brief glimpses of necessary friction as he glided his mouth over hers. There were no thoughts. Only pleasure. Only the building climax threatening to end this moment too soon.

Their tongues tangled, breath mingled, and through it all, he continued to hold her, his hand clutching her nape, his grip on her ass. She was drowning in his love, succumbing to the relief she wasn't sure she was ready to feel.

Her husband was back. Her soul mate had returned. This man was her everything. Her future. His laughter, weaknesses and determination. He was her happiness, and she'd make sure he knew there was never another option than them being together.

"I hope you're not still nervous about being watched," he spoke against her lips.

Her nipples tingled before she had the chance to stiffen. Yes, she was nervous, but exhilarated was more accurate. "Why?"

"Brute seems to like the show."

She shot a glance over her shoulder, meeting the stare of their business partner, who leaned against the side of the bar. His gaze was intense, in complete contrast to the lazy way he lifted the scotch glass to his lips.

"Doesn't that make you feel uncomfortable?" At least she should be uncomfortable, right? She felt far from it. Having Brute's gaze on her was making her breath hitch, her pussy tighten.

"Should it?" He grazed his mouth over hers. "You don't want to know how many times I've watched him with women. It's become as natural as sharing a drink with him at the bar."

"Never again, okay?" She rested her forehead against his, working her hips harder. "If you're down here, I want to be with you. No more watching him without me."

He released a breathy snicker and jerked his hips in a hard thrust. "I can commit to that."

She ground into him, her movements becoming more forceful, her desire growing as his hands ran up her sides, brushing the curve of her breasts.

"I've missed these." He tweaked her nipples, earning a hard thrust in retaliation. "I've missed everything."

He bucked harder, his grip moving to her ass, pressing her down harder on his cock. She began to pant, trying to focus to curb the impending climax. She was so close...almost there.

"Tate." His name was barely audible, a mere whisper against his neck.

He growled, moving his hips in a harsh rhythm as she clung to his shoulders. She couldn't wait. She'd been too long without his love.

"Tate..." Her pussy contracted, erupting in sensation that ebbed throughout her body.

He groaned, digging his fingers into her flesh. Her name whispered from his lips, a repeated caress she'd cherish forever.

"You're never leaving me again." It was a demand. One she would ensure he adhered to.

"I promise." His lips brushed her jaw, her cheek, her lips. "Never again, Cassie."

"You need to stop the divorce. You need to make it go away."

"I will. Don't even spare it a thought."

She nodded, their mouths still pressed together as their movement slowed and silence descended around them. She wasn't sure what she expected. Applause? Cheers? None came. The club continued as if their monumental reunion hadn't existed.

She glanced over her shoulder, to Brute who was still staring at her, Leo and Shay now positioned at his sides. All three of them smiled...

well, Brute's lips lifted slightly. Their expressions of satisfaction filled her lungs with renewed warmth.

"I think they're glad I'll no longer be torturing them with my mood swings," T.J. spoke into her hair.

"And you'll no longer be torturing me by living somewhere else." She nestled against his shoulder and faced the back wall. His length was still inside her, his heart beating into her chest. Losing him scared her. It always would. She could lose the sun, the moon, the breath from her lungs, but as long as T.J. was with her, she'd be happy.

"Are you okay?" he spoke into her hair.

"Perfect." She sighed and nuzzled closer to him.

The pain was easing. The mourning being replaced with hope for their future.

"Take me home, T.J." She pulled back and stared into his eyes. "I want to fall asleep in your arms."

EPILOGUE

"We really need to get these women on a leash," Brute muttered. "Every time I turn my back, it seems like they're fucking up the Vault."

T.J. grinned, unable to drag his gaze away from Cassie and Shay swaying their hips on the small dance floor they'd added to the far corner of the club. The music was low so it didn't disturb the carnal atmosphere, but in his opinion, the slow, sultry songs they'd programmed into the nearby iPhone only added fuel to the fire.

He hadn't been able to move since he'd taken a seat on the leather sofa a few feet away. Neither had Leo, who sat at the other end, his focus trained on Shay as the two women danced around each other.

"I think they're deliberately trying to drive me crazy." Leo scowled.

"Ya think?" Brute chuckled. "It's having the same effect on James."

T.J. and Leo studied the man sitting on a nearby sofa. He had a drink in his hand, and a wolfish gleam in his eye as he observed the dance floor.

"Are you sure he passed the security check?" Leo asked. "I don't like the look of him."

"Me either." T.J. turned his attention back to Cassie. "Make sure his name is taken off the list. I don't want to see him here again." Letting go of his protective nature wasn't easy. Especially not when unfamiliar men were ogling his wife. He was happy for regulars to look their fill. She was a woman made to be admired, but he didn't know this man.

"You can't deny entry to every guy that wants to fuck your wife." Brute stood behind them, looming over the back of the sofa. "If that were the case, I wouldn't be allowed down here either."

"Funny," T.J. grated.

"Not joking." Brute clapped him on the shoulder. "What's with the phone anyway?" He leaned forward and snatched the device from T.J.'s hand.

"Just having a little fun." He'd convinced his wife to wear the sex toy he'd given her years ago. One half of the C-shaped instrument was burrowed inside her pussy, while the other was wrapped around to nestle against her clit. "It's an app for the sex toy Cass is wearing."

He chanced a quick glance over his shoulder at Brute who was focused on the phone. "Every once in a while, I press one of those buttons and it triggers vibrations."

"You've been doing that all night?" Brute asked.

"Mostly." It was thrilling to know he was pleasuring her without anyone else's knowledge. Her pussy was probably dripping, the evidence of her arousal barely contained in the lace G-string he'd picked for her to wear.

"What happens if I press a lot of buttons?" Brute tapped on the screen.

"I think you can figure that out for yourself."

"And you're not worried that I'm going to make your wife come?"

T.J. grinned, still staring at his wife. "Not in the slightest." There wasn't another man who could tempt Cassie. He may not deserve her, but she was committed to him nonetheless. Her love was flowing through his veins, her happiness a constant beat in his heart.

"Go for it." T.J. reclined, spreading his arms along the back and arm of the sofa. She'd know he wasn't controlling the sex toy as soon as she glanced his way, and he had a feeling it would have a positive effect on her.

All three of them watched in silence, the rhythmic tap of Brute's finger against the screen in time with the slow beat of "Gorilla" by Bruno Mars.

"She hasn't even noticed." Leo inched forward on the seat. "Are you sure she's still wearing it?"

"She's noticed." He could tell from the heavy convulse of her throat as she swallowed, the brief, almost unnoticeable way she brushed her arms over her breasts as she raised them over her head in a sultry move. Her feet were closer together, too, allowing her to squeeze her thighs together and disguise it as dancing.

He scrutinized her, ignoring the incessant throb of his cock that hadn't seemed to ebb since he'd moved back home two weeks ago. She licked her lips, her chest rising and falling quicker, her actions becoming slower. "I think she's about to break."

Each day was getting easier. Their passion had reignited as if it had never been extinguished. All they had to do now was wait for the past to stop haunting them. Peace would come with time. But what was more important was the steady ownership of the life they led.

She turned to him, her chin high, her footsteps shaky as she strode forward on her stiletto heels.

"Should I prepare to be slapped?" Brute muttered.

T.J. shook his head. "No." That wasn't anger in her eyes.

She didn't stop her progression. She came at him, climbing onto the couch and straddling his hips.

"Enjoying your dan—"

She cut off his words with a kiss. A wild, passionate kiss that had her tongue sneaking into his mouth to tangle with his. She ran her fingers through his hair, her other hand gripping his shoulder, digging her nails deep.

"Why did you give your phone to Brute?" She moaned into his mouth, her hips gyrating, the vibrations of the sex toy pulsing into his shaft.

"I didn't think you'd mind."

"I don't." She mewled, driving him insane with the rough way she ground against him. "*Oh, God,* I don't."

Leo cursed and Brute's finger began to tap against the screen again.

"Wait. *Stop.*" Cassie glanced up at Brute, her eyes imploring. "Please. Don't turn it down."

Asshole. T.J. knew exactly what his friend was doing.

"Brute," Cassie begged. "I need it harder. *Please.* Do it harder."

"You hear that, Tate?" Brute boasted. "Your wife is begging me to give it to her harder."

"You're fucking predictable." T.J. shook his head, and ground his teeth together. "Would you hurry the fuck up, so I don't make a fool out of myself?"

Brute tapped a few more times, creating a harsh vibration in Cassie's pussy that pulsated all the way through him. He wasn't sure he was going to make it out unscathed. He was dying to have her. To sink into her.

She moaned, her arms gripping tight around his neck. "I can't breathe." She was panting, rocking her hips back and forth, snaking her tongue out to wet her dry lips. "I need more."

"Sorry," Brute grated, the sound of arousal heavy in his voice. "That's as high as it goes, sweetheart."

Shay strode forward, her slender frame coming to stand at Cassie's back. She peered down at T.J., a familiar gleam in her eyes. "Need help?"

Fuck. If Cassie didn't quit gyrating over his cock and come soon, he was going to explode. There was no question about it. He'd either have to take himself in hand or figure out a way to get his wife's underwear off in a hurry. "Yes."

Leo cursed again. This time louder.

Shay turned her focus to her boyfriend and smirked as she brushed the hair back from Cassie's neck. "It's just a kiss." She leaned down, brushing her mouth at the low of Cassie's neck.

"You've got ten seconds to get over here." Leo began counting down, his tone becoming harsher the lower the numbers fell.

"And if I don't?"

"Jesus Christ," Brute snapped. "Would you take this somewhere else? Can't you see I'm trying to work my magic here?"

Shay held up her hands in surrender and sauntered toward Leo, taking her steps nice and slow. "You're on your own, Cass."

Cassie whimpered, once, twice, then sunk her teeth into T.J.'s neck as every muscle in her body clung to him, holding tight. She stopped breathing. Then her body began to shudder, the orgasm hitting her as she rocked into him.

Breathe. Focus. Do not come. Do. Not. Come.

"Just think of me, buddy," Brute whispered in his ear.

That did the trick. Somewhat. He glanced over his shoulder and snatched his phone back, lowering the vibration settings as Cassie began to settle in to his chest, her exhalations a constant stroke over his skin.

He closed the app, locked his phone and threw it onto the seat at his side, mere inches from Leo who now had his girlfriend straddling his lap. Their mouths were joined, their bodies chest to chest as Leo cupped Shay's face in his hands.

"This is getting old." Brute huffed. "I need to go get laid before we close up. I'll see you all later."

T.J. inclined his head and clutched the woman in his arms tightly. He held her close, enjoying the adoration that took over the need for pleasure. They weren't back to normal. They were back at the beginning. Going on date nights, reigniting puppy love and mixing it with the years of commitment they already had.

It was a blessed combination.

"Let's go home," he spoke into her hair.

She pushed her hands against his chest and pulled back to stare at him. "You don't want to stay?"

"Not tonight." He shook his head. They had years to spend in here. To have fun with friends and strangers. He wanted to be greedy. For the rest of the night, he would have her all to himself. And maybe every other night until she grew tired of his affection. "I want to take you home and show you just how much I love you."

Her eyes twinkled. "You haven't stopped doing that for the last three weeks."

"No." He smiled, brushing his lips over hers. "And I never will."

BRUTAL SIN

DEDICATION

For those who like damaged goods. I hope you enjoy Brute.

CHAPTER ONE

*P*amela slid her bare thighs onto the bar stool, feigning relaxation even though the sensation was illusive.

Whimpers and groans filled her ears, along with the rhythmic slap of naked, sweaty bodies. At one time, she'd thrived on this atmosphere. The lascivious environment had invigorated her. Awakened her.

Until the excitement wore off and desperation set in.

Escaping to the Vault of Sin had been her monthly ritual for almost two years. She'd started out optimistic, hoping to replace the void her husband's death had gouged into her chest with the delicious thrill of the exclusive sex club. Now, the bright hope had faded to black, making her bitter and resentful. There was nobody here for her. No one to give her what she needed. What she craved.

"Are you looking for company, sweetie?"

From the corner of her eye, she took in the man beside her. With the gentle tone of one word—*sweetie*—she could tell his aim for the night was to role play in genres unsuitable to her palate. She didn't want to be his good little girl. She didn't require a pedestal or the touch of a delicate hand. Her desires were far more complex than that.

"I'm good, thanks."

It was time to face the harsh reality. Her sex life would forever be on a downward slide. Her marriage to a man who had pinpoint precision on her libido had ruined her for future lovers. She needed to stop wasting time on men who lacked the skill and patience to get her off. She'd squandered enough Saturday nights already, spent months upon months playing with men who refused to take non-verbal cues.

"You sure?" He placed his hand against the ribbons tying the back of her corset, now entranced with the navy-blue flecks in the material sparkling in the bar light. The boned lingerie, along with the silken panties she currently wore, were a present from her late husband, Lucas. One of the last presents he'd given her. "You look lonely."

She sighed. Yep, she definitely needed to move on. Now men weren't even taking verbal cues. "Not lonely. Just alone. There's a difference." She swiveled on the stool and slid to her feet. "And besides, we've been together before. It isn't something I want to repeat."

"Aww, honey, from memory, we had a lot of fun."

"*You* had a lot of fun." She bit her tongue to stop elaborating.

His brows pulled tight, encouraging her to walk away in case he interjected with an insult of his own. When she'd first arrived at the Vault, the other patrons had considered her shy and apprehensive. They hadn't seen past her exterior. They hadn't attempted to look deeper.

To them, she resembled a shallow, neglected puddle, when the reality was an expanse of tumultuous ocean. She knew exactly what she was searching for. The checklist was small but specific. And apparently, each item was more rare than a unicorn.

Her feet stopped of their own accord as she came to the open doorway of one of the side rooms. Zoe, another regular club patron, was on the sofa along the wall, her two men paying homage to her scantily-clad body with such sweet finesse it made Pamela's eyes burn.

The threat of tears wasn't due to weakness or heartbreak. These were tears of frustration. Of utter annoyance and anger. Why was it so difficult to find a man in tune with her needs, the way these men were in tune with Zoe's?

Everywhere she turned, sexual chemistry stared back at her. The bartender, Shay, had it with her manager boyfriend, Leo. Then there was T.J. and his wife, Cassie, along with every other duo inside the secretive walls of the carnal club.

Maybe her appetite was the problem.

Her desires were too specific. She had no use for sweet affection. She craved finesse in a more dominant form. The skill of a man who could inspire an orgasm mentally as well as physically. *Damn it.* Was she being overly critical? It wasn't as if she expected a stranger to learn everything about her in one touch. Problem was, some men still had no clue after three orgasms.

Theirs.

Not hers.

"They're good together, aren't they?" The smooth drawl came from a man at her back. "They adore her."

"Yes, they do." She closed her eyes briefly and forced down the instinct to fling another rejection. "But I'm looking for something a little more…"

"What?"

She shrugged. Pointing out specifics seemed equivalent to gifting a completed puzzle. Where was the fun in that?

"Whatever it is, I'm happy to help."

Her last slivers of hope faded with each breath. "I want to be controlled." The admission came with a wince. She shouldn't be encouraging more opportunities for disappointment. There'd already been enough.

"Hmm." His thighs leaned into her, his unmistakable erection nestling against her ass. "I can control you, princess."

An arm wrapped around her waist. The touch light, delicate—a man playing a dominant role he had no idea how to perfect.

She turned, seeing him for the first time, his hand now draped over the low of her back. He was attractive enough. A soft hazel gaze, smooth skin, and neatly cut brown hair. What he didn't have was the *zing*. The buzz. The commanding presence in his eyes.

"Not tonight." She pulled away, only to be stopped by his tightening grip.

"You'll stay," he ordered.

A shiver ran down her spine. It could've been a delicious thrill, the start of something promising, only his features didn't match his tone. He was a scared kitten behind that hold. There was no conviction. No power.

"Take your hand off me," she grated.

It wasn't easy to play an unfamiliar role. It took balls. Large ones. And the man she needed required cojones the size of a rhino, not a mouse.

"I'm sorry." His hand fell, his balk of regret reigniting her frustration. "I was only trying to—"

"I know." She pasted on a smile, determined to fight her bitchy attitude into submission. "And I appreciate the attempt."

It wasn't his fault she was already edgy from the impending sexual sobriety. She needed to remove her toxic attitude from this place of bodily worship and cut her losses. More hours here would only increase her resentment. She wasn't a bitter old hag. Not entirely. But soon she might be if she didn't stop feeling sorry for herself and move on.

She squeezed his wrist in apology and strode through the main Vault room, giving half-hearted grins to the patrons who looked at her in pity. She didn't fit in with this crowd. A world she'd once dominated was now foreign. She'd become a pauper in a place where orgasms were currency —at least where receiving was concerned.

When she reached the seclusion of the locker room, defeat set in. She'd come so far from the missionary-position woman she'd been before Lucas. Now she'd fallen from carnal grace. Sex was no longer exciting. Her seven-day-a-week habit had died from starvation, and all she could do was move on. Bury the craving, like she'd buried her husband.

"Goddamn you." She opened her locker door and slammed it shut again. The loud bang reverberated through her, hitting her chest, her heart. The threat of tears returned. Angry, scornful tears making the room blur.

She'd thought she'd done everything right. She hadn't jumped into the Vault experience with gusto. Her steps had been slow. Over unending months, she became the ultimate voyeur, not touching another man until she was ready—mind, body, and soul. Then one after another, the club regulars had failed her, leaving unfulfillment to run rampant, all because her husband's prowess was irreplaceable. "Damn you, Lucas."

"Hey."

She stiffened at the sound of Shay's voice and hoped the woman would let her be. "Can you give me a minute?"

"That depends. Are you going to continue destroying Vault property if I leave you alone?" The sound of softly swishing fabric encroached. "What's going on?"

Pamela inhaled deep and turned to Shay, taking in the beauty of a woman who couldn't possibly understand what was going on in her addled mind.

"You look gorgeous. As always." It was a side-step. An optimistic diversion. Chatting about the seductive red dress clinging to the bartender's breasts and flowing into a sexy skirt at her thighs was better than the alternative.

"Thank you. Leo seems to enjoy the easy access." Shay gave herself a once-over before meeting Pamela's gaze. "Now, spill. What's got you slamming lockers and looking like the world's coming to an end?"

Pamela kept her mouth shut, scared of what would come out if her lips parted. Words built in her throat, clogging the small space, the pressure increasing. Venting wasn't an issue. She could share her hardships with her sister tomorrow. Even her mother, if she was truly desperate. But they didn't fully understand her cravings. Her sexuality. Sharing with Shay, a woman who knew this way of life, would be different. And the thought of having her worst fears confirmed wasn't something she could handle right now.

"Come on, Pamela." Shay stepped forward, her gentle eyes coaxing. "Tell me what's wrong."

The need to purge grew. The truth cut off her air supply until she opened her mouth and words tumbled out. "*Everything*. I can't do this anymore. I need to give up before it kills me."

"Take a deep breath, honey, and tell me what happened."

"Nothing happened." Pamela swung back to her locker, pulled out her loose black skirt, and yanked it up her thighs. "The same nothing that happens every time I come here." She shoved her tank top into the handbag sitting in the back of the locker, unfazed by walking out of here with her lingerie on display. God knew the people dancing upstairs would be wearing far less. "Please tell Leo I want to cancel my membership. You won't see me here again."

"Okay... I can tell him." Shay leaned forward, inching her way into Pamela's sight. "But before I do, can you elaborate? I've seen you with different men, so your comment about 'nothing happening' is throwing me."

"I mean, nothing happens for *me*." She waved a hand to encompass her body—the breasts that never tingled from a man's touch, the pussy that didn't throb in arousal. "In all the time I've been here, and all the men I've slept with, I haven't orgasmed once. Not even a tiny bit. Not even close." She reached for her shoes and dropped the one-inch black heels at her feet. "I'm only kidding myself if I keep coming back."

"Didn't Leo set you up with someone a while ago?" Shay frowned. "Yeah. It was my first night down here, and he was playing the role of instructor. Didn't that work out?"

"That was the first time I'd been with anyone since my husband." She yanked her handbag from the locker and pulled the strap over her shoulder. "I faked my way through it, thinking that was necessary to get into the swing of things. Turns out, I've had to fake it ever since."

Shay slumped onto the bench seat in the middle of the room. "Maybe it's too soon for you to move on."

"It's been three years." For others, the timeline of grief was infinite. Not for her, though. She'd been primed to move on for a long time. "I'm ready. The problem is finding the right person."

"Is there something in particular you're looking for? Is it aesthetic appeal? Are the men not your type? Or do you have a specific kink?"

"I know exactly what I want." A carbon-copy of her husband, at least where the sex was concerned. "I want a man who will take me over and control my pleasure. Someone who knows what I want before I want it and doesn't mistake his cockiness for finesse." She sighed and let her tired shoulders sag as she slumped onto the bench beside Shay. "Sorry for the hysterics. I guess frustration finally has the better of me."

"Is that all it is? Frustration?"

Yes...

Maybe...

No.

She stared down at her glossy shoes, the past reliving itself in her mind. "I wasn't married to Lucas for long. We didn't even reach our one-year anniversary. And in that time, he completely changed my sex life. He made me aware of a sexuality I never knew I had. But I didn't realize it was exclusive to our relationship. I thought the physical connection would be replaceable. Maybe not to the exact degree of what we had. I only hoped for something similar. Instead, I'm losing faith in ever finding the part of myself that made me feel most alive."

It sounded pathetic. How could sex be such a significant piece of her? It was only physical exertion, right?

Wrong.

The act was so much more. She needed to be seen without having to wave her arms in the crowd. She wanted to be heard without words. She longed for someone to know her. Yet, she wasn't sure she knew herself anymore.

"Would you trust me to hook you up with a guy who might be able to help?" Shay leaned in and rested her head on Pamela's shoulder.

"I think I'm too far gone. I used to be able to orgasm with the flick of my husband's fingers. Now men need to have mastered the Kama Sutra and bear the scratches of a thousand pleasured virgins before I give them the time of day." She released a half-hearted chuckle. "I'm high maintenance."

"The person I have in mind would see that as a challenge."

"I've been with most of the available men at the Vault."

"You haven't been with him. I'd know." Shay stood and rubbed her hands together. "I have a really good feeling about this. All I need is five minutes to make it happen."

"It's too late. I'm..." An old widow? A born-again virgin? A broken soul?

"In a slump. That's all." Shay started for the door, her face bright with optimism. "And I'm convinced Brute will be the perfect match for you."

CHAPTER TWO

*B*ryan Munro tugged the under-age piece-of-shit through the club by the collar. Standards of Practice could kiss his ass. There was no way he was letting this fucker walk out without being manhandled. If you were cunning enough to pass the bouncer inspection and sneak inside the Shot of Sin nightclub illegally, the last thing you wanted to do was draw attention to yourself by grabbing the first pair of tits that passed your way.

"Come back here and I'll show you what it feels like to be sexually assaulted." He shoved the kid through the open front doors. When the prick righted himself without falling to the pavement, the disappointment was real. "Believe me, some days I miss being in jail. Making you my bitch would bring back memories."

It was a lie. All lies. But the wide eyes of the teen were well worth the pretense.

The bouncer on the door chuckled. "You definitely live up to your nickname, Brute."

"I do." He jerked his chin toward the club. "And if I find anyone else in there who's underage, you'll find out just how brutal I can be."

The guy straightened. "Sorry, boss."

"You should be." Bryan and his business partners, T.J. and Leo, didn't have time for this lazy bullshit. The adjoining Taste of Sin restaurant was being slammed nightly with eager walk-ins willing to beg for a table when the already extended dining hours couldn't keep up with reservations. And Vault of Sin downstairs always came with a heavy dose of drama. He didn't need Shot of Sin to add legal issues with underage drinkers to his list.

"I'll be more thorough." The bouncer crossed his arms over his chest, his lips thin, his frown deep. A picture of clichéd security.

"Make sure you are." Bryan strode back into the club, his bad luck increasing when he sighted Shay leaning against the entry hall in her tempting thigh-high dress. Leo's girlfriend was not only a thorn in his side, but a fucking pinecone up his ass. If he didn't know better, he'd assume her life's mission was to turn him gray. And she was succeeding. "What do you want, wench?"

Her lips quirked as she pushed from the wall. "I need to borrow your cock for a minute."

He raised a brow and came up beside her, stopping close. "You've finally realized I'm a better option than Leo?"

Her smile turned coy, those long brown eyelashes batting up at him. "Not even close." She pivoted on her toes and sauntered toward the dancing bodies, crooking a finger over her shoulder. "Come on."

He growled and followed, pretending he didn't appreciate the way his sexy subordinate ordered him around. She led him through the thick crowd to the Vault entry, guarded by a lone member of security.

"Why are we going downstairs?" He raised his voice over the thud of music. "I'm supposed to be watching the bar tonight."

"Stop bitching. The staff can do their job without you breathing down their neck for a while." She pulled open the door and disappeared into the darkened stairwell.

He gave the security guard a dubious look and contemplated what lay ahead. The barely controlled twitch of the guy's mouth announced loud and clear that the hell-raiser of the club was likely to shank him with a steel dildo once he was in seclusion. "If I don't come out within twenty minutes, call Leo for help."

"Will do."

Bryan strode inside and pushed the door shut behind him. With the click of the latch, the club music disconnected, the soundproofing replacing the loud beat with static. "Hold up."

The eager way Shay bounced down the steps toward the private sex club increased his apprehension. She was excited about something.

Something that involved his dick.

"Shay," he grated, unmoving. "What's going on?"

She turned to him, the overhead lights shining down on her with a heavenly glow that didn't fool him in the slightest. "There's a woman who needs your help."

"Help? Are we talking about a maintenance problem or a woman-wants-to-get-laid issue?"

He had no problem with the former. The latter was entirely different. Apparently, he'd earned a name for himself within the sordid walls of the club. A name that had him at the front and center of every woman's spank bank.

"This situation leans more toward the latter," she said in a rush. "But hear me out."

He glared. "You know my position on this."

"I know. I know. But this is different. You haven't been with her before. It won't break any of your precious rules. She's also not the clingy type."

He'd assumed the same about the majority of women who visited the Vault. Unfortunately, he'd been proven wrong time and time again. No matter how brutally honest he was with his intentions, they always expected more from him once he effortlessly pushed them over the line of orgasmic bliss.

"I'm not the helping type. You should ask Leo or T.J."

She shook her head. "I'm not willing to share Leo. And T.J. is far too sweet for this role."

He trudged toward her, the enthusiastic glow in her eyes lessening with each step he took. "*What* role, exactly?"

"I need you to work your magic on someone who's having trouble in the orgasm department."

His frown was an adequate response.

"Don't look at me like it's a hardship." She swung around and continued bounding down the stairs. "Hurry up."

"Wait." Shay knew better than to play matchmaker, which meant curiosity now had him by the balls, pushing him to catch up to her at the bottom landing. He grabbed the crook of her arm and encouraged her to stop. "Why can't someone else handle it?"

"She's tried everyone. Nobody succeeded."

"Then tell her to come back next time the Vault is open. There's always fresh meat to sample."

"She's been attending for months. Probably years. She's ready to cancel her membership."

"Then maybe that's for the best."

Shay's expression morphed from hope to anger. "Don't be such a selfish prick. I know you've got what it takes."

"I don't doubt it. But I'll repeat—I'm not the helping type."

"Then consider it a challenge. Leo told me you have plans to organize a development night focused on women's pleasure. This would be a great test to your skills."

"I don't need to be tested, sunshine."

"I disagree."

The corner of his lips twitched. "Then drop those panties and allow me to demonstrate."

Her laughter was light and infectious. That was the problem with Shay—she made him feel different, less abrasive, when he much preferred to remain distant and caustic.

"You know that's not going to happen. But I will encourage you to prove yourself with this chick. Every other man here is incapable of making her climax. I'm sure you could outline her problems in some sort of case study and make this the perfect opportunity to show patrons you're fit to teach."

He leaned in, his face inches from hers as he smirked. "I've seen you watching me down here. You know I'm fit to teach."

"Pleasuring innumerable women who are already primed from the Vault atmosphere isn't a valid indication. I doubt you'd have the same results with someone who's highly specific in her needs and no longer wants to be here."

"Highly specific?"

"She wants to be controlled. To be mastered. She doesn't want to draw a road map for every guy who gets between her thighs."

He straightened, trying to fend off the catnip piquing his interest.

She narrowed her eyes and grinned. "Come on. You know you want to. It's a trifecta. You get to pleasure a beautiful woman during work hours. You'll gain a great case-study for your class, while also proving you're the most talented man in the club."

The title wasn't up for debate.

"*Please.*" She clasped her hands together and raised them to her chest—begging with an added hint of cleavage persuasion. "Do this for me."

"I won't make any promises. I need to meet her first."

She nodded and walked backward until she reached the locker room doorway. "Bryan, I'd like you to meet Pamela."

Pamela?

Fuck.

He didn't need to step forward to see what she looked like. A gorgeous blonde with ample curves and deep brown eyes. He'd been drawn to her the moment he'd double-clicked the membership photo that slid into his inbox.

Then he'd read her name, and all interest had vanished like condoms at a frat house.

"Brute," Shay warned. "Hurry up and get in here."

He glared as he walked through the doorway and watched the blonde beauty stand from the bench in the middle of the room. Her limited clothing showed off a figure that hadn't changed since her induction. The dark navy corset clung tight, the breast cups supporting a lush chest while the waist curved to promote a perfect hourglass. She met his feral stare momentarily, then just as quickly, she lowered her gaze.

Submission.

Nice.

Usually, the women in the Vault were overly eager. Bright eyes. Visually defiling stares. The type who expected more from him than he ever planned to give. Rarely was there an opportunity to be with someone less enthusiastic. Sometimes it felt like he only had to blink in the wrong direction and the females started to take off their panties.

Not that he could blame them. He had sexual groupies for a good reason.

He cleared his throat, the deep sound a test to how she'd respond. And just as quickly as her gaze fell, she straightened her shoulders and met him with a narrowed stare, taunting him.

Interesting.

Her defiance conquered the desire to submit.

Maybe she wasn't the easily boxed woman he'd initially thought.

"Have the two of you spoken before?" Shay hovered in the doorway, one shoulder resting against the frame.

"Very little." He'd made sure of it, always happy to distance himself from triggers of his past. "But I processed Ella's application, so I'm familiar with her reasons for being here."

"Pamela," the woman murmured.

He ignored the correction and prowled around the bench seat. From the rebellion in her eyes and the stubborn set to her shoulders, he could tell she wasn't a natural submissive. She wanted the fight. Might even crave it more than the physical pleasure.

"You can leave, Shay." He kept his focus on Ella, taking in the stories her body willingly whispered. She was confident, her posture straight, her chin high and proud. She also came from money. Her shoes were polished and clearly designer. Her corset was made from expensive material, not a cheap knock-off. And her blonde hair was immaculately cut and pulled into a neat ponytail.

"Are you sure?"

"Leave," he grated.

"Pamela?" Shay questioned.

He shot the bartender an incredulous stare. "Leave. *Now*."

She held up her hands in surrender. "I'm going. I'm going."

She muttered something under her breath—an expletive, he was sure—but he let it slide, choosing to focus on Ella instead.

They stood in silence, a few feet apart, sizing each other up. She was trying to predict his failure before he'd even begun. The added challenge made his pulse increase. There was no excitement in her features. Not even a hint of hope. The walls of pessimism were firmly erected, and he'd take pleasure in knocking them down.

"Shay claims no man can get you off."

Her chin lifted. "That's right."

"I beg to differ."

She scoffed and gripped the strap of her handbag, hitching it higher on her shoulder. "Look, this isn't going to work. We're both wasting our time."

"Why is that?"

She swallowed, fear or manners holding her back.

"You can be honest." He wasn't a pussy who could dish out brutal honesty without taking it in return.

"Really?" She quirked a brow. "In that case, I'm not interested in being with someone driven by arrogance. This isn't a game to me. And I refuse to coddle another guy who thinks he's skilled, when reality would prove he's delusional."

"You think I'm delusional?" Her disinterest was cathartic. A breath of fresh fucking air. Maybe he needed to get Shay to start a rumor about him loving the thrill of the chase. That way women would stop stalking him and he could go back to enjoying his time in the Vault.

"I think you're like everyone else here who expects me to give them a quick thrill and a boost to their ego. I assure you, you'll get neither from me."

Feisty. This woman continued to grow in appeal.

"Look..." She sighed. "I apologize for being rude, but this is pointless." She made for the door. "I'm sorry Shay interrupted whatever you were doing."

"Leaving would be a mistake." He didn't turn to her. He didn't need to. Although she was abrasive, her hope was palpable. "I promise I'll give you what you need, but I won't chase you. You walk out the door and I won't follow."

Her footsteps paused and a deep breath whispered into his ears. "How can you promise that?"

"Because what you interpret as arrogance is actually experience. Unlike other men, I know what I'm doing."

Her wide eyes spoke of silent disbelief. He let her mull it over, predicting a number of responses before she finally spoke.

"A long list of conquests won't help. My appetite is more specific than most."

"Have it your way." He strode for the door, eating up the space between them.

Her throat convulsed. Her fingers twitched. "Wait." She held out a hand, her heated palm connecting with his chest, the delicate touch powerful in its gentleness. "How?"

He quirked a brow. "How?"

Her hand fell and she huffed. "How would you make me come?"

"Chitchat isn't really my thing. Why don't you just let me show you?"

"Because every other man who's received the opportunity has crashed and burned."

"It's not my fault you've had bad taste in lovers."

Her eyes narrowed, the callous slits of spite making his cock twitch.

He had her. She may not know it, may not even approve of it, but he'd definitely won.

"Drop the bag." With the jut of his chin, he indicated the leather strap hanging over her shoulder.

She puffed out her chest, and the rebellion spurred his pulse harder. Faster. He was fully invested now, wanting her to continue the game because most women barely tweaked his interest.

"Drop it." His voice was low, the command unmistakable.

She didn't move. Refused to comply.

Silent laughter filled his chest at the obvious way she demanded punishment. Her eyes begged. Her body hummed.

"All right, sweetheart. Have it your way." He encroached, leaning into her. His gaze never wavered as he placed his hand on her upper arm, gliding it over the exposed skin of her shoulder, toward her neck.

He latched onto her throat, her body heat burning his palm. She sucked in a breath, fast and deep, her acquiescence coming in harsh exhalations. Those brilliant eyes sparked before him with flames of annoyance as he held her at his mercy. And still, she didn't back away, didn't even flinch when he tightened his grip.

Any other man might've been put off by her lack of verbal consent. But he didn't care. Not one little bit. He received her permission from the unwavering stare, the lick of her tempting lips, the thrust of her chest.

Her bravado had begun to fracture. It wasn't a large break, merely a fissure to expose how well he'd worked his way under her skin. He wasn't immune either. The increased beat of her carotid against his fingers and the delicate swallow of her throat had his cock twitching against his zipper.

"Drop. It." The words grated from his drying mouth.

She lifted the strap from her shoulder and dropped the weight beside her feet with the clink of loose change.

"Good." He caressed her neck with his thumb and stared into those beseeching eyes. She told him everything he needed to know with that look. She was laid bare. Transparent. "You want this to happen. Want to know how I know?"

Her throat expanded under his palm, her heavy swallow like nirvana through his veins.

He leaned closer, his mouth less than an inch from her ear. "Because I'm listening, Ella. I can hear you. I can read you like a book."

She shook her head. "That's not my name."

He growled at the reminder. "It is tonight."

CHAPTER THREE

*P*amela closed her eyes, sinking into the thrill of the tight grip around her throat. She hadn't had this—the commanding presence, the compelling dominance—in a long time. It filled her with relief, along with other sensations she was truly thankful for. Even if this man did fail to bring her to climax, he'd do it with the slightest achievement.

"Tell me what you like," he whispered.

She stiffened, the hard punch of disappointment hitting her without warning. So much for slight achievements. With the opening of her eyes she was back to square one, not willing to draw a road map.

"Forget it." She shoved at his chest, her hands colliding with unyielding muscle.

He laughed, the humor brightening his harsh features. She didn't care if he could pull off his tailored suit like a *GQ* model, or that his chin-length hair made her itch to run her fingers through it. Hell, she even craved the rough grate of his close-cropped beard against her breasts... But he was a jerk.

A goddamn asshole.

"Move."

He continued to chuckle, the sound fraying her sensitive nerves as she shoved him again. His hands fell, his palms snatching her wrists tight and yanking her into his chest.

"You're touchy," he growled. "All this spite over a rhetorical question."

"It wasn't rhetorical." She tugged in vain to free her wrists.

"Wasn't it? Didn't I just tell you I can read you like a book?" He flashed his teeth.

It wasn't a nice smile. It was vicious. Nasty. And God help her, it made her chest constrict for all the right reasons. Or maybe they were the wrong reasons.

So very, very wrong.

She didn't want to swoon over a guy who could laugh in her face with undiluted smugness. She *shouldn't* swoon over a guy like that. Should she?

"If I were a smart man, I'd pose opportunities for you to show me exactly what you want without asking. Wouldn't I?"

She shook her head in denial. "You're messing with me, and I don't appreciate it."

"Yeah, you do. You're looking for a fight." His fingers pressed into her wrists, his power holding her captive in more ways than one. "That's what you like, isn't it?" His gaze searched hers, back and forth, back and forth, each swipe reading things she didn't want to admit. "Don't tell me other men failed to get such an easy reaction out of you. You're practically shoving what you want in my face."

"Stop it." He was right. So right it hurt. She wasn't usually like this. The need to spar was an anomaly he'd picked up on with flawless precision.

His strong hands turned her around to hitch one arm behind her back, the other forward between her breasts. He pinned her against him, his heated breath brushing her neck.

"I'm only going to say this once," he spoke harshly in her ear. "I don't do safe words. If you want to stop, all you have to do is repeat what you just said and I'm gone. I won't stand here while you kid yourself about your dirty little perversions. If you want me to make you come, you need to own it."

She whimpered. Lucas never made her admit the naughty things running through her mind. He never demanded that of her. To him it was roleplay, a fantasy, while this man made it reality. Being forced to vocalize her desire was torture—punishment of the most delicious kind.

"Tell me you want this." He nuzzled her neck. "Admit you're deliberately pushing because you want me to fight back."

Her heart pounded in her throat. Breathing became an arduous challenge. Her body reacted to him like paper to a flame. She was scorched. Burning. Her edges singed from his affects.

She fought against him, ashamed and achingly aroused as she tried to wrestle her wrists from his grip.

"Good girl." The arrogance tainting his voice made her pussy clench. "I love being right. It makes my dick hard." He proved his point by grinding his cock against her ass.

His large, erect cock.

Damn him. The last thing this accomplished man needed was the asset to back up his ego.

"You're an asshole." She bucked her hips, and his grip tightened to the point of heavenly pain.

"I'm also better than you. At this, I'll *always* be better than you." He nudged her forward, leading her to the lockers. "Put your palms on the metal."

He released her, trapping her between two immovable objects, one devilishly warm, the other chillingly cold. He kept her on her toes. Where had this man come from, and how did he get a cheat sheet on her body?

No. It wasn't her body. It was her mind. He was fucking her from the inside out, his words entrancing her with arousal, his confidence inspiring arrhythmia-inducing hope.

"Put them on the locker, Ella."

She bit her lip and raised her hands, freezing them in place against the metal. There was a heartbeat of silence, the quiet almost deafening when mixed with the rush of blood in her ears.

He lifted her skirt, the hem scratching sensitive skin like sandpaper instead of elegant fabric. Every inch of her responded in erotic fascination—her nipples tightened, her breasts ached, even the hair on the back of her neck rose, eager and greedy for more.

The sensations were foreign. Years had passed since her body had reacted this way. A lifetime.

The smooth graze of his fingers cut across the curve of her bottom, then lower, between her thighs. Slow and torturous.

"You're soaked." His teeth grazed along her shoulder, inspiring a shudder. "But how can that be, sweetheart? I thought you were an ice princess." He nudged aside the crotch of her panties, the slightest brush of her sex sending a wave of pleasure from her core outward. "Turns out you're just as eager for my dick as everyone else."

A hiss of breath escaped her lips. She wanted to hate him. To despise his skill.

The exact opposite happened.

She was indebted to him, her orgasm so frighteningly close she was actually fighting it.

"On second thought, you don't even need my dick, do you?" His derisive chuckle peppered her skin. "I bet I could get you off with one finger."

She closed her eyes, unwilling to admit it would take a lot less.

"Should I prove it?"

A lone fingertip parted her folds, sliding with ease through her arousal. He learned her, trailing inside and out. Back and forth. Around and around. Never penetrating. Only teasing her to the point of silenced hysteria.

He didn't rush, didn't falter in his blissful assault. He was too good, too skilled, and not merely with his touch. His precision came from strategy—a game plan she appreciated whole-heartedly if the lust and adrenaline flooding her veins was anything to go by.

"Enough with the questions." She bucked against him, fighting the mental connection and focusing on the physical. Instantly, she was pushed against the lockers with a responding jerk of his hips. She needed him to do it again, this time with his cock inside her. Over and over. "You talk too much."

"Then I'll stop."

Panic flooded her veins. *Shit.* She wanted his voice. Needed it. The threatening drawl was the cause of her bliss, and she knew he was arrogant enough to withhold it from her. "I take that back. Keep talking... I-I need you to keep talking."

"No, you don't," he whispered into her hair, each word softer than the last.

"I do." She waited long moments, her hips circling to follow the trail of his fingertip. "Please."

Christ, she was begging for sound. Pleading for him.

He didn't respond. Not with words. Only movements. His finger continued to glide around her sex, outlining her pussy lips, then straight down to her core. He circled her opening, painfully slow, deliciously teasing.

She whimpered. Mentally begged.

He felt so good, but she needed the mental stimulation. The dirty words were necessary to get her off.

"Talk to me." She shoved back against his chest. And again, when he didn't answer. "You won't make me come like this."

That finger kept circling, turning her into a liar with the efficient way her orgasm hovered. She shot a pleading glance over her shoulder and their gazes connected in an instant. His confidence washed through her. There was no denying she was in skilled hands. Everything about him hit the right mark.

His touch.

His focus.

His understanding.

He was listening.

Finally, someone was listening. Not to her words, but to *her*.

Pressure slid over her clit, his thumb, the tight press holding the bundle of nerves hostage. A gasp escaped her, and he raised a checkmate brow in response.

Damn him. She turned away, closed her eyes, and rested her forehead against the locker.

His other hand trailed a path around her body, starting at her hip. He drifted over her stomach, through her cleavage, along her sternum to the base of her throat.

Her skin erupted in goose bumps; her lungs tightened. She tilted her head back, offering herself to his mercy. But he didn't take it. He didn't encase her throat in his grip as she wished. Instead, he wove his hand around her neck and fisted her ponytail, pulling tight.

She whimpered.

This man wasn't merely reading her cues and responding, he was taking them a step further. Pushing her. Giving her something she didn't expect.

"Talk to me."

He refused. The only sound came from the upstairs door opening, the blast of dance music filtering in, before an abrupt disconnect. Footfalls and light chatter echoed forth as he pleasured her. People were approaching, and he showed no intent to stop.

"Whoa." A man's voice carried from the door. "Now this is what I call a proper greeting."

A woman laughed, friendly and light.

Bryan didn't falter. Didn't even pause. He kept her hair in his grip, his finger still teasing her pussy. "Evening," he drawled in greeting. "Look, honey, we've got visitors."

She groaned at the gift of his voice.

Could he tell she enjoyed an audience? She didn't know how or why, but this man had already learned so much about her.

"I said *look*."

Her nipples tingled at his command, and she sucked in a breath to counteract the shock. His words made her sizzle. *No.* She had to keep reminding herself it wasn't the words, it was the conviction in his tone. The pure authority. He spoke with no fear of her rejection. He issued directives he knew she wanted to follow.

"Come on now," he purred. "Play nice."

She whimpered and opened her eyes to see the couple standing a few feet away. The middle-aged woman bit her lip as she nestled close to her companion with a mammoth-sized erection tenting his pants.

Oh, sweet heavens.

Her pussy fluttered, her core clamped down. She panted, no longer capable of speech. The man stared at her, his gaze intent, his appreciation clear while Bryan's lone finger continued to torment her pussy entrance.

"Say hello." There was another tug to her hair, the slight pinch only increasing her pleasure. "Don't be shy."

She moaned and refused with a shake of her head.

Bryan's breathy snicker caused a shudder to flow down her spine. He was loving this, thriving on her defiance.

"Now you're just being rude." His beard grazed the skin of her shoulder, and he tilted her head higher.

"Fuck you," she muttered under her breath.

Fuck me.

Fuck everything.

She became mindless with the hunger for penetration. All she needed was...something. Anything.

"You'd like that, wouldn't you?" He ground his cock into her ass and sank his finger deep into her heat. "You'd fucking love it. Coming all over my dick. Milking me with this tight pussy."

She didn't want to show him how right he was, but her body refused the order. She shuddered, a mere breath away from orgasm. He was so fucking good. *Too* fucking good.

Her core throbbed, over and over, igniting a release she couldn't abate.

"Christ." The word was a breathy exhale. It was relief and pleasure and torture. Closure and rapture and desolation.

Pure, carnal release.

She clawed at the locker and failed to keep herself upright as her pussy contracted, tighter and tighter, clinging to the single digit sheathed inside her. She sank one inch, two, only to be pressed harder against the cold metal, his body helping her stand. Her core spasmed on a continuous loop, one convulsion after another as she panted and gasped for air.

"That's it," he coaxed. "Show me how good I am."

She ground her teeth in defiance, but it was too late. He'd already won. The height of orgasm had been and gone, each contraction now shorter than the last.

Everything became heavy—her arms, her legs, her chest. Relief turned into an uncomfortable tightening beneath her ribs. She'd waited so long. Hope had been fleeting. Now... now, this smug ass of a man had reignited her libido, and she couldn't be happier.

She turned to face him and tried to ignore the rapid rise of his appeal. They'd been left alone, their audience nowhere in sight as she struggled to regain normal breathing.

"I guess my work here is done." He winked, his fingers fleeing her panties. "And you thought I wouldn't get a quick thrill or a boost to my ego. Turns out I got both."

She let him revel in his victory, wishing the blissful hum of her body wasn't adding fuel to his blazing bonfire of arrogance. He was a jerk. No doubt about it. But Jesus fucking Christ, he was an accomplished jerk.

Her knees buckled and she slid down the cool metal of the lockers, landing in a heap on the floor. Relief overwhelmed her, making her gasps for air turn into gulps for mental stability.

"I'll see you around, Ella." He backtracked, his heated gaze making her self-conscious about her disheveled state before he turned and strode from the room.

She couldn't even find the breath to correct her name. It didn't matter, anyway. He was gone, the upstairs door to the nightclub soon opening and closing with a burst of loud music.

Questions and eager observations filled her adrenaline-fueled mind as she relived what had just happened. He'd opened his own forum in her brain, a mass of squealing groupies pointing out his achievements like they were worthy of Olympic gold.

He hadn't even sought relief. Hadn't even mentioned reciprocation despite the hard, thick length of his erection that had been an unmistakable presence at her ass.

"You good?"

Pamela blinked from her trance and focused on Shay in the doorway.

"Yeah." She cleared the gravel from her throat. "Better than good."

The bartender sauntered forward, her smile wide. "He did great, didn't he?"

Pamela laughed. She couldn't explain it. Couldn't describe it. She didn't think she even wanted to, because the idea of complimenting the arrogant ass was a despised prospect. Then again, he kind of deserved all the praise bubbling in her rapidly flowing bloodstream. She never would've thought an orgasm with minimal penetration was possible. Not even when Lucas had been alive.

All Bryan had needed was one finger.

One. Damn. Finger.

"I'm glad." Shay held out a hand and pulled Pamela to her shaky feet. "Does this mean you won't be canceling your membership?"

She blinked, too shell-shocked to know the right answer. "It means there's hope. And that's enough for now."

CHAPTER FOUR

TWO WEEKS LATER

*T*he shuffle of footsteps at the open office door demanded attention Bryan wasn't enthusiastic to give. "Did you want something?" He met Leo's stare as his friend leaned against the doorframe." Or are you happy to stand there and admire me in silence?"

"What are you up to tonight?"

Bryan raised a brow. "Probably a whole heap of none-of-your-fucking-business. Why?"

"Shay asked if you had plans to play in the Vault."

Great. Another woman to add to the list. "Tell Shay to get a life. I don't want her vetting questions from the vultures down there."

"Christ, you're in a mood. *Again*."

Bryan sank back in his chair with a huff. He *was* in a mood. This was his night to work the restaurant, and with Taste of Sin now closed, he should already be downstairs relaxing with a beer and a woman. Instead, he battled with annoyance.

He'd finally nutted out the particulars for the development night he would soon run in the Vault. Meticulous detail had gone into the first email to club patrons advising them of what to expect and what they could learn. Yes, he'd expected questions, and yes, there had been many, but all of them had revolved around his sex life and who he'd be fucking in the near future.

"I made the mistake of leaving my phone number on the email I sent to Vault members. Now I've got women hounding my ass. I've had two text me in the last five minutes, asking when I'm coming downstairs."

"Holy shit," Leo exaggerated a whisper. "You poor, defenseless bastard."

Bryan scowled.

"Most men would kill for your position. But not you. For such a hard ass, you really are a pussy when women show any interest."

Yes, he was. A remorseless bachelor for life. He refused to be tied to anyone. Not even temporarily. And if running from commitment-starved women made him a pussy, he'd be happy to wear the title like a badge of honor. "I'm not most men."

"Clearly. But you do realize they'd back off if you settled down with a regular hook-up? If you remain single, they're always going to look for an opportunity."

"I'm not going to let one woman latch her claws for the sake of keeping the rest at bay. They should all know the drill by now. If not, I'll have to give them a reminder."

"Well, it better be friendly. They'll be dripping in their panties if you pull the usual Brute routine." Leo gave a half-hearted laugh. "I don't know how you do it, but they eat up your bad attitude like a vanilla fudge sundae."

That was the vicious cycle. He didn't do nice. Never had. So, whenever he opened his mouth, the females lapped at his hostile sterility. "Do me a favor and don't mention my routine and vanilla in the same sentence. We both know that's more your style."

"You know what else is my style?" Leo countered. "Committing myself to one woman, so the rest know I'm off-limits."

"Everyone knows you're off-limits because Shay threatens to slash them with a broken bottle if they get within two feet."

"Yep." Leo grinned. "She's a keeper." He pushed from the doorframe, making way for the person who entered.

Shit. Janeane. She was one of the text-message hounds. Long brown hair, dark hazel eyes, a body made for sin, and a determination for commitment that made his skin crawl.

"Looks like you've got a visitor," Leo drawled. "I'll leave you two alone."

"You need to hang around." Bryan narrowed his gaze on his business partner, relaying an unmistakable message. "We still have things to discuss."

His friend grinned in return. "I'd love to, buddy, but I'm going to be busy helping my girlfriend get a life. We'll catch up later." Leo gave a salute in farewell, then disappeared down the hall.

Fucker.

"He was in a hurry." Janeane sauntered toward the desk, her hips moving with an exaggerated sway. "How you doin', Brute?"

"Fine." He gripped the armrests on his chair, holding his temper at bay. "You?"

"Good."

He understood the look she gave him. It was siphoning. She was trying to get more sex out of him and wouldn't succeed. He'd already slept with her once. That was the extent of their tally—past, present, and future. "What are you doing up here?"

"I thought we could discuss your upcoming development class. Do you still want me to be your assistant?"

He thought it over. After her text messages, and now the visit into the staff area of the club, he knew he should find someone else. But who? She was a carbon copy of every other woman in the Vault. Once he slept with them, his sperm became a potent commitment supplement making them rabid for more.

He really needed to figure out how to get that shit fixed.

"It's not an assistant, as such." He leaned back in his chair, relaxed, a picture of disinterest. "I only need someone to demonstrate on."

"Then I'm your girl."

Of course, she was.

"But I'd prefer to practice first." She raised the hem of her skirt and started lowering her underwear.

"No need." He pushed to his feet and strode around the desk. "I want the session unscripted."

She batted her lashes and dropped her G-string to the floor. "No problem. Tonight can be just for fun."

"Not interested."

She slid forward and placed her hands on his chest. "Are you sure?"

Her nails grazed a trail down his pecs, over his stomach, to his crotch. "I bet I can convince you."

He'd happily take that wager. He'd even stake his house on it. "You won't win." He eyed her with apathy, knowing his flaccid cock was incapable of resurrection under her grip. He wasn't interested. At all. And if she needed to grope him to get the picture, so be it.

"You're not in the mood tonight?" She pouted. "What's wrong?"

"You know I'm not a repeat offender, Janeane. We won't sleep together again."

Her palm paused on his cock, her brows knit tight. "But the class you're teaching..."

"Is a one-off. It's business. If you want to fuck, go downstairs and find someone else."

Her hand fell away. "I thought—"

"You thought wrong." He didn't want an affiliation with any woman. And he definitely didn't want her to latch her claws any deeper into the assumption that they had something between them. "I suggest you go back downstairs and find a guy who can treat you right."

Her lips kicked in another vain attempt at seduction. "I think we both know that's not how I want to be treated."

Jesus Christ. For the love of promiscuity. He raked a rough hand over his beard, his fingers digging deep when his phone beeped again. This shit had to stop.

Janeane licked her lips, ignorant to the underlying tension in the room. "Come on, Brute. Do what you want with me."

He cocked a brow. "You sure that's what you want?"

"You know it is." Her eyes brightened.

"Okay, then." He gently grabbed her wrist and led her into the hall. "I'll see you later."

Her mouth gaped as he dropped his hold and inched back to slam the door in her face. *Perfect.* Peace and fucking quiet.

"*Brute.*" She banged on the door.

"For fuck's sake." He clenched his teeth. What did he have to do to stop these women from praising the ground he walked on? It was no secret he treated them with contempt. Apart from telling them to fuck off, he'd exhausted all other forms of rejection. But still, they came at him like defensive linebackers on a quarterback. "Unless you're looking for your underwear, you need to leave."

She huffed. "Fine. Keep them as a souvenir."

"Yeah, thanks." He picked the scant piece of material off the floor and threw it in the trash. He didn't need a reminder. She had his fucking phone number and he was sure she wouldn't let him forget.

"Bye, Brute."

He closed his eyes with a sigh. "Bye, Janeane."

Peaceful silence followed, and he welcomed it with building annoyance. The Vault was supposed to be his sanctuary. His domain. He owned the ground it was built on. Literally. He'd spent years cultivating the perfect environment for his gratification, only now, fucking had become a chore. There was no thrill. No chase. Most importantly, there was no respect.

Sex outside of the club wasn't an option. He wouldn't date, and he refused to waste time searching for women morally capable of enjoying an uninhibited one-night stand. He didn't have the patience or the motivation. Instead, he'd had to settle on growing the list of rejected women inside the Vault. The ones who kept coming back for more. Over and over. Without remorse or dejection.

That shit wasn't admirable. And it definitely wasn't attractive. The more a woman chased him, the less respect he gave her in an effort to put her off his scent. Even then, his form of rejection seemed to smell like the latest best-selling fragrance to hit the market.

He couldn't fucking win.

"This is bullshit." He yanked open the filing cabinet and sorted unorganized invoices to distract himself from where he wanted to be. Where he *should* be.

Another slicing beep sounded from his phone, and he slammed the cabinet shut in frustration. He pulled the cell from his pocket, the grind of his teeth harsh enough to cause damage. He'd turn the fucking thing off until morning. Then he'd get the number changed.

He was poised to shut down the device when it started to vibrate, the screen changing with an incoming call from an unknown number. His teeth should've cracked under the weight of his rage.

"If this is another woman..." He pressed connect, his nostrils flaring as he placed the device at his ear. "*What?*"

There was a beat of silence. A delicious beat where he hoped he'd given the caller enough reason to change their mind about asking him to hook up. Or fuck. Or whatever version of a proposition they wanted to use.

"Bryan?"

Yep. Another fucking woman. "Who's this?"

"It's Tera."

Tera?

He frowned. He only knew one woman by that name, and he had less enthusiasm to speak to her than he did with the scavengers at the Vault.

"Bryan?" Her voice was timid, less forthright than he remembered.

He ran a hand over his mouth and contemplated hanging up. "Yeah."

"It's your cousin, Tera." She paused, probably expecting him to spread a welcome mat. The poor thing would be waiting a while. "Is this a good time to talk?"

He scoffed. How the fuck did he answer that? Was now a good time? Really? Was now, more than ten years after being cut from the family, a good time to talk?

"Sure." He didn't hide his animosity. "I've been hanging out for the perfect opportunity to catch up. Who knew it would be a random Saturday night, a lifetime after you all turned your backs on me?"

"Bryan..."

"Don't fucking *Bryan* me. Tell me why you called so we can get this over with."

She sighed. "I called to ask you to come home."

"Not going to happen."

"Not even if your mom is sick?"

The rage disappeared. The bitterness, too. The world stopped. The sound of the club and the echo of his heartbeat pausing along with it. He thought this day would never come. That his family would always treat him like a pariah—unworthy of their attention. After a childhood chasing parents who tried to ignore his existence, he had finally been acknowledged.

"Bryan, are you still there?"

"I'm here." He leaned against the filing cabinet, contemplating the need to hang up. He didn't want to know. He didn't want to care.

"I'm sorry to be the one to tell you this, but she has terminal cancer."

Fuck. He'd wondered if this outcome would ever eventuate from his mother. Not the karma that reared its head in the form of a disease with a death sentence. He'd always wondered about the regret—the moment she would realize she had a list of sins she needed to absolve before she passed into whatever holy land she thought was waiting for her.

"She's been fighting for a while now. I'm just not sure how much she has left in her."

A while. He really shouldn't be surprised. "If she wants to see me, she can call herself."

"She doesn't even know I've called." The words hung like a noose awaiting an unwilling neck. "Nobody does."

In other words—they still didn't care about him. Nobody did.

He gave a derisive laugh. The possibility of death hadn't even inspired affection in his mom. Why, after all this time, did he expect something different from the stone-cold bitch?

"Thanks for the call, Tera."

"Are you going to come home?" she asked in a rush.

"Tampa was never my home. My parents made sure of that." He cleared his throat and tried to clear his mind of the past at the same time. "It's best for everyone involved if you lose this number."

He waited for an acknowledgment of his request—the slight hitch in her breath—before he disconnected the call and pocketed his cell.

He didn't have a home. Didn't need or want one.

He had a refuge, though, and it was time he reclaimed it.

CHAPTER FIVE

*P*amela handed her identification to the security guard at the parking lot entrance to the Vault. She was buzzing, every inch of her alive with possibility.

The last two weeks had been spent reliving what had happened the last time the secret part of the club was in session. The awakening. The pleasure. The pure ease with which she'd come undone under a skillful hand.

"Have a good night." The guard returned her ID and indicated for her to go ahead with a jerk of his chin.

"Thank you." She hitched her handbag higher on her shoulder and approached the darkened stairwell. The sound of moans and grunts became louder the farther she descended, until she was at the bottom step, peeking inside the Vault.

For once, she smiled as she strode by the bar, no longer frustrated at the ease with which women were getting their rocks off. She did the customary disrobe in the locker room, packed away her handbag, and then returned to the main area.

The room held the usual patronage, apart from a few unfamiliar faces who didn't pique her interest. Couples mingled with drinks in their hands, others fucked in quiet corners or blatant positions on sofas.

Nobody paid her much attention. No more or less than usual.

"Pamela," Shay called from behind the bar. "You're back."

"Yeah." She approached the grinning woman and slid onto a vacant stool. "I thought I'd give this another try after the success from the last session."

"I'm glad to hear it. Can I get you a drink to celebrate?"

"Sure. Tequila sunrise, please."

Shay made the concoction while Pamela swiveled on her seat, scoping the crowd. There was nothing new or different about the scene before her. One couple used the sex swing. Singles crowded the open doorways to the adjoining rooms. Some regrouped around the bar.

The only thing missing was her resentment.

"He's not here yet."

She turned to Shay and grasped the drink now placed in front of her. "Who? Brute?"

"Isn't that who you came back for?"

"No." It was the truth. "I have no misconceptions about being with him again." She didn't want to fuel his ego, no matter how skillful those hands were. "Not that I was technically with him in the first place. All it took was a thumb, a fingertip, and some smoothly drawled words."

What made her sashay her butt back to the Vault was the hope that Bryan had opened the floodgates when he'd broken the drought. Hopefully, whoever she decided to play with next would be just as successful.

"That sounds about right." Shay chuckled. "I swear he was born with a gift. He always leaves women begging for more."

"I wish I didn't agree." Unfortunately, she did. He was truly skilled in the art of pleasure. And undeniably undeserving of his talent.

"Then why not try for another round? If you technically weren't together last time, it wouldn't go against his hook-up rules."

"Rules? Really?" Incredulity dripped from her lips. The contrast from his technique to his temperament continued to shock and amaze her. "No, thanks. God knows I wouldn't want to step on his toes."

"He's not that bad. Honestly. I wouldn't have encouraged him to help you out if he was. He knows what he wants the same way you do. The difference is, he never wavers."

"Tell me about it." Pamela took a gulp of her drink. "I wavered like a palm tree in a cyclone. There isn't a guy here who I didn't at least flirt with, all in the name of trying to get a fix."

Shay placed her hands on the bar and gave a sad smile. "Then, honey, can you really blame him for setting firm boundaries? At least women know what to expect from him."

True. Maybe she shouldn't blame Bryan for owning his shit. Self-empowerment and all that pompom shaking stuff. "I guess. Doesn't stop his personality rubbing me the wrong way."

"Who gives a shit which way his personality rubs you as long as those orgasms keep coming? Believe me, if Leo would let me bag and gag every guy who walked in here so there was no annoying small talk—"

A guy sitting two stools down cleared his throat, drawing their attention.

"Oh, come on, Jeff. Don't tell me you're not sporting wood at the thought of being bagged and gagged."

The guy grinned. "Get me a bourbon and dry, and I'll pretend I didn't hear a word."

Shay chuckled as she grabbed the requested liquor bottle. "See? Bag and gag is definitely the answer. But it's not going to happen. This is a sex club, not a bonding retreat, and you pay good money to get in those doors. Make the most of it. Hit him up for a full round. What's the worst he could do?"

Maybe Shay was right. Pamela's decision should revolve around Bryan's skills, not his attitude. "I'll think about it."

"Well, think quick." Shay focused over Pamela's shoulder. "Because the man of the moment has arrived."

The pound of her irregular heartbeat echoed in her ears, the reaction bringing an unhealthy dose of confusion.

She swiveled on her stool and captured the man in her sights. His suit covered him like armor, strong and sure. His shirt was white and crisp, with a gleaming black tie hanging loose around his neck. He must be working, not playing. Otherwise, he'd be in boxers or briefs, as the Vault rules stated.

She grasped her glass, keeping her hands busy while her mind worked overtime. Asshole or not, he'd been blessed with physical appeal. The type that hadn't lessened since learning more about his personality.

His expression wasn't welcoming in the slightest. His eyes were harsh, his face covered in a light, bristly beard that always seemed impeccably trimmed. He had strong shoulders, a solid frame, and a powerful stride.

An emotionless vortex from head to toe.

A shuddering thrill worked through her without permission. She didn't want to be attracted to him. Hell, she'd drink herself under the table in the hopes her sober goggles were adversely affected with a few shots, but the alcohol wouldn't help.

She was intrigued by him.

Attracted, intrigued, and maybe a little curious, too.

"I might go and ask what his plans are." She spoke aloud, hoping it formed some sort of commitment with the universe to stop her from backing out.

He continued toward one of the side rooms, his focus hitting her with a scowl.

She paused, caught halfway off her seat.

She waited for a sign. A spark. An acknowledgment of the monumental zing they'd shared last time she was here.

Nothing.

He glanced away without so much as a twitch to his lips.

"Umm." She turned back to the bar. "That didn't seem friendly."

"That's Brute. One hundred percent asshole, one hundred percent of the time. Doesn't stop him from fucking like a Trojan."

Damn it. Body parts reacted without warning—breasts, tummy, and lower. *Deeper.* When had she become a sucker for punishment?

She chanced another glance over her shoulder and focused on the darkness of the room he'd disappeared into. She didn't want to give this brutal man any power over her, but the truth was, he already had it. He could give her things no other man seemed capable of.

"I assure you, he does know how to have fun. He's just extremely picky about who he lets past his defenses."

A loner.

Like her husband.

The familiarity softened her interest a little. Not enough. The past seemed to repeat itself, and like with her husband, she found herself unable to walk away.

"Are you going to chicken out?" Shay's voice was light, a bare whisper of subconscious thought through Pamela's frazzled mind.

"No. It's all good. I'll go see what he's up to. There's no harm in asking, right?" She sucked hard on her straw, finishing her drink. "Wish me luck."

"Go get 'em."

Pamela gave a chuckle in farewell and slid from her stool, righting her favorite deep-pink corset as she padded in his direction. This situation would be different if he weren't the only man standing after years of unreachable orgasms.

He was a unicorn. That was all.

A vicious, snarling anomaly.

And if she wanted to be brutally honest with herself, she wasn't entirely enthusiastic about propositioning previous play partners. The possibility of repeating the mistakes of her past made her skin crawl.

She stopped in the doorway, taking in the shadowed sight of him as he leaned against the wall, staring at the threesome kissing and caressing on the circular bed in the middle of the room. The appeal of Zoe and her men had always drawn Pamela's attention. Not tonight, though. Right now, she couldn't stop staring at the man who owned her pleasure. The man who made her pussy clench with remembrance.

Damn him.

She came to his side, ignoring the deep, woodsy scent of his aftershave wrapping its potion around her. "Hey."

Ten children could have been conceived in the time it took his gaze to finally meet hers. There were no words. No familiarity or friendship. Only obligation bleached of warmth as he jutted his chin. Not only a cold shoulder, but a cold stare.

Problem was, she was here now, by his side, and she didn't want to walk away with her tail between her legs. Especially not when Shay's words repeated in her head, mantra-style—*doesn't stop him from fucking like a Trojan.*

"Are you working?" She fought to remain detached. "You're still wearing your suit."

"Just finished."

His tone carried a hint of "fuck off." A hint she should take. She should grasp the warning and stride from the room. From the club. From his life. Instead, she let her focus wander along the strong lines of his chest, down to the thick thighs she could still remember pressed against her.

Curse him for being a tease to her starved ovaries.

Those hands had inspired daydreams capable of lasting months. Those legs had helped stabilize her during the most tumultuous orgasm.

He pushed from the wall and walked by her without so much as a farewell.

"Hey." She frowned at his retreating back. "Hold up."

He stopped, his shoulders broad and menacing.

"Are you interested in playing tonight?"

This time the beat of silence rang in her ears like an exploding bombshell. The world collectively held its breath.

Slowly, he turned to face her, the furrow between his brows sharp enough to cut stone. "Have I done anything in the last five minutes to give you the impression I'm interested?"

"Uh..." Her throat dried, cutting off her words.

"The answer you're looking for is no," he muttered under his breath. "I didn't say hello. I didn't even smile. Then I *fucking walked away*. What more do I have to do?"

Shock addled her brain, making coherence impossible. She didn't know whether to apologize or lash out. Whimper or snarl. She'd been in this situation before. Many times. But always in reverse. She'd never been accused of not taking a hint. She was always the accuser. Difference was, she wasn't such an ass about it. "A simple 'no' would've sufficed."

"Then, 'no.'" He raised his voice and his arms at the same time, drawing attention. "I'm not interested."

She blinked on rapid repeat, trying to remain strong while humiliation burned her cheeks. "You're a rude son-of-a-bitch."

She walked past him, unwilling to let him get his belittling fix.

"Hold up." The command reverberated off the walls, stopping orgasms, pausing foreplay. Her cheeks heated as more than one inquisitive stare turned toward them. "*I'm* a son-of-a-bitch?"

Panic clogged her throat. She was confident. Empowered. But up against a man like Brute, her self-worth flickered, threatening to snuff completely.

"That's enough," Zoe's voice carried from the bed. "Whatever this is, it doesn't need to be shared in front of a crowd. Brute, you should know better."

No, Pamela should've known better. She should've listened to her gut and left well-enough alone. Before resentment settled in. Before she'd turned to Shay for help. And definitely before this thug had entered the picture.

"I'm not the only one who should know better." Bryan strode by her. "Ignorance to the club rules is becoming an epidemic down here."

He entered the main area with his smooth gait still intact. Each step he took promoted his control, his self-worth, while her resilience to stand tall teetered on a precarious edge.

This could've been worse. At least he'd confined her humiliation to a small room and a minimal number of witnesses. He could have—

"I shouldn't need to remind everyone in attendance that no means fucking no." He demanded the attention of the entire club with a raised voice. "You take rejection without pause or you get the fuck out of my club. Are we clear?"

Her lips parted, her mortification spilling out with a ragged breath.

There were no words to describe the carnage of his attack. He was deliberately ostracizing her. For what? Because she'd asked him to play?

"You all received my email earlier in the week," he continued. "And I'm fucking pissed that a lot of you took it upon yourself to use my cell number as your personal booty call."

She glanced around, expecting condemnation and judgment. What she found was the same discomfort staring back at him from numerous women. Some looked abashed, others appeared confronted, while men ping-ponged their attention around the Vault trying to determine who'd triggered the earthquake.

Bryan glared, taking the time to pinpoint every female in sight. "That shit has to stop. We have strict rules in place for a reason, and I'll be damned if I'm made to feel pestered in my own club. Respect boundaries and take non-verbal cues or expect to have your membership canceled." He sucked in a breath and let it out with force. "And if I find out anyone has a cell phone in here instead of keeping it secure in the locker room, there's going to be hell to pay."

The silence thickened.

"Thanks for the reminder," Leo called from the bar, a hint of amusement in his voice. "Who wants a drink?"

As quickly as the wildfire had spread, the flames were doused under the offer of alcohol. Couples returned to their canoodling, voyeurs assumed their positions, and exhibitionists sank back into bliss.

The world began to revolve again, circling around her while her feet remained in place.

"I wouldn't take it to heart." Zoe came to stand beside her, the gorgeous woman's brows pinched. "From the whispers I've heard tonight, the outburst was inevitable."

"I...um." Lost for words? Really? The effect of this man had no bounds. She still had no clue what had just happened.

"I'm sure it wasn't supposed to be directed at you." Zoe narrowed her gaze. "Unless you've been calling and texting him to hook up."

"No. *God*, no." If it wasn't for his magic touch, she wouldn't have given him the time of day. "I wouldn't be that stupid."

"You'd be surprised how many women are. I've heard whispers that there's a bet over who can sleep with him next. The members involved aren't shy about it. They're all trying to be the lucky lady who takes him off the market."

"As far as I'm concerned, he's all theirs." The rhythmic sounds of sex and fulfillment built as if they had never stopped. "I just wish I didn't feel like such an idiot." She *had* pestered him and hadn't taken his not-so-subtle cues. "I should've paid more attention to his demeanor."

"Brute's demeanor?" Zoe laughed. "If we all did that, nobody would ever talk to him."

"I guess." She nodded, trying to appreciate the camaraderie even though acid ate through her stomach. "I better get going."

"You can't go now." Zoe turned to the men on the bed and raised a splayed hand, asking for five minutes. "If you leave, his shitty attitude wins. Let's get a drink first."

She wasn't interested in claiming any sort of victory. Besides, she couldn't fight someone who was striding from the room. "No, I've reached my limit." Of bullshit *and* alcohol. "Don't leave your guys waiting."

"Honey, they're not going anywhere."

"Maybe not, but I am. I can't stay here. Thanks for the offer, though."

She didn't say goodbye. Not to Zoe, Shay, or a single soul as she slinked her way through the main room, the newbie lounge, and the entrance hall. She had to get out of there before her head exploded from the vacuum to her pride.

CHAPTER SIX

*B*ryan had his hand in the safe, reaching for his keys, wallet, and cell, when the office door flung open, only to be slammed shut seconds later.

"What the fuck is wrong with you?" Shay came up behind him, a solidified form of indignation and fury.

"The Vault was getting way out of hand. It's time I pulled everyone back into line. I'm not going to apologize for reminding them of the rules."

"I'm not talking about that. I want to know why the hell you would make an example of Pamela when she did nothing wrong."

He winced. That name. It fucking killed him. Every time. "Nothing wrong?" The question came through clenched teeth. "How about calling me a son-of-a-bitch for declining a hook-up?"

"I don't care if she forcibly tried to give you an anal exam. You could've let her down gently. There was no need to make a fool out of her."

"Mind your own business, Shay."

He didn't regret a second of his anger tonight. Especially after he'd been stopped in the Vault stairwell and told about the group of women who had started placing bets on his sex life. That knowledge had been enough to send him nuclear.

The only saving grace was their luck at choosing him as a target. If another man, or woman, for that matter, had been treated this way, he would've gone postal long ago.

"It is my business, seeing as though I was the one who convinced her to speak to you."

His chest tightened, the unmistakable beat of rage clogging his throat. "You told her to hassle me?"

"Hassle you?" She cocked her hips. "She didn't even want to go near you. I had to talk her into it."

He should've known Shay was a part of this. Should've fucking known. "Then you're to blame. Not me. I made it obvious I wasn't interested. I barely said two words to her before walking away. She was the one who followed *me*. She's the one who continued to act like I was a sure thing because, apparently, she got the wrong impression from you."

Her posture shifted, the slightest sign of guilt.

Just because Ella wasn't as forthright as the others who had called or texted, didn't mean she wouldn't be the next time the Vault opened. His announcement had been a caution to every patron who needed to be reminded that hints of rejection were to be taken as seriously as blatant refusals.

"And like I said downstairs, she's not the only one." He lobbed his cell toward her, the device fumbling in her fingers before coming to rest in her grip. "Check the messages. See just how many women from the Vault are trying to ride my dick."

"I don't—"

"*Fucking look*." He didn't care if she thought he was irredeemable. But he sure as shit wouldn't have her thinking the women down there were all sweet and virtuous.

She raised a haughty brow and cocked a hip as she unlocked his screen and navigated to the texts. She scrolled and scrolled, her eyes skimming messages he knew were as vulgar as they were annoying.

"Your girl may not have been a serial offender. But it was only a matter of time."

"She's not like that... Holy shit, I can't believe Elise sent you a nude selfie."

He nodded. Elise had a fine rack, but he would still delete the pic and place her firmly on his shit list. "One of many."

She winced and handed over the phone. "It doesn't mean you have the right to take your frustration out on Pamela. Her involvement was my fault."

"Shay admitting guilt?" He pocketed his cell, along with his keys and wallet. "You must really like this woman."

"I feel sorry for her. She's too young to be a widow."

He'd almost forgotten about the dead husband. Didn't matter, though. The only thing worse than a pushy woman was a pushy woman with baggage. "She's attractive, and new men continue to join the Vault. She'll find someone to suit her soon enough."

There was no doubt. Apart from her beauty, she was passionate and sexual. The top three checkboxes on any hot-blooded male's list.

"And what about you?" Shay crossed her arms over her chest. "After your demeaning display, I think you're going to find it hard to get laid in the Vault. Female solidarity can be a bitch."

"Female solidarity can kiss my ass. It's my club. If I want to wipe the slate clean of women members and start fresh, I will." Culling members seemed like a damn good idea.

"You're not the only one who owns the club. It's Leo and T.J.'s, too."

He growled, his teeth clenched tight. He loved this woman. Really, he did. But holy fuck, he hated her at times. "Tell Leo I'm leaving."

"I don't think—"

He held up a hand. "When it comes to me, don't think. Ever again. You hear me? Stay out of my sex life unless you want me meddling with yours."

Her chin hitched, the expression held for a brief second before she nodded.

"I'm glad we're finally on the same page."

Those arms remained locked tight over her chest as he walked from the office.

He strode into the hall and down the stairs to the bar. The club was in full swing with loud music and a packed dance floor. His peripheral vision caught sight of the opening Vault door, and he paused to make sure he didn't have to hide in the crowd to save himself from another female leech.

The guard manning the entrance stepped aside to welcome someone from the darkness.

Bryan should've kept walking. Should've gone straight to the parking lot without giving a fuck about anyone from the private club. But then it was too late. Ella strode from the shadows, wearing a silky dress barely covering the scant lingerie beneath.

She gave a half-hearted smile to the guard, then worked her way across the dance floor, heading toward the main entrance to Shot of Sin.

"You can't let her walk out on her own." Shay's raised voice came from over his shoulder, having the effect of a surprise enema.

"I'm on it."

There was a reason they'd renovated the Vault to have a parking lot exit. Escaping through a mass of drunken revelers at the front of the club wasn't an option, especially for a woman on her own. She'd have to walk around the building unattended. Unprotected.

"Goddamn it." These women would be the death of him. Or at least his libido. He turned to face Shay. "Go back downstairs. I'll make sure she gets to her car."

"Will you make sure she gets an apology, too?"

He scowled. *Apology, my ass.* "Good night, Shay."

She smiled, big and wide and full of spite. "Night, Brute."

Finding Ella again wasn't hard. She parted the sea of pussy-starved men with a whiplash effect. He followed, hanging back at least ten feet. He wouldn't talk to her. She wouldn't even know he was there. All he would do was shadow her to her car and kiss her annoyance goodbye once she safely drove away.

She reached the club doors, tipped her head so she didn't make eye contact with the bouncer, and walked into the night.

He did the same, approaching Greg a few seconds after.

"Everything okay, boss?"

"Yeah. Heading home." They both stared after Ella.

"A friend of yours?"

"No, she's from downstairs."

Greg nodded, lowering his attention to her swaying ass.

Nobody inside the club knew what lurked behind the guarded Vault of Sin doors. Not the bouncers, not the Shot of Sin staff, and definitely not the crowd who continued to carve up the dance floor on a weekly basis. There was only Bryan and his business partners, along with very minimal bar staff. To everyone else, it was an exclusive VIP area, with the people coming in and out carrying the intrigue of celebrity status.

"Keep your eyes on the door," he growled. "I'll make sure she gets to her car."

"Sure thing."

Ella gained distance, and two men waiting in the crowded line for a cab stepped back to follow her along the building. They framed her, leaning close, making their intentions known as Bryan lengthened his stride.

To her credit, she didn't slink away. She stopped, faced one of the men with a jut of her chin, and announced loud enough for everyone to hear, "I'm not interested."

He could've laughed at the parallels of their earlier situation. Then again, it made him think of the differences, too.

Her position contained vulnerability. His hadn't.

She needed to use aggression to get them to back off. He'd merely done it to cause a scene.

The men took the rejection, chuckling to themselves as they made their way to the end of the cab line. Bryan slowed, waiting to overhear a derogatory comment, a snide remark, anything to give him the justification to break a nose or crack a jaw.

Nothing came.

The men were harmless as well as tactless.

Ella continued along the building, her heels tapping with her sure stride. Once she turned the corner of the building she'd be out of sight from club security. From anyone. Except those who thought it might be a good idea to follow a gorgeous woman into a private parking lot in the early hours of the morning.

With a quick glance over her shoulder, she took a hard left and disappeared from view.

She hadn't seen him. Hadn't paid enough attention to her surroundings to notice he'd followed. Her main focus was on the cab line and the men who had approached her.

Big mistake.

She needed to pay more attention.

He increased his pace, wanting to make sure nobody waited in the darkness. Once he turned the corner, his feet hit the gravel of the parking lot. The crunch beneath his soles was unmistakable.

She heard it, too, if the way she gripped her handbag and riffled through the contents was any indication.

Fuck.

If she turned, he'd have to talk to her. And if she didn't, he'd be stuck with the guilt of knowing he'd unintentionally scared her. Maybe he should call out. Say a quick, "Hey, you fucking idiot, why didn't you use the other exit?"

But he didn't want to speak to her again tonight. Or anyone else, for that matter. The thought of socializing had the appeal of a drug-free circumcision. Not that the feeling was a stretch from any other moment when he had to be chatty.

He ignored the crunch of his footsteps and followed, closing in on her. His pace hadn't increased. Hers had slowed. Why the hell had she slowed?

He was about to announce his presence in an effort to ease her fears, when she swung around, raising a pocket knife in his direction.

Her lips parted at the sight of him, the determined squint of her eyes changing to a widened stare of confusion.

"You plan on using that?" He focused on the knife, the blade barely long enough to cause significant damage. Didn't stop her from squinting at him as if planning the best way to slash and dash. "The Vault has an exit to the parking lot for a reason. You shouldn't be out here on your own."

Her cheeks darkened, in embarrassment or anger, he wasn't sure. But she kept wielding that knife like she had every intention of using it. "You followed me all this way to give me a lecture?"

"I followed you to make sure you got to your car safely."

She scoffed, closing the knife with a confident flick before throwing it back into her handbag. "Chivalry doesn't suit you. It doesn't even make sense, seeing as though you're the reason I felt too humiliated to walk back through the Vault."

The pang in his chest wasn't appreciated.

"Go back inside." She swiveled on the toes of her shiny black shoes and continued along the building. "I don't need your help."

She walked away from him, striding in the opposite direction when every other woman seemed to salivate over the ability to have a conversation with him. Maybe Shay was right. This woman might not be a leech after all.

"That wasn't the case two weeks ago." His retort came from leftfield. An unscripted retaliation he didn't see coming.

She kept walking. One step. Two. Then she gifted him with another swirl, rounding on him, spitting contempt in his direction. "You know what?" She snapped her lips closed.

"What? Let me have it." He shouldn't have found her fury humorous. "Get it off your chest, princess."

Her eyes flared. "Oh, buddy, I don't know where you get off speaking to me like that when I've done nothing wrong. Tonight, you treated me like I was trying to tattoo myself on your charcoal-riddled soul, or steal your cherished bachelorhood."

She stepped forward, straightening her shoulders. Women really needed to get a clue that thrusting their breasts didn't work in their favor. It only made men feel like they'd scored a triple-point bonus during battle.

"Let me assure you," she spat, "I'm not interested in either. In fact, if you were the last man on Earth, I'm pretty sure I'd start fucking livestock to get my kicks just so I didn't have to deal with your bullshit attitude." Her mouth remained open, gaping a little.

Yeah, sweetheart, your diatribe did include a reference to bestiality.

"Good to know." His lips kicked into a smile, and the flare of her nostrils announced she didn't appreciate it.

"This isn't funny."

No, it wasn't. Apart from the enjoyment he received from her annoyance, this wasn't funny at all. He didn't like having his enjoyment of the Vault washed out from underneath him by disrespectful women. He didn't like being railroaded. And he certainly didn't like the reminder that he had a family back in Tampa, ignoring his existence. "No, you're right. After the day I've had, your lack of interest is a fucking relief."

"Well," she grated, walking away, "I'm glad I could ease the tension."

He didn't follow this time. The nagging throb in his chest increased. It wasn't his fault she'd been caught in the line of fire earlier. She'd been collateral damage. A tiny blip on the casualty radar.

All he'd done was announce his disinterest. Loudly. While deliberately drawing the attention of other club patrons.

Fuck.

"I had a shit of a day, okay? I shouldn't have taken it out on you."

She froze, her back still turned. "Was that an apology?"

If it was, it was a shitty one, but coming from him, it was the holy grail of remorse. "It's whatever you need it to be."

She released a sardonic laugh and pounded out the distance to the end of the building.

The ache beneath his ribs grew, demanding more. More what? He didn't know.

"Look, I shouldn't have directed my rant at you." He jogged to catch up, chasing the wanted distraction.

"So you don't regret what you said, just that you included me in it?" She approached the line of cars and slipped between a polished SUV and T.J.'s new BMW.

"Hell, no, I don't regret it. It was a long time coming." He followed her into the small space and stopped a foot away, at the start of her door. "You don't think I have a right to tell women to back off? If it was your private number being distributed around the club and guys started texting at all hours, asking to hook up, while also sending unsolicited dick pics, I'd make sure those fuckers never stepped foot in the club again. Yet, when it happens to me, I'm supposed to be happy about it? Come on. Cut me a break. I enjoy unwanted attention as much as you do."

She opened her door and he retreated a step, not realizing how close they'd become.

"Tell me, Ella. Don't I deserve a break in my own club, or do you think I should keep letting it slide?" He wasn't sure if the question was rhetorical. The only thing he was aware of was the unfamiliar need to keep the conversation going. "Should I keep rejecting the same women over and over again every time I enter the Vault, even though they already know the score?"

"How do they know the score?" Her voice softened, the bitter edge of spite seeping away.

"I always make it clear I don't sleep with the same woman twice. I never leave any doubt." That hadn't changed since the first night the Vault doors had opened.

"You never made it clear to me."

No, he hadn't. Their position was different. "We haven't slept together yet." *Yet*? His subconscious tacked on the additional word without his approval.

"Well..." She lowered her gaze to his shoes. "I guess addressing the issue wasn't uncalled for. But you could've handled it better. You should've been nice."

"I don't do nice."

Her grin produced a dimple, and soft laughter followed.

"You're laughing at *me* now?" He should've been annoyed. Instead, he found himself grinning back at her. It didn't make a lick of sense. Then again, he rarely had women making fun of him. They were always making plans to fuck him. "I thought we weren't allowed to do that."

"I can't help it. You sound like a five-year-old throwing a tantrum. I can picture you using the same tone to say, 'I don't *do* vegetables.'"

"I *do* do vegetables," he countered. "What I don't do is put up with people's shit. I'm just sorry you got caught in the crossfire."

"Really?" She quirked a disbelieving brow.

"Yeah. Really."

She gave a soft snort and threw her handbag onto the passenger seat. "Thanks for letting me know."

"Does that mean we're good now?"

She nibbled her bottom lip. There was no seduction. Only contemplation. And holy shit, it was worth more on a sexual scale than any lip bite he'd previously witnessed. The sight sent his mind into a rapid rewind to the night in the locker room. Her body resting against his. Her moans filling his ears.

"I suppose so."

His dick started cashing checks his mind wasn't willing to pay. "I'm glad to hear it." He backtracked, getting out of there. Fast. "I'll see you around."

"Nope." She slid into the driver's seat. "I won't be back."

"Then, I guess it was nice knowing you."

She chuckled again and began closing her door. "I wouldn't go that far, either."

CHAPTER SEVEN

A shitty mood didn't come close to what Bryan sported when he shoved past the glass doors of the Taste of Sin restaurant the following day. The scheduled lunch shift wasn't the issue. The problem came from his phone.

He'd expected the sperm vultures to have left a message or two while his cell lay dormant overnight. The snatch pics that filled his text box hadn't been a surprise. He'd also expected the abusive message from Leo over what had happened last night.

What he hadn't predicted was the message from Tera—*If you change your mind and want to talk, please call me.*

Oh, hell, no. He wasn't going to let her fuck up another day. As far as he was concerned, his parents were already dead and buried. He assumed the feeling was mutual.

The reminder to change his cell number had him in a shitty mood. But from the sight of his business partners standing beside a table in the empty dining room of Taste of Sin, the worst was yet to come.

T.J. maintained his usual friendly expression—casual smile, laid-back posture. On the flip side, Leo scowled, eyeing him as if eagerly awaiting the start of whatever intervention was on this week's agenda.

"What are you doing here?" Bryan veered to the left, cutting through the tables toward the storage room behind the bar. "I thought you were both working tonight."

"We are." T.J. cleared his throat and shot a glance at Leo. "We have a few things we wanted to discuss with you beforehand."

"Right..." He continued walking, unsurprised when they both followed into the small enclosed area behind the bar. They hovered inside the doorway as Bryan dumped his wallet and keys in the safe. "Hurry up and get it over with."

"You went too far last night." Leo stepped inside and pulled the door shut behind them. "I had no idea of the extent of what happened until after you bailed. Then all hell broke loose, and I had a mass of women nagging me about how I was going to address the situation."

"Address the situation? You're joking, right? I followed club rules. I did everything by the book. The women in the Vault were due for a reminder on club etiquette, so I made a public announcement." No harm. No foul. At least from his viewpoint. "If you'd been getting snatch pics every five minutes and throaty voice messages the next, you would've done the same damn thing."

"I get it." T.J. gave him a placating look, furrowed brow and all. "Leo said a few of the women were hounding you—"

"A few?" Bryan glared at Leo. "If you're going to relay a story, at least tell it right."

"Okay, so a population equivalent to the Chinese army has been begging to nail you. Better?" Leo rolled his eyes. "You already know my feelings on the matter. You can't deny you overreacted."

Bryan ground his teeth. Had his friends already forgotten what it was like to be single in a club of voracious women? Did they even remember why they'd opened the Vault?

No. Of course not.

They were too busy creating memories with their significant others, and in return, shifting the dynamic of the business. T.J. had reconciled with his wife, Cassie, and Leo and Shay were growing closer with every public display of affection. Decisions surrounding the running of Taste of Sin, Shot of Sin, and the Vault of Sin were no longer a closed discussion.

"I go to the Vault to relax," he grated. "I'm not going to put up with any crap down there. It was created for us. We opened it. We made the rules."

"And now it's a thriving business." T.J. leaned against a stack of beer cartons next to the door. "It's moved beyond an irregular night of fun and is growing into something bigger than any of us planned."

"Then maybe it should go back to the way it was." He didn't believe the words coming out of his mouth. He didn't mean them. But something had to change. He just didn't know what.

His friends frowned, matching expressions of disbelief hitting him with their subtle annoyance.

"You're the one who suggested these show nights," Leo bit out.

Demonstrations. They were demonstrations or classes, not shows, but Bryan kept the critique to himself.

"You wanted to increase satisfaction levels and talk about getting women off efficiently. You were the one who suggested a BDSM talk session in the future. Now, all of a sudden, we're moving too fast? You can't have it both ways."

Bryan ran a hand over his forehead and massaged his temples. "I know."

Tera's phone call had him on edge. To the point of angered hysteria. After years of continuously burying the memories of his past, one twenty-second conversation had dragged everything to the forefront.

"Come on, man. You know the Vault is holding its own when it comes to income." T.J.'s voice softened. "Membership has doubled. The nights we open are increasing due to demand. And there's a shitload of interest in the class you've organized."

"There *was,*" Leo clarified. "I doubt it will go ahead now."

"What?" Bryan dropped his hand to his side. "Why?"

He'd put weeks of work into curating the perfect information session. With the influx of new members, there'd been a slight decline in enjoyment from the female patrons. The intention was to encourage men currently more interested in their own orgasms into those who gained greater pleasure in providing them to others.

"You stirred a hornet's nest last night. After you left, half the members were up in arms, screaming for blood."

"Let me guess," Bryan scoffed. "The female half?"

"Nailed it." Leo glared through tiny slits. "So how are you going to fix this?"

Fix this? He balled his hands into fists, the divide between them increased. There was nothing to fix. Not on his end.

"Like I said, I had women hassling me last night. I reminded them of the rules. End of story." He made for the door. "If they can't take a stern warning, they shouldn't be in the club."

"That's not what they're pissed about. They're saying you singled out a woman in one of the private rooms. They're demanding an apology."

"He's not exaggerating." T.J. pulled his cell from his jacket pocket. "I received a few messages about it this morning. Cassie did, too."

Bryan brushed the offered phone away and grabbed the door handle. "Well, then, they're in luck, because I already apologized to Ella last night. This shit is dead and buried." He winced when the words reminded him of his mother.

"Did you really apologize?"

Bryan turned to Leo. "Do I look like I give enough fucks to lie about it?" He was many things, but a liar wasn't one of them. His friends knew it, too.

"Good." The concern in T.J.'s features didn't lessen. "That's a start. They're still going to want a public apology, but if we send everyone an email clarifying what happened in the aftermath of the confrontation, maybe the class can go ahead."

"A public apology?" A public fucking apology? Were they kidding? "That's not going to happen."

"Then neither will the class." Leo spread his arms wide. "You can't have one without the other."

"That's how it's going to be?" Fury slithered through his veins, making his fingers shake, his heart palpitate. He took a menacing step toward Leo, trying like hell to keep his emotions in check. "You're railroading me into doing something I shouldn't have to do?"

"Are you really going to get in my face over this?" Leo raised his chin. "What's gotten into you? I warned you yesterday to keep it friendly. Now look what's happened—the women have quit salivating over your bullshit. Even Janeane has a prickle up her snatch and has refused to be your plaything for the demonstration night."

A prickle, otherwise known as rejection revenge. "I don't need her help." God knew he'd been scraping the bottom of the barrel when it came to his enthusiasm over using someone with claws poised to sink into his skin.

"Well, you're going to need someone, and none of the women in the Vault will touch you. They've already vowed to stick together to make a point."

"We're not the only club in town. I'll find someone else."

"That's beside the point. Nobody will show up to the demo as a spectator for the same reason." T.J. slid his cell into his jacket pocket. "You know I love you, man, but this is our reputation you're playing with. You either need to apologize or get the woman back in here to prove everything's been smoothed over."

"I agree," Leo added. "Or maybe think about stepping away from the Vault until it all blows over."

"Step away?"

Fuck.

He got it, really, he did. The women were playing the emotional, we-did-nothing-wrong card, and all the men were standing beside them because otherwise they wouldn't get laid.

Well played, ladies. Well played.

"I can't do that." The Vault was his go-to. His one hangout. His only refuge. He'd never needed the mind-numbing escape more. "Not right now."

"And why is that?" Leo asked. "You haven't been an eager participant for months."

Now they were keeping tabs on him? "Because Shay keeps asking to ride my dick and I'm just about ready to cave."

Leo glared. "Sarcasm? Now there's something new for a change. You could've simply asked me to mind my own business."

"I'm pretty sure I've done that more times than I can count. It looks like Shay is starting to rub off on you."

"Come on, guys." T.J. pushed from the stack of beer cartons. "We need to sort this mess. The demo is next Thursday night, and we don't have another party planned in the Vault beforehand."

There was no *we* involved. This was all on Bryan's shoulders. Along with all the other shit that had piled on top of him this week.

"Don't worry. I'll work it out." Bryan made for the door, determined to put this bullshit behind him to make way for the more important bullshit.

"Yeah?" Leo followed behind him. "And how do you plan on doing that?"

"It'll be an easy fix." He shrugged. "I'll convince Ella to be my assistant."

CHAPTER EIGHT

Pamela handed the carry-out coffee and muffin to the construction worker who had become a regular customer in her cafe. He was a nice guy. Always placed a generous tip in her jar. Constantly gave her a sweet grin. Never wavered with his manners. "Enjoy."

He inclined his head, backtracking as he increased the sugary sweetness of his smile. "Thank you. I will."

Her sister, Kim, groaned from her position in front of the coffee machine. "The studs are out in force today. I feel like we've hit the hot-guy jackpot."

"He's not *that* hot." Pamela placed the glass dome back on top of the muffin display plate. "Too cute and sweet for my appetite."

"I'm not talking about Muffin Man. I want to latch my nails into the guy out front. He's been standing there on his cell for five minutes, and I'm dying to know if he's going to come inside."

Pamela swung her gaze to the door and swallowed over the gasp threatening to escape her throat. The man's face was annoyingly familiar—the scowl even more so.

Bryan. The asshole who'd kept her up all night pondering hate sex.

"Shit." She scooted behind Kim, hiding from view. It wasn't the first time she'd seen him walk by her little café, but it was the first time he'd stopped.

"You know him?"

"Technically? No."

"But..."

"That's Bryan—the guy from the club I was telling you about." She clutched her sister's arm, dragging her along the counter like a shield.

"The one with superior hands and an unrivaled bad attitude?"

"Yes. Now get me out of here before he sees me."

They shuffled in unison toward the swinging kitchen doors until she safely hid from view. Now all she had to deal with was the raised questioning brow coming from her mother behind the preparation bench.

"Who are we hiding from?" Her mom craned her neck, paused in her task of peeling carrots as she looked out the service window.

"Nobody." Pamela smiled and crossed her hands behind her back. "I just wanted to see what you're up to."

The raised brow didn't waver.

"You're such a bad liar," Kim whispered.

At this point, Pamela didn't care. She just wanted to remain in hiding, not tempting fate, until Bryan continued down the street.

"I think he's gone." Kim nudged the door open, peeking out the small space. "I can't see him anymore."

Relief, thick and delicious, pulsated in Pamela's chest. "Thank God." She didn't have the energy to deal with assholes today. Not even good-looking ones. But just to be sure, she glanced through the slight part of the doors and scanned the sidewalk.

Nope. Not there.

"Wait." Her sister indicated a man at the counter, his back toward them. "Is that him?"

The guy she pointed to had a similar build—broad shoulders covered in a tailored suit. Only the blond hair was all wrong. Too short. No beard.

"No. That's not him."

"You sure? Isn't he the guy who was out the front?"

"What guy out the front?" Their mom squeezed between them, her voice a conspiratorial whisper.

"Forget it." Pamela stepped back from the door, her cheeks warming. Was she hallucinating now? She could've sworn she'd seen Bryan. Then again, her thoughts had been obsessed with him since he'd broken her non-masturbatory orgasm drought. Not even his nastiness had abated the X-rated daydreams.

"I must've been mistaken." She leaned against the counter beneath the service window and winced. "That guy doesn't look anything like him."

Kim frowned at her, the glance speaking of a shared concern to Pamela's mental stability. "I need to get back out there. We'll discuss this later." She pushed through the doors, disappearing into the main room of the café.

"Did you get enough sleep?" Her mother scrutinized her, the concern in her eyes a familiar sight since Lucas died.

"I slept fine… Or maybe I didn't. I don't know." She shrugged. "I'm at that age where sleep is more of a luxury than a necessity."

The close examination continued. "You had another bad night."

This time it wasn't a question. After Lucas passed away, her mom had become a master at reading all the things Pamela tried to keep to herself. And years later, the game of hide and seek hadn't ended.

"I went to the club last night. That's all. You know I don't get much sleep when I've been out."

"It seems like more than that to me."

She waggled her brows, hoping to kill the questions with her mother's discomfort. "Maybe I got laid."

"The luggage under your eyes isn't the I-got-laid type. But you know I'm here whenever you're ready to talk." Her mother returned to the preparation bench and picked up a carrot from the chopping board.

Pamela stood there, hard bench behind her, concerned parent in front. She didn't want to talk anymore. There'd been years and years of it. All conversations revolved around Lucas and how she needed to live her life now that he was gone.

Like her time at the Vault, she needed to move on and realize this new chapter wasn't a failure. It was merely going to be different. Devoid of sexual motivation, but not necessarily crummy.

Oh, who was she kidding.

Her sex life had taken a nose-dive and she was still cleaning up after the crash and burn, hoping to salvage something from the charred remains.

"Thanks." She gave her mom a sad smile and pushed from the counter. "I better go and help Kim."

"Ella?"

Holy shit.

Her eyes widened as the masculine voice washed over her, the dominant presence tickling the back of her neck.

Her mother paused, carrot in hand, and glanced through the service window. Pamela didn't need to turn around to determine who owned the deep growl.

Then again, maybe this was another hallucination.

She swung around, coming face to face with Bryan standing on the other side of the window.

"Have you got a minute?" The question came casually. As if they were friends. As if she should've expected him to walk back into her life today.

"Do you know him?" her mother hissed, dragging Pamela's attention back to maternal eyes now twinkling with appreciation for a man who was completely undeserving.

"Unfortunately."

Appreciation turned to excitement. "Come in. Come in." Her mother waved a hand, her matchmaker switch well and truly engaged.

Oh, no.

No, no, no.

"*Mom.*"

The warning was ignored, the kitchen door swung open, and the devil entered, shrinking the room with his presence.

"Morning, ma'am." Bryan smiled at her mother.

Smiled and used the word *ma'am*.

What the hell was he playing at? The contrast from the stuck-up, superior man she knew didn't compute. Not in the slightest. This guy had a casual air of the-boy-next-door, with a smooth swagger and gentle eyes.

"Morning, Ella."

She didn't offer a greeting. Not in words. Her frown posed as a technicolor response.

"Can we talk?"

She worked the question over in her mind. Back and forth. "Didn't we speak last night?"

His lips twitched, a tiny hitch of mirth. "We did. And now I have something else I want to discuss."

"Take a seat in the café," her mother offered unwanted assistance. "I'll help Kim for a while."

Bryan raised a questioning brow to confirm the option.

"No," she growled. "We can speak here."

He sucked in a slow, deep breath, showing his displeasure with a subtle expand of his broad chest. "Sure." His gaze leisurely glided from her to her mother, back and forth. "Are we still good after last night?"

"As good as we're going to get."

There were no grudges. Not really... Okay, she hadn't slept a wink due to her body wanting him and her mind hating him. With time, her annoyance probably would've faded. But less than twenty-four hours had passed, so he was out of luck.

"Hint taken." His tongue worked over the words like he was seducing them. Or her. She feared he succeeded in both. "I have a proposition for you."

She shook her head. "Not interested."

"You don't want to hear me out?"

"I ditched the sucker-for-punishment attitude twelve hours ago."

Another glance went from mother to daughter before his expression changed. It was slight. The minute squint of his eyes, the tiniest tilt of his chin. "This has nothing to do with punishment." He stared at her, stared so hard her betraying nipples tingled. "It's the opposite."

The opposite of punishment?

She shuddered. Her built-up tension and annoyance formed a concoction that resembled arousal. All the while, her mother remained quiet. Still a few feet away. Still mesmerized by a man who deserved far less scrutiny.

"On second thought, let's take this outside." She dragged her feet to the kitchen doors, shoving through them to enter the dining area.

It wasn't safe to be caged in the small kitchen with him. Fresh air became necessary. Space, too. She walked onto the street and took a seat at one of the steel-frame tables that were usually only occupied during the really busy times when customers had nowhere else to sit.

He followed, and the split second when he loomed close, about to take his seat, was a threatening taunt to all her needy senses. She wanted him over her. Under her. Inside her.

Christ.

"What do you want, Bryan?" Her voice cracked with the built-up tension clogging her throat.

He sat opposite her, dwarfing the setting, the metal table and chairs appearing toy-like under his large frame.

The problematic situation only intensified when Kim strode onto the sidewalk, a notepad in hand, and stopped at their table. "May I take your order?"

Pamela scowled. They didn't provide table service. Never had. "No, Kim. We're good."

"I'll get a large coffee, strong, with cream, thanks." Bryan held her focus while he ordered. Asserting his authority. Vocalizing his confidence.

Wrong decision, buddy. He'd flaunted his head-strong independence in the wrong place. Especially when it came to her protective sister.

"Sure thing." Kim scribbled on the notepad. "I'll be back in a second."

Pamela focused farther down the footpath, unwilling to stare into his deep blue eyes. It didn't make sense that she could loathe and lust for a man, all at the same time. She wished one emotion would hurry up and claim victory because this seesaw was exhausting.

"We're not good, are we?" He leaned back in his chair. "Even though you said so last night."

"Last night we were good because I never thought I'd see you again."

His mouth tilted as if she'd paid him a compliment. Sharp eyes turned gentle. Harsh lips became inviting. "What if I decided I'm not finished with you yet?"

She laughed, a cold, bitter laugh she hoped sounded convincing. It wasn't the first time he'd said 'yet' and had it sound like a sexual promise. Both instances had been equally confusing. "Then I'd take pleasure in letting you down gently. Just like you did to me last night."

"I see you like to hold a grudge."

"Only as much as most women."

He gave a breath of a chuckle, the sound lacking humor. She waited, hoping to see a believable smile pulling at that lush mouth.

Nothing came.

Nothing but her sister who slid a take-away coffee in front of him with a slight curtsy. "Here you go, Bryan. Enjoy."

"Thanks." He focused on the container as Kim walked away, his hand snaking up to rub over his beard. "She knows my name?"

"She knows a lot of things." There were no skeletons left hidden to her family. No rock left unturned. Pamela rarely had anything to be ashamed of, and even when she did, telling her sister seemed like a form of penance.

"So, it's likely she spat in my coffee."

"No, it's not likely." She spoke with solemn sincerity, allowing him the time to relax and reach for his take-away cup before she added, "It's a certainty. There is no way in hell that coffee doesn't contain some sort of retribution."

His smile turned to a grin. When laughter hit her ears, she sat back and stared. Carefree Bryan was remarkable. A picture of charming severity. The playfulness in his eyes swept away his hostility, those flawless white teeth no longer vicious.

He placed the cup down as his happiness dissipated and the man she knew returned, this time less harsh.

"Are you ready to tell me why you're here?"

He raised his gaze to her, those blue eyes lingering on her lips longer than necessary. "After we left last night, some of the Vault members announced their annoyance at how I spoke to you. In fact, a lot of the women are up in arms, demanding a public apology."

"Public apology?" She glanced around, hoping he had no intention of making a scene in front of her café.

"Don't worry, I already told my business partners I've done the necessary groveling. I don't plan on doing it again."

She rolled her eyes. "Why am I not surprised?"

"I'm hoping it's because you realize we've already resolved the situation and dragging it out would be bullshit."

"Okay." She shrugged. "But you still haven't answered my question. Why are you here?"

"Did you get the email I sent about the class I'm running next Thursday night? A guys' tutorial on the female—"

"Yeah. I got it."

"Then, you'll also know I plan on having a demonstration assistant."

She remembered. Her imagination had run wild with the thought of watching the instructional performance. "And?"

"And Janeane, the woman who was supposed to play the role, is one of the people demanding an apology. I need someone to take her place."

"That shouldn't be difficult. Not with women scrambling to climb on your junk."

He nodded, as if pondering his immense self-worth. "Finding a willing woman wouldn't be too hard. I'm more concerned with finding the right one. That's why I'm here."

She laughed. He had to be joking. There was no way in hell a man could have balls big enough to ask that of her after the way he'd treated her. "You want *me* to be your assistant?"

"Yes." The answer came strong and sure. No doubt. No guilt.

Another laugh escaped. "Are you kidding?"

The tight set of his jaw implied he wasn't.

"Is this some sort of game? You thought I was interested in you, so you shot me down in flames, and now that you realize I have no intention in joining your drama-llama lifestyle you decide you want my help?" She pushed back in her chair, ready and oh, so willing to bail.

"I came here because you're the perfect fit for this demonstration—"

"Out of all the women at the Vault, *I'm* the perfect fit?"

"There's no one else." His nostrils flared and he stilled, taking precious moments before he said, "What happened last night has ensured nobody else will help me. Not without the public apology I refuse to give."

"Oh." She batted her lashes, the picture of sweet innocence. "I get it now. You *need* me," she enunciated the words, letting them dance over her tongue. "Isn't this a delicious curve ball?"

"I don't need you, Ella. I can cancel the class. It's no skin off my nose. But working together would benefit us both."

"No." She pushed back in her chair, preparing to stand. "It wouldn't benefit me at all."

"Are you sure about that?" His tone dropped, having a torturous effect on her belly. "You came to the Vault in search of something. And you know I can give it to you."

"You *could*," she corrected. "Back when you hadn't grated every one of my nerves. For me, mental stimulation is ten times more effective than physical. There's no way you could get me to cross the line now I have a clearer picture of who you are."

"Don't assume to know me." He held her captive with his fierce stare. "We've spent little more than an hour together."

An hour that packed the punch of a three-year obsession.

"Look..." She sighed. "Maybe if last night hadn't happened, I'd consider it. But I didn't exaggerate what I told you in the parking lot."

She wasn't interested. She couldn't be.

He raised a brow. "Not even about the livestock?"

She snorted over his unexpected humor. "Okay, so maybe I exaggerated about the livestock. But that's all. You're not my type and I'm definitely not looking for complications." She'd had enough to last a lifetime. "Enjoy your coffee. I need to get back to work."

She pushed from her seat and stepped away, only to be stopped by a large hand clasping her wrist, the fingers delicate in their hold.

He glanced up at her. "I don't need to be your type to get you off."

He was right. So damn right her uterus squeezed, begging her to concede. Every part of her reacted to him in an unforgiving way. Her skin buzzed. Her heart fluttered. The nerves he'd grated to stubs were waving wildly with energetic excitement.

"Yeah, you do." She knew her sexual limits, even if her body wasn't predictable at the moment.

"So, your rapid pulse is from what?" He tilted his head. "And the goose bumps?" He trailed his thumb along the inside of her wrist. Teasing. Tormenting. "You may not like me. But you're still attracted to me."

He released his hold and stood. All male. All muscle. "What happened the night in the locker room is a drip in the ocean to what I have planned for the class."

A drip?

She kept her chin high, even though her breasts ached. All she could do was shake her head, no longer able to voice a rejection.

"I've proven you wrong once before. Give me the chance to do it again."

"While under the scrutiny of a crowd at the club? No, thanks." She walked for the café doors, even though her libido remained begging at his feet. Her interest was temporary. A sleep-deprived delusion. There was no doubt he'd be unsuccessful a second time around.

Okay, maybe there was a little doubt.

A teeny, tiny bit.

Not enough to justify further humiliation, though.

"What if we had a test run?"

His question pulled her up short. She turned, finding him clutching the backrest of his metal chair.

"A test run?"

"I can open the Vault tonight. For the two of us. That way we can see who's right or wrong."

"I know my body." At least she had, until Bryan had scorched her with his touch.

"I remember you thinking the same thing in the locker room."

She scoffed, wishing she had a smart quip to shove in his face. Unfortunately, they both knew he was right. He'd tweaked parts of her she'd thought died years ago.

"You like to keep throwing that in my face, don't you?"

"If it helps me get what I want." He shrugged. "I'll do whatever's necessary."

Her chest squeezed with the close proximity to defeat. "I'm not going to the club. If you want to do this, we do it my way." The response felt like surrender. Tantalizing, erotic surrender.

"I'm listening."

She approached, taking one cautious step after another. The ball rested in her court; all she needed to do was determine what she wanted to gain.

His discomfort.

The tiniest taste of retribution.

"You need to meet me at my apartment." Where he'd be surrounded by her things and would no doubt feel uncomfortable in a scary, relationship-type setting. If they were going to do this, he needed to hate every single minute of it.

He didn't flinch. "Your place, it is. Would you also like to dictate the time?"

"Seven." The power trip was invigorating. "I'll get a piece of paper to write down the address."

"Don't worry about it. I have all your details at the club."

So, that was how he'd found her.

He released the back of the chair and straightened to his full domineering height. "I'll see you tonight, Ella, and I'll bring dinner."

Dinner? Like a date?

He pulled a wallet from his back pocket and retrieved a ten-dollar bill. "For the coffee."

"I don't want your money." She didn't even want his conversation. All she was willing to gain from her time with him was orgasms.

"Thanks." He encroached, putting her on edge. His aftershave danced around her, the slightest scent of sexuality teasing her senses. "I guess I'll pay you back tonight."

She wouldn't shudder. She refused. "We'll see."

"Yeah." His eyes danced, devilish, predatory, and so damn cocky. "We will."

CHAPTER NINE

𝓑ryan reached her doorstep five minutes early, bottle of wine under one arm, bags of Chinese take-out in the other. He'd made the right assumption about her wealth. She lived in an expensive suburb, her complex surrounded by manicured gardens and an impressive security system.

It got him thinking about where she got the money. It was either Daddy's or the dead husband's. You didn't get digs like this on a barista's paycheck.

He knocked on her door with a gentle knuckle, knowing she'd already be waiting after having to buzz him into the building.

Seconds later, the door opened and Ella stood before him, one hand clutching the handle as she rocked a loose grey shirt and a pair of cotton, sporty short-shorts.

"You found the place easy enough?"

"No problem at all."

He hadn't expected this—her no-fucks-given attire, the lack of seduction. She dressed simple. Carefree. There was no hint of her trying to impress him, and funnily enough, she had anyway. He couldn't even smell perfume. Only the faint hint of citrus soap mingling with the Asian spices wafting from their dinner.

"Something wrong?" She frowned, her questioning eyes reading him.

"I'm surprised, that's all. I didn't know what to expect when I arrived."

"You thought you'd get lingerie and scented candles?" She nailed it with a smile. A cute, light-hearted lift of sweet lips. "Let me remind you, you're not the stud you think you are. I get that you're the king of orgasms in the Vault. But out here, in the real world, you're kind of a dick."

"So you keep telling me." He held up the bags containing their dinner. "You going to let me in before this gets cold?"

"Oh, sorry." She stepped back, sweeping her hand to the apartment behind her as if he were royalty. "I guess I was expecting you to pound your chest and demand entry."

"Very funny."

"I thought so."

Her apartment was pristine. Nothing out of place. Pillows lined her brown leather sofa. Magazines were neatly stacked on the coffee table. The carpet had fresh vacuum marks, the furniture was polished. She had her shit together, at least better than he did.

"Where do you want to eat?"

"Dinner table."

He continued ahead to the open dining and kitchen area, placing the food and wine on the large wooden setting.

Ella busied herself riffling through cupboards and drawers, then came to stand beside him with plates and cutlery. "Do you think you ordered enough?" Her sarcasm was rich as she helped him place the containers in the middle of the table.

Truth was, he hadn't known what she'd like. He didn't even know if she enjoyed Chinese food, so he'd ordered a variety to satisfy every palate. "You can't order Chinese without leaving enough for leftovers. They're the best part."

She nodded, buying his bullshit. "What would you like to drink? I don't have beer, but I have some of Lucas's scotch and bourbon hidden in the kitchen somewhere."

"I'm happy to share the wine with you."

She eyed him skeptically. "Sure."

"Something wrong?" he mocked, taking on the same tone she'd used earlier.

"Yeah. You're being nice."

"How?"

"The wine. The mass of Chinese food. What gives?"

She was right. This moment escaped his typical normality, but he wasn't willing to admit how badly he needed her to smooth things over at the Vault.

"Sweetheart, there's nothing nice about it. I'm starving, and I need as much alcohol to get through this as you do."

"And there he is, the Brute I've come to know and despise." She slid into her seat across the table, dragging a plate and cutlery in front of her. "But you know what? I think you're making excuses, because deep down you think I'm super-dooper awesome." She waggled her perfectly manicured brows.

He couldn't tell if her pretty smile was annoying, or way too endearing. Either way, it had an effect on his chest he wasn't used to. And he was surprised her laugh didn't make him want to shudder. "You're not too bad."

She chuckled and dished food onto her plate while he poured the wine. They didn't talk for long moments. Strangely enough, they didn't need to. He had no desire to fill the silence. And going by the pleased look on her face, she had no problem with the absence of conversation, either.

While they ate, he took the time to read her. Finding out tiny snippets of her character with the visual sweep. She chewed slowly. Unrushed bites with dazed contemplation. She didn't gulp at her wine as if consumed with nervousness. She didn't fidget or fiddle. Despite having a low tolerance to his attitude, she seemed to feel comfortable with him.

"Have you lived here long?" He had a sudden urge to learn more. To dig deeper.

"About a year."

"And you've been a widow for how long?"

Her fork slipped, missing food and splashing sauce onto the table. She stared at the dark brown droplet now marring the wood and frowned. "Long enough."

The vibrancy of her eyes turned bleak. Her smile faded, and in its place, sorrow grew. She cleared her throat and ran a lazy finger over the dribble, bringing the liquid to her lips to lick away the mess. For a second, he became mesmerized by her far-off contemplation. She was emotionally bare, her pain almost tangible.

He shouldn't push, and not merely due to manners. He didn't want to give her the wrong impression and make her think he gave a shit. But he needed answers, for no other reason than to understand who this woman was.

"How long were you married?"

She reached for her wine, dragging out the seconds as she took a long gulp. "Eleven months."

"You must've been young." He was fishing for answers because he hadn't had time to re-read the finer details of her file when he snooped for her café address.

She barked out a laugh. "How old do you think I am?"

Good question. *Tricky* question.

He scrutinized her—the young eyes, the ruby lips. She didn't have a wrinkle in sight, yet she grasped her sexuality like a woman far older than her appearance suggested.

"Late twenties?"

Her mouth quirked and he had the sudden urge to kiss her. There was no romance about it. He wasn't interested in a chaste kiss. What he pictured was something harsh and unforgiving. Something dirty to wash away the tainted widow.

"You just earned yourself a gold star." She placed her fork on her plate and inched them both toward the middle of the table.

"I'm right?"

"No. But I'll take it as a compliment." She pushed to her feet. "Do you want seconds, or should I put the containers in the fridge?"

"I'm good." Too good.

He enjoyed knowing they were closer in age than he'd previously assumed. But again, the added information only increased the need for more. He wanted to know everything. Was she still hung up on the love of a dead man? How had she found his sex club? And how did she plan to sate her sexuality if she didn't return to the Vault?

He shoved the last piece of honey chicken into his mouth as she stacked containers back into the bag. Her loose top gaped at the front, the fucking brilliant view of her bra-covered tits staring him right in the face.

From any other woman, he would've considered the act a blatant attempt at seduction. From Ella, he didn't get that vibe at all. She was oblivious to her temptation and confident enough in her own right not to be embarrassed about a glimpse of intimate skin. It was clear she also had no clue of the filthy thoughts rapidly building in his mind—the need to prove her wrong, to make her fully aware of the control he could gain over her body. He wanted to have her pussy clamping around his fingers. Her thighs clenching around his head. Her lips parting to call his name, louder than she'd ever called before.

Because that was what he was good at.

The only thing he was good at.

He snatched the wine bottle from beside her and filled their glasses. The comfortable silence had turned chaotic. A hint of panic tinged the air, or maybe it only lingered in his blood.

"How many times have you done this?" He needed to know where he ranked on the list. What was his number in the line?

"Had wine and Chinese food?" She didn't meet his gaze as she lifted the bag and made for the kitchen.

"Brought someone from the club back to your apartment?"

She shrugged. "This is the first time I've had any man in my apartment."

"The first?" He followed, dirty dish and full wine glass in hand. "I thought Shay said you'd been a widow for years."

"And now you're taking the invitation as a compliment?" She opened the fridge, shooting him an unimpressed glance over the top of the door as she placed the food inside. "Don't. Believe me, you're not special. I just haven't had much luck with men since Lucas passed."

With every insult, he struggled to hide his smirk. Her compounding disinterest had the opposite effect on him. A dangerous effect. For once, he felt a strange pull for more.

"Maybe that will change after the demonstration night."

She closed the fridge and came toward him, taking the plate from his hands to place it in the sink. "You've gotta get me there first, bucko."

"I guess you're ready for me to prove my worth. Tell me where you want to do this and we'll get started."

"Now?" She turned from the sink, her eyes wide. "God, no. I just ate a truckload of food. Unless you have a pregnancy fetish, you're going to have to wait until my belly settles."

No, no pregnancy fetish, but he was starting to think he had a thing for kitchens.

He could picture her bent over the sink. Slammed up against the fridge. Splayed on the counter. He didn't want to wait. He had to get this over and done with before his needs became demands.

"Can we sit for a while?" She made for the dining table to claim her wine glass, bringing a waft of heavenly scented citrus air as she scooted past. "I've been on my feet all day."

He huffed. He didn't even try to hide it.

Her responding chuckle only increased his annoyance.

"Is it going to threaten your bachelor status if we sit side by side on the sofa?"

"Doesn't worry me in the slightest."

"Liar." Her mouth curved in a knowing smile, the wine glass raising to those tempting lips. "I knew being here would make you uncomfortable."

"We'll see who's uncomfortable once you're naked and writhing. I figure the apology you're going to owe me for doubting my skills will be hard to spit out."

"I'm never going to apologize for not being endeared by your shitty attitude." She strode into the living room, an added sway to those hips. "If you can work any sort of magic it will merely be a payoff for the crap you've put me through."

His gaze strayed to her ass encased in those tiny sports shorts. If anyone was going through crap, it was him. He was the one who had to figure out how to get her off while holding his own lust in check. Lust that rapidly morphed into a driving force.

He followed her, choosing to stand by the stacked bookshelf while she lazily slumped onto the three-seater sofa. She kicked her feet onto the coffee table, spreading long, smooth legs before him like an appetizer.

"So..." He turned to the bookshelf, taking in the middle shelf stacked wall to wall with cancer information. A cold ache formed under his sternum at the thought of the nightmare his parents were enduring. He wanted to familiarize himself with their suffering, to pretend he was involved somehow. "That's a lot of books."

There were emotional titles—*When Breath Becomes Air, Everyday Strength*, and *How to Help Someone with Cancer*. Research titles—*Radical Remission, What You Need to Know About Cancer, The Facts 101*. Even those that promoted alternate therapies.

"Lucas had terminal cancer."

He'd guessed as much. "I'm sorry you had to go through that."

"Don't be. It's not your fault."

He pulled a title from the shelf and stared at the couple on the cover —*Supporting Someone with Cancer: A Loved One's Guide.*

He wondered if his father had this book filed neatly on their perfect shelf back in Tampa. Had he purchased all these titles for the woman who made his life worthwhile?

"How much time did you have with your husband after his diagnosis?"

"Eleven months."

He frowned and shoved the book back into place. "I thought you said you were married for eleven months."

"I did." She sipped from her glass, her eyes trained on his. "It's a long story."

"Do you mind if I ask what it's like?"

"Cancer?" Her forehead wrinkled.

"Yeah. What's the process? The end game?"

Her mouth opened and closed. Her eyes remained wide.

"Sorry, is that a shitty question?"

She snorted through a sip of wine, then placed the glass down on the coffee table. "I guess it depends why you're asking."

He could've given a lame excuse. He could've lied. "My mother has terminal cancer."

"Oh, Bryan. I'm so sorry." Her face scrunched with genuine sympathy, masking all her beauty and replacing it with pathetic emotion.

"Don't be." He stepped over her legs and took a seat beside her. "We're not close."

"But still, she's your mother. The news must be devastating."

The fact his mother had withheld the information from her only son was more traumatic.

"Feel free to take any of the books home with you. They're no use to me anymore."

"No. I'm good." He could ask a question or two to feel connected to a family who disowned him, but he refused to spend hours researching his mother's downfall. He never should've mentioned her in the first place.

"Well, I'll leave the offer open if you change your mind." Her voice turned somber, her expression, too. "I've been meaning to get rid of them for years. Having the reminder stare me in the face every day is getting a little old."

"Thanks." He concentrated on her fingers, noticing how they dug deeper and deeper into the sole of her foot, as if trying to massage the pain away.

"Do you want to talk about it?" She flashed him a look, one that told him she'd battle through this painful conversation, if only for his benefit.

"No." He shook his head. "Not at all."

"Okay. I get it." She flexed her feet, feigning relaxation. "So, tell me, why a class?" The pain didn't leave her features as she blatantly changed the subject. "What will you get out of it?"

"Satisfaction." At least that's what he'd told himself in the planning stages. He'd wanted to tweak the club on the most intimate level. To mold the greedy Vault patrons into more selfless participants.

But that aim didn't hold his interest anymore. Now, the only thing he wanted from the demonstration night was a one-way ticket between Ella's thighs. To sink under her skin, the same way she was crawling under his.

"I don't buy it."

"I don't need you to."

"That's exactly my point. You don't seem the type to willingly help others for the sake of it. And you already have a posse who think you're the messiah of the female orgasm."

"You've got me pegged. After what? Two conversations?"

Her lips curved, the grief gradually seeping away. "Don't you think I deserve to know, considering I'm contemplating helping you?"

"Helping me? We both know this is mutually beneficial." He jerked his chin toward her feet and indicated for her to lift them in his direction with a crook of his hand.

She frowned, remaining immobile.

He slapped his lap, trying not to make a big deal out of the offer. He wouldn't be able to stop fixating on his parents until she stopped thinking about her husband. And neither thought process was conducive for what he had planned. "Put your feet up here."

Her lips worked over silent contemplation until finally she turned on the sofa, placing her heels on his thighs. "Your fixation on this being mutually beneficial is a load of bull. It's not like I can't get an orgasm without you. I can do the work myself."

"And you're satisfied with that? You don't need a guy to break the monotony?" No matter how she responded, he knew the truth. A woman with her sexuality and passion could never be entirely satisfied with masturbation. It might dull the ache, but she needed to be fucked. There was no substitute for skin on skin.

"I have toys."

He didn't appreciate the visual. Actually, his body appreciated it too damn much. His cock stirred, the hard length nudging against her heel. "I'd like to see that."

"I know," she drawled. "And you wouldn't be the only one."

No doubt. He could sell tickets at the Vault and pack the room with willing voyeurs. She'd enjoy it, too. This woman would love to be the center of innumerable fantasies. She deserved to be.

He grabbed one of her feet, distracting himself as he worked his thumb along her inner sole.

"Oh, God." She groaned. "That feels good."

Shit.

As far as distractions went, this one was counterproductive. Her throaty moans and the arching of her back made his cock push harder against his zipper. And those toenails. Jesus. He'd never spent much time admiring a woman's feet. It wasn't his kink. But he understood it now.

Those dainty, delicate toes.

The feminine light pink polish.

He was in fucking trouble.

How many men came home to this every day? A beautiful woman. A nice meal. Light-hearted conversation. And the promise of a sweaty, energetic fuck.

"I don't get you, Bryan."

Not surprising. He didn't understand himself. Maybe they could work out his insanity together. "What's not to get?"

"You bought me dinner and wine. You're being kind. Well, way beyond civil, anyway. And now you're massaging my feet."

His skin itched with the influx of reality. He'd stopped pretending this woman annoyed him sometime in the last hour. Probably earlier. This afternoon could've been the culprit.

He shrugged it off, determined to snap back on track. "You're not a vulture. It gives me the freedom to relax."

"So, this is the real Bryan?" She scrutinized him, her brows pulled tight. "Far from the brute who torments everyone?"

"I don't torment anyone. Neither do I pretend to be someone I'm not." Not really. He lowered his focus to her feet, gently curling her toes under. "This is me. And the guy you met at the Vault is, too."

She remained quiet, and he didn't dare look at her to fill the void.

"I'm not an asshole, Ella. Not entirely. I just have a low tolerance for bullshit."

She tilted her head, pondering, and he knew exactly what skittered through her mind. He knew it even before she opened her mouth. "Why El—"

"Are you ready to get started?" He tapped her ankles, indicating for her to move. He liked her, but not enough to field questions about his reluctance to say her name.

"Ahh. Sure." She placed her feet on the floor and sat up straight. "How do you want to do this?"

"Let's start with where."

"The bedroom?" Her face remained impassive. "Just in case I get bored and want to take a nap." Her lips twitched, breaking the tension building in his chest.

"The bedroom, it is." He stood, offering her a hand. "And don't worry—you won't be nodding off any time soon."

CHAPTER TEN

The back of Pamela's neck tingled as she led Bryan down the hall. Nervousness had set in, the shaky, uncomfortable feeling an unwanted blast from the past.

"Is something wrong?"

"No, why?" She stopped before her open bedroom door and faced him.

"You were walking like I had a gun at your back."

Why did he care? Before today, she would've assumed it was to exploit her discomfort. But from the way he'd acted tonight, she wondered if the question came from true concern.

"There's a lot of pressure on my shoulders." She hadn't been anxious about sex in a damn long time. Not that this was anxiety as much as it was nervous anticipation.

"There's no pressure." He led the way into her room, not bothering to turn on the light. "All you have to do is relax and let me work my magic. Once I'm done, you can sing my praises, and then I'll leave. Simple as that."

She wasn't going to encourage his confidence. Nope. Not at all.

"I see you hiding a smile under those tight lips." He smirked over his shoulder. "We both know I'm right."

She ignored him and padded to her nightstand to flick on the lamp. The dim light only endeavored to highlight the devilish appeal of his features. His expression spoke of passion. Pleasure and dominance.

Everything she'd been searching for since Lucas died stared her in the face, waiting to be grasped in both hands.

If he demanded things of her, things she wasn't necessarily prepared to give, she'd succumb anyway. No doubt. Something inside her had become starved for his approval. She wanted to make him smile again. To ease the sterility that coiled around him with suffocating efficiency.

He inched closer to the bed, his suit pants brushing against the mattress. "Take off your shirt."

Her lips parted in shock, but they shouldn't have. Pleasantries weren't a part of the deal. Neither was foreplay.

She grasped the thin material of her shirt, pulled it over her head, and dropped it to the floor. She stood before him, black lace bra and old cotton shorts. Her chest expanded with the need for more. More air. More control. More noise to fill the tense silence. "Better?"

"Not quite. But we're getting there." His scrutiny raked her. It wasn't a light caress of his attention. It was brutal, like his nickname demanded. Those eyes turned molten, the heat of promise burning bright. "Shorts off, too."

"Wait." Her nervousness came out of hiding, nudging anticipation out of the way. "Should we discuss a rough timeframe to end this?"

He frowned.

"I mean..." She sighed. "If this doesn't seem to be working, should we have a set time in mind to stop? Unlike you, I don't like hurting people's feelings, but I also don't want you all up in my bits, working long hours like a miner, when you're getting nowhere. So, maybe we need a deadline."

He lowered his gaze, paying too much attention to the rapid rise and fall of her chest. "Sure. If it'll make you comfortable, we'll put a fifteen-minute timeline on this."

"Fifteen minutes?" Was he kidding? "I won't even be turned on in fifteen minutes."

He smirked, that wicked lift of lips telling her he already knew she was simmering. "Trust me." He tapped the mattress, encouraging her approach. "I've got this covered."

Her heart kicked.

Parts lower, too.

"Not only will fifteen minutes be enough," he drawled, "but I'm willing to wager I'll get you over the line in less than ten."

"Now you're delusional." She crossed her arms over her chest. "If you're not going to take this seriously—"

"Who's really the delusional one here?" He approached, his sure stride eating up the distance in less than a heartbeat. "The woman who says no man can make her climax?" His hand raised, gently gliding stray strands of hair from her cheek. "Or the guy who achieved it with one finger?"

Her cheeks heated. "Stop bringing that up."

"Why? It was some of my best work."

Some? Whisper-thin threads of jealousy came to life in her chest. She shouldn't have forgotten his efficiency was equally brag-worthy with other women. It was pathetic to even care.

"Are we doing this or what?" She shoved at her shorts, letting them fall to her feet, then climbed onto the bed. "Hurry up. The clock is ticking."

"Not yet, it isn't. We still have the finer details to sort out." He grabbed her ankle and tugged, dragging her toward him. "I've got a ten-minute deadline in this wager. All you need to do is tell me what you want to bet."

She scowled, trying to determine how to dent his arrogance. Their egos were on entirely different playing fields. He was in the pros. She was warming the bench in adolescent D-grade. "If you lose, you spend the night."

No denting occurred. His expression didn't falter.

"In my bed," she continued, hoping to inspire panic. "Like a man who doesn't have a million commitment issues."

The anticipated revulsion didn't reach his features. She hadn't even laid a finger on his bravado.

"Deal."

Was he kidding? Where the hell did his confidence come from?

"And if I win," he purred, "you need to admit, in graphic detail, how my prowess is unlike any other."

"I didn't think you were the type for accolades."

"For you, I'll make an exception." He tugged her closer and let her legs fall over the edge of the mattress.

She clenched her teeth, hating how he'd already made her wet. Her body didn't comply at all. The men she'd wanted to succumb to had no effect, and the one man she didn't want anything to do with was like a sexual healer. Her very own Marvin Gaye. Or was she Marvin in this situation?

Shit.

She couldn't think through the lust fog.

"Any other rules before I start?"

"Yes. I don't kiss on the mouth." She'd had the same stipulation since Lucas died. She didn't want that connection from someone able to walk out the door without a backward glance. The next man she kissed would care for her. He'd cherish the ground she walked on.

"No problem." He splayed a hand over her upper thigh, his thumb pressing temptingly close to her pussy. "Only touch."

"Good." Her voice croaked.

"Anything else?"

She shook her head.

"Anal? Oral? Foreign objects?" He raised a brow. "Pain? Submission?"

"Now you're just teasing," she murmured. "I'd be surprised if you had time for even one of those in the ten minutes you've allocated."

He snickered, the sound sinister. "Maybe that can be a wager for another day."

Strong fingers gripped the waistband of her panties and tugged. With bold finesse, he exposed the trim strip of curls above her entirely bare pussy and dropped the material to the floor. For long seconds, he stared at her. At *that* part of her, his nostrils flaring, his jaw ticking.

This could be where she gained the upper hand.

She inched back, lying down against the covers, and slowly spread her thighs.

His visual admiration turned to humor, his lips lifting as if he knew her game.

Damn it. How was he so good at this?

"It looks like it's time to start." He glanced at her bedside clock. "It's eight fifty-three."

"Eight fifty-three." She swallowed over the desire clogging her throat.

She was wound tight, eagerly wondering how he planned to win this battle in ten minutes. And if he didn't, how would he deal with a night in her bed? Hell, how the heck would she handle it?

He slid his palm along her leg, toward the apex of her thighs. He held her gaze as the heat of his touch came closer.

A finger, or maybe it was a thumb, skirted gently over the edge of her pussy lips. Delicate and oh, so light. It could barely be considered a touch. It was a breath. A whisper of sensation through the slickness of her arousal.

"I'm surprised you're this wet. Seeing how you're not interested and all." His touch gained pressure, parting her, tempting her opening.

She wanted more. Needed more. "I never said I wasn't interested."

"Right..." Back and forth, his touch raked over her slit, teasing and torturous. "You just lacked faith in my ability."

She opened her mouth, poised to respond when two fingers slid deep, penetrating her, making her back arch off the bed. He curled those digits inside her, finding her sensitive spot faster than she ever found it herself.

No fair.

She clamped her thighs together, tight, and rocked into the rhythmic stroke against her G-spot.

"Still think I can't get you there in another eight minutes?"

"Goddammit. Shut the hell up."

He chuckled, and she didn't understand how he could be unaffected. Maybe that was the reason he kept rejecting women in the Vault. Did he have erection issues?

She lowered her gaze, down his pristine, white dress shirt, to his waistband, then his crotch.

Nope. His reluctance definitely wasn't an arousal issue. The hard, thick length of him strained against his zipper.

He wanted her.

Or maybe he just wanted sex.

Either way, it didn't matter. The thought of his desire made her squirm. Made her throb. Pressure landed on her clit, the spark of enthusiastic tingles taking over her core. He was succeeding. Winning. Not that she wanted him to fail. She craved another of his masterful orgasms.

"You're gorgeous."

The solemn compliment fractured her bliss and she blinked away the confusion to find him visually worshiping her body. The glide of his attention raked her skin, causing havoc, inspiring hysteria.

"The worst part about this agreement is the inability to fuck you." His free hand splayed across her stomach, creeping higher.

"What? Why not?"

"That's not part of the deal." He grasped her covered breast, working the cup down to brush his fingers over her nipple. Back and forth. Up and down.

"Forget the deal," she panted, arching into his touch.

"I wouldn't have time." He grinned, but this curve of lips was half-hearted. "There's only six minutes left."

She whimpered and he responded to her unspoken plea by adding another finger to her pussy. He stretched her, the muscles of her core protesting with a delicious twinge.

"I want your feet on the bed. Soles on the mattress."

She complied, lifting her legs, bending her knees, willing to do anything to continue the bliss.

"Ass up. I want to see you."

Her cheeks warmed as she obeyed, raising her butt off the bed to give him a better view.

"*Fuck.*" It was barely a word, his voice more of an incoherent growl. "Tell me what you're thinking. I want to hear those dirty thoughts."

She shook her head, speechless at the ferocity in his eyes. She couldn't think past his touch, the wicked stroke of her G-spot, and the palm massaging her breast. She kept her ass off the bed, each second making her climb higher in search of more.

"Tell me." He glanced at the clock, unhurried as he massaged and coaxed.

They had to be running out of time, but he didn't rush. There was no frantic pace, only a slow build to the perfect rhythm.

"Fucking tell me, Ella, or I stop." His movements slowed, inspiring panic.

"No, don't." Her voice broke. "I want this," she admitted. "I want you."

"*How?*" he snapped.

She continued to shake her head. If she pictured the ways in which she needed him—visualized the two of them together—she'd come. And she wanted that... But she didn't want it, too.

Not yet.

He growled and shoved another finger inside her, her pussy now stretched around four digits. He worked her hard, making her legs burn, her body sweat. He slid his other hand from her breast, over her collarbone, this time stopping at her throat. He held her there, pushing her toward mindlessness with the tight grasp of dominance.

She was close. Her orgasm within a flick of those fingers.

Then he paused.

Fucking stopped.

For seconds or minutes, she didn't know.

"If you don't tell me your dirty thoughts, I don't make you feel good." He appeared to lack concern over the approaching deadline, even though his chest heaved and his eyes blazed. "So, keep talking, sweetheart, or this ends."

"Oh, God," she pleaded, the tingle of bliss fading. She couldn't let it go. Refused. "I never want you to stop touching me. I want to feel you everywhere," she rambled. "I want you to fuck me. And I want it to be hard. So hard it hurts." She wasn't a masochist. Slaps and pinches weren't her thing. The excitement revolved around harsh penetration and vicious thrusts. The thrill of helplessness in the arms of a strong man. "You'd fuck my pussy... My mouth."

His nostrils flared as he groaned. Slowly, the grasp around her throat tightened, increasing her heartbeat. Then the fingers in her cunt twitched. Both sensations were profound on their own. Together they were an exquisite surge of sensation.

She bucked, demanding more. "Then you'd fuck my ass."

The pulse inside her quickened. The squeeze at her throat tightened. His focus held more intent than she'd ever received from him before. Frustration and delirious lust built in those eyes—over her.

He wanted to be inside her, just as much as she needed him there.

She grinned with the knowledge. The pleasure doubled. Multiplied. His fingers kept pace. She whimpered, the sound turning into a mewl. A scream. She tensed, every inch of her becoming a slave to the first pulse of orgasm bursting forward, making her buck.

He didn't stop as she spasmed, calling his name, arching her back. Over and over, he continued to work her, until the pulses lessened. Even then, he didn't stop. In fact, he did the opposite, pressing harder on her clit, spreading her pussy wider.

Another wave hit, blindsiding in its attack.

This orgasm was short but more surprising. The pleasure a breathtaking hit before an equally shocking vacuum. She was capable of multiples now?

She panted through the delirium and slumped against the mattress. When he released her throat, she fought not to show her disappointment. That hold had been transforming. A grasp of nirvana. And those fingers. *Damn him.* They still gently stroked inside her, not letting the bliss entirely fade while his other palm trailed along her sternum, her stomach.

Too much talent had been given to this man. Too much god-like finesse for someone entirely undeserving.

As if reading her mind, his lips quirked. "Are you ready to apologize for doubting my skills, Ella?"

CHAPTER ELEVEN

He'd thrown the bet.
He'd deliberately thrown the whole fucking thing.
She didn't even know yet. She just lay there, blinking up at him with sated, euphoria-glazed eyes.

He hadn't been able to talk himself out of it. She'd been at the mercy of his touch, her perfect body writhing and contorting with each of his movements. Then he'd paused, unable to stand the thought of her coming so soon.

He'd known how much time he'd had left. He'd known exactly how long it would take to get her back to the peak, too, and he'd stopped anyway.

For what? A handful of seconds of her at his mercy?

He couldn't remember a woman ever ensnaring him with erotic fascination. She wasn't merely sexual, she was sensual. A combination of vulnerability and confidence. Carnality and trepidation.

Obviously, he suffered from a case of temporary amnesia. He'd played a hand in innumerable sexcapades. His sexual bucket list had been ticked off long ago. But this was different somehow. If only he could pinpoint the why of it all.

The lust-filled decision to throw the bet was a mistake. And now he was staring down the barrel of an overnight stay in a barely-known woman's home.

He pasted on a fake smirk, needing to dissolve the blissful state of her features. "Are you ready to apologize for doubting my skills, Ella?"

The daze didn't fade. Instead, she smiled, those ruby lips making his dick twitch. "Hmm?"

He removed his fingers from her body and fought the need to lick away her arousal. "I'm waiting for you to admit you were wrong."

She chuckled. Breathy. Barely audible.

She was a pliable kitten.

He felt the same.

"I was wrong." She pushed to her elbows, then her knees. She straightened before him, putting her bra back in place, then glanced over her shoulder. "But it's five past nine. You didn't win the bet."

He could've talked his way out of it. Probably could've convinced her she'd been lying in a trance for more time than she had, but again, that amnesia had him questioning why he wanted to leave in such a hurry. "I guess I'm not quite as good as I thought I was."

She tilted her head, blinking up at him. He itched to loosen the top button of his shirt, to adjust his cock. She had him in all sorts of discomfort, and he'd be damned if he showed it.

"Are we done here?" She raised to her elbows.

"I don't know how to answer that."

She'd come. He'd felt it. Her pussy had spasmed around his fingers. More than once.

She'd bucked.

Writhed.

Shit. He needed to get the memory out of his head.

Her smile increased, her lashes still batting in a lazy, content rhythm. "It was a subtle way of asking if *you* were done." She pushed to her elbows, her thighs closing slightly. "I mean, can I return the favor?"

"*No.*" God. No. The last thing he needed was to be force-fed more temptation. "This isn't a favor. This is..."

Torture. Pure and simple.

She stiffened, and finally that daze fled the scene like an Olympic sprinter.

He wanted to fuck her in so many ways he'd be able to publish a sex guide to rival the Kama Sutra. But before he did all that, he wanted to spank the look of rejection off her face. "Fucking you is a bad idea, that's all."

She nodded, sat up straight, and then swung her legs off the bed. "Don't elaborate. I've already taken the hint." She reached for her bedside table, pulled open the top drawer, and removed a large expanse of shiny black material. A robe.

In seconds, she was covered, her beautiful body hidden from view. She tied the thin belt around her waist with jerky movements, then clutched the lapels to hide her cleavage. "I'm going to freshen up. You don't have to hang around. I'm not going to hold you to the bet. Feel free to leave whenever you're ready."

He nodded, remaining silent as she strode for a door at the side of the room and closed herself in.

This was what he hated. The bullshit. The ping-pong match of hurt feelings and expectation. His dick didn't seem to care, though. The rock-hard part of his anatomy soldiered on, determined not to stand down until it glimpsed the front line.

He should leave.

It was the sensible option. He should walk out of here before she returned. No explanation. No goodbye.

He wouldn't have even contemplated his options if it were any other woman. He'd be out the door, down the hall, and driving back home without a second thought.

A toilet flushed, followed by a rush of tap water.

Leave or stay, Bryan? Leave or stay?

Shit.

It wasn't like she was an emotional threat. She had no interest in him. But why the fuck was he considering staying, anyway? For the bet? Maybe. He'd never backed out on a wager before. Problem was, he didn't know if it was more than that.

He closed his eyes and pinched the bridge of his nose. He was overthinking this when he shouldn't be thinking at all.

A cupboard closed in the adjoining room. The water stopped. The door reopened and the light spilling in from behind created a flawless silhouette. Her hair sat against her shoulders, the thin robe pulled tight at her waist. She looked like a model. One with beautiful curves and slightly faltering confidence.

"You're still here." She switched off the light and padded into the room.

He didn't bother fighting the laugh that escaped. "Yeah, sweetheart. Still here. I want to clear up the reason why fucking you is a bad—"

"Please don't." She held up a hand as she approached the bed. "I think I'm at my quota for your honesty."

He growled. If she didn't wipe the backslap of rejection off her face, he was going to do something he'd regret. Something they'd both regret. "The reason fucking you is a bad idea," he grated, "is because I can't sleep with a woman more than once."

Why *the fuck* had he said that?

She rolled her eyes and pulled back the coverings. "I also don't need a refresher on your rules. Shay gave me the Cliffs Notes."

He ground his teeth and wished he was the brute she thought he was. At least then he wouldn't feel obligated to give her an explanation.

"An incapability," he clarified. "*Not* a rule."

Her brows pulled together, the pinch of her forehead taking seconds, if not minutes. "You can't..."

"Get an erection? Wood? A hard-on? Whatever you choose to call it, I can't get it more than once for the same woman." He let the information sink in. The private, close-kept secret he'd never told a soul.

"Wow... So, you haven't slept with a woman more than once for how long?"

"Over twelve years."

"Holy. Shit." She drew out the words as she stared at him with a mix of fascination and concern. "Have you been to see anyone about it?"

"Oh, no." He shook his head. "Don't go thinking there's something wrong with my dick. There's no problem as far as I'm concerned. It's a skill. A talent that took years to master. It's my insurance policy."

"Insurance," she repeated slowly.

"Yeah, to protect the commitment phobia you seem to think I have."

"*Seem* to have?" Her lips quirked. "Is there really any doubt? You're seriously messed up."

"You won't hear a denial from me. But the reason for the explanation is to set things straight. The lack of fucking has nothing to do with you and everything to do with me needing to remain interested for the demonstration night."

She climbed onto the bed, her brow regaining its furrow. "You know, Bryan, I never took you for the it's-not-you-it's-me type."

Because he wasn't. Never had been. She inspired anomalies. "And I never took you for a woman who could come with a mere twist of my fingers. I guess we both made inaccurate assumptions."

He kicked off his shoes and placed his socks inside them.

"You're still staying?"

"We made a bet. I'm not a sore loser."

This was a mistake. A huge mistake. His dick stood rigid as fuck. His restraint was equally vulnerable. Yet, for some unknown reason, he wasn't sprinting for the door.

He undid the top button of his shirt, moving down, one by one. Her hungry gaze ate up each new inch of exposed skin. He could practically feel those eyes sending their laser beam of fascination down his chest. The distraction should've made him stop and throw this upcoming train wreck in reverse.

"Want me to turn off the living room lights before I climb in?" He shoved the material off his shoulders, letting it fall to the floor.

"No." She shook her head. "It's early. I just want to lay here a while." She pulled the covers to her chin, snuggling farther into her pillow.

The entire scene before him seemed like a parallel universe. He didn't do this shit—not the sleepovers or the dinner. Definitely not the wine. And, Jesus Christ, if he thought about throwing the bet one more time, he'd probably throw his cookies, too.

But every time he blinked, he appreciated the sight he opened his eyes to. She looked natural. Relaxed. She didn't attempt to seduce him. She was just a woman, without flaw, and he was just a man, with many.

"So, who was she?"

He paused in the middle of unbuckling his belt. "She?"

"The woman who turned Bryan to Brute."

"There's no woman," he lied. "Like I said, I haven't been with anyone more than once since my school days." He released his belt, undid the zipper, and shoved his pants to the floor. "You really need to stop searching for excuses to explain who I am. There aren't any."

She made a noise. An *mmph* of disapproval. "We're all shaped by our experiences."

"If you say so." He averted his gaze, unable to look at her while he climbed into bed beside her. Out of all the sexual things he'd done over the years, this, by far, seemed the strangest.

Then again, it wasn't sexual.

This part was due to the bet.

A bet he'd thrown.

"If there's no woman, then tell me about your upbringing. Have you lived in Beaumont all your life? Do you have family here?"

Well, that was a sure-fire way to instigate a limp dick. "Grew up in Florida. Had a good education. Excelled in math and science. Hated my parents, like every kid my age." Problem was, his parents had hated him back.

"Do you go home often?"

"Not at all. A while ago I bought an apartment in Tampa, thinking I'd eventually revisit where I grew up. But..." What the fuck? This wasn't a shrink session. He didn't need to rehash the past to fill the silence. "I have no plans to go back now." He cleared his throat, rested back against the pillow, and stared up at the ceiling. "How 'bout you? What are your issues?"

"You already know mine." She released another noise, this time a tired moan. "Dead husband. Kinky proclivities. Inability to orgasm."

"You orgasm just fine."

Her chuckle was a puff of breath. "Spoken by the only man capable of making it happen."

"You'll figure yourself out soon enough." With another man. Maybe in another club.

"Yeah... I know."

He remained quiet through her long yawn, hoping she fell asleep and brought an end to the ocean-deep conversation.

He watched her from the corner of his eye, her hair splayed across the pillow, her blinks closing for longer and longer, until finally they closed for good. Tiny moans escaped her, the barely audible sounds sinking under his skin. His cock twitched again, the softened length making a comeback with renewed enthusiasm.

If she didn't stop, his ability to sleep would sit somewhere between not-likely and never-going-to-happen.

Not unless he took the edge off.

He stared at the clock, passing the whimper-filled minutes as he glared at those numbers. Each second provided a new rush of blood to his dick and a renewed sense that something was seriously off-kilter in this situation.

She hadn't tried to seduce him. She hadn't even stayed awake past ten o'clock.

He let out a silent puff of laughter. This woman was the best damn distraction he could ask for. But he couldn't stay here. Not in her bed, lusting over her with perversion while she slept. Nope, he needed to get up and disperse the blood pooling in his groin.

He slid from the mattress, his dick leading the way as he escaped down the hall, in search of...something.

There were innumerable offerings to appease his interest—the television remote, the magazines on the coffee table—and still, he found himself back at the bookshelf, his fingers skimming the spines of medical texts.

Even with the grim reaper hovering over his shoulder, his dick remained adamant. A trooper. The fucker had no plan to give up the fight.

He pulled the books from the shelf, one by one, and stacked them near the front door. She didn't want the reminder, and it wasn't like he had anything better to do. Apart from her. So, he kept going, his cheap workout continuing until every book on cancer sat waiting for him to leave.

And he *should* leave.

He hovered at the door, his issues resembling those of a teenager trying to sneak out for the first time.

"Fuck this." He wasn't a pussy. He could handle a sleepover. Especially when there were no claws sinking into his balls. She was asleep, for Christ's sake.

He padded back to the bookshelf, his attention snagging on the top shelf and the photos spaced evenly along the wood in silver frames. All the images were stereotypical happy families. Mother, daughter, and sister, in varying degrees of happiness.

Would their bubble ever burst, like his had?

He shook his head at the stupidity.

He'd never had a bubble to begin with. The script of his life had the fairytale set with a cast who never showed.

He slid two of the frames to the side and grabbed a shiny pink album stashed behind. He opened the cover, the pages flicking through his fingers, highlighting Ella in all her beaming glory. Her mother and sister played a leading role in the documentation of her life. But it looked like she'd hidden the shots of her husband. Or maybe those were reserved for the privacy of her bedroom.

There were birthday photos. Holiday happy snaps. More images with her sister. With Animals. At different locations. With sexy clothing. Then a fucking bikini.

He slammed the album shut and shoved it back onto the shelf. With every breath, he could taste her, smell her. His limbs tingled with the need to walk down that hall and give her what she'd asked for.

The one-fuck rule must have started to take its toll. The quality-over-quantity diet had turned him bat-shit crazy. So crazy he had to clench his fists to keep from palming his dick.

Alcohol. He needed alcohol.

He strode for the kitchen and grabbed the almost-empty wine bottle from her fridge. The lid was thrown aimlessly, the liquid contents sliding down his throat like the first taste of water after a year of dehydration.

He gulped. He chugged. He downed that motherfucker until the bottle was dry and he leaned against the sink, sucking in breath after breath. And still, his erection wouldn't admit defeat.

His mind was in on the act, too. Images of Ella flashed before his eyes. He could see her ass swaying as she dropped dishes in the sink. Could see her bending over to place food in the fridge.

He gripped the counter for grounding and pressed his erection against the cupboards, hoping to discourage the growing pulse.

The pressure increased.

He couldn't fight the need to palm himself through the thin material of his underwear, his fingers clutching tight. Every time he blinked, she was there—in the Vault, at the lockers, splayed beneath him on her bed. He heard her words, too. All those rasped pleas to be fucked. Hard. And the whimpers.

Jesus Christ.

He increased the severity of his hold, gripping his dick like he was trying to choke a snake. Damn thing wouldn't die. The harder he squeezed, the better it felt. The pain was the best part.

One day, he'd return the favor. He'd torment her like she currently tormented him.

The tight grasp became a stroke, the first glide of friction bringing a heavy dose of pure relief. He bit his lower lip to stop a groan escaping and closed his eyes to concentrate on the childishness of his actions.

The darkness didn't help. Within seconds, he'd wrenched down his boxer briefs, leaving them to cup his balls as he spat on his hand. The first slide of his saliva-slicked palm was hell—pure torture and defeat, rolled into a package of fucking bliss.

Fighting was pointless. Instead, he squeezed his eyes tighter and punished the shit out of his dick, jerking it with harsh strokes, squeezing it with a tight fist. Back and forth he worked the length, each glide getting shorter. Sharper.

He growled through the pressure building in his balls, wanting to get this over and done with. He raised onto his toes, disgust turning his stomach as he blew his load in the sink. Burst after burst of white liquid shot from him, and still she didn't leave his mind. Pulse after pulse of release splattered the stainless steel, increasing his self-loathing, and all the while, she was still there.

Those eyes.

Those whimpers.

Those pleas.

He didn't understand it. Didn't want to.

"Fucking hell."

He rammed his softening dick into his underwear and washed his lack of restraint down the sink. This was Tera's fault. His family had shoved their way back into his life, destroying all the barriers he'd tried hard to erect. Annihilating his sense of worth. His focus. Maybe even his confidence.

Bet or not, he had to leave.

If Ella woke and gave him another whispered proposition, he'd cave. He'd buckle like a cheap belt. And he didn't want to risk dragging anyone else into this regression.

He stalked into the living room, found a piece of paper and a pen, then scribbled his cell number in large font along with the message —*Next Thursday. 8 p.m. The Vault.*

He dropped the note beneath her glowing bedside lamp, tiptoed around the bed, and grabbed his pants off the floor. The loud clink of his buckle was a major "fuck you" from the universe. The noise shot through the silence and she whimpered in reply. He froze, pants halfway up his thighs, his dick beginning to reawaken like an energetic puppy.

"You're leaving?"

He tugged his pants to his waist, zipped, buttoned, and secured the belt. "Yeah. It's too damn early for me to sleep."

"Sorry." She turned toward him, cuddling her pillow as she blinked with lethargy. No woman had ever looked so feminine. So pliable. So breakable.

He only had to say the word and she'd be on her back, arms open, thighs spread. The thought should've been enough to turn him off.

Why didn't it?

Why was his blood rapidly regrouping in his dick?

He snatched his shirt off the floor and stabbed his arms through the sleeves with enough force to rip the material. Every second that drew closer to her proposition made his pulse quicken with anticipated relief. She was going to beg him to stay. She was singular breaths away from transforming into another groupie. Just like everyone else.

"Can you lock the door on your way out?" She stretched, the curve of her breasts straining against the sheet.

What. The. Fuck?

He frowned, confused by the awkward mix of beauty and rejection. "Sure." His fingers tripped over the remaining buttons. "I left a note on your coffee table. It's got my cell number on it. Message me if you've got any questions about the demonstration. Otherwise, I'll see you there."

"Who says I've made up my mind?"

"You'll be there, Ella. And you'll do a great job." He grasped his pockets, making sure he had his wallet, cell, and keys. "Thanks for tonight."

Thanks? For what? The erectile dysfunction and new kitchen fetish? Who the hell was he?

"Thanks?" She smiled. "Are you being polite again?"

"Nope." He made for the bedroom door, ready to run. "I got another cheap thrill and a boost to my ego. What's not to be thankful for?"

"Jerk," she whispered with sleep-addled humor.

And don't you forget it, sweetheart.

"Night, Ella." He stopped himself from turning back for one last look.

"Night, Brute."

The use of his nickname didn't escape him. She'd finally realized who he was. What he was. And even though hearing his title didn't bring the usual thrill, he knew the emotional distance would be nothing but a good thing.

CHAPTER TWELVE

𝒯he café's dining room was empty, spare a few women sharing their usual mid-afternoon coffee. The lull always hit hardest on Tuesday afternoons, which made for really crappy timing since Pamela's mind was mimicking an attention-starved toddler.

"Drop the dishcloth and nobody gets hurt."

Her hand paused mid-circular motion on the counter, and she glanced over her shoulder to see Kim holding the window spray as a weapon.

"What are you doing?"

"Mom and I have been patient, but your time is up. You need to stop the manic cleaning so we can have a serious conversation."

Pamela released the cloth and wiped her hands on the ass of her black leggings. "What have I done?"

"It's been two days."

"Two days," her mom parroted from the kitchen.

"Since?" She stalled, praying they weren't going to bring up the person she'd been trying desperately to forget. It had been two days since Brute. Two days since Chinese, orgasms, and a formidably sexy body in her bed.

"Don't play dumb." Kim crossed her arms over her chest. "We've given you space to digest whatever happened, and now we want the dirty details."

"Not today." She reclaimed her cloth and continued with the calming circular motions. "I don't want to talk about it."

"Since when?" Kim hissed. "You always tell me everything."

"Yeah...well, maybe it's time I stopped oversharing."

"Did he say something? Or do something?"

Pamela scoffed. "From now on, take that as a given. But after the other night, I've got bigger problems than his insults."

"I knew it." Her mother shoved through the swinging kitchen doors. "I never would've picked it from such a handsome boy, but I told Kim I had a niggling feeling about those marks on your throat."

"Mom," her sister warned. "We discussed this and decided it was a rash."

Oh. Shit.

Pamela's hand instinctively snapped to her neck, covering the thin scarf strategically placed around the fading red fingermarks.

"Or am I wrong?" Kim went from chastisement to fire and brimstone with the widening of her eyes. "Did he force himself on you?"

"No. *God*, no." How did she admit to loving every second of his strong hold around her throat? How could she make them understand she'd never been more turned on than in that moment? "The marks are..."

"Damn it, Pamela. Just tell us what happened." Her mother's concern came with a volatile voice. "Is everything okay?"

"Yes." She sucked in a breath and slumped with the exhale. She'd been dodging this conversation for a while. "Actually, no." She didn't want to admit what happened—the monumental stupidity. Problem was, she knew this drill. They weren't going to leave her alone until she blurted the truth. "I fell for him."

They stared.

Unmoving.

Unblinking.

"It's idiotic, I know." She winced through the words. "It must be something hormonal."

"I thought you said he was a dick." Kim lowered her voice and did a visual scan of the few remaining customers.

"He is." *Oh, God, he is.*

"Then there must be a reason."

There were many. The pathetic excuses swiftly formed a list in her mind—his touch, his voice, his body. He was gorgeous—*oh, so, gorgeous*—with his tough-man beard, scrutinizing eyes, and talented hands. Visually, he was perfection. And those books. He'd cleared the shelf that had served as a constant reminder of the months of cancer and misplaced hope. The realization had brought tears, happy ones.

And sad ones, too.

"I can see your brain running a mile a minute." Kim narrowed her eyes. "He did something to win you over, didn't he?"

"No. Not really." Definitely nothing worthy of the plaguing heart palpitations she'd been battling. "He was the same asshole, for the most part."

"And the other parts?" Her mom reached over the counter, tidying the sugar packets in an unconvincing act to appear unfazed. "Could there have been a deeper connection on some other level, maybe?"

Pamela rolled her eyes. "Wow. You slid off your protective suit and seamlessly pulled on a matchmaker cloak in record speed."

"I'm not matchmaking," her mom scoffed. "I'm only suggesting there may have been more of a connection between you than you think."

"Come on." Kim waved her on with a swirl of her hand. "Break it down. Tell us what happened. Start to finish."

Her mom cleared her throat. "Apart from the juicy stuff, of course."

"Of course." Jesus Christ. If she ever heard the word 'juicy' from her mother's lips again it would be too soon. Especially when referring to sex.

Her sister and mother had continuously supported her. They had her back even though they didn't understand her enjoyment of adult clubs or any of the facets within them. They listened without judgment. The only thing they didn't do was hide their confusion over it.

"He turned up at my apartment with food and wine. I think there may have even been a smile on his face." Yes, there'd definitely been a smile. A self-assured curve of his lips. "We talked over dinner, and he was friendly. Even a little funny. Then he helped clear the table and gave me a foot massage."

He'd shown his charm and more of that willingness to physically please. And one by one, the opposing list of negative attributes had begun to diminish under the weight of his allure.

"A foot massage? Is that a fetish thing?"

"There's no foot fetish." Not that she knew of. "He was being nice. He even opened up to me about a family struggle he's having."

Kim's brows pinched. "Then maybe you fell in love with him because—"

"Oh, no. No, no, no. This is *not* love." She snatched the dishcloth and twisted it in her hands. This thing wasn't anywhere close to the L-word. It didn't even nudge the edge of the greedy emotion. What she felt for Brute was something less vulnerable...but equally cloying.

"Then how hard was the fall?"

Pamela turned to scrub at a non-existent mark on the counter. "I don't know. Maybe it's nothing. There hasn't been anyone in my life since Lucas. Not other than physically." But he'd shown her a glimmer of the man beneath the mask. He'd given her a peek at the soft, gooey center, and it kinda seemed comparable to her favorite peppermint-filled chocolate. "This could be a simple case of enjoying the attention I've been starved of. I just wish I could get him out of my head. I need to stop thinking about him."

"Because he's allergic to commitment?"

She paused, wondering if her situation would be as dire if that was the only issue. "Because I'm supposed to be his assistant for this demonstration night, and I'm not sure I can hide the way I feel. The last time I showed any sort of interest, he confronted me about it in front of the entire club. I've never been more humiliated, and back then, I didn't think of him as more than an asshole. Imagine how he'd react now."

Kim cringed.

"See?" It was a problem. A big problem.

"Tell him you can't help with the class thingy," her mother offered. "Call and say you're busy."

"If I call him, he'll expect an explanation." And if they spoke, she'd cave under the dominance in his voice.

"Then don't call." Kim shrugged. "Send a message saying something came up and you can't make it. Don't elaborate. Give him the bare minimum details and leave it at that. You don't owe him anything."

No. She supposed she didn't. Aside from a one-sided orgasm tally, there was no commitment or binding agreement.

"Where's your phone?" Kim glanced beneath the counter, pushing aside her mother's handbag.

"Under the register."

Her sister scooted farther along, retrieved the device, and handed it over. "Send it now."

Pamela sucked in a slow breath and eyed her mother, who nodded in solemn agreement. "Do you really think this is the best way to go about it?" Guilt took over her stomach, making it roil and rumble. Or maybe that was the fear of missing out on another life-changing orgasm.

"Do you have his number?" Kim asked.

"Yeah." She'd saved his details under Brute. Not Bryan. She'd even quit using his name in the hope the reminder of his attitude would kick her out of her stupidity.

The plan had turned out to be highly ineffective.

"Go on." Kim spurred her on with the jut of her chin. "Do it."

Pamela lowered her gaze to the cell in her hand and typed without thought. If she paused, even for a second, she wouldn't go through with it.

Something came up. I can't be at the Vault next Thursday. I'm sorry.

She clicked send and swallowed over the squeeze in her chest. *Bye, bye, beautiful orgasms.* "There." She handed the device to Kim. "Done."

It didn't feel *done*. Her heart beat in a fractured tempo. Her chest grew heavy. She hadn't liked a man in years. She hadn't felt anything apart from pure frustration toward the opposite sex since Lucas died. Which made shoving Brute away seem comparable to punching herself in the vag.

"I'll silence the ringer." Kim pressed buttons on the screen, then returned it to its place under the counter. "If he calls, ignore it. If he messages, delete it. You don't need another emotionless ass in your life."

Ouch. The insult hit her in the chest. "Lucas wasn't an ass."

"No, sweetie." Her mom gave a sad smile. "But he didn't love you either. You deserve something better this time."

Yeah, she knew she did. Her problem was her inability to attract anything other than two distinct categories of men—those who could work her body into a frenzy and leave her heart stone-cold or those who warmed her heart and lacked any understanding of her sexuality.

"Come on." Kim inclined her head in the direction of the dining room. "Help me clear these tables to get your mind off him. And while we're at it, I can tell you about those online dating sites I've been researching."

. . .

$\mathcal{S}$he established a routine for the remaining two hours of her shift—do five minutes' work, check her phone, ponder why Brute hadn't responded, then do another five minutes' work. The cycle was vicious. Then again, maybe his lack of response was a relief.

"See? There was nothing to worry about." Kim flicked off the kitchen lights and headed for the front door. "He probably doesn't care at all."

Her mother had said the same thing before she'd finished for the day.

"Yeah. Maybe."

Brute didn't seem like a man who wouldn't care about a cancellation. Or more specifically, a rejection. He seemed the type to demand explanations and berate unworthy responses. "At least I'll sleep better tonight."

"Do you want to come over and watch a movie? We can get pizza."

"No, I'm good." Pamela pulled the café keys from her handbag as her sister opened the front door. "I think a bath and an early night is what I need."

She stepped onto the sidewalk, dragging the door shut behind her. With a jab of the key and the flick of her wrist, the lock was secure and she could finally go home.

"Sorry to interrupt, ladies."

She turned at the unfamiliar male voice and found a dose of cuteness staring back at her. "Muffin Man."

Kim snorted at her side.

"Muffin Man?" His hope-filled expression fell.

"Sorry." She slapped a hand over her mouth and tried to ignore the heat setting her cheeks to flame. "I... Um..."

"You're a regular." Kim chuckled. "But we didn't know your name. So, Pamela dubbed you Muffin Man."

"I did *not*." It had been Kim. All Kim.

The guy glanced between them, a smile gently spreading his lips. "It's Callum." Humor tinged his voice, friendly and sweet.

Too friendly and sweet. If only he had a fierce streak, then her uterus would be doing tumbles.

"Nice to meet you, Callum." Kim backtracked, removing herself from the equation with stealthy finesse. "But I'm going to have to run."

She finger-waved. "I have an appointment with my personal trainer. I'll talk to you later, sis."

Pamela glared at her lying sister's back until she lost sight of her in the busy foot traffic. When she turned to Callum, he was staring at her, his brown eyes filled with nervousness.

"Well, it's great to formally meet you, Callum. Was there something I could help you with?"

He rubbed the back of his neck. Nibbled his bottom lip. The apprehension may have been endearing to someone else, but she'd always admired confident men.

"Yeah, I've been hanging around, waiting for you to finish for the day. I thought, maybe, I could buy you a drink or two."

"Oh." Her brain seized. "Um..." She hadn't been expecting an invitation. Especially not from a man who seemed puppy-like in his timid nature. "I..."

"I know it's out of the blue." He gave an embarrassed chuckle. "It's taken a while to work up the guts to speak to you."

Again, she should've been charmed. Even a little flattered. He seemed like a nice guy.

Evidently, her libido didn't do nice.

"Tonight?" She glanced along the pavement, caught between voicing a gentle dismissal to appease her disinterest, and an unwanted acceptance which would finally see her sampling a different sort of male.

Who knew? Maybe this timid guy had the occasional anal orgasm in his repertoire.

"I, umm..." She focused on the people passing by—the businessmen, the couples, the kids. Now was as good a time as any to try something new, right?

She opened her mouth, poised to accept, when her gaze snagged on the man leaning against his car a few yards down the street. As if pulled from her fantasies, Brute stood there, arms crossed over his chest, his stance casual as he pinned her heart like a preserved butterfly.

"I'm sorry, Callum." She turned back to meet soft brown eyes. "I can't tonight."

He shrugged, his smile now painted on. "That's okay. I know it's late notice. Maybe another night?"

"Sure." Who knew what the future held? One day soon she seriously had to quit the infatuation with emotionless men and fall for someone like Callum.

Someone sickeningly sweet and drama-free.

Just not today. Not when a man entirely opposite stood close by, invigorating her bloodstream with his annoyance.

"Have a good night." Callum inclined his head in farewell, waved, then turned in those big workman boots.

"You, too." She plastered herself against the glass doors, refusing to look at the man who approached. The closer Brute came, the harder it became to breathe. Her skin prickled. Her throat tightened.

"Is he the reason you're leaving me high and dry?" he growled in greeting.

Her heart beat harder, the mix of attraction and his anger sizzling all her nerves. "What are you doing here?"

"I thought I deserved an explanation."

"You could've called."

"I thought the same about you. After the orgasms I've dished out, you'd think the last thing I deserved was a few vague words via text."

Oh, boy.

Mentally, she had her hands on his shoulders, pulling him in for a harsh kiss that would end with her knee in his junk. Physically, though, she had her teeth clenched and a scowl firmly in place.

Nothing about this moment could end well. Especially when she couldn't voice the real reason for her cancellation, and she didn't have a fake excuse on stand-by.

"So, I'll ask again." He beamed down at her. "Is that guy the reason you're leaving me high and dry?"

She wrinkled her nose. "No."

"You dating him?"

"Is that any of your business?"

"If you keep coming to me complaining you can't get fucked properly, then, yeah. It sure is, 'cause that guy is never going to do you right."

"Keep coming to you?" God, this man made her blood boil and her pussy contract, all at the same time. "You want an explanation for why I canceled? Maybe check your attitude."

"Bullshit. You've always known my attitude. If it's not that guy, my next guess is your husband."

Her mouth gaped at the insertion of Lucas into the conversation.

Seconds ago, Callum made her flat-line with disinterest. In a heartbeat, this callous man had given her a major case of arrhythmia.

"The other night," he continued, "you said you hadn't had anyone over since he'd died. So, if it's not the pretty boy, I'm guessing it's a guilt thing."

"This *is not* a guilt thing," she grated.

"Then what?"

She sucked in a deep breath, let it out slowly, and fought against the warring emotions bubbling in her chest. She hated this sparring match. Loved it, too. She wanted to claw his eyes out. Wanted to fuck his brains out. This situation was a whirlwind of confusion.

"I already told you I need to give up the Vault. Going back for one last time is a stupid idea."

"Instead, you expect this new guy to rock your world?" He ran a rough hand over his beard, his scowl unwavering. "You're making the wrong decisions."

"And you're an expert on love now?"

He screwed up his perfectly perfect face. "I'm not talking about love. This is about fucking. You can't seriously believe that guy would have the first clue about getting you off."

"They say it's the quiet ones you need to look out for."

"They're wrong." He stepped forward, getting in her face, a mere breath away. "The quiet ones bring shock value because they're boring as hell. What you need is someone who lives and breathes to fuck. A guy who can match your appetite. Someone who can push you. Test you. You don't need a guy who doesn't have the balls to tell you he'd like to see your sweet little cunt riding his dick all night."

She shivered. Head to foot. He stole her breath. Infused her with adrenaline. Oh, God, her panties were damp.

"Go home, Ella." He stepped away and made for his car, leaving her reeling with the abrupt end to the conversation. "Get dressed and meet me out in front of your building at nine."

"Excuse me?" Her hands shook. Her brain stopped firing on all cylinders. There were many things to hate about his statement—the authority, the self-righteousness. Yet, her libido only focused on the sexy dominance. "Why?"

"I'm taking you out. It's about time somebody taught you how to find the right hook-up."

A whimper formed low in her chest. *Reject, reject, reject.* She couldn't go ahead with this. She refused. "Don't worry about me. I know what I'm doing."

"Your history at the Vault proves otherwise." He pulled open the driver's door and looked at her over the roof of his shiny car. "Nine, Ella. Be ready."

Then he was gone, leaving her to become overwhelmed by excitement and pure, undiluted fear.

CHAPTER THIRTEEN

Five past nine came soon enough for Bryan not to have to think too much about what the hell he'd instigated. He had better things to do than teach a woman how to listen to her own instincts. But here he stood, leaning against his car, in front of her building while he stared at his watch.

He didn't expect her to be early. Didn't even anticipate she'd be on time. She'd need to retaliate, at least a little, before she gave in and realized she wasn't going to find the right guy without assistance.

She needed his help, maybe even wanted it. The confusing part was why he gave a shit. He supposed he didn't like anyone leaving the Vault unsatisfied. The low enjoyment rating came as a personal blow as much as a professional one. And he still needed her assistance for the demonstration.

So, technically, this was business.

He'd scratch her back. She'd scratch his.

She was also a distraction. The only thing capable of keeping his mind off Tampa, family, and throat-clogging hate. Annoying Ella made the other shit in his life disappear. At least temporarily. The time alone, backed up against his car, made all the thoughts flood to the forefront.

He stared at the yellow glow from the window he guessed was hers and waited for the lights to fade.

They didn't.

Not after one minute. Not even after five.

His cell vibrated in his back pocket, the intrusion a mental *and* physical pain in his ass, but a better source of entertainment than a pane of glass. He pulled out the device, scowled at Leo's name, and pressed connect. "Yeah?"

"Shay thinks you're high on the latest designer drug because of your unnaturally good mood this afternoon. What gives?"

Bryan thought back on the last six hours and refused to acknowledge what might have made a big enough change in his attitude for someone to notice. There was only one thing. More specifically, one person. "I've been testing a new powder on the market," he drawled. "I thought about selling it on the sly to the younger ravers."

There was more than a beat of silence. "You're joking, right?"

"What do you want, Leo? I'm busy."

"Doing what?"

"Your mother. So, if you don't mind, it's time to lube up."

"Fucking Shay," Leo muttered. "I don't know why she thought you were acting oddly cheery lately. You're still the same asshole you've always been."

Bryan grinned. This was how they rolled. Their friendship grew with the help of cheap shots and quick comebacks. "Is that the only reason for the call?"

"No. I wanted to know what steps you've taken to fix the issue in the Vault."

"I'm working on it." He kept staring at Ella's window and wondered about the seductive possibilities of what she might be wearing.

"How? I need details. Cassie and T.J. want an update."

"I told you Ella would do the demonstration, and she will." He swallowed, clearing the dryness from his throat. For once, confidence didn't coat his tone. His words fell flat under uncertainty. "I'll confirm the deal tonight."

"Confirm the deal? Is that what the kids are calling it these days?" Leo chuckled. "She's the reason for the drug high, isn't she? Does the big, bad Brute have a crush?"

Bryan scowled, wishing the look could make its way through to Leo's phone. "This big, bad Brute is going to crush your face if you don't leave me alone to fix this mess."

The chuckle turned into unrestrained laughter. "I nailed it, didn't I? You like this woman."

"Of course," Bryan grated. "You nailed it just as hard as I'll nail Shay the next time you work a late shift."

The delirious mirth increased. "Are you on a date?"

"Goodbye, Leo."

"It *is* a date."

Bryan disconnected the call and pocketed the cell. Ten seconds passed before the first text message vibrated from his back pocket. Then another and another.

Fucking Leo.

The squeak of the apartment building door disturbed the night air, and he lifted his gaze to find Ella's familiar silhouette exiting the lobby. The outside lights bore down on her, giving him an unforgiving view of the skin-tight red dress that ensured no man would need the use of his imagination tonight.

Her blonde hair danced over her shoulders, along with a white scarf trailing into the deep-V of her cleavage revealing a mass of creamy skin, while her cherry-stained lips matched her seductive stiletto heels. But it was her eyes that slayed him, and the nervous sweep of her lashes, exposing the slightest need for validation as she approached.

"You're late," he muttered.

"You're lucky I'm here at all."

Her stride didn't falter as he pushed from the car and opened the passenger door. "If you didn't show, I would've figured out a way into your building and dragged you out myself."

"I know. That's the only reason I came."

"Sure it is." He didn't believe her for a second. Not when she'd gone to so much effort to look drop-dead gorgeous. Every inch of her made his cock fill with interest. Especially those heels.

If he were the one taking this woman home tonight, he'd make sure those shoes remained firmly in place while he sank between those thighs. She'd be splayed across his bed, completely naked, all bar those ruby, fuck-me stilettos.

And hadn't that image just given his dick the green-light to adolescence.

"Nice heels," he grunted.

"Thanks. You look good, too." Her sarcasm was flamboyant, letting him know his compliment about her shoes was far from worthy. "I like the suit. I bet it's a carbon copy of every other one you've worn for the last five years."

He beat back a grin. "You can't ditch a classic."

She stopped in front of him, placing her hand-held clutch to her hip. "No. But it wouldn't hurt to change things up a bit. You're starting to look like a control freak with the constant stiff-suit ensemble."

Stiff suit? Control freak?

She had no idea.

He stepped toward her, hovering close, dragging her sweet scent of lust and beauty deep into his lungs. "You ain't seen nothin', sweetheart. Imagine how wet those panties would get if you had a full dose of my control."

She chuckled, batting away his arrogance with a sly tilt of her lips. "Well, we better not test that theory." She pushed past him, pausing to whisper, "Because I'm not wearing any panties."

He snapped his mouth shut and took the sucker punch to his balls head on. She was messing with him. He knew it. She knew it.

It didn't stop his gaze from landing on her ass in search of a panty line, though. A non-existent panty line.

Get a fucking grip.

He wasn't going there. Not tonight.

"Get in." He made his way around the car and yanked open his door.

This excursion was about teaching her how to read men. To determine the wheat from the chaff. The sexually experienced from the ignorant.

She needed to trust him, not only to get her laid, but to change her mind about the demonstration night. Time was running out, along with his patience, and there was no way he could miss next Thursday's session in the Vault. He needed to be between those sordid walls. He craved the grounding. The connection.

And, if he was being honest, he wanted to see if the image of Ella, naked and in front of a crowd, was as perfect in real life as it was in his mind.

If he fucked her now, his limp-dick insurance policy would steal all that away from him. The class wouldn't run with the enthusiasm it deserved. His interest in her would plummet, if not vanish entirely. There'd be no buzz. No thrill.

He'd make a fool of them both.

This constant state of arousal around her would work much more favorably. His intuition would be flawless with his current level of interest. All he had to do was keep riding this wave of erection-inducing torture until next week. Then he'd reward himself with one hot and heavy fuck and be done with her.

His insurance policy would make sure of it.

He slid into the driver's seat and shut the door behind him. "You ready?"

"Do I have a choice?" She ran a hand down her thigh, straightening non-existent wrinkles in her dress. "Where are we going, anyway?"

"To a bar not far from here." He started the ignition and pulled onto the street. "I know the guy who owns the place."

"Will there be music and dancing?"

He could see her cleavage from the corner of his eye. The lush curves were enough to drive him to distraction. "You don't want music. Dance floors are for guys looking for an easy lay. What you need is someone willing to hold a conversation. If they don't bother learning who you are, they won't bother learning what you want."

"But I like dancing."

And his dick loved the thought of seeing those hips sway. "Not tonight, you don't."

She sighed and rested her head against the passenger window. "If you say so."

"Yeah," he muttered. "I say so."

The drive was quiet, the soft hum of her voice underlining every song on his playlist. This time he itched to fill the void. He had questions. He had suggestions. But every time he thought of something to say, he fell into a pathetic hole where he analyzed the necessity of every word.

He questioned himself.

Over her.

What the hell?

"So…" He pushed through the analytical crap like a motherfucker and focused instead on his building jealousy. "The guy from this afternoon, are you seeing him?"

Her head snapped around. "What guy? Callum? No." The questions shot at him. "He's a regular at the cafe. This afternoon was the first time he's spoken anything other than a drink order to me."

"He asked you out, right?" He hadn't needed to hear the words to read the man's shit-scared demeanor. "What did you say?"

"Why do you care?"

"I don't. I'm only trying to get a feel for how you vet potential lovers."

She focused out her window and spoke softly. "I politely declined."

"Good." The guy wasn't her type. Anyone with a spine as languid as a snake would be an unworthy match for her. She craved strength and dominance. Not a hesitant guy who rocked from foot to foot while talking to his crush.

"For now," she added. "I think I might need to reassess after tonight."

"Why?" He maneuvered through the light traffic, taking in sideglances of her as he went. "What's going to happen tonight?"

"I don't know." She shrugged. "I think I need to stop focusing all my attention on a sexual connection. It's time to lean more toward a mental bond."

"That sounds dreamy," he drawled. "Let me know how it feels when your hymen grows back."

She gave a breathy snicker. "You're such a dick. Just because you enjoy solitude doesn't mean everyone else has to."

"One doesn't have to be the loneliest number. To me, it's the most reliable."

"We'll have to agree to disagree." She shot a glance over her shoulder, giving a quick inspection of the car's interior.

He held his breath and clenched the steering wheel when her eyes widened. For fuck's sake. Why couldn't he catch a break?

"You kept the books?" she asked.

"Yeah."

"I wasn't sure if you were going to keep them to read or—"

"I'm not. I planned on throwing them in the nearest dumpster, but turns out those books are fucking expensive. I read the price sticker on the back of one and couldn't bring myself to trash them. So, I'm waiting for a spare afternoon to drop them at an oncology ward. Or somewhere else they might be of use."

She didn't reply for long seconds that felt like unending months. In that head of hers, he figured she was creating a punishing reply.

"You had no intention of reading them, but you took them anyway?"

He ground his teeth.

"Thank you, Bryan."

Shit. Shit. *Shit.*

She was back to using his name.

"Don't mention it," he muttered and wanted to back it up with, "No, really, don't fucking mention it. *Ever.*"

"You can be a sweet guy, you know that?"

"Yeah. The perfect gentleman," he mocked. "Especially when I have my hands around your throat and your tight cunt around my finger."

She gave a breathy chuckle. "Are you trying to shock me with dirty talk?" She clucked her tongue. "Amateur."

He was. Around her, at least.

"It's hardly dirty talk." He turned onto their street, thankful for the upcoming escape from the confined space. "I should give you a lesson on that, too." No. *No,* he couldn't. What the hell was he thinking?

She sighed and remained quiet.

Crisis averted.

Thank fuck.

"We're almost there." The looming threat of rain had made for less foot-traffic. Not many people were around. Then again, it was nine on a Tuesday night. Not really the hour for raving. "This is the place."

He took in the two-story building as he turned into the parking lot entrance. The front facade had received a facelift since he'd last been here. The dark brick was now matched with black guttering, giving a Gothic feel, while the warm yellow lights brightened up the interior.

"You like it here?" She fumbled with the ends of her scarf.

"Yeah. It's a low-key version of Shot of Sin."

"How so?"

"There's booze, soft music, and rooms for hire upstairs." He parked at the back of the lot and cut the engine.

"Rooms for...?"

"Privacy. Playing. Fucking. You name it." He turned to her, taking in the slight hitch to her chin and her sharp inhale. The mental image had turned her on, which meant his dick wanted in on the action. "Are you ready?"

She held up her clutch and nodded. "All set."

His palms began to sweat as he took in all the visible assets other men would soon be ogling. "Lose the scarf."

Her mouth gaped. "Why?"

Because I want to see more of you. "It doesn't match the dress." *And every time you touch it I think about tying you to my bed.*

Her hand shot to her throat. "I need to wear it."

"Because?"

Her lips worked around silent words before she sighed. "Because I have marks on my neck that I couldn't cover with make-up."

He scowled. "A rash?"

"No." Her focus shot to his. "I'm talking about your fingermarks all over my skin."

"I hurt you?" Snapshots of remembrance peppered his vision—his hands around soft flesh, her moans, the involuntary spasms of her pussy.

He closed his eyes and ran a hand over his face. *Don't think about it. Don't picture it. Just forget the whole scarf thing and get the fuck out of this suffocating space.*

"Not enough," she murmured.

Jesus. It was time to bail.

"Good." He shoved open his car door and escaped the confines of the car.

She followed and met his gaze over the roof. "Do you understand why I have to wear it now?"

"Yeah." He didn't need a reminder staring him in the face all night long, either. "It looks fine."

He didn't watch her as he slammed his door. He didn't need to confirm an eye roll accompanied her scoff; he was already sure of it.

"You realize *fine* is far from a compliment." She shut her door and rounded the hood. "Just for future reference, I mean."

It wasn't like he lacked the ability to compliment her.

He could praise the ever-loving fuck out of her if he wanted. He could tell her how the mere peripheral vision of her gave his dick an aneurism. He could point out how perfect those breasts were—plump and full. Or count on his fingers the amount of times he'd wanted to bend her over different objects and fuck the frustration from his system.

Didn't mean those words would ever pass his lips, though.

"Duly noted."

He started for the front of the building, the gravel of the parking lot rolling under his soles. She wobbled with her first step, her thin heels losing traction.

"You okay?" The instinct to reach out and secure an arm around her waist was a mistake. Yet another idiotic move when it came to this woman.

"You don't need to hold onto me." She inched forward. "I can manage."

He didn't doubt it. But now he had the feel of her embedded into his side, and he wasn't willing to let go. He could smell her hair, the floral scent more of an aphrodisiac than a gut full of oysters. "I insist."

He held her gaze, catching every flicker in her expression as he tightened his hold. She swallowed. Straightened. Lifted her chin. Those lashes even beat with timid lethargy.

"Doesn't it defeat the purpose of trying to pick up another man if I walk in with your hands on me?"

He didn't care. "Doesn't falling face first into the gravel and skinning your knees defeat the purpose of that sexy dress?"

She blinked. Balked. Gaped.

He had no clue why.

"Sexy dress?" One perfectly shaped brow arched.

He huffed and ignored the grin spreading those red lips. "Come on." He led her forward, her waist burning a hole through his palm, until he dropped his grip at the start of the sidewalk. "Have you got it from here?"

"I always had it, Brute." She strutted those toned legs in front of him, making her way to the entrance before he snapped out of his stare and quickly caught up.

"Where do you want to sit?" She glanced around the room, eyeing the booths along the back wall, then the cushion-lined sofas near the front windows, her attention finally coming to rest at the stools lining the bar. "Should we stay close to the booze?"

"That sounds like a good idea." A fucking brilliant plan.

She continued forward while he hung back, waiting in case those gravity-defying heels slipped out from beneath her as she slid onto the closest stool.

"So, tell me your type." He positioned himself beside her and swung around to face the room. It took less than five seconds to deem every guy here as an unworthy conquest. "What are you looking for?"

"Well..." She followed, placing her back to the bar. "Sexually speaking, I want someone confident and—"

"I know what you need sexually." The reminder was a mental stroke along his dick. "What are you after outside the bedroom? I'm talkin' looks, income, race, religion."

"None of that matters to me."

"Looks don't matter?" He raised a fuck-off brow. "Looks always matter."

She shrugged and jutted her chin to the left. "The guy in the back is attractive."

"The one with the Van Dyke beard?"

"Yeah. I don't mind a bit of facial scruff."

His hand itched with the need to palm his jaw. He'd bet she'd prefer a full beard when it was grazing the sensitive flesh of her inner thighs. "How about his wedding ring? Does that bother you?"

Her nose wrinkled, her gaze snapping to his. "How did you even notice that?"

"It's not what you notice, it's what you need to look for. Wedding bands or a tan line on the appropriate finger are a good place to start."

She nodded and sat up straight, ever the eager student. "What else?"

He became fascinated by the way her attention strayed around the room, scoping potential lovers. "The guy you're looking for will be paying you attention. Watching you. Trying to work you out before you even notice him."

Just like I am.

She continued with her search, her shoulders drooping moments later. "Well, I guess I'm out of luck." She turned to face him. "Nobody in here is looking at me."

He wasn't going to prove her wrong. Pointing out all the men who'd already mentally stripped that dress from her body was a conversation for later. When he'd had enough time to determine who would be the right fit for her. "It's early. Don't give up yet."

She nodded, the defeat still a slight groove between her brows. He itched to smother the expression. Wipe it away. With his hands, his mouth, his dick.

Goddammit.

"What do you want to drink?" He yanked his gaze away and raised a hand to call the bartender.

"Tequila sunrise, please."

He placed the order and focused on the drink preparation to ensure he didn't drag her ass out of here for his own fulfillment. He'd already started contemplating the possibility of a different demo assistant. Someone who could take Ella's place so he could sate the rabid hunger tonight and let his insurance policy kick in before this got out of hand.

He didn't care about the female Vault members boycotting the class. Or how Leo and T.J. would want to kill him. All the reasons from needing her assistance disappeared under the chokehold of lust.

His level of investment in this woman was too fucking high. He was beginning to enjoy being around her. The rollercoaster rise and fall of her smile kept stealing his attention. And that dress...

Shit. This wasn't right.

"What's wrong?" she asked. "You look like you're sulking. If you want to go home..."

Take the offer. Get out of here. "We're not leaving."

"Then cheer up, buttercup. You're scaring away any potentials." She waggled her brows and the sultry curve of her lips pummeled another meaty fist into his crotch.

"Here you go." The bartender slid over their drinks.

"Thanks." He snatched at his beer and enjoyed the liquid solace gliding down his throat. He needed to take the edge off. To snuff the burn.

"What's the craziest thing you've done, Brute?" Ella nibbled on the straw sticking from her drink, her head cocked as those eyes bore through him. "I bet you've got a lot of stories to tell."

He shrugged. "Nothing comes to mind."

"You own a sex club and nothing comes to mind?"

He took another long pull of beer. Conversation became difficult—the grasp for coherence almost impossible when her lips were a tempting breath away. "Sex isn't crazy. It's natural. People have been screwing since the dawn of time. What I find hard to justify are those who skydive or participate in adrenaline-fueled sports." He pointed a finger at her. "Or those who get married. Now, if you ask me, making a commitment like that is fucking insane."

She stared at the bar, a far-off gleam in her eyes as she smiled. "My marriage was far from conventional."

"Why is that?"

Her lips parted and silent words hovered out of reach until she sighed. "Hold on a sec." She leaned forward and focused on the bartender. "Excuse me. Can I get a shot of tequila, please?"

"Shots?"

Her fingers tapped against the bar, her leg jolted.

"Have I missed something?" he asked.

She gave a bark of laughter and grasped the shot glass sliding toward her. She downed the contents in one winced gulp and kept her focus on the bartender. "You might want to fill that up again, please. I think I'm going to need it."

"What's going on?" He didn't like the change in her demeanor. He also didn't like the rapid approach of lowered inhibitions. He was already battling enough for them both.

She licked her lower lip, sweeping the remnants of alcohol away. "There was no commitment when I married."

"You had an open relationship?" Her husband must have been one laidback motherfucker. To share a woman as beautiful as Ella was a risk. You'd never know when another guy would throw club etiquette to the wind and steal her right out from beneath you.

"It's a long story."

"Then hurry up and get on with it."

She eyed him, up and down.

Shit. He pulled back, unsure when he'd inched close enough to hear the hitch in her breath.

"Go on." He turned to the bar, palmed his beer, and took a gulp. "We've got all night." At the very least, until he drowned his dick in liquor.

She fiddled with the refilled shot glass, running her finger around the rim. "I met Lucas on one of those European bus holidays. I was doing the touristy thing with Kim, and he was traveling alone. We got to talking and eventually hooked up. It wasn't anything romantic. Just sex." Her shoulders slumped with a deep exhale. "*Amazing* sex."

"I get the picture."

"No, you don't." She spoke to the glazed wood of the bar. "I'd never been with anyone like him before. He taught me things. He knew my body better than I did, which was strange because we rarely spoke. He kept to himself a lot and we only caught up at night."

Bryan gripped his beer, his focus on the liquid. For a fleeting second, his chest constricted with jealousy, but he doused that fucker with the remainder of his drink and quickly ordered another with the raise of a finger.

"When the tour ended, we went our separate ways and neither one of us looked back. I didn't ask for his number, and he showed no interest in keeping in contact. At least, not until he turned up on my doorstep a few months later."

Made sense. The guy must've realized his mistake. Ella was a different sort of woman. Sexually confident and inquisitive. A catch. Anyone who let her walk deserved to wallow in regret.

"Couldn't live without you, huh?" He welcomed his new beer with a deep pull, determined to douse the discomfort under his sternum.

"Actually ..." Her voice turned somber. "He told me he wouldn't be living at all in the near future. He found out about the cancer a few weeks after he returned from Europe."

Bryan dropped his glass to the bar and turned to her.

"It wasn't the happiest of reunions." She shrugged. "But I'm glad he found me."

"That's when you got married?"

"Pretty much. He didn't want to die alone, and I didn't want that for him either. He deserved to have someone by his side."

"What about his family or friends? Couldn't they have looked after him? You said the two of you barely spoke."

"Apart from work colleagues, Lucas didn't have anyone to rely on. His mother had health problems of her own back in Chicago. He didn't even tell her about the cancer. She thought he was going on another vacation. Instead, he came to find me."

"*Jesus.*" He blindly swiped for his beer and knocked back another gulp. "That's a lot of pressure to put on a stranger." The guy seemed like a dick. A selfish, emotionless asshole.

"It was. But I was financially compensated. Our marriage became the equivalent of an employment contract. I quit my waitressing job to concentrate on his health, and when he passed, I became the sole beneficiary of everything he left behind."

She dipped her finger into the tequila, then sucked the moisture away. If their conversation hadn't been about cancer, chemo, and all things melancholy, he would've blown his load then and there.

"His money allowed me to buy this apartment and my cafe. It gave me the opportunity to help my sister who had mounting educational debts, and my mom who'd struggled since my father left. Not that they wanted anything to do with the inheritance. They disagreed with what I did."

"Because you were financially compensated?"

"No." She nibbled her bottom lip and shook her head. "Because at that point, Lucas and I weren't emotionally connected, and they knew it wouldn't end that way. They could see me falling for him, without those feelings being reciprocated."

His chest constricted, the building jealousy hitting harder the further they sank into this conversation. "And you put your life on hold anyway."

"And I'd do it again. There's no way I could've let him die alone. How could I live with myself if I let him walk away? I knew what I was getting myself into. I made the decision on my own." She shrugged. "In the end, they were right. I started hoping for more."

"More what? Time?"

"I don't know." She cringed. "Everything was complicated, especially with my extreme naivety. I've grown up a lot since then."

"Shit." He rested an elbow on the bar and looked at her. *Really* looked at her. "Didn't knowing the end game make it easier to close yourself off emotionally? At least to some extent?"

"How do you close yourself off emotionally, Bryan?" She met his stare. "How do you stop caring? God knows I couldn't figure out how."

She dipped her finger back into the tequila and swirled the contents with her fingertip. "Our days were spent between doctors' appointments and living out a fast-tracked bucket list. We also rekindled the physical relationship when he was able. It became hard building walls against something that monumental." She fell silent, stealing his fascination with each passing minute. "I ended up loving him… In my own little way."

He kept staring at her, kept blinking, kept breathing. He couldn't think past the need to do something, anything, to wipe the pained look off her face.

"Sorry." She winced. "I really won the award for Most Morbid Change in Conversation, didn't I?"

He swiped the shot glass out from beneath her hand and downed the contents in one regrettable swallow. "Yep. And now you're cut off." He cleared his throat to dissolve the burn. "You're a depressing drunk."

Her eyes widened, then a chuckle broke free. "Not usually." She nudged him with her elbow. "I blame the company I keep."

She could blame him all she liked, as long as the smile continued to stay plastered on those dark lips.

"Yeah, well, you need to shape up before your drinking privileges are returned."

"That's rich, coming from Mr. Moody."

"Moody? I'm pretty sure I stick to the one mood ninety percent of the time."

She quirked her lips as she pondered his response. "I guess you're right."

And just like that, her eyes lost the darkened shade of mourning and brightened to a mesmerizing blue.

"Okay." She rubbed her hands together. "Let's get this conversation back on track. We need to focus on getting me laid."

He palmed his beer as the added layer of history tugged at something other than his lust. The additional reminder of why they were here didn't fill him with warm and fuzzies, either. He didn't want to send her home with someone else. He didn't want to send her back to her apartment at all. "Maybe tonight's not the night for this."

"Of course it is." She grabbed his arm, those fingers searing skin and nerves. "Seriously, I need to get lucky. I'll take whatever help I can get."

She batted her lashes, and his dick shoved hard against his zipper, expecting a high-five.

"I'm eager for your expertise." She swiveled, turning her back to the bar. "What about that guy?"

*F*or the next hour, he went through the pros and cons of every male in the building. The pros were few and far between. For good reason. He couldn't find anyone to entrust with her pleasure.

A third of them wore wedding bands. Others leered with no manners or respect. Another chunk of potentials were wiped from the board because they simply didn't look good enough.

He didn't know what it would take to earn his respect, but nobody here had even a glimpse of it, which was becoming harder to explain to Ella, who seemed to have slid on intoxication goggles and considered every man who walked through the door a potential candidate.

He'd had to point out the gay guy who only had eyes for his friend's ass.

He'd had to discuss the downfall of being with someone who spent ten minutes staring at the drink board. Because, seriously, if it took you more than two minutes to figure out your own needs, there was no point wasting a lifetime trying to determine Ella's.

The man she currently ogled wore a plaid shirt, dirty faded jeans, and muddy cowboy boots. Which, realistically, wasn't a bad thing. He looked like he had a good work ethic. But... "If you're still into fucking cattle, go for it."

She snorted, her happiness springing through him like a gunshot. "That's an unfair assumption."

He didn't give a shit.

"What about him?" She tilted her chin toward the man at the far end of the bar.

"You've gotta be kidding." The guy had stuck-up-suit written all over him.

"What's wrong with him?" she slurred through bubbles of laughter, and he immediately regretted reinstating her drinking privileges. "He's cute. He also has good fashion sense. Hell, I could ask him to strip and simply touch him for hours." She slapped her hands together in prayer. "Please, Brute, let me touch his nakedness. I can't remember the last time I got to put my hands on a guy's body."

His nostrils flared. "A few nights ago doesn't ring a bell?" Why didn't she just punch him in the dick? The injury would've hurt less than the insult.

She balked. "I barely got to touch you. Hell, girlfriend—" she waggled her head at him, "—if I had the chance to sink my nails into you, you'd know it."

"Girlfriend?" He pushed from his stool. "You're too drunk for this. Either sober up or I'll have to take you home."

She pouted. "Okay, daddy."

Fuck. Me.

She snorted again. "I'm joking. Stop glaring at me like that. Christ, you throw in a daddy line and everyone gets offended."

Yeah, he was fucking offended, because any other reaction while imagining spanking her over his knee wasn't goddamn appropriate. If only his cock would get the memo.

"I'll be back in a sec. Behave while I'm gone."

He needed a bathroom break.

An *Ella* break.

She wasn't the only one who needed to sober up. The alcohol heating his veins spewed some pretty crazy shit into his mind.

Jesus Christ, he could fucking taste her with every swallow.

Good news was, he hadn't thought of his family. Not until now, when his lust dissipated with each step.

He hadn't contemplated why his dying mother couldn't gather a glimmer of affection to call her only child to say goodbye. He hadn't pondered why his father hadn't picked up the phone—now or in the past months. He didn't think about how the two people who were supposed to love him the most hadn't given a fuck about him at all, because his concentration kept focusing back on Ella with pinpoint precision.

He shoved into the bathroom, stood in front of the basin, and stared at his reflection in the dirty mirror.

Something wasn't right.

Lust had never felt like this before. It had never started in his chest and worked its way down.

At the bar, he'd tried to convince himself it was the alcohol, or the sob story about her husband that pulled at his usually non-existent heartstrings. This was supposed to be about Ella finding someone to fuck. It was about getting her to participate in the demonstration. It was about business. But in here, facing himself, it became harder to live the lie.

He liked her. He fucking liked her. "Damn it."

He ran his hands through his hair, entwined his fingers at the back of his head, and placed tight pressure on his skull.

This was Tera's fault. In one phone call, she'd fucked with him, messing with his head in so many ways he couldn't think straight. She'd reminded him of his childhood, and how he'd once believed in happily-ever-afters and all that naive, fairytale bullshit.

It had to stop.

He couldn't do this to himself.

He couldn't do it to Ella.

She had baggage. Issues.

The appeal didn't make sense. Yet, it was there, building from a molehill into a mountain, right before his eyes, and there was only one way to make it stop.

CHAPTER FOURTEEN

Pamela waited until Bryan disappeared into the bathroom before she slumped against the bar and released her pent-up nervousness in an audible sigh.

This was hell. She wasn't entirely sure which of the nine circles she currently resided in—either lust or greed—but it was hell nonetheless.

Not only did she have to continue the let's-get-me-laid charade, she also had to pretend she wasn't sliding headfirst into deeper feelings for a man who'd made it clear he was off limits. She'd even stooped to the low of bringing up her late husband in the hope the tragic topic would break the early descent into puppy love.

The diversion hadn't worked in the slightest. The conversation had only achieved additional respect for a man who seemed to have more layers than puff pastry.

He'd listened to her. He'd comforted her with soft, simple words. And when the conversation became too emotional, he'd shut it down in typical Brute fashion, which made the depression instantaneously vanish.

Now, leaving wasn't an option. Being alone in a car with him was too much of a temptation to her diluted sanity.

She wanted Bryan.

She wanted Brute.

She wanted whatever she could extract from the big grizzly bear of a man and didn't care about the consequences.

"Hey, sugar."

She glanced from her empty glass to find another flannelette-wearing cowboy at her side. He was broad, tall, and tanned, with an uber smirk to boot.

"You look like you need another drink."

She gave a false smile. "I'm fine. Thanks."

He inclined his head. "That you are, but I insist." He knocked his knuckles on the bar. "Bartender, get this pretty lady a glass of bubbles."

Bubbles?

"I, um…" That went against rule five-hundred and fifty-five in the Brute's Fuck Buddy Guidebook—a potential lover should nail your drink order before he nails you.

A mini bottle of champagne cracked open before her, the contents poured into a slim flute. She should've declined with more enthusiasm. Should've, could've, would've if numbing mindlessness wasn't a mere drink away. Tomorrow, she'd pay for mixing drinks. For now, she'd take whatever relief she could get.

"Here you go." He lifted the glass from the bar and handed it over. "Something sweet for someone sweet."

She cleared her throat. "If you came here looking for timid and cute, I'm not your girl."

"You're the naughty type?" He eyed her with lust-filled appreciation. "Tonight is my lucky night."

A laugh escaped. She couldn't help it. In a game of hot and cold, this guy was so far from getting lucky he'd need a snow suit.

"I can't believe a woman as fine as yourself would be out on her own."

"She's not." Bryan came up behind her. "Take a hike, buddy."

"*Bryan.*" She snapped her head around, scowling. "You don't have to be rude."

"My apologies. I didn't realize this was the type of guy you were looking for."

Was intoxication playing tricks on her, or did he seem unmistakably jealous? Her stomach flipped, and all the liquid she'd consumed went with it in a nauseating roll.

"Hold on a minute." The cowboy held up his hands. "She was sitting here on her own. I didn't know you two were together."

"We're not," they spoke in unison.

"Right." The guy retreated a step. "I guess looks can be deceiving."

Heat crept up her throat, soaking through her scarf.

"We're leaving." Bryan stared at her, demanding compliance.

Shit. He must have finally cracked the code on her not-so-subtle feelings.

"Sugar," the cowboy started. "If you're in trouble—"

"Trouble?" He thought she was in danger? From Bryan? Okay, so maybe the brute was clenching his fists and breathing heavier than normal, but that was only because she'd broken her promise not to fall for the commitment-phobic jerk. "No. I'm okay. This is what he's like. All bark. No bite."

Bryan growled. Actually growled.

"We're leaving," he repeated. "Unless you want to hang around with a guy who doesn't give you the respect of finding out what you're drinking. But, hey—" He shrugged. "—I'm sure he's a keeper. You've got great taste in men, after all."

She scoffed and downed half the champagne in one fast swallow. He itched for a fight—she could see it in the flash of anger in those deep blue eyes. She had no plan to leave him unsatisfied.

"My taste in men shouldn't be any of your business." She shoved from her stool and wobbled with the landing.

"Fucking hell." He flung out a hand to catch her.

"Don't speak to me like that." She slapped his hold away and got in his face, allowing his dark, masculine scent to mess with her senses.

"Then stop doing stupid shit."

She heard the words, and the only thing that sunk in was his protection. His authority. His claim for territory. *No*. The alcohol played tricks on her.

She stepped back and turned to Mr. Cowboy. "Sorry 'bout that." She snatched her clutch from the bar and put the champagne flute in its place. "Thanks for the drink."

The guy's eyes widened. "You're leaving with him?"

Yes. *No*. The answer didn't matter because she couldn't think without fresh air.

She hustled outside, her short, sharp toe steps making the support of her stiletto heels unpredictable.

"What the hell are you doing now?" Bryan followed, keeping a thankful yard of distance between them on the sidewalk.

"Leaving. Isn't that what you wanted?"

His fury tickled the back of her neck in the form of a snarl. She hated that noise. Hated it so much her pussy contracted and released enough times to mimic an orgasm.

"When it comes to you, I get nothing I want."

His retort hit her like a slap across the face. She swung around, teetering again, her heels producing the same stability as cooked spaghetti. "Then what *do* you want, Bryan? Tell me."

He crossed his arms over his broad chest, making his jacket gape and the material of his shirt temptingly tighten over the muscles beneath.

Oh, dear God.

The entire world conspired against her attempts to dislike him. Every time she erected blocks to combat the attraction, he'd shove them down again in one mighty Hulk smash.

"I want you to fucking listen." His breath came in exhausting huffs. "I'm trying to show you how to find a guy who deserves you. Someone who's going to give a shit about what you want. And the minute I turn my back you're hooking up with Cowboy Bill."

"Hooking up?" *Hooking up?* "He offered to buy me a drink. I declined. And he didn't take no for an answer. I didn't even take a sip of the champagne until you came back and inspired the need for alcoholism."

He glared, those blue irises harsh with menace.

"Come on." She sighed. "What's this really about?"

"You know what this is about." The words grated through perfect teeth, across lush, smooth lips.

She wanted to nod and confirm that, yes, this was about feelings neither one of them could ignore. This was about something more than friendship or sex or the Vault. This was about sparks and connection and heart-clenching emotion.

"This is about needing a demonstration assistant," he snarled. "That's all this has ever been."

Her nose tingled, throat pinched. "I know that." But she hadn't. Not really. She'd tried to forget. She'd ignored the entire purpose of them being together while becoming overrun with the allure of romance.

Again.

This was Lucas on repeat.

"Good," he snapped.

"*Great*," she mimicked.

He approached, getting in her face. His nostrils flared, his lip curled. "*Fucking* perfect."

She'd never wanted to kiss him more. The thrill of having his beard scratch against her mouth, her neck, her breasts. Her heart thundered. Her throat pinched tighter. She whirled on her toes and escaped in the opposite direction, the *click, click, click* of her heels a panicked staccato.

"God, I wish I knew why you were such a grumpy jerk." She approached the edge of the building and turned into the darkened parking lot, remaining close to the brickwork in case she needed the support.

"Slow down. You're going to wind up on your ass."

"Stop it, okay?" She glared over her shoulder. "Stop the back and forth. The Jekyll and Hyde. The kindness and severity. I'm sick of it." Her ankle rolled, the sharp twinge of pain shooting up the outside of her leg. She tilted, the threat of falling on her butt replaced with something even more threatening—his hold.

He grabbed her, tugging her against his strong chest and lunging her into the brickwork. She was boxed in, caught between two layers of cold sterility. But that wasn't what stared back at her. Those blue eyes weren't barren. She could see everything peering down at her—his affection, his lust, his hopes for the future. Then, in a blink, they disappeared.

"Jesus Christ." He held her upright, keeping her caged. "I never should've brought you here."

Regret took over his expression. Annoyance, too. Her delusional fairytale of what they'd shared became tarnished by the frustration staring down at her.

"I'm sorry."

His brows pulled tight. "Why?"

"I don't know." A breath shuddered from her lungs. "I feel like I need to apologize. I've never offended anyone as much as I seem to offend you." She had to keep talking, if only to make sure he remained nestled against her, his warmth finally sinking in. They'd never been this close. Not emotionally. "I guess I lost sight of this being about your job. I began to think we were friends."

His body relaxed.

No, it deflated. His shoulders slumped, his face fell. "You don't offend me, Ella."

"Then what is it?" she whispered.

He turned his head away, the tension building in his frame until he loomed over her as he focused on the street.

"Bryan?" She reached out, her fingertips tingling the closer she came to his beard-covered cheek. Her palm slid over the coarse hairs, and everything inside her crumpled. She'd never touched him. Not like this. Not with her heart in her throat and her feelings exposed in the brief connection.

She guided his face back to hers and pleaded with her eyes. "What's this all about?"

The hardness of his jaw became more defined. "It's about wanting to fuck you. I've gone insane for the last five hours, fighting the need to get you under me. And the five days before that." He stepped forward, squeezing her tighter between the hard wall of the building and the harder wall of his chest. "Even before that, Ella. Since the first night I touched you in the fucking locker room."

Hope took the reins and ran. Everything inside her ignited, emotions and body parts all combusting to cause a mass of burning, tingling flesh.

She had to kiss him. Had to taste those lips and feel them devastating hers. And that was exactly what they'd do—devastate her. Destroy her. Because one passionate kiss would be so much more than she'd had from her husband.

He rocked into her, the solid length of his shaft making itself known against her pubic bone. She couldn't breathe. Couldn't think. All she could do was become ensnared as his mouth called her name like a siren's song.

She smashed her lips to his and immediately drowned in the intensity of his reciprocation. His hand flew to her hair, sliding over her scalp, holding her close. His arm wrapped around her waist, squeezing life back into her. Every part of him touched her. Every inch of her body remained at his mercy, while his tongue parted her lips and delved deep.

He took over. Made her hyperventilate. All with one kiss.

With only his beard, lips, and teeth.

When he pulled back, they both panted into the small space between them. "We should get out of here."

She nodded.

His hand left her hair, snaked down her arm, and entwined with her fingers. He didn't acknowledge the intimacy, didn't even look her in the eye anymore. Instead, he turned and led her to the car, not stopping until they stood at the passenger door, his free hand poised on the handle.

He remained close, frozen against her, as if the world had stopped for them to have this moment. At least that was how it felt, until comprehension dawned.

"You can't drive, can you?"

He released her hand and wiped a rough palm over his mouth. "I've had too much to drink."

He remained pressed against her, the teasing torment of her feelings flickering between them like rapidly igniting sparks. She tried to think of a sensible way out of this situation. Something that wouldn't leave her broken tomorrow. But want and need fried those rational thoughts, leaving her alone with the chemical imbalance driving her to clutch his shirt and pull him closer.

"Do you want to catch a cab?" She lifted her clutch over her shoulder and placed it on the roof of his car.

A lifetime of racing heartbeats measured the seconds they remained close, the intoxication rapidly leaving her system in a passion-induced detox.

"You know I don't." His touch returned to her hip. "Not yet."

The pulse of his dick nestled against her. The thickness, the length, made her salivate. She couldn't budge. It wasn't the inescapable cage of his arms. It was his nearness. His proximity. The promise of more.

"Are you sure you want to do this now?" he asked, his breath drifting over her cheek, inspiring exhilaration, goose bumps, and nausea in overlapping doses.

She was entirely wrecked by this man.

"Are you sure you want to finish this here?" He nuzzled into her hair, his nose teasing her neck, his beard scratching her skin. He gripped her chin, guiding her gaze to his penetrating eyes while his thigh parted hers, his weight pinning her to the car.

"Yes." The word was a breathy exhale. "Here. Now."

He ground into her, tearing a whimper from her throat. He was already so close to fucking her, a mere unbuckle of his belt and the raise of her dress. She could sense how cataclysmic the penetration would be. How perfect. But... "I'm scared this isn't going to end well."

She needed his reassurance. Craved it as much as she craved his cock.

"Doesn't matter. We both know this is inevitable," he countered, gripping her dress.

She couldn't stop him. There was no will. Her body gave her no choice.

All she could do was stare into that fierce face as he focused on her with pure ownership and lifted her hem. Inch by inch, the tight material crawled up her body, exposing her flesh with agonizing lethargy. The cool night air seeped into her thighs, her hips, her sex. And still, those eyes pinned her, reading the reactions she tried to hide.

He released the fabric to bundle at her waist, then slid his hands down her bare skin, searing the flesh he touched.

"You weren't lying about not wearing underwear."

"I have no reason to lie to you." She could've laughed at the hypocrisy. She'd been lying to him all night. This afternoon, too. She'd lied about her feelings. About her intent. She'd lied and lied and lied. Even to herself. "This dress doesn't look anywhere near as sexy with visible panty lines." She lied again. The lack of underwear had been to tease him. To see if he was affected by her the way she was by him.

"Well..." He grinned. "I've never appreciated honesty more than I do right now." He gripped her chin, demanding her attention. A gentle fingertip glided over her tingling lower lip, the connection more painful and emotional than anything she could've expected.

Her insides waged war. Half of her screamed to take all she could get. The other ached to tell him what another kiss would mean. To make him understand. Even though nobody else ever had. Not even her mother or Kim.

This time when he leaned in, she held her breath, waiting for his next move. Those tempting lips approached, only to veer at the last second and plague her cheek with the burn. "I could've sworn you weren't the type to fuck in a parking lot," he whispered against her skin. "But you have a habit of surprising me."

His beard grazed each place of impact, along her jaw, then further, to the sensitive spot below her ear. She wanted to hate the misplaced sentiment. Wanted to hate him in general. But those light kisses turned into nibbles, the nibbles transforming into bites and sucks, until he ravaged her neck with such erotic efficiency she clung to his shoulders for more.

"Take off the scarf." He ground into her, his erection thick and pulsing between them.

"If I take it off, are you going to leave more marks?"

"Without a doubt."

Oh, God. She couldn't have asked for a better response.

She slid the silk from her neck. The delicate glide inspired goose bumps. Her skin erupted in a mass of tingles. She held the material out to him and pretended it didn't affect her when he placed his hand over hers, stealing the scarf from her grip.

"Now, open your mouth."

She recoiled. "Excuse me?"

"Trust me, you're going to want something in that mouth to stop you crying out."

"I'll be quiet."

"Really?" The silk fell to his side while his free hand skimmed the trim patch of curls at the apex of her thighs. With a quick slide of his fingers, he grazed her clit and parted her folds, teasing her slit. She moaned with the sharp infusion of pleasure. The noise was long, low and entirely out of control.

"Do you want to rethink that promise?" He pulsed the tip of two fingers at her entrance, eyeing her with confidence while he worked his magic.

Her chest exploded, the shrapnel shooting to her breasts, her abdomen, her core.

"How do you think you're going to react once I slide my cock in here?"

He raised the scarf and a confident brow at the same time.

Damn him. For everything.

"Fine." She jutted her chin, waiting.

His eyes blazed as he removed his fingers from between her legs to place the material in her mouth. She bit down while he crossed it behind her neck, then guided it forward to hang over her chest.

"Now give me your wrists."

She shook her head, working the material from her mouth. "No."

"Don't trust me?"

"No. I don't. Not out here. Not when I'm already vulnerable enough."

A flash of rejection marred his features. "I wouldn't hurt you, Ella. Not like that."

Not. Like. That.

Just in every other way imaginable.

He worked the silk between her lips and tightened the knot behind her neck. "There. Pretty as a picture and even more inviting now that you can't talk."

"You're a piece of work, you know that?" The words were mumbled into utter incoherence.

"What was that?"

"Fuck you."

He smirked. "You'll be doing that soon enough."

A hand glided between them, those talented fingers rediscovering her entrance, spreading her folds. This time, her accompanying whimper barely sounded, smothered by delicate material.

"That's better." He bent forward. "Now I won't have to hold back."

She would've hated if he had. She couldn't wait to see his mindlessness. His restraint and subsequent surrender.

"I love how you're always wet for me. Are you like this for everyone?"

She shook her head. *No.* Nobody but him.

"Good." He trailed two fingers around in circles, not stopping the motion as he retrieved a wallet from his back pocket, flipped the leather open, and rested it against his hip to pull a condom from the notes section. Once he had what he wanted, he dropped the wallet to the ground, his cards, coins, and notes scattering across the asphalt.

He didn't seem to notice. Didn't seem to care.

He placed the condom packet between his teeth and unbuckled his belt one-handed. The *clink, clink, clink* of metal on metal broke the quiet night air, followed by the grate of his zipper. She watched, her breath catching as he shoved at his waistband and fisted his erect length in his palm.

She was really doing this. Really shoving herself into a situation that could only end in heartbreak. *Again.*

But who cared?

She'd recovered before.

She reached out, trailing her nails along his shaft, then gripped the base with a tight squeeze.

"Fuck." The curse was guttural, defenseless, and entirely perfect.

Behind the scarf, she smiled.

He released his dick and spat the condom packet into his palm. "So, you want me to blow in your hand, is that it?" He closed his eyes and dropped his head back. The worst part was his fingers sliding from between her thighs. "Come on, sweetheart. You need to let me suit up. Neither one of us want to see me finish like this."

Maybe she did.

Maybe it was best for them both.

He was under her control, susceptible to her touch, just like she was to his. The knowledge made her attraction all the more punishing. He was so beautiful, his face a mix of tension and control as moonlight beamed down on those harsh features.

"*Ella*." The way he said her nickname—the plea, the passion, the lust. "This isn't what you want... You need my hands on your ass... My mouth on your neck... My cock in your pussy."

Her lips burned with dryness she couldn't lick away. All she could do was bite down on silk and whimper.

"You've got five seconds," he murmured. "Four..."

She trailed her touch to the head of his shaft and rubbed the moisture beading at his slit.

"I lied." He gripped her wrist and dragged her hand away. "You're done." His other arm snaked behind her back, lifting her off the ground. "Legs around my waist."

She complied without thought, her ass sliding against the side of the car, his dick poised at her entrance as he worked the protection over his length in efficient strokes.

All too soon, he was ready and looking at her as if asking permission.

"Do it," she mumbled around the gag. "Just do it."

His jaw clenched. "You sure?"

Goddamn him and his sweet concern.

She threw her hands around his neck and sank her nails deep. If those scars weren't enough to convince him to hurry, the buck of her hips should've been.

He slid his hand to the top of his shaft, working the tip back and forth along her entrance. She didn't know where to train her gaze—on his impressive cock, his muscled chest, or those penetrating eyes now framed by strands of loose hair.

He blinked at her, sweat beading his brow as he snaked his tongue out to moisten his gorgeous lips. She became lost in the moment. Lost in him.

He thrust home in one long, punishing shove of his hips, stealing all the breath from her lungs. All the thoughts from her mind. There was only friction. Only pleasure.

She cried out, her head falling back, her fingers clenching tight into his neck. The heat of him enveloped her chest, the weight pressing deep. His hips rocked in a slow, torturous rhythm and she whimpered with each undulation, the sound ringing louder and louder in her ears.

"Hey." He placed his mouth a breath away from hers. "Keep it quiet, sweetheart. You're not going to find a friendly audience in this shoddy neighborhood."

Her breathing quickened with her jerky nod and she bit around the silk to sink her teeth into her lower lip. She wiggled, trying to seat her ass on the edge of the window and slipped.

"It's okay." He gripped her tight. "I've got you."

Did he? Really?

Physically, he was there. But emotionally, she wasn't sure he existed.

"Fuck." He thrust. Again and again. Each pleasure-induced pulse followed with a panted breath against her lips. "What are you doing to me?"

She closed her eyes, wishing she could close her ears, too, because his words were sinking into her soul, never to be removed. *So damn good... Drive me crazy... Fuck... Best damn thing...* She wanted to scream for him to stop and beg for this to never end.

He kissed her neck, her shoulder, then the deep V of her dress, marking the curves of her breasts with lips and tongue and beard. She'd never been more alive. More hopeful. She wanted to share the world with this man and believed he craved the same thing. Maybe not on the surface, but deep down. Deep, deep down. Almost within reach.

"I want to do everything to you." He thrust hard. Over and over, each undulation growing in force.

"Yes." She gasped around her gag. "More."

She was close, already. He had a way of knowing her. Of sensing where to touch. Where to focus.

He grazed her nipples through her dress. The first time was too light, the second too hard. The third and every time after was utter perfection. He was Goldilocks. Testing everything. Finding the right fit. He even had the hair to prove it.

"What are you smiling at?" His nose brushed hers.

She couldn't explain, even if she was physically able.

"I love your smile." He nuzzled her cheek, his beard leaving its mark. "Prettiest damn thing I've ever seen."

Her grin vanished, pure shock taking its place. *Oh, God.* Her heart stopped. It didn't start again—just remained idle as his mouth trekked her mouth, finally coming to rest on the corner of her lips.

"What?" He pulled back. "What is it? Have I done something wrong?"

He kept compounding her awe. Kept showing a side of himself even more alluring than what she'd already fallen for.

He froze, those sexy undulations ceasing to exist. "Ella?"

She worked the scarf from her mouth, no longer caring if she drew a crowd because she couldn't go a moment longer without his kiss. "You've done everything right."

She shoved a hand through his hair and dragged his face to hers, stealing his lips. Their connection ignited, the mix of tongues and teeth and renewed thrusts building to a crazy intensity that had every inch of her in love with every inch of him.

He kissed her as hard as his cock fucked her. He worshipped her just as sweetly, too. His touch was a fine contrast to all the slamming body parts.

"You're going to make me come." She spoke into his mouth, pulling his hair.

"I fucking hope so."

Her pussy contracted around his length, tiny spasms quickly building to impending bliss. "Bryan..."

"I got you."

He did. He really did.

She came undone, the whimpered noises building in her throat, only to be smothered by his mouth. He continued to kiss her. To love her like nobody had ever loved her.

"*Shit.*" His fingers dug into her ass, marking flesh she never wanted to heal. He pistoned his hips, extending her orgasm as he came, thrust after torturous thrust.

He bit and sucked and licked. Bucked and caressed and squeezed.

Her world became one mass of tingling sensation. Then just as quickly, it faded.

Starbursts turned into twinkles. Pulses lessened to twinges. She pulled back, panting into the night air while his rhythm lessened to a slow dance.

She slumped against his shoulder, his scent filling her lungs, his sweat coating her cheek.

One moment, bliss conquered. The next, the hard weight of reality made her numb. She hadn't merely fallen a few steps for this man—she'd toppled down a slope the size of Everest.

"Ella," he whispered into her neck, a hint of regret tinging his voice.

She closed her eyes, not wanting to know the harshness inevitably due to follow all the sexy sweetness she'd received. "Mmm?"

"I'm sorry this had to end."

Her heart swelled as she worked the tight silk from around her neck. "*Had to* end? What do you mean?"

He spoke in past tense, like this was already over. As if it had been a foregone conclusion that they would share a monumentally deep connection, then wave each other goodbye.

He settled her on her feet and stepped back, frowning. "You knew this was the end, right?"

Her eyes seared, threatening to betray her.

"Ella?" His voice turned into a warning. "You knew this game was over once we fucked."

She blinked and blinked, trying to hide her cluelessness while he righted his clothing.

"I told you from the start. I tell *everyone* from the start."

"Yeah." She swallowed. Licked her lips. "I knew. I just..." She tugged down the hem of her dress and snatched her clutch from the top of the car. "I didn't—" She clamped her mouth shut and inched away, taking close, cautious steps.

"Wait." He reached out and the connection of his hand missed its mark. "I thought you understood. You spoke about this not ending well. I made sure you wanted to finish this *here. Now*. I asked you, Ella. I thought we were both on the same page."

She hadn't even been in the same book.

She'd momentarily forgotten his rules and regulations, too blinded by the dreamy thoughts of what could be. She'd made herself believe that something special was a possibility. Just like she had with Lucas.

"We were," she lied with a jerky nod. "We *are*."

"Then why are you looking at me like..."

Don't say it. Please don't say it.

"Why are you backing away from me?" he amended.

"Because that's what you want." She stopped, commanding her feet to remain in place even though she itched to kick off her heels and sprint. "I'm giving you space. I know how much you hate clingy women."

He winced, and for the briefest second she expected him to tell her to come back into his arms.

Yet again, she was wrong.

Why did she keep getting this so wrong? She pinned her hopes on love when it was nowhere in sight. She continued to fall for men who had no intention of falling for her.

"Did you expect this to turn into something more?" His jaw tensed as his hands stabbed through his hair. "I can't fucking read you."

"*No*," she lied and scrambled to come up with solid reasoning. "I just didn't think you'd be fucking me one minute and kicking me to the curb the next." She backtracked, each step bringing more necessary space. "But I get it. You made your position clear. And I certainly don't want to be classified as one of your groupies."

"*Fuck*." His curse rang through every inch of the parking lot, startling her. "Just stop." His hands fell to his sides. "I don't want you to be pissed at me."

"Why does it matter?" Her question held too much heartache, the weakness ringing in her ears. "You know I want to cancel my Vault membership. After tonight, you'll never see me again. So, who gives a shit if I'm pissed?"

He clenched his teeth. "I do, okay? I want you back at the club. I want to help you find someone."

"No, thank you." Not when she wanted that someone to be him. "Your help tonight was enough."

He stepped toward her and froze when the crunch of plastic sounded under his sole. "*Shit*." He crouched to pick up his wallet and the scattered credit cards. "Look, Ella, I've got a truckload of bullshit on my shoulders. My family is fucked. The guys at work are on my back about the argument we had at the club…"

"And the last thing you need is what? Me causing you problems?" When had she become a liability instead of an asset for his demonstration?

His lips parted, but an answer hovered out of reach. *Everything* hovered out of reach. If only she had the heart to stretch a little further. To find the perfect words to make him realize. To do something, anything, to make him wake up and see the possibilities right in front of him.

"You're a great guy, Bryan," she whispered. "But I deserve better than this."

He scoffed, his hand paused on a dirty business card, his hair framing his gorgeous face. He didn't look at her. Didn't move. "Ain't that the truth." His voice was barely audible, the softness far more punishing than if he'd growled at her.

He sat back on his haunches, those brilliant eyes hitting her with feigned sincerity. "What a fucking mess, right?"

She slowly nodded through the disbelief. "Yeah…"

What else could she say? She wasn't going to stand here and argue with him while her heart slowly bled out. "I'm going to catch a cab." A chill took over her skin, sinking deeper to penetrate bone. She wanted to hate him and couldn't. Wanted to stop adoring him and failed at that, too.

"Wait." He rushed to pick up more of his scattered belongings. "Let me get all this shit first and we can leave together." He snatched at the coins, notes, and credit cards strewn across the asphalt. "Give me a second."

"No. You want this to end now. At least let me have the dignity of walking away."

"You can, *after* I get you home safely."

The concern was a weighty sucker-punch. He cared about her, but not enough to ditch his stupid rules. "I've been single a long time. I'm sure I'll be fine on my own."

"*Ella.*"

The word tore her apart—her skin, her ribs, her heart. She gave him one last look, taking in all the severity framed by pure gorgeousness and turned on her heels. "I've told you before, that's not my name."

CHAPTER FIFTEEN

*B*ryan kept his attention on his computer as Shay came to stand inside the doorway of the Shot of Sin office. Her presence was never a good thing. Not lately, anyway.

"We're ready for the management meeting. When are you coming down?"

"I'm skipping it." He didn't raise his focus. "Take notes for me."

"You already missed last week's meeting. And the one before that."

He slid his palm over the pen laying on the table, his fingers clutching the flimsy plastic in a death grip. "And if I want, I'll miss the next one, too. You know you don't need me to participate."

"Brute..." She approached his desk.

"*Shay*, I'm not in the mood."

"You know they're only going to bring the meeting up here if you don't get your ass downstairs."

His friends must have reached the threshold of his bullshit. About time, too. He'd expected them to cave more than a week ago, and he still hadn't been able to pull himself out of the spiral of bad behavior.

"Was that your brilliant idea?" He pinched the bridge of his nose, already knowing the answer.

"You know I'm always trying to figure out how to get more Brute time."

He sighed and rested back in the chair. He'd been ignoring everyone for weeks, successfully keeping enough distance to avoid their nagging eyes. "I'll be down there in a minute."

"Good." She boasted her victory with a slight quirk of her lips. "You still doing okay?"

"Why wouldn't I be?"

"Do you really want me to spell it out?"

"What I want is for you to get the fuck out of my office." And for Ella to get out of his mind. It seemed he was destined to give a shit about women who didn't give a shit about him. First his mother, then the sexual goddess in the Vault who had his gray matter running a minefield of pathetic emotions.

"I will, as soon as you follow me downstairs." She smiled, big and broad, and backtracked toward the door. "Come on."

"I said I'll be down in a minute."

He needed to pull his shit together before the inevitable slew of questions. He'd left everyone in the lurch for almost three weeks without explanation or remorse over why he'd bunkered down in the office, demanding to be the reclusive office bitch.

He'd played Tetris with the once-perfect work roster, moving employees around like puzzle pieces to fill the holes his absence made. All he could handle were emails, stock orders, and bookwork. Everything else had been left to T.J. and Leo, along with a disgruntled team of staff who'd never liked him anyway.

Most of the time he sat staring at his phone, waiting for calls that never came. One from Tampa. The other from Ella.

Neither connection seemed likely to happen, and each day of radio silence made him more annoyed. At himself. He should've known better, on both counts, than to expect a different outcome.

But he'd still texted Ella days after their night in the parking lot. It hadn't been much in the way of communication. A few sentences to encourage a conversation that never eventuated—*I gave your books to a local oncologist. He appreciated your donation and said he'd pass them on to interested patients.*

He couldn't blame her for cutting him off. That was what he'd set out to achieve when he slept with her. *That*, and to get her as far away from the dick at the bar who couldn't spare five seconds to ask what she wanted to drink.

She deserved better.

Truth be told, she deserved better than someone who would call her out in the middle of a sex club. Or fuck her in a dark parking lot in a shitty neighborhood. Or let her catch a cab home on her own after she'd been drinking.

He was no better than the champagne-buying prick.

And her lack of reply was a good indication she knew it, too.

"What's going on with you, Brute?"

"*Shit*." He startled at Shay's voice. "Why are you still lurking?"

She cocked her head and scrutinized every inch of his face. "Something really bad is up with you, isn't it?"

"Apart from my annoyance levels from your constant nagging, no." The cloying thoughts of going back to Tampa didn't help. He'd contemplated making the trip every damn day. There was a hatchet to bury, if only for his sake, because his parents made it clear they still wished he'd been swallowed instead of conceived.

But it was about closure, right?

Or something similar. He'd read a convoluted online article outlining paragraphs of psychological drivel stating all the reasons to be the better person. All of which made a lot of sense. Just not enough to convince him to pack his bags.

Not yet, at least.

"You sure? You haven't been brutish lately. I was thinking of changing your nickname to melon."

He scowled.

"Because you're so melancholy," she explained.

He pushed all the air from his lungs. Before Ella, Shay's taunting had kept him on his toes. She was an annoyance he enjoyed reciprocating. Now, all he wanted to do was sink his head back against the chair and go to sleep. "Get out, Shay."

"See, that right there is a stellar indication of your melon state. Brute would've told me to try it and see how I liked the unemployment line, but this melon uses a defeated tone to tell me to leave."

"I don't have time for this."

Her expression stilled as she contemplated him, then slowly her face fell and a potent look of concern bore down on him. "Now I'm really starting to worry."

"Look, I'm fine, okay? I've got shit going on. Personal shit. But it's nothing I can't handle."

"You know you can talk to me if you need someone."

He glared. "Seriously?"

"Don't be like that. We're friends. I care about you."

He closed his eyes and massaged his lids. "I'm not the talking type. You know that." At least he hadn't been. Not until Ella. That woman seemed to bring out the verbal diarrhea in him. She currently knew more about his life than his closest friends.

"Well, maybe you should be. It wouldn't kill you."

"It might."

She chuckled, the sound half-hearted. "Have it your way. But just so you know, if you're not downstairs in five minutes, I'm bringing the team up here."

"Yeah, I heard."

Her footsteps faded down the hall, allowing the shit running through his head to reassemble and gain traction. This whole situation had started because Shay had wanted him to help a random chick obtain an orgasm.

But Ella hadn't turned out to be a random chick, and what he'd given her hadn't merely been an orgasm. She'd taken much more from him. Too much more. And he had no idea how to get those parts of himself back.

He was stuck feeling too hollow and too heavy, at the same time. There was darkness, as well as picture-perfect clarity. Unpredictability and painful routine.

He pushed from his chair and made his way downstairs to fast-track the punishment. There was no point holding out any longer. His friends had been patient, far more than he would've been in return.

They all sat in a line, positioned across the stools at the main Shot bar. Leo, Shay, Cassie, and T.J.—all of them holding matching blank expressions as he walked behind the bar to face them head on.

"You're late." Leo slid a stack of mail across the counter. "And you might want to consider checking the mail every once in a while if you plan to continue being the office bitch. This must've been sitting in our box for weeks."

"It was on my to-do list." He grasped the envelopes and flicked through the pile, finding a mass of potential bills and one hand-written address.

"You seem like you've been busy in the office." T.J.'s statement sounded like more of a question.

"How are you handling the detox from the Vault?" Cassie asked.

"It's a piece of cake." It wasn't a lie. He hadn't stepped foot inside the sex club in weeks and had no interest in going down there in the near future. Not until he got his head sorted out. His dick, too.

"Speaking of to-do lists." Leo cleared his throat. "Did you refund everyone's money for the demonstration night?"

The reminder made him tense. "It's done." He ripped open the first envelope and retrieved the folded invoice inside before discarding the rubbish onto the counter. "I've refunded everyone involved."

"Did you explain the cancellation?"

"It's nobody's business."

"Not even ours?" Leo stared him down. "What happened, Brute? We've handled you with kid gloves for weeks, but now it's time for an explanation. I thought you were determined not to let the women win."

"They didn't win. I needed a break from the Vault." Not only the setting, the carnality, and the people. He needed a break from the reminder of what had driven him into this mind fuck. "And Ella couldn't participate either. So, the cancellation worked for both of us."

"Did you refund her membership?" T.J. asked. "It would be a nice gesture of goodwill."

His hand paused in the middle of tearing open the second envelope. "I'm not kicking her out of the club. She can return whenever she wants."

"She's not coming back," Cassie spoke softly.

He continued to open the envelope, his gaze focused on the shredding paper. A tight restriction took place behind his sternum, the pain intensifying with the need for answers to questions he didn't want to voice. Tighter and tighter his lungs squeezed, until he couldn't hold it in anymore. "You've spoken to her?"

"I called her," Shay answered.

He emptied the invoice from the envelope, threw the rubbish to the counter, and then started the process all over again. "I didn't realize the two of you were friends."

"We're not. Not really. But I wanted to check on her."

"How'd you get her number?" He couldn't hide the pathetic jealousy in his voice.

"I looked in the Vault database."

His foot to tapped against the polished floorboards, the rampant beat out of his control. "You were on my computer?"

"She was on *our* computer," T.J. corrected.

"Right." He slashed another envelope and turned back to Shay. "And she said she isn't coming back?"

The nod and accompanying look of pity were enough to send his fingers tearing through the paper.

"Did she say why?" He already knew her original reason—nobody interested her in the Vault. But he'd hoped her mind would change with time.

"Are you asking because you hope we don't know the answer?" Cassie rested her elbows on the bar, leaning forward, fully invested. "Or do you truly not know?"

He shredded another envelope and kept his mouth shut, not wanting to admit he was to blame. He didn't need to exacerbate his pathetic existence.

Shay sighed.

Leo crossed his arms over his chest.

Cassie glanced at T.J., while her husband pinned him with a sympathetic stare.

He opened three envelopes in quick succession and pulled out the accompanying information. "What's next on the agenda?"

Uncomfortable silence fell until T.J. had the balls to fill it. "We still haven't resolved the current topic. Are you able to refund her membership? Maybe write a check and put it in the mail?"

Another envelope died in his hands, the front half ripping in two. He didn't want to think about her any more than he already did. He didn't want to look up her details on his computer. Or scribble her name on a check. But taking this route and getting his friends off his back was the lesser of two evils. "Yeah. No problem. I'll sort it out."

"Great. We can move on, then." Cassie gave her co-conspirators a warning look, wordlessly reiterating how pathetic and temperamental he was. "Next on the list is the possibility of an under-age dance night."

That was his cue to zone out of the conversation. His field of fucks was well and truly barren. Everything felt raw and uncomfortable. Even answering the simplest of questions. All because of Ella—a woman who hadn't called and evidently had no plans to see him again.

She'd forgotten him.

And with all his determination and focus, he still couldn't seem to do the same with her.

Turned out, his insurance policy was a piece of shit.

He tore open the last envelope, this time slower, drawing out the need to keep his hands occupied. There were no folded pages this time. He parted the opening and sank his hand in to retrieve the tiny slip of paper buried inside.

A newspaper clipping.

He read the heading and wondered if he'd fallen into a momentary hallucination. He blinked, blinked again, and re-read the words. He stared for long moments, his chest tightening, bile rising in his throat.

"Brute?" Shay's voice was distant. A million miles away.

"*Bryan?*" Cassie pleaded. "What is it?"

He slid the paper back into the envelope and ran a hand over his beard, hoping to encourage his lunch to stay in his gut. "Nothing." His response was static. "Can you finish up without me? I need to sort out this mail and get started on the refund for Ella."

Ella. *Fucking Ella.* At a time like this, she was still at the forefront of his mind.

Pinched brows aimed at him. Worried eyes, too.

"What's going on?" Leo glanced at the envelopes in Bryan's hand. "Is there something in the mail I need to know about?"

"No." He was on his own with this. Like he always had been. Like he'd always wanted to be. He never should've contemplated a deviation. "I'll fill you in later if anything becomes important."

He made for the upstairs staircase. Once he was out of view, he ran, taking the steps two at a time, pounding out the motions until he was behind the closed door of the office and leaning against the hard wood.

He was done. So fucking done with life and work and people.

The mail crunched in his closing fist as devastation seared a scorching trail through his veins. Every inch of him was out of control—his mind, his pulse, his tingling limbs.

He'd never needed something more than he did right now. And for the life of him, he didn't know what that something was. He only knew there was a hole in his chest. A massive, gaping crater, screaming to be filled.

He couldn't breathe through it. Couldn't think around the pain of it.

Everything was closing in—his mistakes, his insecurities. Every little thing he hated about his existence bore down on him with enough force to crush him.

Nothing gave him hope.

Not. One. Thing.

All he had was the dizzying punishment of all the mistakes he'd made.

He rushed toward the desk, grabbed a fresh envelope from the drawer and scrawled *Pamela* across the front. Those six letters were a death sentence.

No. They'd been a life sentence. Years upon years of unwanted sterile independence.

He transferred the newspaper clipping into the unripped envelope, making sure not to read the words demanding his attention, then encapsulated the information by sealing the back. He stood staring at the name, hating it, his anger building, growing.

He tore his attention away and scoured the perfect alignment on the desk. The pens, Post-Its, and stationery items all had their own place, their own function in the world. While he remained in limbo, stuck thinking about what he was good for.

In one harsh swipe of his arm he sent everything flying, the symmetry transforming into a scattered mess on the floor. The destruction brought relief, the tiniest flicker of havoc sating his self-loathing.

He did it again, this time pulling the drawer from the desk and throwing it across the room. And again, with the second drawer. And again, with the filing trays.

His blood raced with dizzying speed, the lightheaded delirium righting some of his wrongs.

Most, but not all.

Ella still stared back at him from his mind. Taunting him. Reminding him of his biggest mistake. He never should've touched her. Never should've given a shit. Because now she was stuck in his head. Unable to get out.

All he wanted was for her to get out.

To leave him alone.

To stop torturing him with the one thing he wanted but nobody could ever give him.

"*Fuck.*" His shout echoed off the walls.

He had to find a way out of this. To make his head stop pounding. He spun around, his gaze catching on the bookshelf, the parallel lines of immaculate book spines taunting him with their equilibrium.

"Fuck you," he spat.

Fuck their easy existence and harmonious balance.

Fuck their effortlessness and their calm.

Fuck everything and everyone, because he couldn't take it anymore.

Breaths heaved from his lungs. His limbs ached. His forehead heated with sweat.

"*Fuck. You.*" He stormed toward the bookshelf and gripped the heavy wood in his hands. Then in one effortless pull, he created more destruction.

CHAPTER SIXTEEN

$\mathcal{P}$amela raised her gaze to the person walking into the deserted cafe. "What can I get—" The words died on her lips, the familiar face bringing memories she eagerly tried to bury.

"Hi, Pamela." The blonde gave a half-hearted smile as she clutched a large wicker basket in her hand. "I'm Cassie from Shot of Sin."

"I know. We've met before." The woman was T.J.'s wife and a regular participant at the Vault.

"Sometimes we're not easily recognizable with our clothes on." The faux tilt of her lips increased.

"I suppose so." Pamela grabbed the portafilter from the coffee machine and dumped the used puck into the refuse chute. "What can I get for you?"

"Actually, I've got something for you." Cassie raised the basket and placed it on the counter. "This is yours."

"Why?" She paused the cleaning routine and scoped the contents of the basket from the corner of her eye. Inside lay an array of different items. Two bottles of wine. Chips. Bar nuts. A small bottle of vodka. Along with other things hidden beneath.

"I hoped you might be able to tell me the answer to that. Bryan asked me to deliver it to you."

"Bryan?" She raised a disbelieving brow. "He asked you to deliver me a basket of goodies?" The same Bryan who had been nicknamed for his brutality? The same Bryan who told her their time together was over? "Sorry. I think you've got the wrong person."

The woman broke eye contact.

"Why are you really here, Cassie?" She shoved the portafilter back into the machine and slid along the counter, meeting the woman face to face. "We both know he didn't send you here."

There was a beat of silence while T.J.'s wife turned a bright shade of pink. "Wow." She gave an awkward chuckle. "I thought this would've played out a little longer than five seconds."

"Bryan playing Santa is as far-fetched as it gets." Pamela struggled to keep her tone friendly.

"I guess. I just thought things between the two of you may have been different."

It was Pamela's turn to crumple under the burn of reddening cheeks. "Nope. You're wrong there, too." She glanced away, meeting Kim's gaze as she strode from the kitchen. "Bryan has no need to get back in contact with me."

"That's not entirely true." Cassie reached into the basket and pulled out a pristine envelope. "He wanted you to have this."

"I'm sorry, I don't bel—"

"Look, it even has your name on it. It's a refund for your membership. He wanted to make sure you were reimbursed."

Pamela crossed her arms over her chest, determined not to buy what she was selling, even though her heart wanted to. The only communication she'd had from Bryan was a lone, emotionless text. He hadn't mentioned what they'd shared or how he felt. He'd only spoken about her books. The damn cancer reminders.

"I promise he wanted you to have this." Cassie handed it over. "He just may have planned to mail it to you. That's all. The basket was an excuse for me to see you."

"And why would you want to do that?" She ignored the offering as Kim came up beside her, hovering close.

Cassie eyed them both, appearing more fragile than deceptive. "Have you got time to talk?"

"Not really. I'm working." She ignored the empty cafe and the fact it was less than thirty minutes from closing.

"*Please.*" It wasn't a request. It was a plea. "It's important."

"Hear her out." Kim nudged her elbow. "You're not going to sleep tonight if you send her away. Listen to what she has to say, and we'll deal with it from there."

"It won't take long," Cassie added.

Pamela closed her eyes, silently praying for strength. It wouldn't need to take more than five seconds to cause mayhem. She'd already hovered on the precipice. The last few weeks had drained her. She constantly analyzed what they'd shared and what she could've done differently. She couldn't stop thinking that there'd been more. More emotion and affection. More connection sizzling under the surface.

Yes, she'd thought the same thing about Lucas, but once he'd passed, those feelings had, too. The reality of their marriage had bled into her memories, allowing her to see how wrong she'd been to expect anything more than friendship and sex from her husband. He'd been explicit. Not only in his words, but in his actions. He hadn't wanted anything from her. Not love. Not affection. Just someone to care for him in his final months. And not once had he wavered.

But with Bryan, she couldn't let go.

Everything between them was different. He contradicted the space he tried to place between them by selflessly pleasuring her, by listening to her past marriage problems, by taking the books that served as a painful reminder of Lucas and giving them away respectfully. He'd flirted with her, laughed, joked, bought wine and dinner. He'd taken her out. He'd desired her.

And those kisses. Every brush and sweep of his tongue had told a story about something more than sex.

"Whatever happened between you two, he's not coping, Pamela."

That made her eyes open and her heart climb to her throat. "What do you mean?"

"He had a scare today." Cassie straightened to her full height. "A panic attack. A complete meltdown. Or something similar. And he won't talk to any of us about it."

The heavy doses of affection for a man she'd tried to forget came rushing back in a torrential flood. "A panic attack?"

Cassie sighed. "It might not seem like a big deal, but for Bryan—"

"No. I get it." He was bound by control. Entirely guarded. If he'd broken, she knew it must be due to something unfathomably horrible. "What happened?" She didn't want to care, but she did. She cared so much her chest fractured a little.

"He left a work meeting early, which wasn't unexpected with his recent mood. He's been grumpier than usual since he canceled the demonstration night."

He'd canceled? Her insides grated over exposed heartstrings.

"You didn't know?" Cassie scrutinized her.

"No." Pamela shook her head. "But I'm nobody to him. There's no reason I should've known."

"I thought the two of you were close. Shay told me he had dinner at your apartment and took you to a bar. To him, that's—"

"Our time together was an effort to convince me to be his demo assistant. That's all. Nothing more."

"Right..." Cassie straightened. "I just thought—"

"Maybe something happened with his mother." She was sick of the speculation. Each question only made her stupidity more apparent. "He had a lot on his mind about his family."

"He told you about them?" Cassie frowned.

"Only about his mother's cancer. Maybe she took a turn, and he isn't taking it well." She shrugged, becoming increasingly overwhelmed with the layers of confusion and annoyance beaming back at her.

"He told you his mother has cancer?"

"Yeah... Why?" She shot a glance at Kim, wordlessly asking for emotional backup. "Doesn't she?"

"I don't know. Bryan has never spoken to me about his family. And from what T.J.'s mentioned, he hasn't brought up his parents in years."

"Oh..." Her mouth formed a circle that cemented in place.

"Yeah, *oh*. You seem to be the only person he's opened up to in a really long time."

"He didn't open up." The tiny glimpse of insight hadn't been anything remotely monumental. "It was a brief mention."

"A brief mention that his mom has cancer?" Cassie raised her brows. "Pamela, believe me, if he even mentioned his parents, he was opening up. He doesn't share information about his past. He barely shares anything at all."

The woman sighed and relaxed her worried expression. "Like I was saying, he left the meeting early and retreated to the office where he's been hibernating for weeks. Five minutes later, we hear a huge crash and rush upstairs to find him tearing the place apart. There were books and files everywhere. The desk had been cleared with everything shoved to the floor. Including this."

Cassie handed over the envelope again, and this time Pamela took it. "Is he okay?"

"Physically, yes. But mentally? Emotionally? No." She shook her head. "I don't think he is. Not at all. But he won't talk to us. So, that's why I'm here. While the two of you were spending time together, he was happy."

"He told you that?"

Cassie released a huff of laughter. "No. Like I said, Bryan doesn't open up. We have to watch and take subtle hints. He started smiling instead of bearing his usual scowl. He was joking around a lot more, too. Leo and T.J. tracked his unusual behavior, and you were their conclusion." Cassie paused, probably waiting for a reaction Pamela wasn't willing to give. "You're the only one who's been close with him lately. Which is why I thought, if I came here and begged, maybe you'd speak to him."

Kim cleared her throat, the noise a subtle warning not to take the bait.

"Look, I understand your position and the concern." Pamela shot a look at her sister, then returned her focus to Cassie. "But what Bryan wants is for me to stay away. He made that clear."

"Are you sure? Telling you about his mother is a huge move for him. It's more than he's ever given me, and I've been his friend for years."

"Cassie, he literally slept with me and five seconds later told me our association was over. Five seconds," she repeated. "Maybe even two."

The woman winced.

"See?" She slid back to the coffee machine to keep her hands busy. "I'm sorry I can't help you."

"You won't even try?"

"Why is she obligated to?" Kim grated. "He discarded her like garbage."

"Don't—" Pamela pressed her lips tight, breathing through the need to defend him. Kim was right. But her stupid, idiotic heart didn't like hearing the truth from someone else.

"You like him." Cassie's expression softened, the friendship turning to compassion.

"Understatement." Kim scoffed.

"*Kim.*" She scowled at her sister. "Go finish up out back."

"Sorry. Was that supposed to be a secret?"

No. But it was personal. She didn't want Cassie sliding her into the Brute-groupie category, even though that was exactly where she needed to be. "Give me a minute, okay?"

Her sister sighed and made for the kitchen doors.

"I'm sorry. I didn't mean to make this harder on you." Cassie's voice held sincerity. "If it makes you feel any better, I think you're the reason he's been in seclusion for the last few weeks. He's showing signs of heartbreak."

"Pfft. I'm not convinced he has a heart at all."

Cassie's lips thinned into a sad smile. "Do you really believe that?"

Yes.

No.

Christ, she didn't know what to believe anymore. "I think you need to ask him about his family. Maybe then he'll talk to you about his mother."

"Okay." Cassie gave a solemn nod. "But I still think he'd really appreciate seeing you."

"If he needs me, he knows where to find me."

"You've gotta understand, a man like Bryan won't ask for help in words. He's not going to blurt it out. What he's doing is showing how badly he needs someone, and the four of us—Shay, Leo, T.J., and myself—aren't good enough. He needs you."

"This isn't fair." If he'd made a mistake and wanted to see her again, he needed to come crawling back. Not the other way around.

"He's a good man, Pamela. He's one of the best. He just doesn't like to show it."

"I know." She'd figured that out herself, which had made his rejection all the harder to bear. He was a great guy, who shared a sexual attraction with her, and still he preferred to be alone.

Cassie backtracked toward the door. "Well, if you change your mind, or want to talk, you can always find me at the club."

"Wait." Pamela grabbed the envelope and rushed around the counter. "I don't want this."

"Then give it back to him. Or rip it up. Either way, I don't want it either." She continued onto the sidewalk. "It was nice seeing you."

Cassie gave a gentle finger-wave, then walked out of view, leaving numbness in her wake.

There was no point running after her. There was no strength or energy.

"Goddamn it." Instead, she pulled the cafe doors shut and flicked over the closed sign.

"You're thinking about going to see him, aren't you?" Kim spoke from the kitchen.

"I can't help it." She rested her head against the glass. "If he's going through something..."

"What?" The swinging kitchen doors whooshed open. "What are you going to do for him?"

"I don't know." She turned and dragged her feet back to the coffee machine. "What if Cassie's right? What if he needs me?"

"Pamela." Her name was a placation.

"I know. I know." She pulled the basket toward her and peeked inside. "You think I'm doing the same thing I did with Lucas."

Kim approached, meeting her gaze from the other side of the counter. "Aren't you?"

"It's different."

"How?"

The one-word question required a far bigger answer. One she wasn't sure she could convey with conviction when everything was uncertain.

"Pamela? Explain it to me. Make me understand why you're doing this to yourself again."

"Because this time it was real," she admitted. "With Bryan, it wasn't just about hoping for more. I could actually feel it. I could've sworn he felt the same way."

She placed the envelope back in the basket.

"You were wrong before. You thought the same about Lucas."

"No. I expected the same from Lucas. But I never felt it, and he never once showed it. I stupidly thought he owed me his affection after everything I did for him. I became infatuated with the thought of us being in love. I know that now."

"And maybe in a few years' time, you'll have the hindsight to explain this situation, too."

Pamela cringed. She didn't want to think about Bryan for years. Not if she couldn't be with him.

"I want you to be happy." Kim gave a half-hearted smile. "After everything you've been through, you deserve someone who adores you."

"Then what should I do?"

"We should upgrade your standard pity party into something sponsored by your sexy club. Look." She pulled out one of the bottles from the basket. "We've got vodka."

"And wine."

"Two bottles." Kim waggled her brows. "And your light ass wouldn't even need one." She continued looking through the basket, her fingers pausing on the envelope. "Do you mind if I take a look? I've always wanted to know how much you pay to get laid."

Pamela rolled her eyes. "Go for it." She was curious to find out the monetary value herself. What price had he placed on her broken heart? Had he refunded her membership for the exact number of months she wouldn't attend? Or would he add more insult to her emotional injuries by giving her added compensation?

Kim carefully opened the back and pulled out a slip of paper, the piece no bigger than a business card. "Are you sure there's supposed to be a refund in here?"

"That's what Cassie said." She pressed onto the tips of her toes, trying to catch a glimpse of the contents.

"Well, this definitely isn't a check." Kim placed the paper back inside the envelope and handed it over. "Take a look."

It was a standard size, nothing special, apart from her full first name scribbled on the front. There was no nickname this time. And there was no check inside, either. Not even cash.

She retrieved the scrap of paper and felt the blood rush from her face. "A funeral notice..."

Her heart squeezed, tighter and tighter until she couldn't take it anymore. She blinked through her rapidly blurring vision to read the heartbreaking words resting in her palm.

MUNRO, *Pamela Sue of Tampa aged 55 years.*

Dearly loved wife of Raymond Thomas Munro. Mother of Bryan Munro. Cherished sister to Andrew and Kylie, and aunt to Silvia, Tyler, Jackson, and Tera.

Relatives and friends are respectfully invited to attend a funeral service for Pamela, which will be held in the chapel at 17 Day Street on the 1st of May, commencing at 10 a.m. to be followed by interment in the cemetery.

No flowers by request. Donations to your preferred cancer charity appreciated.

"His mom," she whispered. That's why he'd always called her Ella. "She must've died weeks ago. Around the same time I ignored his text message." Guilt and regret bubbled inside her, coming out in the form of a dry sob.

He'd reached out. He'd wanted a shoulder. And she'd ignored him.

"Hey, now. Don't get crazy." Kim came around the counter. "I'm sure he's fine."

"But he's not. Didn't you hear what Cassie said? He's falling apart and won't even talk to his friends about it. They don't even know his mother died."

"And what makes you think he'll talk to you? You're only going to get hurt."

Too late. She was already straddling heartache and limbo. "I need to see him."

"Sweetie..." Kim placed a gentle hand on her elbow. "Please don't."

"You know I have to do this. I can't keep questioning myself. Either way, I have to get answers." She grabbed her handbag from under the register. "Would you mind closing up for me?"

"Only if you call as soon as you finish talking to him." Kim placed her hands on her hips. "And grant me permission to knee-cap him if he upsets you."

"He's grieving—"

"Kneecaps or no deal."

"Fine. You can do whatever you like if this turns sour." She'd deal with the possibility of having to lie to her sister later. For now, she had to get to the club. To ease her pain, and hopefully his. "I'll call you as soon as I'm done."

CHAPTER SEVENTEEN

Bryan stared at the mess once known as the work office. He'd lost his mind. Momentarily. Now the remnants of their once tidy work space lay scattered across the floor in a mangled heap that mimicked his life.

All because of a death notice.

A death notice he couldn't fucking find.

"It has to be here somewhere." The new envelope was missing. The one he'd written on. Those six letters to name the person who left his life long ago, but shaped every decision he'd ever made. She was the reason he'd never had a relationship. She'd created his paranoia over love and commitment, and molded him into the man who refused to let down his guard.

All for what? Stubborn pride? Superiority? To continue a fight with his parents, when the assholes didn't even know they were still at war?

They never gave a shit about the years he'd spent distancing himself from others in retaliation to what they'd put him through. They didn't care enough to pay attention.

The ongoing barrage of reminders made him want to tear apart the office all over again. He wanted to destroy everything. Most of all, his mother. But evidently, she was already dead, and probably looking up from hell with just as much disdain for him as she always had.

"It's not in here, man. Maybe Shay or Cassie thought it was rubbish."

Leo kicked at a splayed book on the floor. "What was in the envelope, anyway?"

He huffed out a breath. "Nothing." He wouldn't check the bin for a third time when the first two attempts came up empty.

"You lost your shit looking for an envelope with nothing in it?" T.J. shot a glance at Leo, the two of them sharing a silent communication.

"Yeah, I guess I did." He strode for the door, still incapable of revealing the bullshit clogging his veins. He couldn't talk about it. He didn't even understand it. "I've gotta get out of here. I'll clean this mess up later."

They didn't stop him. Didn't say a word. Their kid gloves were well and truly in place, with neither of them willing to give him the verbal beatdown he deserved for destroying their space. Shay and Cassie hadn't chastised him when they'd walked in on his meltdown, either.

He fled down the hall, then took the stairs to Shot of Sin two at a time. He should've run. Instead, he decided to hide. He practically jogged across the empty dance floor, unlocked the Vault door, and descended the next staircase in darkness.

He didn't bother with the lights. He hoped he'd fall. A few broken bones and a heavy sedative seemed preferable to the punishing void consuming him.

His mother was dead, and the web-thin ties connecting him to the rest of his family had been severed. The news should've brought delirious joy. Somehow, it didn't. Now, there was another layer to his lack of worth. Another brick to add to the wall around him.

He reached the bottom of the stairs intact and slammed his way through the next pin-code door until he reached the newbie lounge. After a slap against the light switch, he continued into the main room, then straight behind the bar.

Instinct had him reaching for a bottle of scotch, dragging the soothing liquid to stand on the counter in front of him. He stared at the alcohol, his body begging for a taste, his mind pleading for the escapism.

He wouldn't be defeated.

This time, he'd savor the new invisible scars his parents had inflicted on him with pure lucidity. He'd relish the pain. He'd make the torment solidify his strength and wash away the momentary lapse when he'd stupidly decided to give a fuck about someone.

He became infatuated with the bottle, entranced by the possible solace for minutes. Maybe hours. Then the main entrance door squeaked and he closed his eyes, not wanting to face whoever came to break his solitude.

"I thought I'd find you down here."

Cassie.

Out of all the people to disturb him, it had to be her.

They should've sent Shay. He'd have no hesitation in giving Leo's girlfriend a piece of his mind. But Cassie was different. She was soft. Kind. A fucking burst of unwanted sunshine.

He opened his eyes and visually defiled the scotch. "This is the only time I'm allowed down here, remember?"

"I was under the impression the hiatus was your choice."

"My choice?" Maybe it was. If only he hadn't pissed off the women of the Vault in the first place. If only he'd sent one of the security team after Ella that night in the parking lot instead of indulging his unprecedented interest in someone of the opposite sex.

"I thought you were hiding from something," Cassie hedged. "Or someone."

He squeezed the neck of the bottle, not appreciating her accuracy.

It wasn't that he was hiding from Ella. He knew he wouldn't see her again. Instead, he supposed he was withdrawing from anyone or anything that reminded him of his mistakes.

"I just want to be left alone."

Slowly, she came toward the bar, her eyes bleeding with concern as she took a seat on the stool opposite him. "I went to see Pamela today."

Every muscle snapped rigid. The anger and self-loathing fled under the weight of panic. Pure fear. "Why?"

"I thought I'd make things easier on you and drop off her refund."

"Thanks," the word grated through his teeth. "But I could've done it. It was only a case of writing a check and putting it in the mail. I wasn't going to see her."

Cassie shrugged. "I figured as much. That's why I knew it was the right decision. We were all concerned that things didn't end amicably."

He narrowed his eyes, giving a voiceless warning.

"Not between you and her," she quickly amended. "Between the Vault itself. You know how much we pride ourselves on the club's reputation."

His jaw ached under the pressure of his clenched molars. "I hope you were smart enough to mind your own business, Cass."

She broke eye contact, her chin hitching in the slightest show of remorseful defiance.

"*Cassie?*" His blood surged.

Her cheeks turned a warm shade of pink, and the delicate column of her throat rolled with a heavy swallow. "You haven't been yourself lately. I thought she was the cause."

"But now you know better." It should've been a statement. He should've spoken with conviction. Instead, he was stuck sounding like a jackass as he waited for her to spill whatever news she had about the woman who hijacked his masculinity.

"Now I know something special happened between the two of you. You like her, Bryan. I know you do. And when I handed over the check you wrote, I could tell she was upset by the formality."

There were many things to hate about her statement, but his focus pinpointed the abnormality. "I didn't write a check, Cassie. I hadn't gotten around to it."

Her eyes met his, her brows knitting tight.

Something was wrong with this situation. Something his intuition had already begun to digest with nauseous anticipation.

"I found the envelope you addressed to her. It was on the floor in the office."

On the floor.

In his office.

There were no words. Only panic. Only volatile anger.

"Bryan?"

His lungs heaved with each breath. His limbs shook. He gripped the counter behind him with his free hand, that liquor bottle burning a hole through his other palm. "It wasn't a fucking check."

The bottle threatened to slide from his grip. He tightened his hold, clutching the glass to stop himself from throwing it against the wall.

Ella had his mother's death notice.

"Did you see her open it?"

She shook her head.

Maybe there was still time to get the envelope before it was opened. To reclaim his privacy.

"Go get it." He glared to reiterate the demand.

"I'm sorry, Bryan. I thought I was doing the right thing."

"No, you didn't. You didn't give a shit about the right thing. You only wanted to sate your curiosity."

She cringed. "You've never made friends with a woman before. Not like this. At least, not that I've ever known. And you were happy. Then, all of a sudden, you cancel the demo night and start falling into a spiraling depression. I wanted to know what happened. We all needed to make sure you were okay."

He stepped toward her side of the bar, raising to his full height. "Get it back. *Now*."

"I..." She cleared her throat. "It was almost closing time. She wouldn't be there anymore."

"Then find her. Get in your car and don't come back until you have it."

Her eyes glistened, the slight sheen of approaching tears kicking him square in the balls. *Fucking hell.* He swung away, facing the back of the bar, the bottle now a serious temptation in his closed fist.

If he started drinking, he wouldn't stop. Not today. Not tomorrow.

"What was in the envelope? What's so important?" Her voice shook. "And why didn't she know the demonstration night was canceled? What happened between you two? One minute you were dating. The next you were—"

"We weren't dating." He hung his head.

"I disagree." Her voice continued to waver, but there was backbone in her words. "You told her things. You cared for her. I didn't need to see the two of you together to come to that conclusion. I've heard parts of what happened. You went to her cafe, and her house. You brought food and wine. Then a few days later, you're taking her to a bar. How isn't that dating?"

He didn't know. He'd never dated before.

"You chased her, Bryan. You went after her because you like her. You may have blamed it on a million different reasons, but you enjoyed her company and you wanted to keep—"

"Enough."

"No. You need to realize—"

"*I fucking realize, okay?*" His head pounded through the admission, each heartbeat bringing the threat of a stroke. "I know."

"So, you realize you like her?"

Christ, did she want him to carve the declaration into his flesh? "I *realize*."

"And you're going to let her get away?"

"She's already gone." He shrugged. "There's nothing I can do."

"You pushed her away. But I don't think it was hard enough to be permanent. You could get her back."

Why? For what reason other than to drag her down to his heartless level? "I don't want her back." He only wanted to know what she'd said. How she'd said it. And what she'd looked like when those words had left her lips.

"Why?"

He scoffed. There were a hundred and one reasons. A thousand. Many more. "Because it's a waste of time. Everyone walks away in the end."

"How can you say that? Especially after everything T.J. and I went through. We went to hell and back, and now look at us."

He should've clarified—everyone walked away from *him*. His parents. His aunts and uncles. His cousins.

He turned to face her, taking in the determined set of her shoulders. "Cass, T.J. tried like hell to leave you behind."

"You know that's a lie." Her eyes sparked with defensive rage. "He was only doing it to protect me."

The inside door squeaked again, making his exhaustion peak. If Shay added to this bullshit, he'd lose his fucking mind. More than he already had.

"You need to get my envelope back." He jerked his chin toward the internal door to the upstairs staircase. "And take whoever that is with you. I'm not interested in company."

A curvy figure came to stand in the doorway to the newbie lounge, the familiarity setting his vision to flame.

Fuck. Me.

He stumbled back to the counter and gripped the scotch like a lifeline. His throat threatened to close. His lungs demanded more air.

Cassie swiveled on the stool, the name she spoke slicing through him like a sword through silk. "Pamela."

"Hey." The response was the sweetest form of torture. A punishment he couldn't keep his gaze from.

"What are you doing here?" The question was born from habit. He already knew the answer. He just needed to fill the void of restricting silence. "I thought you weren't coming back."

"I heard you had a bad day." She held up the envelope in her hand. "I read about it, too. But don't worry, I overheard you say you didn't want company. I promise I won't stay long." She was fragile—her eyes, her lips. Even her skin seemed like porcelain. Her attention gently raked over him, tearing through skin, ripping through flesh. "Can we talk?"

He couldn't deny her. He couldn't watch her walk away again. Not yet, anyway. "Give us a minute, Cass."

"Okay." She gave a hollow nod and slid from the stool. "Please make sure you don't run out of here without saying goodbye."

He couldn't make any promises. Not that it would matter. By the time he was ready to flee, Cassie would have Shay, T.J., and Leo positioned at the exits, ensuring he couldn't escape unnoticed. "We'll catch up later."

"Thank you." She strode for Ella, giving the other woman's shoulder a squeeze as she passed before disappearing into the newbie lounge.

The room closed in around him, those eyes reading him and finding the truth.

He couldn't do this. Not today.

He cracked the cap of the scotch and took a long pull. The burn lessened the emotional carnage staring him in the face, but one taste wasn't enough. He feared the whole bottle wouldn't dint the surface of the shit-storm about to descend.

"Did you tell them?" Slowly, she approached the bar, her work pants stained with coffee, her white button-down wrinkled at the ends. He loved that she wasn't picture-perfect. Mascara smudged her eyelids. If she'd worn lipstick today, it was nowhere to be seen. Not that she needed it. Her lips had always been her most endearing feature. Hypnotic and too damn influential.

"What's there to tell?"

"You've kept the information to yourself this whole time?" She rounded the bar, stopping a few feet away.

"This whole time?" He gave a harsh laugh and downed another gulp of awaiting solace. "I guess I enjoy my privacy too much."

"Then I assume you didn't want me to have this." She placed the envelope on the counter, her hand lingering against the name written on the front.

"Cassie had no business going to see you."

She winced, the slightest furrow marring her brow. Her pain was more torturous than the threat of Cassie's tears. Ella's discomfort tore at him, demanding apology, which he beat back with another quick pull from the bottle.

"You should slow down with the alcohol." She eyed the sloshing liquid. "You're going to feel crappy tomorrow. There's no point making it worse."

"There are only two things I need at the moment, and one of them is booze." Lucidity was no longer an option with her here. She was still fuckable. Still irresistible.

"And the other?"

"Sex."

It was a taunt. He couldn't help it. Making the conversation interesting saved his mind from the dark and dreary cave of reality. And, truth be told, even though they were discussing his mother, he wasn't even thinking of her. There was only Ella.

"Well, you've got a bar full of booze." She glanced around the room, probably searching for a diversion. "And you've already made it clear I can't help with the other matter. So, I guess you want me to leave."

He couldn't tell if she was itching for a fight or an excuse to run. He could never tell with her. "I'm not going to kick you out. Feel free to pull up a stool and take a front row seat to my impending alcoholism." He swung the bottle to his lips, watching her as he took another long pull. "You'll probably enjoy the show after all the shit I've put you through."

"What shit?"

He released a breath of a laugh. "I don't need to paint you a picture. We were both there."

"Oh, no." She shook her head and crossed her arms over her chest. "That's not what I meant. I'm just trying to figure out which shitty moment you're referring to."

This time his laugh was audible. "I appreciate the honesty."

"I'm not going to coddle you." She approached, her steps still slow and cautious. "But I do think you need to add some water to your intake." She reached out, her warm fingers brushing his to grip the bottle neck. "Let me take this."

She kept their hands fused, their eyes, too. "Please." She tilted the scotch, inching it toward her chest. One hard tug had it slipping through his fingers, and she placed the bottle gently on the bar beside them.

He could give up the liquor if he didn't lose the heat of her. Denying himself both didn't seem fair.

"Bryan..."

The whisper of his name brought pain. Nobody had ever spoken to him like that. Not without desire or need. She was selflessly here, dealing with his shit, and he couldn't understand why.

"Why do you care?" He inched closer, his thigh brushing hers, the zing of atomic attraction washing away the fucked-up reasons that drove him to drink in the first place.

She didn't retreat, only hitched her chin higher, refusing to look away. "You need water."

"It doesn't even rank in the top twenty things I need."

"Really?" This time she stepped back, and he countered with an arm around her waist, keeping them close.

"Yeah. Really."

She elbowed him, soft but blunt. "You're looking for a distraction, which will only be temporary. You need to talk this out. If not to me, then your friends. Tell them about the cancer. Tell them about the funeral."

"I didn't go."

She balked, her lashes rapidly beating in a show of shock.

The seconds of silence were punishing. For once, he didn't want her thinking he was a callous asshole. He didn't enjoy the judgment staring back at him. He wanted to be better. To be worthy. "I didn't know about it. They didn't tell me."

"They didn't tell you when they were holding the funeral of your own mother?"

No. For the first time, someone in his family had heard his voice, even though his request had been a painful backlash. They always found his weak spot, no matter how he acted.

"They didn't tell me she was dead."

Her expression fell, her throat churning over a heavy swallow. Breath by agonizing breath, her devastation reigniting his own. "When did you find out?"

"A few hours before you did."

Her gorgeous face bleached, all color and compassion. She turned away, gripped the counter, and released a long breath before sucking in another lungful of air.

"Ella?" He placed the bottle beside her and ran his palm over her arm. "What's going on? Why are you upset?"

"Why?" She slid farther along the bar. "I'm devastated for you. You don't deserve this. They put you through enough already. I don't understand..."

He became lost in her words and the tears now staining her cheeks. She was crying. Not because of something he'd done. Those tears seemed to be due to something she felt.

For him.

She cared?

About him?

"There's no point crying a river, sweetheart. It's not like I want to bring her back. My mother is exactly where she deserves to be."

"Oh, God." Her eyes widened. "Don't say that."

"Why? I didn't kill her. I'm just not sorry she's gone."

"You're grieving, Bryan."

"Not for her." He shook his head. He felt something, but it definitely wasn't grief for the woman who'd birthed him. "I swear I couldn't give a shit about her passing."

"Then what happened earlier today?"

Earlier today? He ran over the day's events, pinpointing the only thing worthy of making the rumor mill. "Fucking Cassie. What did she say?"

"She was worried about you."

"Well, for the sake of my sanity, can we please ignore every other motherfucker on the face of the planet for the time being?"

"*I'm* worried about you."

Jesus Christ. Where the hell did he put the scotch?

"I don't know what else to tell you." He ran a hand through his hair, unable to explain his confusion. He'd never given a shit about his mother. He didn't care about her death. It was something else. Something he couldn't pinpoint.

"When Lucas died, I cried for days, even though we were never close." Her voice came in slow, soft bursts. The depressing lilt reeked of despair. "It wasn't until a week later that I realized I was grieving more for what could've been. I was hurting because the dreamy relationship I fought for us to have would never happen. I'd tried so hard to get him to love me, never giving up hope it would happen one day. Then he was gone. And so were all the fairytale dreams." She lowered her gaze, staring at her feet. "I grieved for what could've been. Not the man who died... If that makes sense."

He froze, her explanation sinking down to his marrow.

It was such simple insight. So easily spoken. Yet, it was exactly how he felt. He didn't give a fuck about his egg donor. The thing tearing him apart was what he'd missed. What most people took for granted.

A pained laugh escaped, the action dislodging the ache behind his ribs. He couldn't fathom the brilliance of this woman. He didn't know why she knew his thoughts, or how she'd become abnormally insightful. He just loved the fact she was here, with him, pushing away the hollow feeling that no longer dictated his chest.

"Did I overstep?" She glanced up at him through thick lashes, the sight of her concern depriving him of words. "I'm sorry... I should go."

He couldn't make her stay.

He *shouldn't*.

"Again," she added softly, "I'm sorry for what you're going through. It gets easier. I promise." She made for the end of the counter, her retreat encouraging the return of his hollow torment.

He needed her here. And yet, he didn't have any way to encourage her to stick around.

There were no bonus points for enduring his company. He didn't have the kindhearted nature of T.J. or the smooth sophistication of Leo.

Only a shitty attitude and an even shittier outlook on life.

"Don't." That was all he had. One word. One pathetic, timid syllable.

She paused, her back to him, her hands limp at her sides. He could feel her slipping away, moving closer and closer toward an escape even though she remained in place.

"Stay a while." He came up behind her and wove a hand around her hip.

The only asset in his arsenal was sex.

Carnal finesse.

The gift of orgasms.

She gave an audible swallow, and he fought the need to cringe.

Everything about her spoke of discomfort—her stiff spine, her rushed breathing, her silence.

She turned, her hip brushing his crotch with painful effect. The slight connection had his cock filling with rapidly-pulsing blood. Those dark lashes beating up at him made coherence difficult.

"You want a distraction?"

"I want you." He pulled her tight against him and clasped the back of her neck with his free hand.

"What about your insurance policy?"

He scoffed. "Turns out all bets are off when you find out your mother is six feet under."

She cringed. Maybe she didn't appreciate his callousness, or sensed his lie. But the evidence stood thick and heavy between them, his dick taking center stage as he leaned in to slant his mouth over hers.

The kiss was utter finesse—smooth swipes of lips and a gentle dance of tongues. He wanted to tattoo this moment on her soul. To engrave himself in her memory, like she'd carved a hole in his.

"Stop." She placed her hands on his chest. "I still don't think this is a good idea."

The rejection stung deeper than it should have. "Why? It's not like my track record has provided anything but satisfaction."

She scowled. Scoffed. The two reactions kneeing him in the conscience.

"*Fuck*." He stepped back. "I'm sorry. I'm shitty company today... As opposed to every other day, right?"

He waited for her to retaliate. For those eyes to continue spitting fire.

"I never minded your company, Bryan."

"Skip the placations, sweetheart. We both know I pissed you off more often than not. It's what I do."

Her shoulders slumped, his words defeating her in a way he didn't understand. "You're nicer than you think you are."

"Then sleep with me," he begged. The sorry sack of shit he'd turned into pleaded to get laid. Not by anyone. Only her. Only because he presumed he'd never get the opportunity again. "Neither one of us has anything to lose."

Her smile was fake. Maybe even reminiscent. "Bryan, if I tell you what's going on in my mind, it will reinstate your insurance policy."

"Then don't." He slid toward her, smashing his lips to hers, lifting her off the ground. "Don't say a word."

"I can't keep this to myself." Those determined hands found his chest again, pushing. "If we don't see each other again, I want to make sure this is out in the open."

She was seeing someone. Fucking someone.

Christ, he didn't want to know who.

"Bryan?"

"Yeah?" He placed her on her feet and reached for the bottle of scotch, letting the burning liquid unleash on his throat.

"You're not going to want to hear this."

He nodded, his focus on the dwindling scotch.

She was right. He was already prepared to tell her to leave without explanation. He didn't want to hear the details of who she'd hooked up with. Could it be the cowboy from the bar? Or the weak bastard who fumbled over his words out the front of her cafe? Maybe it was someone with worse qualities.

God knew she had shitty taste in men.

"All right. Let me have it." He raised the bottle again, this time holding the liquid in his mouth, letting it sauté his tongue.

"I like you."

The alcohol gagged him, choking the air from his lungs. "What?"

"When we first met, I promised I had no interest in you—not because I knew that was what you wanted to hear—I actually didn't like you. I thought your attitude was toxic and your confidence grated on my nerves. But the man I got to know is nothing like the brute everyone claims you are." She nibbled her lower lip. "I don't see that guy when I look at you. I see someone I want to spend more time with. Someone I fell for. Someone I could see myself falling in love with."

He dropped the bottle to the counter, still clutching the neck for grounding.

"Don't get angry." She held her hands up in surrender. "I know it's the last thing you want to hear. And that's why I didn't tell you the night in the parking lot. I walked away, just like you wanted me to. But I can't be with you tonight and pretend I feel differently. I can't lie by omission."

He wanted to believe everything he heard. If it wasn't for the alcohol, the nervous breakdown, and the fucked-up news about his mother, he probably could've convinced himself this wasn't a hallucination. Problem was, it seemed too coincidental to have the one thing he wanted laid out before him within accessible reach. It was too good to be true.

"Say something," she pleaded.

"Give me a second." His head spun, liquor and disorientation having their wicked way with him.

He wanted to sober up. He *needed* to sober up.

He side-stepped to the sink, snatched an empty glass from the rack, and filled it with water. Gulp after gulp, he downed one glass, then two, his impatience making the numbing intoxication a heavy liability.

"Don't worry about it." Her voice drifted. "I'll see myself out."

"*No.*" God, no. He just needed a minute.

He gripped the counter, lowered his head and breathed deep.

"It's okay. This response is better than the rage I anticipated. I thought you'd yell at me."

Because that was what he'd done in the past. It was all he knew how to do.

Focus.

He mentally repeated a suitable response, over and over, to make sure it seemed worthy. "I feel the same way."

She was quiet, deathly silent.

He glanced from the corner of his eye to find confusion staring back at him. He didn't know if he'd spoken aloud or if the mantra in his head had grown in strength.

She didn't acknowledge him. She probably didn't know what he was talking about because all the things she'd said were a figment of his imagination.

Fuck.

"Ella?" He straightened and told his insecurities to fuck off. "I feel the same way."

CHAPTER EIGHTEEN

Pamela held herself in check.

Bryan was drunk and on emotional life-support, making her blurted confession a disaster waiting to happen.

"It's your turn to say something," he whispered.

Her lips quirked, the burn of tears returning to her eyes. "I'm still trying to digest what you said."

"Why?"

"You're confused—"

"About the way I feel?" He spoke with vehemence. "No shit. I've spent the weeks trying to figure it out, and it still doesn't make sense."

All her needy insecurities latched on with energetic force. "You've been thinking about me for weeks?"

"You sound pleased to know I haven't had a lick of sleep since I last saw you." He bridged the gap between them, the tips of his shoes nudging hers. "And people think I'm the brutal one."

This time her smile flourished, spreading across her face in unmanageable enthusiasm. "You're not brutal."

"Don't go ruining my reputation, sweetheart." He backed her into the counter, his hips rocking into hers. "You've done enough to me already."

His strength seeped into her, calming the frazzled nerves and heartache. She wanted to fall deeper into him, to sink, to drown. But she couldn't. Not yet.

"Can we put this on hold for a while?"

He slid his hands into hers, entwining their fingers against her thighs. "You still think this is a reaction to grief?"

She nodded. "A little."

"That's okay." He grinned, surprising her with the impressive display. "I still think it's a drunken hallucination."

He pressed his lips to hers, stealing away the negative thoughts with his patented kissing style. He licked her thoroughly, patiently, their tongues sparring and dancing. She ran her hands along the lapels of his suit, holding him close, but a distant sound disturbed her concentration, the murmurs of conversation building with every second.

Bryan broke the kiss to glare over her shoulder. "Your cavalry has arrived."

She frowned and turned to find Leo, T.J., Cassie, and Shay striding into the main room, only to freeze in place, one after the other.

"Whoa." T.J. shot a glance at his wife. "This isn't what I expected to find."

"What *did* you expect?" Bryan caged Pamela in place from behind, one hand on the counter at either side of her hips.

"I, umm..." Cassie blushed. "I thought it was a good idea to do a welfare check. Things were tense earlier."

"We're okay." Pamela straightened, keeping the heat of Bryan tight at her back. "Everything is fine."

Cassie nodded while Shay crossed her arms over her chest.

"Cue the questions," Bryan muttered in her ear.

"Is your mom okay?" Shay asked. "Apparently, you told Pamela she was sick."

"*Shay*," Cassie hissed. "That was private."

Shit. Bryan remained quiet, his warmth turning to icy steel.

"I'm sorry." She turned in his arms. "I mentioned it to Cassie earlier. I assumed they already knew." She held her breath, waiting for his anger.

"Don't worry." He gave her a thin-lipped smile. "Shay snoops like a P.I. She would've found out sooner or later."

His easy acceptance only compiled her guilt. It also made her want to kiss the breath from his lungs.

"Is she okay?" Leo asked.

Bryan kept his focus on her, not acknowledging his friends as he announced, "She's dead."

She didn't wince. Didn't flinch. She began to think the brutal replies were the only way he knew how to respond. Maybe it was a coping mechanism, or something he'd been taught since childhood from his heartless parents.

"Oh, shit." T.J.'s voice sounded over the numerous gasps. "What happened?"

Bryan's composure fractured, his forehead creasing with deep wrinkles.

"It's okay." She could be his strength. At least, she wanted to be if he'd allow her. "Let me take care of it." She faced his friends with a sad smile. "She lost her battle with cancer at the end of April."

"April?" Shay accused. "She died last month and you couldn't tell us?"

Pamela flinched, her blood boiling over the insensitive reaction.

"Let her go," Bryan mumbled in her ear, his arm weaving around her waist. "I get too much satisfaction watching her make an ass of herself."

"Brute?" Shay snapped. "What the hell?"

"You've gotta admit, this is unfair," Leo added. "We've given you space for weeks, letting you dump the workload on our shoulders. I don't doubt you needed time, but you could've told us before today. We had no idea what was going on."

Bryan began playing with her hair, acting as though the heated conversation was a casual chit-chat. "This pretty little lady was the cause of my issues. Not my mother."

"Me?" She peered over her shoulder. "Why?"

"I told you—you were messing with my head. I couldn't concentrate. I had to bow out of dealing with customers because my public relation skills became less than stellar."

"They've never been anything to write home about," Shay muttered.

He smirked, the expression quickly fading. "I didn't find out about my mother until today."

"Oh, shit." Leo palmed his stubbled jaw. "Who the fuck does that?"

"My family," Bryan offered. "But on the bright side—one down, one to go."

They all cringed.

Leo held up his hands in warning. "Don't say shit like that. You're gonna go to hell."

"At least my family will be there to greet me, right?"

"Bryan..." Her plea whispered between them. She couldn't handle his detachment anymore. It wasn't healthy. She needed them to be alone so she could comfort him the way women do—with affection and understanding and love. Not the careless back and forth between friends.

Cassie met her gaze, her eyes questioning. "We should go back upstairs..."

"*Yes. Please,*" she mouthed, appreciating the woman's intuition. "*Thank you.*"

"Good idea. We'll give you two a few more minutes alone." T.J. placed a hand on his wife's hip and guided her toward the exit. "If you need anything..."

"I'm good." Bryan's lie was convincing. If only she didn't know better.

"Yeah." Leo nodded. "We're here, buddy. Just say the word."

The four of them filed through the entry to the newbie lounge, their footsteps fading until the deafening click of a door latch sealed her fate.

The room remained silent, the emptiness closing in on her as Bryan's heartbeat echoed into her back. She sensed he wouldn't fill the void. At least not with honesty or emotion. If she left the conversation up to him, she was certain there'd be more dark humor to mask his feelings. She craved his trust and wished he would open up to her. Even if just a little.

"You joke about things that upset you."

He nestled his forehead into her hair. "It's what I do."

"If you talk it out, it might get better." She stared across the room, knowing he'd loathe her suggestion.

"I prefer my way. It works for me." A way that kept his heartbreak hidden and slowly building. God forbid he ruined his reputation. "For now," he added. "Who knows what girly things you'll talk me into if we start spending more time together."

"Is that what you want?" She turned, becoming ensnared in the emotional depth of his eyes. There was no more dark or callous banter. He was bare, vulnerable, and oh, so beautiful. "The time together, not the girly part."

"That's what comes next, right? I've never done this before."

"That's not what I asked. I want to know what *you* want."

One side of his lips gradually kicked, his smirk building as he pressed his hips harder into hers. "In that case, I think we both know the answer."

"*Bryan*." She struggled not to laugh. "I'm serious."

He stared at her mouth, his thumb lifting to trace her lower lip with feather-light pressure. "You still want to wait?"

"That depends..."

His gaze snapped to hers. "On?"

"On whether you want me to feel secure in what's going on between us. The physical part has been easy. Why don't we give ourselves time to work on everything else?"

"You're trying to appeal to logic over my libido?" He clucked his tongue. "Stupid move, sweetheart."

It wasn't stupid. She wanted him to be of sound mind the next time they slept together. For her sake, and his. Regret was the last thing either one of them needed if he woke up tomorrow and decided he'd made a mistake. "I just thought waiting would be best."

He ignored her and leaned in to trek his lips along her jaw, to her neck, then the sensitive spot below her ear.

Alcohol. Bereavement. Heartache. She reminded herself of the aspects shaping his decisions.

She shouldn't encourage his heavenly seduction. Not when he was finally where he was supposed to be. She should hold out, for her heart's sake. For one more day. At least until morning.

"Tomorrow, you'll have more clarity. More stability." She sighed as his mouth found her collarbone, the rough scrape of beard adding a touch of friction to the exquisite softness of his kisses.

"Right."

His thigh parted hers, the rub against the crotch of her pants grazing her clit. Tingles spread through her abdomen, the tendrils of pleasure creeping higher and higher. Slowly, her brain switched gears, sliding commonsense to the sideline and yanking gratification to the forefront. She needed more touches, more kisses, more endorphins.

He pulsed his leg between hers, taunting her pussy. "More security?"

"Mmm hmm." She closed her eyes and whimpered. Hope was lost. Not one single part of her body wanted to be apart from this man. Not one finger. Not one nerve.

Rational thought became suffocated by lust.

They could work out the important stuff tomorrow.

After.

"I guess I've been wrong before." Christ, she was such an easy mark. Such a groupie.

He didn't acknowledge her surrender, only continued the delicious trail of his mouth. She undid the top button of her shirt, then the next, exposing her cleavage to his mercy.

"I've dreamed about these." He slid his hand into the cup of her bra and brushed her nipple between his fingers. "My imagination didn't do them justice."

He kissed her sternum, the curve of her breast, then yanked at her bra to suck her nipple into his mouth. Wildfire flickered to life under her ribs. Passion collided with happiness.

For one tiny moment, everything was perfect. They were synced—movements, heartbeats, intensity. Mind, body, soul.

He paid homage to her breasts. His thigh teased her pussy. Every nerve tingled under his mastery. She could almost come like this, from friction and suction.

"We better get going." He straightened and stepped back, his lust seeming to vanish in an instant while she spun from the stronghold. "Let's get out of here."

"Excuse me?" She licked her drying lips as he grabbed the bottle of scotch and placed it in a cupboard under the bar. "What just happened?"

"You don't want to have sex. So, let's go."

"But..." How did he jump from the sizzling depths of carnality, to the freezing icecaps of chastity? "What? Why?"

"Your rules."

"Wow." Her mouth gaped. "You're horrible."

A picture-perfect grin beamed back at her. "Just in control for now."

"For now?"

"Yep. It doesn't always happen around you." He fastened her shirt buttons, the composed action a physical brag about his discipline. "Did you really think I'd risk all that stability and clarity you were mumbling about?"

"Then why start?"

"I'm not a priest." He winked. "You might dictate the rules, but I know how to play the game." He grabbed her hand and dragged her forward.

"That's a really nasty thing to do." Her panties were damp. Her breasts screamed for more. "I don't want to forgive you."

"I'm drunk and emotional, remember? Go easy on me."

"You're drunk, emotional, and soon to be neutered if you don't quit dragging me around."

"Neutering me would mean coming in close contact with my dick, and that's off limits. You can't break your own rules." He kept tugging, leading her around the bar toward the cement staircase leading to the Shot of Sin parking lot. "And besides, you like holding my hand."

"I can't believe you played me." She glared through an unwanted smile. "This isn't fair."

But it was. For once, everything seemed fair, and honest, and fun. Breathing him in, feeling his strength, knowing he cared—the happiness of it was overwhelming.

He paused at the foot of the staircase, the atmosphere changing as he focused into the darkness ahead. "Ella?"

His ominous tone killed her playful heartbeat. "Yeah?"

He shot her a glance over his shoulder, his features tight. "I can't promise I won't fuck this up."

Her heart swelled, the rush of blood struggling to get through. "I know."

He gave a sharp nod and continued forward, his fingers gently squeezing hers.

"Bryan?"

"Mmm?" He kept walking, bringing them to the top of the staircase and the door leading outside.

She wrapped her arms around his waist and nuzzled her head into his neck. "I can't promise I'll walk away the next time you ask me to."

"I can handle that."

"No." She shook her head. "I mean it. I'll put all those other sex hounds to shame."

He laughed and pushed opened the door. "Come on. Let's get out of here."

"I'm serious." She followed him into the dwindling daylight. "If you ever break up with me, I'll stalk you."

His snicker was awkward.

"And if you leave me, I'll slash your tires." She swung their joined hands with delight. "After all this time, destiny has finally brought us together." She grinned as he slowed his stride, his posture stiffening. "Do you think it's time to start discussing matching tattoos?"

He stopped, his gaze taking long seconds to meet hers. He scanned her face, searching her expression.

"What's wrong?" She blinked up at him. "Are you scared of needles?"

His eyes narrowed, and he yanked her into his chest. "You're playing games with me?"

"Maybe." She chuckled. "You started it."

"I'll finish it, too." He pinned her hands behind her back and smashed his mouth to hers, punishing her with bliss.

She wiggled, not wanting to succumb a second time. "Don't start this again."

"I won't." He stared down at her, his gaze raking over her eyes, her nose, her lips. Each feature was treated to the same visual affection. "I think I changed my mind."

"About?" She gave his gorgeous face the same tender inspection, taking in the kindness of those deep blue eyes and the dark tempting lips.

"I'm not going to fuck this up, Ella."

"You know what, Bryan?" Her heart swelled again, pumping tingling blood through every inch of her, filling her with confidence. "I believe you."

EPILOGUE

*P*amela slid her bare thighs onto the bar stool, feigning relaxation even though the sensation was illusive. Whimpers and groans filled her ears, along with murmured chatter, soft laughter, and the occasional clink of a glass as Vault patrons socialized around her.

"I didn't expect to see you down here." Shay retrieved a tall glass from the clean rack. "Tequila sunrise?"

"Yes, please." On second thought... "Make that a double."

Shay eyed her with suspicion. "Nervous to be back?"

"I'm not sure." She hadn't stepped foot inside the sex club in months. Not since the night she'd vowed never to return.

Life was different now. *Everything* was different. And knowing what to expect once she walked down the dimly lit Vault staircase had become an elaborate guessing game.

"Bryan told me the two of you stopped dating." Shay continued her scrutiny as she pulled a bottle of orange juice from the fridge under the counter.

"He did?"

"I didn't get the details. He only said the first date failed with fucking brilliant efficiency, and he wouldn't be doing it again."

Pamela winced at the memory. Their meal at an exclusive restaurant had been a nightmare of awkwardness. "We didn't even make it through dinner."

"Was it that bad?"

"Yeah, it was." She could've enjoyed his monumental discomfort and considered it a sweet serve of karma, but she hadn't. He'd fumbled with the cutlery, guzzled the wine, and hadn't taken a bite of any of the extremely expensive meals. "He's not the dating type."

Shay slid the tequila sunrise across the bar but continued to grip the glass. "I gather things ended amicably if he reinstated your membership." She continued holding the alcohol hostage. "But if you being here is some form of retribution, I'm going to have to ask you to leave. I don't want any drama on his first night back."

"Drama? I'm not here to—"

"I like you." Shay lowered her voice, shooting a conspiratorial look over Pamela's shoulder as she released the glass. "Please don't make me kick you out."

"Kick who out?" Bryan's delicious, deep growl tickled her neck, the sound having the ability to burst ovaries in a ten-mile radius. "What did I miss?"

He swiveled her stool, dragging her attention to his ruggedly perfect face. His beard had been cropped, the blond strands shorter, revealing more of the man he hid beneath. She'd never get sick of staring at him, not when he looked at her with affection and ownership. Tonight, there was something else, too.

Was he nervous?

"Apparently, our break-up." She feigned a glare. "You told your friends we weren't dating anymore?"

His lush lips curved, setting off a chain reaction to transform his features into something entirely stunning, and maybe even a little sweet. "We're not."

"True." She leaned in, swiping her mouth leisurely across his. His responding growl carried into her belly, tickling all the way down to her pussy. "But I think you've given them the wrong impression."

"You're still together?" Shay shrieked, stealing the attention of the room.

Numerous people stopped what they were doing—the drinking, the kissing, the fucking—and turned to face them.

"Subtle," Bryan grated. "Real fucking subtle, Shay."

Pamela wove a hand around his neck and kept him close. She loved this man. Not that he knew it. The L-word was extremely significant to him. Without the love of his parents, he considered the emotion to be the holy grail of humanity. She didn't expect to ever hear the declaration from his lips. But she took solace in telling herself his adoration and commitment were signs of something parallel.

"Why did you give your friends the wrong impression?" she whispered.

He'd changed during their time together. Each day, he opened up a little more, sharing tidbits about his past, giving enough to satisfy her concern. Apparently, that translucent behavior ended when he came to work.

"I had to keep you to myself for as long as possible." He leaned back to stare at her. "I didn't want to keep fielding questions about us every time I took a breath. I needed it to be you and me for a while."

"What the hell is going on?" Shay slapped her hands against the bar.

"See?" he drawled. "She's a hemorrhoid we'll never get rid of."

"I am not," the bartender snapped. "You're too secretive. Maybe if you shared every once in a while."

Bryan shook his head, his nose brushing Pamela's. "I don't want to share."

"You're lucky you're cute." She nibbled his lower lip. "But it's time to tell her. Don't be mean."

His chest rumbled, the predatory sound tickling her nipples as he slid his hands around her hips and cupped her ass. "We're not dating, Shay," he muttered between kisses. "We're living together."

Pamela smiled and sank into his affection while the bartender flung questions their way, over and over, one after another, until her voice approached a yell and Leo, T.J., and Cassie joined the inquisition. Not once did Bryan allow their kiss to break. He kept their bodies fused—lips and hips—while his tongue teased hers with gentle swirls.

She couldn't get enough of him or his arrogant demands. Not now, and definitely not when he'd dragged her from their first date and announced they needed to skip the irritating formalities and move in together.

Bryan hadn't functioned well under his preconceived notions of what a romantic relationship should be. He'd needed to create his own rules. And the unscheduled fast-forward into a cemented commitment had worked for them both.

She loved the stability and devotion. He enjoyed keeping her on her toes.

Not once had they looked back.

He wasn't anything like she'd anticipated. She'd already known they'd set sheets aflame in the bedroom. But away from the sex and the seduction, he was the most attentive and protective man she'd ever met.

Selfless, too.

Tonight, he surprised her all over again with his gentle devotion. In a sex club, for the first time as a couple, she'd thought he would've been in predator mode—all hands, teeth, and gyrating body parts.

This smooth tenderness was a million times better.

He inched back, those blue eyes slaying her with their passion. "Are you ready for the inquisition?"

She nodded, taking the seconds of their locked gaze to try to read him. When he swung toward his friends, she remained clueless.

T.J. and Cassie huddled beside them near the stools. Shay and Leo stood behind the bar.

Shay cocked a hip, a manicured brow rising. "You've got some ex—"

Leo clapped a hand over his girlfriend's mouth, softening the restriction with a kiss to her forehead.

"Are you happy?" Cassie asked over the growing enthusiasm in the room.

"That's your first question?" Bryan scoffed. "Great. This is going to take all night."

"That's our only question," Leo clarified. "You don't like to share, and we don't need to pry. We just want to make sure you're happy." He dropped his hand from Shay's face and poured himself a glass of bourbon. "Isn't that right, Shay?"

She grunted. "Speak for yourself. I want all the gory details."

"There are no gory details." Bryan wrapped a hand around Pamela's waist, squeezing tight. "Dating didn't work, so we moved in together."

"But you're happy?" T.J. asked.

"Yes." His response was simple. No inflection. No emotion. No bullshit. "Are we done now?"

Pamela hid her disappointment. She didn't want him to gush and brag about their relationship. She just wanted... Something. Anything to match the man he became in the privacy of his own home. Here in the bar, he'd regressed to being the closed off, tight-lipped guy she first met. Even his posture seemed stiff.

Leo inclined his head, raised his glass in salute, and then walked for the end of the bar.

Discussion over.

"Yep. That's all." Cassie beamed. "I'm so pleased for you both." She clapped Bryan on the shoulder and strode away, dragging her husband along with her.

Shay did a repeat of her eye-roll, not saying a word as she sidestepped and requested a drink order from a waiting patron with a jerk of her chin.

That was it. The inquisition had finished before it had begun.

"You hid our relationship because of that?" she asked.

"That's not normal," he muttered. "I think they're lulling us into a false sense of security."

"Is that why you're anxious?"

He stiffened, not meeting her gaze.

She'd nailed it. He *was* anxious. "What is it? I thought you were excited about tonight."

They'd discussed the complexity of returning to the Vault. It was their first major test. The trust and responsibility of being committed while participating in a sex club wasn't something to disregard without a second, third, or fourth thought.

He frowned. "I don't know what you're talking about."

Now he was lying? "Bryan? What's going on?"

"*Shit*," he muttered under his breath. "Look, I have something planned. I'm just not sure how it will turn out."

Her stomach flipped. What plans could put this experienced man on edge? "You're never nervous when it comes to sex."

"Exactly." He cleared his throat and stood tall. "*Hey*." He raised his voice, cutting through the moans and whimpers. "I need everyone's attention."

Her heart fluttered as the room fell under his command. Couples stopped fucking. People stepped out of the adjoining rooms to hear what he had to say. Even Cassie and T.J. looked on in confusion from the far corner.

"As you all know, this is my first night back—"

Wolf whistles and cheers sliced through the air.

"Come on, guys." He hushed the excitement with raised hands. "As I was saying, I haven't been down here since before I canceled the demonstration night. Unfortunately, the original plan didn't work out, but tonight I'd like to give you all a taste of what's in store when I reorganize the class."

He faced her and held out a hand.

"Bryan?" She glanced around the room, unsure what was going on. "What are you doing?"

"I need you to help assist me in a tiny preview."

She shook her head. *No.* No, no, no. She'd barely been prepared for what could've happened in the dark shadows on their own, let alone under a microscope.

Everyone stared at them, the simmering excitement in the air tickling her skin.

"I don't think I'm ready for this."

His anxiety faded under the brilliance of his smirk. "You will be." The promise was wicked. Confident. Entirely undeniable.

She reached for her drink and gulped some of the liquid.

"Don't drink too much." His heat closed in to envelop her, his lips finding her neck. "You don't want to be numb for this."

Yes, she did.

If it weren't for his anxiety, she would've indulged in the upcoming naughtiness with bounding delight. Her nipples already tingled. Her panties had turned into a Slip 'N Slide. She loved every opportunity to be an exhibitionist in the safe environment of the Vault.

But Bryan was worried about something. The fear pulsed off him in waves.

"We should talk about this first." The weight of the room's interest bore down on her.

"Trust me."

"This has nothing to do with trust. I've never seen you anything other than one hundred percent confident when it comes to sex. Whatever you're concerned about is starting to concern me."

"Come on," a man called from the back of the room. "Bring on the demo."

Bryan slid a hand into her loose hair and cupped the back of her head. "I was worried about dumping this on you. That's all. I didn't want you to anticipate what was coming, and not telling you made me feel like a guilty little bitch."

She studied him, unsure what to believe. "Are you bullshitting me?"

"When have I ever done that?" He smirked, making it ten times harder for her to trust her intuition.

"Are you sure everything is okay between us?" That was all that mattered. She didn't care about anything else.

"We're exactly where I want us to be at this point in time." He entwined their hands and tugged her from the stool. He led her through the mingling crowd, weaving through the condensing throng without effort. "The sooner we get this over with, the sooner I get you all to myself."

Leo and T.J. quickly rearranged furniture, creating space. Ottomans were shoved toward the wall. Sofas were turned and swiveled. Everything was strategically placed to face the large bed in the center of the room, the cream satin sheets gleaming under the overhead lights.

Bryan stopped at the side of the mattress and kissed her knuckles. "You're not going to fuck this up. However this turns out, it's because of me, okay?"

She nodded.

"Okay?" he growled, his drawn brows demanding a vocal response.

"Okay, you big brute."

With a subtle glide, his expression transformed from tight concern to gentle appreciation. Maybe even pride. "And don't you forget it."

"I already have." She knew him better now, better than anyone who believed this man was harsh and heartless. Past his sterile exterior, he was the exact opposite.

"All right, everyone." He scoped the audience of half-dressed patrons. "This is only going to be a taste of what's to come. On the actual demonstration night, I plan to discuss a range of different techniques. We'll go over the benefits of edging, and how consistency or surprise can affect women in different ways. But tonight, it's all about reading signs."

He crooked a finger at her, encouraging her onto the bed. "Lie down close to me. You need to stay in reach."

She stood immobile, her heart galloping into her throat. This would bring her exhibitionism to a whole new level—from amateur to professor.

"Don't worry." He held out a hand. "I promise to look after you." His grin was sly and cocky, the opposite of reassuring.

He didn't make sense. One moment he seemed restless and skittish. The next he exuded his ingrained confident sexuality without flaw.

"You're going to have a lot of explaining to do later. You know that, right?"

He inclined his head. "I know, sweetheart."

She slid her palm into his and allowed him to help her onto the raised bed. He guided her to lie close to the side of the mattress, the tiny overhead lights beaming down, bathing her in a glow before the shadowed audience.

"Gorgeous." Appreciation ebbed off him. "I think you're going to have more than a few admirers after this."

Her cheeks heated, from his words and the crowd's whispers of affirmation.

"Your blush does things to me, sweetheart."

"Me, too," another man muttered.

She chuckled and shook her head. "Just get started, would you?"

"You all heard the lady. We need to get this show on the road." He pivoted to the crowd of thirty-odd people, all of them silent with expectation. "Your job tonight is to study this flawless woman. I want you to be able to pinpoint those barely recognizable signs to learn just how subtle a partner can be during sex."

Their scrutiny bore down on her, tickling her skin and heightening her awareness. She breathed in their interest, letting it coat her in tingling carnality. But something else made the pressure between her thighs intensify. Something she'd grown to crave each day from this addictive man.

"See that?" His short, sharp glance captured everything. "Her breathing has increased, and I haven't even touched her yet. Can anyone tell me why she's already aroused?"

"Alcohol?" someone asked.

"Nope," Shay called. "She didn't even finish her first drink."

"She's in a sex club. Of course she's aroused," a man drawled.

"Wrong." Bryan verbally slapped away the comment. "She isn't new to the scene. It's not like watching you fool around is going to send her into a panting mess. Try again."

"The anticipation?" a feminine voice asked.

"Maybe, but I wouldn't bet my house on it." He held Pamela's gaze, deciphering every move she made. Every breath. Every thought. "Anyone else have a suggestion?"

Silence followed, not a whisper of an answer coming forward.

His focus held her in a trance, her breaths becoming gasps.

"Your eyes," she admitted. "Your confidence."

"I hoped you'd say that." He gifted her with a subtle grin. "Most women are attracted to knowledge. Problem is, every woman is different, which means nobody can become complacent. There's always a learning curve with a new partner, no matter how good you think you are. The trick to becoming an expert is to read who you're with. Never stop searching for signals."

He took a step toward the end of the bed, aligning himself with her feet. "You have to acknowledge what isn't being said, because your partner may lie for numerous reasons. Maybe they lack confidence. Or don't trust you enough. Maybe they're shy. Or don't want to hurt your feelings."

His hand reached out, the approach a slow, tormenting tease. She could feel his touch before the lone fingertip grazed her ankle, the slight brush scorching in its wake.

"Nothing is more rewarding than a sexually satisfied woman." He spoke softly, the trail of fire ascending along her calf. "Take your time exploring their body. Make her think it's a game, when all along, you're creeping further and further under her skin. Learning her secrets."

She tried not to move, not to flinch. Staying quiet became difficult. The further that lone fingertip trailed, the more her body reacted without her permission, jolting and glitching like a Richter scale in an apocalyptic earthquake.

"How do y'all think I'm doing so far?"

"Her breathing is still getting faster," Cassie offered.

"Yes. But what else?" His caress crept higher, over her knee, along the inside of her thigh. "Has anyone noticed her muscle spasms? They're flowing along her leg, preceding my touch, anticipating my next move."

"She's tilted in your direction, too," T.J. added. "Not much, but a little."

"Those are the tiny signs you need to look for. Anything deliberate could be a lie, for the reasons I've mentioned. These almost imperceptible changes are the things that mean the most. Especially those beautiful eyes dilating."

She was ready to ditch the imperceptible signs and drag him to the bed by his hair. How could a lone finger torment her like this?

No. It wasn't the solitary stroke. She couldn't forget that. It was his stare. His voice. His infallible expertise. The list increased with every blink.

His aftershave. His dress sense. His erotic selflessness.

There wasn't one thing about this man that didn't turn her on.

Not one thing that didn't encourage her to want to grind her thighs together.

She cleared the gravel from her throat and swallowed to soothe the burn.

He paused in his moment of sexual prowess, giving way to sweet sincerity. "How are you doing?"

"Fine, thanks." Her betraying voice broke.

People chuckled, some snorted, while Bryan grinned down at her, his admiration a living, breathing thing.

The fire reignited at mid-thigh, sliding to her garter.

She licked her lips, overheating, hyperventilating.

Everyone watched them, their fascination rushing through her. There was no condemnation from the group, only awe and enjoyment. Every single person had pinpoint focus on her gratification.

He slid a finger under her garter and pulled tight to release it with a snap.

"Ouch," she hissed.

"Now, that right there is a blindingly brilliant display of something I've done wrong. And I'm not talking about the verbal cue. Yes, she also flinched, which is another obvious sign, but if she was shy and tried to suppress her reactions, we'd still be able to rely on the rigidity of her posture and the way she tilted her legs away."

"She pulled back into the mattress, too," a woman offered.

"Exactly." Bryan slid his finger along her garter, soothing the sting beneath. "Even if she did gasp or whimper or moan, her body is pulling away. This is when you check your ego at the door and acknowledge your partner didn't enjoy what you dished out."

Pamela froze, not realizing the signals she was sending. Her cheeks tingled. Her chest and belly, too.

"Now," he continued, "once you fuck up, you need to make amends. Mistakes are common. All you need to do is work them to your advantage."

He added another finger to the soothing slide along her garter. Gradually, those searching digits skimmed higher and higher, gliding inward to the sensitive spot where her inner thigh met the crotch of her panties. She jolted, overwrought with twirling knots inside her pussy.

"All better?" he teased.

"You're a horrible man." She glared, earning herself another laugh from the crowd.

His touch delved under the elastic and hovered in place, not advancing to his prize. Back and forth he rubbed right beneath her panty line, turning the erogenous zone into an orgasm trigger set to detonate. He was going to make her come without penetration.

Again.

"I want to keep hearing observations. Call them out. Tell me what you see, because from my point of view, she's a kaleidoscope of signals."

She whimpered and sank her teeth into her lower lip.

He was there. *Right* there. Less than an inch from her pulsing pussy. Yet, he seemed a mile away. The confidence in his focus told her the height of her bliss would come when he allowed it.

"Her back arched," a man called.

"She thrust her breasts."

"Her eyes rolled."

Breathing became difficult as overlapping observations filled the room.

"She's panting."

"Clutching the sheet."

"She keeps swallowing."

Bryan encroached, those fingertips nudging closer and closer until finally he slid through her arousal, the smooth glide exquisite. Almost perfection. Just not quite enough.

She needed a little more. The slightest penetration. A swipe across her clit.

"Her hips are lifted toward you."

"She's shaking."

"She closed her eyes."

Oh, God.

He stopped. The heavenly glide ceased. Those wonderful fingers escaped her panties.

She blinked up at him, collapsing into the mattress as frustrated tears blurred her vision. This was torture. Pure, hysteria-rich suffering.

"Not yet, sweetheart." His own suffering bled through his words. "There's one more thing I want to do before I have you all to myself."

"Please, Bryan." She clenched her thighs together. "This is killing me."

"I know."

He reached out a hand and she grasped his offering, allowing him to guide her into a seated position.

"I'm giving you all one last chance to analyze her." He sat on the edge of the mattress and patted his thighs. "Come here."

She frowned, frantically trying to figure out what came next.

"It's okay. This won't take long." He grabbed her wrist and led her to sit on his lap, facing the crowd.

Her limbs trembled with need. A sheen of sweat coated her skin. It took all her self-control not to turn and bury her face in his neck. One more whispered plea and she knew he'd give her what she needed. He'd end both their torment.

He parted her thighs with his hands, encouraging her legs to drape over his, exposing the soaked crotch of her panties.

She vibrated, thrummed. She'd been infused with hyper-sensitivity. Even the subtle scratch of his suit material made her whimper.

"I want you to watch her closely." His voice became low, brutal in its command. "I need you to focus and make sure you read all those signs."

Her breath hitched, the anticipation killing her. Her heart threatened to explode, the pulsing muscles on fire behind her ribcage.

"Are you ready, sweetheart?"

She nodded as he guided her loose hair away from her shoulder to place his lips at her ear.

"This time the test comes in words," he whispered. "Let's see what reactions I can inspire."

She nodded, ready and oh, so willing to hear his dirty talk.

"You sure you're ready?"

"Yes," she gasped. She was ready for this to be over so she could jump him, smash her lips to his, and drag his body beneath hers.

"Okay."

She heard his swallow and felt the tease of his beard against her cheek.

"Ella..." His voice was barely audible, leaving everyone clueless to their conversation. "I've been wanting to tell you this for a while. But I didn't know how you'd react."

She nodded, the frantic bob of her head trying to encourage a speedier outcome.

"Ella..." He stopped, sighed, those hands on her thighs becoming sweaty. "I love you."

Arousal vanished. Noise, too.

There was nothing.

No thoughts. No comprehension. Only a slow repeat of his gentle declaration through her mind.

"That doesn't look good." Distant words fractured her daze.

"Whatever you said wiped away the lust."

"You blew it, Brute. She's not horny anymore."

Those three words had been a dream she never thought she'd experience. They were too important to him. Too special. Three words fractured her, making everything unstable—her heart, her mind, her emotions.

Strong hands gripped her waist, lifting her, turning her limp body to sit sideways on his lap.

"Ella?" His blue eyes blinked through apprehension, his vulnerability unmasked for everyone to see. "I should've kept my mouth shut, shouldn't I?"

"No." She shook her head. Her tongue tangled with all the things she needed to say. All the things he needed to hear. "Not at all."

"What happened?" a woman yelled. "What's going on?"

His nostrils flared, the harshness returning to his features. "I should've done this somewhere else."

"Why didn't you?" The question tumbled from her mouth. "Why now? Why here?"

She didn't understand. It would've been so much easier for him to share this moment in private. Alone. Without a mass of scrutiny.

"I can read your body like it's my own, sweetheart. But when it comes to reading your emotions, I'm clueless. I needed their help to gauge your reaction." He released a caustic laugh. "I guess it didn't work in my favor."

"Of course it did. I'm just shocked. That's all."

"You're about to cry."

"No." She swiped at the lone tear that broke free. "I'm not."

He raised a brow, silently calling bullshit.

"Well, I am, but it's because I'm happy. I never thought I'd hear those words from you."

He stiffened. "Because I'm a heartless asshole?"

"Bryan, I know that declaration means the world to you. And I..."

"You didn't realize you mean more than the world to me?"

Her chest heated, warmth and relief flooding her in equal doses. "I wasn't sure."

"Be sure, Ella," he whispered. "There's nothing more important to me than you. No matter how you feel in return."

His fingers glided along her jaw, holding her in place as he leaned in for a chaste kiss. The brush of lips lasted a second before he pulled away.

No. She wanted more. Needed everything.

She stood, changing her position to straddle his lap.

"That poor excuse for a kiss isn't going to satisfy." She poked him in the chest, earning a snicker. "Not after you've teased me to mindlessness."

"Welcome to my life. That's what it's like living with you every damn day."

She smiled and leaned her head against his shoulder, running her arms around his waist while his wove around her back.

His feelings mimicked her own. Her adoration and affection were reciprocated. The brutal man she'd once thought heartless was more tender and loving than anyone could imagine.

"Are we still supposed to be watching?" someone asked, the silence of growing confusion changing the once heated atmosphere.

Neither of them responded. They didn't move, didn't speak as they continued to pretend the world didn't exist.

For her, nothing existed.

Only him.

Only her.

"Bryan?" she whispered.

He placed a delicate butterfly kiss to her neck. "Yeah, sweetheart?"

"I love you more."

Every muscle beneath her tightened. His arms tensed around her back.

"Oh, shit," someone muttered from the crowd. "What the fuck is going on?"

"I'm confused. Is this part of the demonstration?" a woman asked.

"I don't think so." Leo's voice carried over the growing speculation. "That's it, folks. This is the end of the show. Let's give them some privacy, okay?"

Shuffling feet moved around the bed. Murmured words brushed her ears. But she didn't let him go. She didn't flinch in her unwavering hold as the room returned to its usual broadcast of dirty talk and indulgence.

"Nobody has said that to me before." His hold tightened, squeezing her like a lifeline. "I never knew what it would feel like."

"What does it feel like?"

"I don't know." He shook his head against hers. "I guess it feels like I'm not alone anymore."

"You're not. You never will be." She'd make him see. One day at a time. No matter how long it took. "Take me home, Bryan. I don't want to be here right now."

"Good decision." He kissed her forehead and stood, keeping her locked around his waist like a child. "But first, I want to hear those words again."

"What words?" She grinned, unsuccessfully playing dumb.

"You know what I'm talking about."

"I do. But I want you to ask properly."

His jaw tensed, but he faced the vulnerability head-on, tilting his chin as he stared her down. "Tell me you love me, Ella."

Pain exploded in her chest. The most delicious and fulfilling pain she'd ever felt. "I love you, Bryan Munro. I love every damn thing about you."

ALSO BY EDEN SUMMERS

HUNTING HER SERIES

Hunter

Decker

Torian

~

RECKLESS BEAT SERIES

Blind Attraction (Reckless Beat #1)

Passionate Addiction (Reckless Beat #2)

Reckless Weekend (Reckless Beat #2.5)

Undesired Lust (Reckless Beat #3)

Sultry Groove (Reckless Beat #4)

Reckless Rendezvous (Reckless Beat #4.5)

Undeniable Temptation (Reckless Beat #5)

~

Information on more of Eden's titles can be found at www.edensummers.com or your online book retailer.

ABOUT THE AUTHOR

Eden Summers is a bestselling author of contemporary romance with a side of sizzle and sarcasm.

She lives in Australia with a young family who are well aware she's circling the drain of insanity.
Eden can't resist alpha dominance, dark features and sarcasm in her fictional heroes and loves a strong heroine who knows when to bite her tongue but also serves retribution with a feminine smile on her face.

If you'd like access to exclusive information and giveaways, join Eden Summers' newsletter via the link on her website - www.edensummers.com

For more information:
www.edensummers.com
eden@edensummers.com

CPSIA information can be obtained
at www.ICGtesting.com
Printed in the USA
BVHW071242281220
596559BV00003B/506